A NIGHTINGALE CHRISTMAS CAROL

by

Donna Douglas

Magna Large Print Books
Long Preston, North Yorkshire,
BD23 4ND, England.

British Library Cataloguing in Publication Data.

A catalogue record of this book is
available from the British Library

ISBN   978-0-7505-4506-8

First published in Great Britain by Arrow Books in 2016

Published in Large Print 2017 by arrangement with
Random House Group

Magna Large Print is an imprint of Library Magna Books Ltd.

Printed and bound in Great Britain by
T.J. (International) Ltd., Cornwall, PL28 8RW

Acknowledgements

Many thanks as always to my editor, Jenny Geras, and team at Arrow. I would also like to thank my agent, Caroline Sheldon, for her endless support and good advice.

As far as research goes, I gained a great deal of information about POWs from Eden Camp in North Yorkshire, and the wonderful Imperial War Museum.

I would also like to thank my family – my daughter Harriet for listening to my ever-evolving plot ideas, and my husband Ken, for his support and his encyclopaedic knowledge of World War II. I knew it would come in useful one day...

To Rebecca and Wayne, wishing you happiness
in your married life.

Chapter One

December 1943

'Only you would come out in the middle of an air raid to look after a ruddy cat, Dora Riley!'

Dora didn't look back at her husband. She could hear the gruff exasperation in Nick's voice, so she could well imagine the look on his face. She kept her eyes fixed instead on the bomb-scarred ground in front of her; a freezing fog was descending, and it took all her concentration to pick her way over the treacherous cobbles, pitted with craters. The streets looked nothing like she remembered them. Most of the houses were gone, destroyed in the Blitz.

'It wasn't a very big one, and the all-clear sounded half an hour ago,' she called back over her shoulder. 'Besides, I didn't ask you to come. You could have stayed at home.'

'And let you walk the streets by yourself?' Nick sounded outraged. 'It'll be dark soon. It ain't safe.'

Dora smiled to herself. Bless him. Nick had been away fighting for nearly four years, and she could count on one hand how many times he'd been allowed home on leave. How did he think she'd managed without him in all that time? Like all the other wives and mothers left alone to cope in the East End, she'd learned to live with the fear, and the blackouts, and the nights spent hiding away in

9

damp air raid shelters, wondering if they would have a home to return to in the morning.

And being a nurse, she'd also come face-to-face with some truly horrifying sights, images of injured soldiers and bomb victims that still haunted her nightmares.

But now Nick was home, and he wanted to protect her, and she knew she had to put aside her independence and let him be the husband he wanted to be.

She was so happy to have him home. Even now, nearly two weeks later, she couldn't stop smiling at the memory of opening the front door to find him standing on the doorstep in his uniform, his kitbag slung over his shoulder. He'd been sent back from Italy on a troop ship to Scotland, and it had taken him two days to make his way back to Bethnal Green.

Now it was the day before Christmas Eve, and it was going to be the happiest Christmas Dora had had in a long time.

The twins seemed to pick up on her lighter mood, too. It had been so long since the children had seen their father, and they had been painfully wary of Nick at first. But now they couldn't leave him alone. They'd begged to come out with their parents this afternoon, Walter riding high on Nick's shoulders, while Winnie roamed ahead, bold beyond her six years, her keen gaze darting around, searching for lost treasure.

'Be careful,' Dora called out to her. 'Remember what I told you. Don't pick anything up.'

Winnie paid her no mind, criss-crossing the pavement, still looking here and there.

'She's turning into a proper little tomboy, ain't she?' Nick said fondly.

'That's our Alfie's doing,' Dora replied. 'He's always bringing home bits of shrapnel to show her, and pointing out the different aeroplanes. I swear they'd both be out in the air raids if I let them...' She stopped short, a nameless fear choking the words in her throat.

Nick seemed to understand. He lengthened his stride to catch up with her, then reached for her hand and tucked it into the crook of his arm, pulling her close to him. Neither of them spoke. They weren't much for flowery words, either of them. But their silences spoke volumes.

Dora tightened her fingers around his arm, feeling his solid strength through the thickness of his coat. She might have learned to cope alone over the past four years, but now he was here, at her side, she wondered how she had ever managed without him – and how she would manage when he was taken away from her again.

Because he would have to go away again, sooner or later. Until this wretched war was over, he would never be hers.

As if he knew the direction her thoughts were straying, Nick began to grumble about the weather again. Dora knew he was trying to distract her.

'Remind me again why we've come out in the freezing cold on this fool's errand?' he muttered under his breath, his coat collar turned up so Dora could hardly see his profile buried inside it.

'I promised Mrs Price.' The old lady had been in such a state since she was admitted to the isolation ward. She was very poorly with influenza, but she was more worried about her precious cat than herself. In the end, Dora had had to swear she would go and feed the creature just to get her to stay in bed.

'Couldn't you just tell her it ran away? She'd never know.'

'How could you suggest such a thing?' Dora stared at him. 'I couldn't live with myself, knowing the poor thing was alone and starving.'

Nick shook his head. 'Typical,' he muttered. 'That's your trouble. You spend too much time thinking about everyone else.'

'So what if I do? Shame you don't try it sometime, Nick Riley,' she replied primly.

'Look after number one, that's my motto.' He did his best to sound brusque, but Dora could see the faint smile lifting the corner of his mouth. Nick preferred to hide his kind heart under a hard shell. Very few people had ever been allowed close enough to see what he was really like.

'Mrs Price was our neighbour once,' she reminded him. 'Of course I'll do a good turn for her if I can. She did enough for us.'

'Not me. She never had a good word for me or my family. Nor did the rest of them.'

Dora sent him a quick look. It was true, the Rileys had always been outcasts in Griffin Street, thanks to Nick's violent father and his drunken mother. Growing up, he had always been surly and troublesome, ready to start a fight at the drop of a hat. It was only Dora who had been allowed to see the hurt, angry boy inside.

He was doing his best not to show it, but Dora

12

could tell he was struggling with the idea of returning to Griffin Street. The place held no happy memories for him.

'Are you sure you want to come?' she said. 'I really don't mind going by myself–'

'I told you, I ain't having you walking round these streets on your own.' Nick's expression was grimly determined. 'Anyway, we're here now. Let's just get it over with, shall we?'

She could feel his tension as they turned the corner into Griffin Street. She had returned to the area several times since that fateful night during the Blitz, but Nick hadn't seen the devastation for himself. Now he stopped dead, and Dora heard his sharply indrawn breath.

The street they'd grown up in was barely recognisable. It wasn't as bad as it had been, just after the bomb hit it. The mountains of debris, the brick rubble, shattered wood and glass and broken roof tiles, had all been cleared away over the past two years. But somehow it was all the more heartbreaking for that. Now there was nothing but a yawning gap where their houses had once stood, with jagged points of broken wall still standing at odd angles. Thin wisps of fog threaded between the skeletons of the houses, giving the street an eerie, haunted look.

Here and there were touching reminders of the people who had once lived in the street – a fluttering pennant of flowery parlour wallpaper, the remains of the pigeon loft where Mr Prosser kept his birds, the broken wooden stump of what had once been a washing line. And there, over by the broken-down back wall, was the outline of the

13

coal cellar where Nick's younger brother Danny had sat and waited for his brother to come home until the night the bomb came down...

Dora was always careful to avert her gaze from the spot, but Nick's eyes were fixed on it, almost as if he was testing himself to see how much pain he could bear.

'Where are we, Daddy?' Walter's piping voice broke the tense silence.

Nick cleared his throat. 'This is where we used to live,' he said in a low voice. 'Me and your mum grew up here.'

'Where?' Walter wanted to know. 'Where did you live?'

'Just there.' Nick pointed towards the gap. 'Your mum lived at number twenty-eight, and I was next door.'

'Where is it now?'

'They've been bombed, silly,' Winnie answered for them as she scrambled up the crumbling edge of a wall. 'The Germans knocked them all down in the Blitz. They came over in their planes, hundreds and hundreds of them, bang, crash, bang–'

'Stop it!' Dora snapped, more harshly than she'd meant to. 'And get down off that wall before you tear your coat. You won't get another one if you ruin it.'

Winnie shot her a sullen look, then climbed down and darted off.

'And stay where I can see you,' Dora called after her. But Winnie had already disappeared into the gathering gloom.

'You can't blame her,' Nick said softly. 'They've grown up with the war. It's all they've ever known.'

'Don't I know it?' Dora muttered. It broke her heart to think that her children couldn't remember a world when air raid sirens didn't wail in the sky, or the simple pleasures of waking up on Christmas morning to a stocking filled with presents. They were six years old, and their innocence was already gone.

'Come on,' Nick tugged at her arm. 'Let's go and see about this cat before it gets dark.'

Mrs Price's house stood in isolation at the end of Griffin Street, the only house still intact, apart from a large dent in the roof and half the outside privy missing.

Nick squinted up at the house. 'Look at all those tiles missing,' he said. 'And that chimney's going to come down, too. It must be bloody freezing in there. Damp too, I shouldn't wonder.'

'I expect that's why she's in hospital with flu.'

He shook his head. 'How does the old girl live here all by herself? I'm surprised it's not been condemned.'

'I think they tried.' Dora remembered what Mrs Price had said to her, her wrinkled face lit up with determination.

'My house is still standing, and so am I. The Germans didn't get me out of it, and neither will the corporation.'

'I think she's planning to be here when the war's over, so she can put out the flags,' Dora said.

'She always was a tough old boot!' Nick was grudgingly admiring. 'Just like all the other women in Griffin Street, eh?'

He grinned at her, and Dora did her best to smile back. The truth was, she didn't feel very

15

tough any more, but she didn't want to show it in front of Nick. He had enough to worry about.

'I think I might take a look at that roof first thing tomorrow, see if I can stop some of the rain coming in,' Nick said, squinting up at the crumbling chimney.

'Oh yes? What happened to looking after number one?' Dora asked.

Nick's mouth twisted. 'You must be a bad influence on me,' he muttered. 'Now come on. Let's find that ruddy cat and get out of here before the fog comes down and we can't find our way home!'

They searched for ages, wandering around the wrecked houses, calling out the cat's name.

'Timmy? Timmy? Come out, mate. I've brought you some nice fish heads.' Dora's voice echoed around the empty street. 'He must be inside the house,' she said. 'Poor little thing, I expect he's terrified.'

'More likely out hunting!' Nick grimaced. 'There must be enough rats around here to keep him going for months.'

'Don't say that!' Dora shuddered. 'Find Winnie, would you? I don't want her getting bitten.'

Nick peered into the gloom. 'It's all right, I can see her. She's just over there, where the Prossers' privy used to be–'

But Dora wasn't listening. She was staring at Mrs Price's back door, swinging open on its rusting hinges.

'What is it?' Nick asked behind her.

'It looks as if someone's been in here.'

Nick stepped forward, taking charge. He lifted Walter from his shoulders and dumped him on

16

the ground. 'You stay here,' he said. 'I'll go in and have a look.'

'But–'

'Stay here!' he ordered.

Dora frowned at his back as he opened the door and stepped inside. He might be used to giving orders, but she wasn't used to following them. Clutching Walter's hand, she stepped after Nick into the gloom.

Chapter Two

It was just as she'd feared. The tiny kitchen had been turned over, tables and chairs upended, the dresser that had once housed all Mrs Price's fancy china thrown on its side.

Dora froze, staring at the mess around her. 'What the–'

'Someone must have realised the place was empty.' Nick's face was grim. 'You stay here, I'll take a look in the other room.'

He disappeared up the darkened passageway. 'What's happened, Mum?' Walter asked, looking round.

'I–' Dora opened her mouth to answer him, but words failed her.

Nick appeared again in the doorway. 'I've looked in the parlour,' he said. 'It's the same in there. And I found this...' He held up a wooden jewellery box, the lid gaping open to expose its faded silk lining. 'They've taken everything that wasn't nailed

17

down, I reckon.'

Dora's knees weakened and she stepped backwards, feeling the cold stone of the sink at her back.

'How could they?' she whispered. 'How could someone do this to a poor old lady?'

'You'd be surprised how low some people will stoop,' Nick muttered.

'Yes, but...' Dora looked around. This was the East End, people stuck together here, they helped each other out in times of trouble. They didn't turn on each other like dogs fighting over scraps.

'It's the war,' Nick answered her unspoken question. 'It does strange things to people.'

The bloody war. Anger welled up inside her. She was sick of hearing about it, sick of living through it, sick of the way it twisted people and tore the heart out of communities like Griffin Street.

'How am I going to tell her?' she said, looking around at the broken remains of Mrs Price's home. 'She's already lost so much. Her husband, both her sons...'

'Don't say anything,' Nick said. 'Not until she's strong enough to take it. Now, let's find that cat and a box to put him in, and we'll take him home.'

Dora stared at him blankly. It took her a moment to remember why they'd come.

'Oh no,' she said. 'Mrs Price said not to move him. She said he wouldn't like it–'

'To hell with the cat!' Nick cut her off. 'I ain't having you coming back to this place every day, d'you hear me? Not with thieves roaming around the place.'

Dora straightened her shoulders. 'They won't

be back, if they've taken everything,' she said. 'Besides, they don't scare me.'

'I don't care, I still don't want you round here on your own–'

Just at that moment the door swung open behind her and Winnie appeared, looking pleased with herself.

'Look what I found!' she cried.

Dora turned around, expecting to see the cat in her daughter's arms, and instead caught the dull glint of dirty metal in her hand. Before she'd had time to think about what she was doing, she had let go of Walter and thrown herself at it, snatching it away from her.

'What did I tell you?' She shoved Winnie out of the way and flung the lump of metal out into the street as far as she could. 'I don't want you digging things up. They're not toys, do you hear me? You're not to play with them!'

The world seemed to blur before her eyes, and it wasn't until she heard Nick's voice, firm and low, that she heard her daughter crying and realised she was shaking her like a doll.

She released her abruptly, numb with shock. Freed from her mother's grasp, Winnie gave a sob and rushed off. Dora went to follow her, but Nick held her back.

'Leave her,' he said. 'She won't go far.' He held Dora at arm's length, his eyes meeting hers. 'It was just an old shell case, Dora. It was harmless.'

'She didn't know that when she dug it up, did she? It could have been anything.' She paused, fighting for control. 'We had a kid from Russia Lane in the other day, brought home something he'd found on an old bomb site. It turned out to be an unexploded incendiary.' She kept her voice flat, neutral. 'I'll never forget his dad carrying him in his arms, his clothes all soaked through with his blood...'

'Don't.' Nick flinched.

'What if that had happened to our Winnie?' Dora said. 'What if it wasn't a harmless shell case she picked up? What if it was a – a–' Fear gripped her chest so tightly she couldn't speak.

'I'm sorry,' Nick said. 'I'll have a word with her, all right? Make sure she knows not to pick anything up – Dora? Dora, are you crying?'

She turned away from him sharply towards the window. 'No,' she said, but the thickness of tears clogging her throat gave her away.

'You are.' Nick turned her to face him. 'Come on, this ain't like you. What's wrong?'

'What's wrong?' Dora echoed in disbelief. 'Look around you, Nick. Look at this place. Can you imagine anyone robbing their neighbour before this rotten war started? And look at our kids. Winnie's fascinated by bombs and planes, and Walter wets the bed because he's so terrified. Now Christmas is coming, and there's no presents and nothing to eat, and not even enough coal for the fire. I spend all my time worrying and waiting for the next disaster to befall us. And you ask me what's wrong!' She laughed harshly.

'I know it's bad,' Nick said. 'But you've got to keep going–'

'Why?' She gestured around the poor, upended remnants of what had once been Mrs Price's home. 'Look at this place. Mrs Price tried to keep going, and look what's happened to her.' She shook her head. 'I'm sorry I'm not doing what Lord Woolton and Mr Churchill and all the rest of them tell me, keeping my chin up and putting on a brave face and everything else. But I'm tired, Nick. Whatever it was that's got me through the past few years, I'm starting to run out. This war has taken everything away from me.'

'You've still got me.'

'Yes, but for how long?'

Dora saw his face change, and knew the strange, heavy feeling in her gut had been right. There was something Nick wasn't telling her.

'You're leaving, aren't you?' she said dully.

'We always knew I had to go back–' Nick started to say, but Dora cut him off.

'When?'

His gaze dropped to his hands. 'Tomorrow afternoon.'

'Christmas Eve...' She paused for a moment, taking it in. 'How long have you known?'

'Dora–'

'How long?'

'I got my embarkation orders a couple of days ago.'

'Why didn't you tell me?'

'You seemed so happy... I didn't want to upset you.'

Dora wanted to rage, but then she saw his beseeching expression, and tried to hold herself together.

'So you won't be staying for Christmas?' she said quietly.

'I'm sorry, love.'

'You can't help it. I s'pose we should count ourselves lucky we've had this time together. There's plenty of women round here haven't seen their husbands for years.' She looked around. 'We'd better get this place sorted out. I don't want Mrs Price to come home and find it like this.'

Nick was very quiet as they straightened the furniture, and Dora wasn't surprised. He rarely saw her upset. Like all the other women in the East End, she preferred to keep her chin up and battle on regardless. If she had any doubts or fears, she kept them locked inside.

She didn't know why she'd allowed herself to weaken. Perhaps it was because Nick was there, reminding her of everything she was missing. But she was ashamed of herself for showing her feelings in front of him, because whatever she was going through, she knew he was going through far worse. She might whine about rationing and blackouts and the daily fear she had to cope with, but it was nothing compared to the real dangers he faced day after day on the front line.

And now she'd made him feel worse. She watched him from across the room, and a chill ran through her. She knew there was a real chance she could lose him, and she didn't want him to go away thinking that he had to worry about her.

She approached him as he heaved the dresser back into place against the wall.

'I'm sorry,' she said.

He straightened up and turned to look at her. 'What for?'

'I shouldn't have carried on like that. I feel like such a fool.'

His eyes were wary. 'I didn't know you were so upset.'

How can I be anything else, she wanted to say. But instead she smiled and said, 'Oh, don't worry about me. I'm just having an off day.'

Her smile didn't fool him. Nick's frown deepened. 'You will be all right, won't you? I don't like to think of going off and leaving you...'

'I'll be all right, honestly,' Dora said. 'Don't give it another thought. You just worry about yourself.' She paused. 'Do you know where they're sending you?'

He turned back to the dresser, leaning his weight against it to push it into place. 'Somewhere on the south coast is all we've been told.'

And they couldn't let you have one more day at home? Dora bit back the complaint that sprang to her lips. She had already said far too much.

'And then on to France, I suppose?' she said.

'I don't know. And even if I did, you know I wouldn't be able to tell you.' Nick's face was a blank mask. Dora knew that like her, he was trying to play down his feelings.

Then he smiled, and said, 'But if I do end up in France, I promise I'll bring you home a bottle of fancy French perfume, as a late Christmas present.'

'I don't want any perfume. I just want you to come home safe.'

Her anxiety must have shown on her face, because Nick grinned and said, 'I'll be all right.'

If only that were true. Without thinking, Dora's gaze dropped to the place where the bullet had torn through his chest, missing his heart by inches.

23

He still had the scars, the flesh puckered and silvery under his shirt. Dora couldn't bear to touch it, because it reminded her how close she had come to losing him.

He followed her gaze downwards. 'That'll teach me to run faster next time!'

He laughed, but Dora didn't. Her throat tightened, and she felt like crying again. But this time she managed to hold it in.

Nick reached for her hand. 'I'll be back, I promise,' he said.

'Do you? Do you really promise?'

'You know I will. I'd never leave you. And I want you to be here waiting for me when I come home, too,' he joked. 'No running off with any handsome GIs, do you hear me?'

That brought a reluctant smile to her lips. 'What kind of a girl do you think I am?'

His intense navy blue gaze met hers. 'My girl,' he said softly.

For a moment they were caught, trapped in a moment together. Then suddenly, Winnie's voice interrupted them from outside, breaking the spell.

'Look what I've got!'

'Oh Lord, what's she found now?' Dora hurried to the back door, Nick at her heels, in time to see her daughter staggering across the yard, her arms full of hissing, spitting ginger fur.

Winnie beamed at them, pleased with herself. 'I found Timmy!' she announced.

'So you have.' Nick went to take the cat from her. 'Give him here before he scratches you to ribbons. Come on, we'll find a box to put him in.'

As he went outside, Nick turned to look back at

24

Dora. 'It'll be all right, you know,' he whispered. 'Just keep your chin up, for my sake.'

Dora smiled back 'I will.'

It was only when he was out in the yard that she allowed her smile to drop.

Chapter Three

June 1944

'Have you heard the news, Nurse? The Allies have landed in France.'

Mr Hopkins the Head Porter stuck his head out of the window of the porters' lodge. His eyes gleamed with fervour above his bristling moustache. 'This is it, Nurse,' he said. 'It's finally started!'

'So it has, Mr Hopkins.' Dora tried to smile, but unease was already uncurling itself in the pit of her stomach.

It's finally started.

She had lain awake most of the night, listening to the planes going overhead. There seemed to be many more than usual, and now she knew why.

The Head Porter puffed out his chest and gazed up at the cloudy grey sky. 'It's a big day for all of us,' he declared in his sing-song Welsh accent.

Dora gazed past him into the lodge, where two more porters sat hunched over the wireless set, sharing a cigarette, laughing and joking. It was all

25

right for them all to look pleased with themselves, she thought. They weren't the ones risking
their lives.

'Just think,' Mr Hopkins went on, 'at this very
moment, our brave boys are on those French
beaches, ready to give those Germans what for–'

'One of our windows is cracked,' Dora interrupted him shortly.

Mr Hopkins frowned. 'I beg your pardon,
Nurse?'

'On the emergency ward. One of the panes of
glass has cracked, and it's letting in a terrible
draught. Could you do something about it?'

The Head Porter drew himself up to his full
height, which was barely taller than Dora. 'I'll see
what I can do,' he sniffed.

'Thank you, I'd appreciate it.'

As she walked away, she heard him saying, 'Well
I never! Did you hear that? The news we've all
been waiting for finally comes, and she's not even
interested!' He tutted. 'Downright unpatriotic,
that's what I call it.'

Dora stopped dead, rage singing in her ears. She
had half turned to go back and give him a piece of
her mind, then she forced herself to carry on walking.

It wasn't Mr Hopkins' fault, she told herself. He
was just excited that the waiting was over. Ever
since the Russians defeated the Germans on the
Eastern Front, the newspapers had been calling
for the Allies to take the fight to them in the west.

But Mr Hopkins didn't have someone he loved
in that fight. He didn't have to lie awake at night,
worrying that they wouldn't come home.

Of course she wasn't the only one. Nearly everyone she knew had a husband, or a son or a brother out there fighting. And a lot of people were much worse off than her. Poor Mrs Price had lost both her sons, one at Dunkirk and the other in North Africa.

She remembered her promise to Nick. *Keep your chin up.*

You need to stop feeling sorry for yourself, Dora Riley, she told herself sternly. It was a bad lot, but she had to pull herself together and get on as best she could.

But it wouldn't be easy. She was afraid if she uttered Nick's name she would lose the fragile self-control she had been holding on to so grimly for the past six months.

The squeak of her shoes echoed in the empty passage as she made her way into the main hospital building. Once those same passages would have been busy with nurses hurrying to start their morning duty. But ever since the gas explosion two years earlier which had destroyed half the hospital building, most of the wards had closed down and the patients transferred out of London to a hospital in the Kent countryside. Most of the doctors and nurses had been sent away too, while others had signed up for military service.

Only Dora and a handful of other nurses, medical students and VADs had been left behind to man the Casualty department, the male and female emergency admissions wards and the few outpatients clinics that remained.

She missed the hustle and bustle of hospital life, the nurses and the doctors, and the orderlies going to and fro with trolleys. She even missed the stern ward sisters in their grey uniforms and white bonnets. The empty wards seemed almost eerie, their rows of bare metal beds like ghostly skeletons.

Kitty Jenkins, the junior nurse, was already on the male emergency admissions ward when she arrived, chatting to Miss Sloan, one of the VADs. They looked odd together, young Kitty so dark and petite, in contrast to Miss Sloan's awkward height and long, clumsy limbs. Dora could tell from their excited faces that they were discussing the news.

Kitty fell silent the moment Dora appeared in deference to her rank, but Leonora Sloan continued to chatter on, oblivious as ever to the niceties of hospital etiquette. She was a middle-aged music teacher, a well-meaning soul who had joined the Red Cross Voluntary Aid Detachment to do her bit for the war effort. She could be more trouble than she was worth at times, but Dora couldn't fault her redoubtable spirit. Every morning without fail, Miss Sloan cycled in from Essex, paying no attention to blocked roads or air raids, snow or thunderstorms.

Now she hurried up to Dora, her broad smile exposing her prominent teeth. 'I say, Nurse, have you heard the news? The Allies—'

'Yes, I've heard.' Dora kept her own smile fixed in place.

'Isn't it marvellous?'

'Yes, it is.' Dora turned to Kitty. 'It looks as if it was a busy night last night, Jenkins?'

'Yes, Staff. Five admissions, according to the night nurse.'

'Where is she? I'll take report from her.'

As the weary night nurse went through the details of the cases that had been brought in overnight, Dora was aware of Miss Sloan's huffy expression at the corner of her vision. But she tried not to pay attention to it as she concentrated on the appendicitis, the suspected heart failure and the burns case that she would have to deal with that day. Not to mention the two sailors with toxic gastritis who had arrived in the early hours.

Dora sighed. 'Let me guess – they'd been drinking in the White Horse?' The night nurse nodded. 'When will they shut that place down?'

She had lost count of the number of men they'd had in after drinking there. The locals all knew to avoid it, but off-duty sailors and soldiers couldn't believe their luck at finding gin and whisky so freely available. It was only when they woke up in hospital that they discovered the booze they'd been enjoying was actually heavily disguised methylated spirits.

'One of these days that landlord is going to kill someone,' Dora said. 'You'd think the police could do something about it, wouldn't you?' She smoothed down her apron, then turned to Kitty. 'Right, let's make a start, shall we?'

Dora might have managed to avoid Miss Sloan's chatter, but she couldn't stop the patients talking about the invasion. As the morning passed, conversation went back and forth across the ward as the men discussed the news and what it might mean.

It was only a matter of time before one of them asked if they could have the wireless on.

'Come on, Nurse,' they urged Dora. 'You want to know what's going on same as the rest of us, don't you?'

Dora hesitated. The truth was, she was torn between wanting to know and being afraid to find out.

'Of course we should have it on,' Miss Sloan stepped in. 'I don't know about anyone else,' she glared at Dora, 'but I certainly want to know what's happening to our brave boys.'

Kitty looked sideways at Dora. 'Would it be all right, Staff?'

Dora summoned a smile. 'Of course,' she said.

After all, she reasoned, surely the truth couldn't be half as bad as the dark pictures her imagination was summoning up.

For once, Kitty Jenkins was grateful for Leonora Sloan and her forthright manner, otherwise Nurse Riley might never have agreed to having the wireless on. Kitty was conscious of the senior nurse quietly going about her business, sitting at her desk writing up her reports as the rest of them listened avidly to the hourly bulletins.

It was strange, really. Kitty knew Nurse Riley's husband was away fighting in France. If it was her, she thought, she would have been glued to the wireless, wanting to know everything.

But then she remembered how she hadn't been able to look at a newspaper for weeks after her own brother Ray was killed. Over a year later, her mother still flinched whenever she heard of another boat being lost in the North Atlantic.

But there was no getting away from the news

30

this morning. And of course, everyone had an opinion on it.

'Of course, the Germans ain't going to take this lying down,' one of the men said, as Kitty helped Nurse Riley prepare him for an injection. 'I reckon we're going to be for it now. There'll be some heavy bombing coming our way, you mark my words.'

Kitty's hands shook as she cleaned the needle. She tried to block out the man's voice, but it droned like an annoying wasp at the edge of her consciousness.

'Oh yes, they'll be bombing us every night, I shouldn't wonder,' he continued. 'We'll be back down those air raid shelters every night.'

Kitty's heart started to crash against her ribs. Air raids had terrified her ever since she got caught in one with no chance to get to shelter.

'Although I've also heard tell the Germans have invented a super weapon that can destroy the city of London in one night,' the man went on. 'It'll make the Blitz look like a tea party, so they say...'

The needle slipped from Kitty's fingers and fell to the ground.

'Oh Lord, I'm sorry...' She fumbled to pick it up, but Nurse Riley's hand came down on hers, warm and steady.

'Take your time, Jenkins,' she said quietly. Dora Riley was no beauty, with her snub nose, square chin and broad, freckled face topped off by a curly thatch of red hair. But the kindness and under-standing in her muddy green eyes transformed her, making her seem quite lovely.

'We're all in a bit of a state today, aren't we?'

she said softly.

Kitty swallowed hard. 'Yes, Staff.'

She quietly set about preparing the needle again, trying to shut out the man's voice as he described the dastardly new weapons the Germans had in store for them, and how they would all surely perish.

'Mind you, they wouldn't have had time to invent them if our lot had got their fingers and out launched this invasion sooner,' the man said as he rolled over on the bed to await his injection. Now it was Dora Riley's turn to tremble, Kitty noticed. But one look at the staff nurse's set face and Kitty knew it was suppressed rage and not fear that was making her hands shake.

'If you ask me, some of our boys have been treating it like a holiday,' the man went on. 'I've heard what they've been getting up to in Italy, sunning themselves and enjoying the local hospitality – ow!' He yelped in pain as Dora jabbed the needle into his bare buttock. 'That hurt!'

'Did it? Oh dear, I'm sorry.' But Nurse Riley didn't sound in the least bit apologetic. In fact, she was smiling as she handed the needle back to Kitty.

'I should think so, too,' the man muttered darkly. 'It's a pity they can't get any proper nurses in here, instead of leaving it all to you lot!'

Kitty glanced at Dora, waiting for her to snap back. But the senior nurse's face was a mask of composure as she applied a dressing to the injection wound.

Dora Riley was too experienced a nurse to get a simple injection wrong, Kitty thought. Which meant she must have done it on purpose to shut him up.

And Kitty didn't blame her, either. If her husband was out there fighting for his country, she would have probably wanted to puncture the opinionated oaf where it hurt, too.

Just before midday, the green line bus arrived to transport the patients down to the country. Kitty's brother Arthur was one of the porters who came up to the ward with a trolley.

'You've heard the news, then?' he grinned, barely able to suppress his excitement. 'They've taken a couple of the beaches already. Now they're making their way inland, and the Germans don't stand a chance!'

'Shh!' Kitty glanced back at Dora. She was busy dealing with the burns patient, but Kitty knew she would be listening to every word. 'I'm not supposed to talk to you while I'm on duty, remember?'

Arthur shrugged dismissively. 'Oh, I'm not bothered about her. You should have heard the way she spoke to Mr Hopkins this morning. Almost like she didn't care about what was happening. He was very put out about it.'

'I expect she's got a lot on her mind,' Kitty murmured. But there was no telling Arthur. He might be five years younger than her, but that didn't stop him knowing everything.

'Anyway,' he went on, 'if what I hear is right, you might not have to work with her for much longer.'

'Why? What have you heard?'

'Oh, so you want to talk to me now?' Arthur gave her a maddening smile. 'I've a good mind not to tell you...'

'Arthur Jenkins!' Kitty hissed, exasperated.

He laughed. 'Oh, all right, then. Mr Hopkins reckons we'll be getting some military patients soon.'

Kitty stared at him. 'They're coming here?'

'It makes sense, doesn't it? We've got all these wards standing empty. And there are bound to be a lot of casualties coming over, after what's happened today...'

Dora Riley approached them. Kitty saw her glowering expression and quickly shushed Arthur.

'We have patients ready to go and a bus waiting downstairs, when you two have finished gossiping?' Dora said, her sharp gaze moving from one to the other.

Out of the corner of her eye, Kitty saw Arthur's face change, and prayed that he wouldn't be cheeky to Dora. Her brother could be his own worst enemy sometimes.

'I was just saying, Nurse, we'll have some more patients for you soon,' he said, in that cocky, confident way that always made Kitty cringe. 'Injured soldiers, back from France.'

Kitty saw the colour drain from Dora's face, her freckles standing out against the milky pallor of her skin. But then she collected herself.

'Let's hope for their sake you're not responsible for bringing them up to the ward, or they'll never get here!' she retorted. Then she turned to Kitty and added, 'Don't you have anything to be getting on with, Jenkins? Because I'm sure I can find a job for you if you haven't'

'Yes, Staff. Sorry, Staff.' Kitty bobbed her head

apologetically and scuttled off. As she reached the doors, she saw Dora saying something to Arthur. She hoped he would have the sense not to answer back for once. Arthur was like their father; he always had to have the last word.

But the news he'd given her stayed on Kitty's mind. Later, when all the patients had gone and they were cleaning the empty ward, she plucked up the courage to talk to Nurse Riley about it.

'Staff, do you think it's right what Arthur said, about us getting military patients?' she ventured, as she swung the buffer to and fro to polish the floor.

'No one's said anything to me about it,' Dora replied shortly.

'What's this?' Miss Sloan glanced up from her cleaning. 'Did you say we were getting military patients here? Oh, that's marvellous news!'

'It's not definite,' Kitty said, her wary gaze still fixed on Dora. She was on her hands and knees, head down, scrubbing away at a bed wheel as if her life depended on it. She had never known a senior nurse so willing to get her hands dirty. 'My brother just told me they might be opening up some of the wards–'

'Oh well, it must be true,' Miss Sloan said, pushing her spectacles up from the end of her long, hooked nose. 'The porters know all the news before the rest of us, don't they? I hope it's true. I would relish the chance to help our brave soldiers. Wouldn't you, Nurse Riley?'

Dora still didn't look up from her scrubbing. 'I think we have our hands full enough looking after our own patients, Miss Sloan,' she said quietly.

35

'Hardly,' Miss Sloan dismissed. 'I mean, look at this place. The patients are barely in their beds for five minutes before they're transported off. It isn't exactly real nursing, is it?'

Dora sat back on her heels. 'Real nursing?' she echoed.

Kitty heard the chill in her voice. Even Leonora Sloan, who wasn't known for her sensitivity, faltered slightly.

'You know what I mean,' she murmured.

'No, Miss Sloan, I don't think I do.' Dora got to her feet, her scrubbing brush still in her hand. 'What exactly do you know about real nursing?'

'Well–' Miss Sloan started to say, but Dora cut her off.

'No, you listen to me. Just because the Red Cross has seen fit to give you a uniform and a few weeks' training, that doesn't make you a nurse. You don't know the first thing about real nursing, otherwise you wouldn't be standing there spouting this nonsense.' Her green eyes glinted with anger. 'I'm sorry if you don't think making beds and sweeping floors is exciting enough for you, but it's as much a part of nursing as mopping soldiers' fevered brows.'

'I didn't say it wasn't,' Miss Sloan said in an injured voice, but Dora ignored her.

'And as for you,' she turned her angry green gaze on Kitty, 'I'll thank you and your brother to keep your rumours to yourself. And pay more attention to what you're doing,' she added. 'You're supposed to be using that buffer to polish the floor, not dancing with it!'

She dropped her brush into the bucket and

36

picked it up. 'You two can finish cleaning this ward. And I want to be able to see my face in that floor when you've finished. Because if I can't, you'll be doing it all over again!'

She stormed down the length of the ward, slamming the double doors behind her.

'Well, I never!' Miss Sloan turned to Kitty, bristling with indignation. 'I don't think we deserved that, do you?'

'No, we didn't.'

'I mean, I know she's under a lot of strain with her husband being away and everything, but all the same...' Miss Sloan shook her head. 'I do hope she isn't going to carry on like this.'

Kitty stared at the double doors. 'So do I,' she said. Otherwise she really would be volunteering to nurse on the military wards.

Chapter Four

It seemed as if Kitty Jenkins was right. As the days passed, wards that had lain empty since the Blitz were reopened, their curtains taken down, mattresses aired and windows flung open to let in the fresh June air. More VADs arrived, scrubbing floors, climbing up ladders to damp-dust light fittings, and making up beds.

Soon after that, a steady stream of nurses from the Queen Alexandra Imperial Military Nursing Service began to appear at the Nightingale. The hospital passageways bustled with a sea of scarlet and grey uniforms.

Dora watched from the window as a new linen order was unloaded from the back of a lorry.

'I don't know,' she sighed. 'I've been asking for new bed linen for six months but everyone said it couldn't be found. And now look!'

'Yes, well, it's for the soldiers, isn't it?' Miss Sloan said piously. She had been very tight-lipped with Dora since her outburst a few days earlier.

Dora still felt ashamed when she thought about how she'd lashed out at them. Poor Miss Sloan didn't deserve it, and neither did Kitty. She had apologised to both of them the following day, and even though they seemed to accept it Dora could tell they were still wary of her.

She didn't blame them for being so bewildered. She had always done her best to be firm but fair with them, so for her to snap so harshly was completely out of character.

She only wished she could explain to them how frightened she was. The idea of nursing injured soldiers might seem noble and wonderful to them, but all Dora could think of was that one day those doors might open and it might be her own husband brought in on a stretcher, close to death. The fear haunted her so much she could barely think of anything else.

It was a warm day in the middle of June when the first of the wounded soldiers began to arrive. Dora and Kitty were on their way down to lunch as the military ambulance rumbled into the courtyard.

'Here they come,' Kitty said.

'So I see.' Dora went to hurry past, but Kitty

slowed down to watch as half a dozen QA nurses swarmed towards the rear of the ambulance, preceded by orderlies bearing stretchers.

Dora followed the junior nurse's avid gaze. 'I suppose you'll be asking Matron for a transfer now?' she said.

Kitty didn't reply at first, but a tell-tale blush crept up her neck from under her starched collar. 'I wouldn't do that, Staff,' she said loyally. 'Not while you need me on the emergency admissions ward.'

Dora smiled. Her outburst had obviously shaken the poor girl. 'But you'd rather nurse soldiers?'

Kitty's chin lifted, her eyes still fixed on the ambulance. 'It's what I've been training for, Staff.'

Dora glanced sideways at her. She had known Kitty Jenkins for many years, long before she had started her training at the Nightingale. Their families had lived around the corner from each other in Bethnal Green, and Kitty was a close friend of Dora's younger sister Bea. It was a surprise to everyone when the girls were conscripted, and Kitty had decided to sign up as a nurse instead of following Bea into factory work. No one, least of all Dora, had imagined she would finish the training, but Kitty had proved them all wrong.

She had done well so far, but Dora knew from her own experience that nursing patients with fevers and failing hearts was a lot different from dealing with injured soldiers.

'It's not easy,' she warned her.

'I'm not afraid of hard work.'

'I'm not talking about physical work, although once you've lifted a full-grown man in and out of

39

bed a few times you'll know about it! No, I mean it gets you up here.' She tapped her temple. 'You see some terrible sights, men with their limbs hanging off, their skin and hair burned away... Some of those scars are so horrible they'll stay with you forever.'

'Surely I'm the last person to worry about that?'

Kitty put her hand up to her left cheek, where the starched edge of her cap met her dark hair. Dora saw the gesture and could have bitten off her tongue.

'Jenkins–' she started to say, but Kitty cut her off.

'Sorry, Staff, I've just remembered my mum asked me to pass on a message to Arthur,' she said. 'Do you mind if I go and do it now?'

'No, of course not. I'll see you in the canteen...'

But her words were lost on the air as Kitty hurried away across the courtyard in the direction of the porters' lodge.

Dora watched her go. The poor girl, she couldn't wait to escape.

How could she have forgotten the terrible scars Kitty had suffered from that air raid three years earlier? She carefully hid the side of her face under her hair, but the withered flesh on her left arm was still visible whenever she had to roll up her sleeves.

Dora knew how sensitive she was about them, and she was mortified at her own thoughtlessness.

She looked back towards the ambulance. The orderlies had opened the back doors, and Dora could see the first of the men being taken off, their khaki uniforms stained brown with blood. She averted her eyes and hurried past.

The hospital dining room, as Dora had once known it, had long gone, destroyed by a German bomb shortly after the start of the Blitz. Since then, the nurses and doctors had been fed from a mobile canteen set up by the WVS in one of the basement rooms. It was dark, damp and crowded. But as Matron was always reminding them, it was better than nothing.

Today, as usual, she joined the queue in front of the worthy women of the WVS in their green uniforms, who were handing out thin-looking paste sandwiches.

Dora looked down at her tray. 'No hot food today?'

'We've lost power in the kitchen again,' one of the WVS women told her apologetically. 'Someone is trying to get the emergency generator going, but it might take a little while. You can have a cup of tea?' she offered, pointing to the large urn on the end of the counter. 'It's a bit stewed, but at least it's warm.'

While Dora waited for the woman to coax tea from the steaming, spluttering urn, she looked around the basement. Once upon a time, when she first started training at the Nightingale, the dining room upstairs would have been arranged with rows of tables, each occupied by different nurses according to their rank. There were still a few tables in the basement, but now they were mostly occupied by QAs.

It was nice to see the hospital so busy again, but she missed seeing the ward sisters, and the staff nurses, and the nervous probationers in their striped uniforms. She missed the familiar faces of her friends, the girls she'd trained with. Mealtimes were when they could all meet up to chat and gossip, to share the gruesome stories of what they had done and seen, or to console each other over Sister's latest telling-off. Whatever happened, they generally ended up laughing about it...

Her roaming gaze suddenly snagged on a particular face sitting among the QAs at a corner table. Dora squinted, not sure whether she was seeing things. It was as if she'd summoned the young woman up from her memory and made her into a living, breathing being.

It couldn't really be her, could it? Surely not. The last time Dora had seen that face, she was waving her off on a hospital ship. As far as she knew, she was still there. Surely she would have written to let her know if she was coming home, especially if she was returning to the Nightingale?

But that face did seem very familiar...

'Your tea.' The WVS woman planted the cup and saucer down in front of her, making her jump.

'Thank you.' Dora turned to put it on her tray. But when she turned back again, the young woman had gone.

Dora gazed around and saw her heading towards the door, her tall, graceful frame setting her head and shoulders above the other QAs. This time there was no doubt in her mind it was her.

'Dawson?' She abandoned the tray without thinking and hurried after her, ignoring the WVS woman's cry of protest.

'What about your tea? You can't just waste it, you know. There is a war on!'

Dora pushed her way through the throng of

QAs and hurried out into the passageway.

'Dawson!'

Further down the corridor the young woman stopped and swung round slowly to face her.

'Riley?' Dora saw her mouth forming her name, and hurried towards her, edging past the QAs making their way towards the canteen.

She had changed. Dora could see it as she drew closer. Helen Dawson had always been slender, but she'd lost so much weight, her eyes were like huge, dark pools in her drawn face.

The other QAs drifted off, leaving one scowling, dumpy girl still standing at Helen's side.

'Fancy seeing you here!' Dora grinned.

'You too.' Helen looked as surprised as Dora felt. 'I didn't realise you'd still be here. I thought they'd moved all the Nightingale staff down to the country with the patients?'

'What, me leave the East End? That'll be the day!' Dora shook her head. 'No, there are still a few of us here, battling on. But what about you? When did you get back from North Africa?'

'A few days ago.'

'And they didn't send you straight off to France?'

'I—'

'We were transferred back to England to deal with the casualties.' It was the other girl who spoke for her. Her voice was so loud and brusque it took Dora by surprise.

Dora turned back to Helen. 'How's David? Did he come home, too?'

Helen's smile faded. 'No, he – didn't.'

Dora saw the sadness on her friend's face.

43

'I know how you feel,' she said quietly. 'Nick's out there, too.'

Helen opened her mouth to reply, but once again the dumpy girl stepped in. 'We should be getting back to the ward, Dawson,' she said. 'Those patients should be arriving soon.'

'Yes. Yes, of course.' Helen gave Dora an apologetic smile. 'It was nice to see you again, Riley.'

'You too. I daresay we'll be running into each other a lot, since we're both working here. Perhaps we could go out for tea...?'

But Helen had already gone, hurrying in the wake of the other girl's brisk footsteps.

'Who was that?' Clare wanted to know as they walked away.

'An old friend of mine, Dora Riley. We shared a room together while we were training here.'

Helen glanced back over her shoulder at Dora. Seeing her again, it was as if someone had turned on a tap, letting all the memories rush out, filling her mind with pictures. That draughty attic room, with its three narrow beds. The hours they'd spent there, poring over their textbooks, desperately testing each other before their State Finals. Dora and Millie, their other room mate, standing on their beds, craning their necks to blow cigarette smoke through the skylight so the Home Sister wouldn't catch them. Coming home after lights out and clambering up the drainpipe, hoping someone had remembered to leave the window open...

'I suppose you must have had some high old times here as a student?' Clare guessed her thoughts.

44

Helen smiled. 'Yes, we did.'

The Nightingale was where she'd grown up. Up until the time she'd arrived as a student, she had led a sheltered life under the control of her domineering mother. But here she'd learned to be independent, to make friends, to fall in love...

She'd had mixed feelings about coming back. There were so many memories for her at the Nightingale. This was where she'd had some of her happiest times, and some of her most heartbreaking.

But now it all seemed like a lifetime ago. So much had happened to Helen since then, it was as if she was picturing a different person's life.

The Nightingale was different, too. With its crumbling walls and bombed-out buildings, nothing was as she remembered it. She had spent the whole morning getting lost in the unfamiliar passageways.

Perhaps it was for the best, she thought. Some memories were better left in the past.

'Are you going to tell her?' Clare's next words were like a blow, shocking Helen back to the present.

Helen looked at her sharply. 'Who?'

'Your friend Riley. Are you going to tell her what happened?'

'No!'

'But surely if she's such an old friend of yours...'

Helen looked back down the corridor to where Dora had stood, even though she had long since disappeared from view. 'I don't want anyone to know,' she said.

Clare nodded. 'I think it's probably for the

best,' she said. She patted Helen's arm. 'That's why you've come here, isn't it? To put everything behind you and start again.'

Helen smiled sadly. If only it was that simple, she thought.

Chapter Five

Lily Doyle was in one of her moods again.

Dora felt it as soon as she came into the house. Her nanna was sitting at one end of the kitchen table, shelling peas while her sister-in-law sat at the other, staring blankly into space and ignoring her little daughter Mabel who was clamouring for her attention.

Dora felt an instant surge of irritation at the sight of Lily, her head drooping like a flower on her slender neck. But then the twins came rushing in to greet her and she forgot all about her sister-in-law as she cuddled and fussed over them.

Her mother appeared in the doorway to the scullery. 'Cup of tea, love?' she offered. 'It's just brewed.'

'Yes please, Mum.' Dora followed her into the scullery, Walter and Winnie still clinging to her skirt.

'What's up with Lily?' she asked.

Rose Doyle sighed. 'God knows. She's been sitting there all day, looking like a wet weekend. It's been driving me mad, to tell the truth.' She stirred the leaves in the big brown teapot.

'She wants to get off her backside and get a job, then she wouldn't have time to feel sorry for herself.'

'Oh, she'd never do that.'

'I don't see why not. There's work to be done, so why shouldn't she do it?'

Her mother shook her head. 'She ain't like the rest of us, Dor.'

Dora glanced back through the thin curtain that divided the kitchen from the scullery.

It was true, Lily Doyle certainly wasn't anything like her in-laws. The Doyle women were all born grafters. Even Nanna Winnie – old, arthritic and nearly blind as she was – still did her bit to help around the house.

But Lily used the fact that she was the mother of a young child as an excuse not to do war work, even though it was usually Dora's mother who took care of Mabel while Lily moped around the place, not lifting a finger.

Dora had tried to be patient with her, but Lily and her moods were beginning to get under her skin.

'She's delicate,' Rose said.

Dora laughed. 'Delicate, my backside! She's just idle, if you ask me.'

Rose chuckled as she poured the tea. 'You might be right, there.' She handed Dora a cup. 'How was your day, anyway?'

'Oh, the usual. A few broken bones and a woman who fainted in the fishmonger's queue.'

She didn't tell her mother about the patient with peritonitis who'd died in front of her because there was no doctor to operate on him, or the shy young

47

wife who'd been too ashamed to go to the doctor about her venereal disease until it was too late.

Nor did she tell her how many times she'd thought she'd seen Nick being brought in on one of the military ambulances. Rose Doyle had enough to deal with, without Dora loading her misery on her shoulders.

'I'm not surprised,' Rose said. 'D'you know, I waited nearly two hours to buy a lump of cod this morning?'

'And I bet when you got to the front of the queue they were sold out?' Dora finished for her.

Rose looked rueful. 'I probably would have fainted with shock myself if they'd had any left!'

They both laughed. Then Dora said, 'How were the twins? I hope they didn't play you up too much?'

'Not at all.' Rose smiled. 'They were little angels, as usual.'

'More like little monkeys, I'll bet!' Dora ruffled her son's hair affectionately.

Rose poured another cup of tea. 'I'll just take this in to your nanna–'

'I'll do it,' Dora picked up her cup. 'You've been on your feet all day.'

'So have you.'

'Yes, but my legs are younger than yours.'

Back in the kitchen, Nanna Winnie was show-ing Mabel how to shell peas.

'Use your thumb, like this,' she was saying to the little girl, who perched on her knee. 'That's it, you've got the idea.'

'Mum, look!' Mabel held up a handful of peas.

'Very nice.' Lily didn't bother to look up, much

to Dora's irritation.

'Good girl,' Nanna said encouragingly to Mabel. 'Now you've got the knack, you can shell all the peas. Make yourself useful.' She glared at Lily when she said it.

'I'm glad someone is,' Dora said, setting down the cup in front of Nanna.

Lily looked up at last. There was no denying she was a pretty girl, even with her sulky, turned-down mouth.

'I can't help it if I'm too tired to lend a hand, can I?' she said. 'If you must know, I didn't get a wink of sleep last night.'

'Really?' Dora shot back. 'That's funny, I heard you snoring all night.'

Lily ignored her. 'I don't like sharing a room with you and the children,' she complained. 'I'm such a light sleeper, the slightest noise wakes me up.'

'I don't like it either,' Dora said. 'But we've got to put up with it, haven't we? There's nine of us crammed into two rooms, in case you haven't noticed.'

Lily sighed. 'I wish we still lived in Griffin Street. There was much more room there.'

'If wishes were horses, beggars would ride,' Nanna Winnie muttered.

Dora glanced at her grandmother. Nanna Winnie had her head down, her swollen fingers busy shelling peas, but Dora knew Lily's comment would have hurt her. Nanna had lived in Griffin Street since she was a young bride, and she felt its loss more deeply than anyone.

Not that Lily would have thought about that

49

before she opened her mouth. She never thought of anyone but herself.

'But it was such a lovely house,' she sighed. 'We had that nice room all to ourselves, Peter and Mabel and me. And we knew all the neighbours. It wasn't like round here, where we don't know a soul–'

'Why don't you lay the table?' Dora cut in desperately.

Lily sent her a long-suffering look. 'If I must.'

Dora watched her sister-in-law dragging herself off to the scullery as if her legs were made of lead.

'Perhaps she needs a tonic?' Nanna suggested.

She needs a kick up the backside, Dora thought. She would have given her one, too, but she didn't want to create more bad feeling in the house.

Dora's sister Bea returned home just as her mother was putting the pot of corned beef hash on the table. She came in like a whirlwind as usual, casting off her hat and coat and complaining about the terrible day she'd had at the factory.

'Honestly, I worked my fingers to the bone,' she said. 'Look–' she held out her hands. 'Have you ever seen blisters like it? And my nails are broken.' She examined her thumb sulkily.

'Poor you,' Dora said. 'I'm surprised we didn't see you in Casualty.'

Bea sent her a sharp look, sensing sarcasm. 'Don't you start with me, Dora Riley, or I've a good mind not to give you this...' She reached into her coat pocket and produced a bar of Fry's chocolate, which she tossed on to the table.

Dora stared at it. It was so long since she'd seen a bar of chocolate she'd almost forgotten what it looked like. 'Where did you get that?'

'A friend gave it to me last night,' Bea said.

'Some Yank, I'll bet,' their brother Alfie said, snatching up the chocolate bar, and turning it around in his hands. From his wide-eyed expression, he could hardly believe what he was seeing either.

Bea clipped him round the ear. 'That's enough of your cheek! And you're to share it with the little ones, mind.'

Alfie pulled a face. 'There won't be much to go round.'

'Oh, I'm sorry.' Bea looked mock contrite. 'I'll tell my friend not to bother next time, shall I?'

'Is he right, Bea?' Rose asked. 'Did you get it off an American?'

Bea's chin lifted defiantly. 'What do you think? I didn't go and buy it down the Co-op, did I? Oh, don't look so worried, Mum!' she grinned. 'They've got loads to spare. You should see them at the club. Their leftovers could feed us lot for three days!'

She glanced at the pot her mother had placed on the table, and Dora saw her sister's lip curl. Bea had always been a little madam, but she'd changed even more since she started volunteering at the American Red Cross Club in Mayfair. Two nights a week she trotted off up West, high heels on and dolled up to the nines. She swore she only cleared plates and served drinks, but Dora was worried about her younger sister.

And her mother clearly felt the same. 'I'm not sure I like you taking presents off strange men,' Rose said. 'Especially not Americans. You hear

51

such stories about them, don't you?'

'Don't worry, Mum. I can look after myself.'

'Yes, but you don't want to get a name for yourself, do you? You know how people talk.'

'Oh, it's all different these days. Girls can go out and have fun without anyone saying anything.' Bea helped herself to a piece of chocolate and put it in her mouth.

'I can't remember the last time I had a bit of fun,' Lily said mournfully.

'You should come out with me,' Bea said. 'I'm going dancing with Kitty at the Palais tomorrow night. Why don't you come with us?'

'I might just do that.' Lily turned to Rose. 'You wouldn't mind looking after Mabel for a couple of hours, would you?'

'Why should she? She looks after her every other hour God sends!' Nanna mumbled.

The thought of a night out seemed to brighten Lily's spirits no end. Straight after tea, she disappeared off with Bea to plan what they were going to wear, leaving Dora and her mother to wash and dry up.

'Her Ladyship seems in a much better mood,' Dora observed as she scrubbed at a pan.

'Thank Gawd for that!' Rose sighed. 'That face could curdle milk.' Her expression grew serious. 'I'm not sure I agree with this business about her going out dancing, though. Surely it ain't respectable for a married woman to go gadding about, especially not with her husband away serving his country. As I said, people talk.'

Dora thought about the young woman with gonorrhoea in Casualty, and how she'd wept in her arms.

'It was only one night,' she'd cried. 'I didn't even see him again. I never thought I'd catch anything ... what will people say?'

But even Lily wouldn't be that daft, she thought. 'She's only going out dancing. And Bea and Kitty will be there to keep an eye on her, make sure she doesn't get into any trouble.'

'I suppose you're right,' Rose sighed. 'Anyway, at least it means we won't have to look at her miserable face for another night!'

Lily was asleep when Dora got up for work the following morning. So much for her being a light sleeper, she thought.

Kitty Jenkins was waiting for Dora when she came on to the ward.

'We're to report to Matron's office straight away,' she said.

Dora looked at the junior nurse's face, all lit up with hope, and knew exactly what she was thinking. This was the summons she'd been waiting for.

Matron's makeshift office was situated in what had been the sister's sitting room off the children's ward. Her original office was long gone, destroyed in the blast three years earlier that had killed the Assistant Matron, Miss Hanley.

Her surroundings might have changed but Miss Kathleen Fox was as cool and implacable as ever as she sat behind her desk in her black uniform, her face framed by an elaborate starched headdress. If she looked closely, Dora could see the lines of strain around her grey eyes, and the threads of white in her chestnut hair, but Matron's indomitable spirit and energy were still there. And Dora still felt as nervous as a probationer as she and Kitty stood on the other side of the desk, waiting to hear their fate.

'As I'm sure you are aware by now, the Ministry has requested that this hospital be used for the treatment of military casualties,' Matron said. 'These wards would usually be staffed by QAs, but with so many still away in Europe, they have requested help from some of our experienced nurses.'

Dora felt Kitty's excitement beside her. The young girl was fit to burst. 'Yes, Matron,' she said.

'With that in mind, you will both be transferring to one of the military wards as from tomorrow morning. Nurse Riley, you will be senior staff nurse, acting under the instruction of a QA. I believe you already know Nurse Dawson?'

'Yes, Matron.' Dora smiled. That was something, at least.

'She will be acting as Sister for at least two other wards, so I daresay she will rely on your judgement and experience to help her,' Miss Fox went on. 'You will also have Nurse Jenkins and two VADs to help you.'

'Thank you, Matron.' Kitty was beaming from ear to ear, but Dora was still troubled.

'Excuse me, Matron, but what will happen to Casualty, and the emergency wards?' she asked.

Miss Fox's brows puckered in a small frown. 'We will still continue to run a Casualty department, but any emergency admissions will be sent to the City Infirmary before they are transferred down to Kent,' she said. She must have noticed

Dora's expression because she added, 'I know the situation is not ideal by any means, but the needs of the military must come first.'

'Yes, Matron.' Dora could feel Kitty's sidelong glare fixed on her.

'As I said, you will be transferring to your new ward tomorrow morning. We will be using what was Wren Ward, Nurse Riley, if you could see that it is stocked and all the beds made up?'

'Yes, Matron.' Dora surreptitiously wiped her clammy hands down her apron. She was aware of a strange chill on the back of her neck. 'Will the patients be arriving tomorrow?'

Miss Fox nodded. 'Either late tomorrow, or the day after.' She paused, her gaze dropping to the blotter in front of her. 'There is something else you will need to know,' she said at last. 'I feel it only fair to warn you, these particular patients might not be what you're expecting...'

Chapter Six

'They're making you nurse *Germans?*'

Kitty stared down at a faded patch on the chenille tablecloth. She didn't dare meet her father's eye.

'They're prisoners of war, Dad,' she said quietly.

'They're still our enemy! It just ain't right they should be under the same roof as our brave fighting men. Why haven't they got their own hospitals?'

'They do at some camps,' Arthur put in, chewing on a piece of boiled mutton. 'The Red Cross run them. Mr Hopkins told us.'

Horace Jenkins turned his accusing gaze on Kitty.

'Well? I don't know, do I?' she said. 'All I know is what Matron told me.'

Kitty shot an appealing look at her mother. Florrie Jenkins was very quiet, her head down, seemingly absorbed in her meal. No one else but Kitty seemed to notice she wasn't eating anything.

'Mr Hopkins thinks it's a disgrace,' Arthur said. 'He says he's a good mind not to let us set foot on that ward.'

'He's got the right idea,' their father said. 'I think it's disgusting to waste our time and our medicine on them when one of our own boys might be in need.' He pointed his fork at Kitty. 'You want to do the same, Kit. Tell them you won't do it.'

'I've already tried. Matron says I've got no choice.'

Kitty had summoned up the courage to go back and see Matron that afternoon, to request a transfer to another military ward. She had tried to plead her case, even explained how her brother Raymond had been killed.

Miss Fox had listened, her face sympathetic as ever, but she had been implacable: Kitty had to do as she was told. Matron was sorry, but as she pointed out, Kitty wasn't the only person to lose a loved one. This war had come at a great cost, and they were all grieving someone. But they could not and should not let that stop them doing their duty.

'We'll see about that,' her father declared, throwing down his knife and fork with a clatter. 'I'll go down to that hospital tomorrow morning and have a word...'

'Don't do that, Dad, please,' Kitty begged. She could just imagine Matron's face if her father stormed into her office, banging on the desk and shouting the odds as usual.

'Well, something has to be done. I'm not letting you nurse Germans, and that's final!'

'I'll go and see Matron again,' Kitty promised. Anything to keep her father from making a scene.

'Well, those Germans needn't think I'm going to fetch and carry for them, whatever anyone says,' Arthur declared.

'Quite right, son. I'm glad someone in this family's got some sense!' Kitty felt the full force of her father's accusing stare.

'You don't want to get into trouble at the hospital,' she warned her brother quietly.

'What can they do? They can't give me the sack, there ain't enough men to fill the jobs as it is.' Arthur's chin lifted. 'Besides, by Christmas I'll be old enough to sign up and then I'll be gone.'

'Let's hope it's all over by then,' Florrie Jenkins murmured.

'I hope not!' Arthur said.

'Listen to him,' Horace Jenkins said fondly. 'The lad's desperate to go and do his bit.' He reached across the table and ruffled Arthur's thatch of hair. 'He wants to go and give those Germans what for, don't you, son?'

'I'll say, Dad. They won't know what's hit them when I get my hands on them!'

'That's the spirit. You go and make your mum

57

and dad proud, eh? Just like your brother–'

Florrie Jenkins shot to her feet and began collecting up the plates. 'I'll go and see about pudding,' she mumbled.

Kitty followed her mother out to the scullery, where she was going through the cupboards, muttering to herself.

'There isn't much,' she was saying. 'I only managed to get one tin of fruit at the grocer's this morning. And there's no cream to go with it–'

'I'm sure that'll be fine, Mum.'

'Yes, but you know how your father likes his cream.'

'He'll have to go without, won't he?'

Her mother shot her a fearful look. 'I suppose I could use the top of the milk,' she said. 'That would do, wouldn't it?'

She rummaged in the drawer and took out the tin opener, but her hands were shaking so much she couldn't work it. Kitty stepped forward and took it from her.

'Here, let me do it,' she said gently.

'Thank you, love.' Florrie Jenkins brushed a mousy brown curl off her face with the back of her hand. 'Honestly, I don't know what's the matter with me today. I'm all fingers and thumbs...' Her voice trailed off, and Kitty read the weary despair in her mother's eyes.

'Don't upset yourself, Mum,' she said. 'Arthur won't need to go away.'

Her mother's smile trembled. 'I hope not, love. I don't know what I'd do if...'

She didn't need to say any more. Raymond's death had hit them all hard, but her mother had taken it worst of all. Overnight, Florrie Jenkins had turned from a cheerful, capable mother to a nervous, shattered wreck. It broke Kitty's heart to see her laid so low.

And hearing Arthur and her father talking about going off to fight didn't help, either. Kitty wished she could explain to them how much they were hurting her mother, but she knew neither of them would listen.

They ate their pudding in silence, the four of them sitting round the table, all lost in their own thoughts. Once upon a time, when Raymond was with them, mealtimes were lively affairs. Everyone would be talking at once, and Ray would be entertaining them all with his funny stories. Her father and Arthur would be roaring with laughter, and her mother would chuckle and shake her head and say, 'Get on with you, Ray! You must be making it up.'

'It's true,' Ray would insist solemnly. 'True as I'm riding this bike.'

But no one told funny stories any more. There was no laughter or lightness in the house. They didn't even have any friends or neighbours dropping in. Now no one bothered to call because her mother was too frail and her father too bad-tempered. Even Arthur was no longer the happy-go-lucky kid he used to be. Losing his older brother had made him angry and vindictive.

The Germans did this to them. Kitty pushed her meagre portion of fruit around her bowl, her throat so closed up she couldn't swallow it. The Germans had taken away her brother and torn her family apart.

And now she had to nurse them.

As her father said, it just wasn't right.

Bea Doyle was late as usual. Kitty stood outside the dance hall for twenty minutes before she saw her sauntering down the road, arm in arm with a slim, dark-haired girl.

It always gave Kitty a jolt to see her friend. Bea looked so like Nurse Riley, with her curly thatch of red hair and freckled face. But that was where the similarity between the sisters ended.

'There you are,' Kitty peeled herself away from the wall to greet her. 'I thought you weren't coming.'

'Better late than never, eh?' Typical Bea, she was never one to apologise. 'This is Lily, my brother's wife. I told her she could come out with us.'

Lily nodded a quiet greeting. Her name suited her, Kitty thought. She looked as beautiful and fragile as a flower, her small, pointed face dominated by a pair of wide brown eyes.

The dance hall was almost deserted when they went inside.

'Where is everyone?' Lily looked around, her mouth turned down. 'There's no one here. I thought you said we were going to have fun.'

'It's early yet,' Bea said. 'Wait and see, it'll liven up soon.'

'I hope so,' Lily pouted. 'Otherwise I might as well have stayed at home and played whist with your nanna!'

Kitty looked at her and felt an instant dislike. 'It's hardly our fault all the men have been sent to France, is it?' she said.

She was being sarcastic, but Lily just stared at her blankly. 'Bea promised me we were going to have fun,' she insisted stubbornly. 'She said we could go dancing.'

Before Kitty could reply, Bea tapped her shoulder. 'Don't look now, girls, but I think we're in luck,' she said, nodding towards the door.

Of course they both swung round straight away and looked at the trio of young men in khaki uniforms who had just swaggered in.

Kitty automatically reached up and smoothed her hair down over her temple. Her long sleeves already hid the scars on her arm, but she tugged at her cuff to reassure herself.

'Oh, they're looking round. Quick, look as if we're doing something else.'

Bea turned her back on them, but Lily continued to gawp, as if she couldn't bear to tear her gaze away. 'They're coming over!' she squeaked.

'For heaven's sake, Lily, I told you not to look!' Bea snapped. 'Now don't look too eager,' she warned them all in an undertone, as the men sauntered over.

'What have we here?' one of them said in a deep Scottish accent. 'Surely you pretty ladies can't be alone?'

Bea affected a careless shrug. 'It looks like it, doesn't it?'

'And why's that, I wonder?'

'Perhaps we're particular about the company we keep.'

The young man's smile widened. He was the most handsome of the group, his black wavy hair carefully Brylcreemed into place. The friends who flanked him were the complete opposite to each other, one tall and lanky, the other stockily built.

'So does that mean you wouldn't let us buy you a drink?' the dark-haired man said.

'Oh, go on, then. You can buy us all a port and lemon.'

'I'll just have a lemonade, please,' Kitty put in.

'Take no notice, she'll have the same as us,' Bea said dismissively.

Kitty glared at her as the young man headed off to the bar. 'I can't go home tipsy, my dad will have something to say about it,' she hissed.

'We've come to have some fun, haven't we?' Bea whispered back.

'What's your name?' the lanky man asked Lily, when his friend had gone to the bar. Like his friend, he sounded Scottish.

'That would be telling,' she replied archly.

'Then I'll just have to call you sweetheart, won't I?'

It was hardly the wittiest comment in the world, but Lily still giggled. She kept her left hand down by her side, hidden in the folds of her skirt, Kitty noticed.

The stocky young man turned to her. 'I'm Mal,' he said, holding out his hand. 'And you are...?'

'It's Kitty,' Bea chimed in before she had a chance to answer. 'But she's a bit shy,' she added.

'Is that right?' Mal smiled at her as they shook hands. His grip was firm and strong, and lasted a fraction longer than it should have. 'Well, as it happens I like shy girls.'

He wasn't bad-looking, Kitty thought. He was well built and muscular, with light brown hair and a nice smile. Just her type, in fact. But that only made her feel more flustered.

The dark-haired man returned with their drinks. 'Sorry,' he said, handing the glasses round. 'The barman says they're out of alcohol. It's just lemonade after all.'

Bea pulled a disgusted face, while Kitty tried to hide her relief.

They found a corner table to sit down. Bea made sure she was sitting next to the dark-haired man, while Lily wedged herself in next to Len, the taller of the other two. She still kept her left hand folded in her lap.

Kitty stared into her drink, feeling at a loss. Across the table, Bea and Lily seemed to know exactly what to do, flirting and laughing and teasing with the soldiers.

Once upon a time, Kitty might have been just the same. But the accident had changed her, made her shy and self-conscious. Now she sat rigidly, her shoulders tensed in case she accidentally brushed against Mal at her side.

'I can't believe there's no whisky,' Len muttered from across the table. 'I told you we should have gone to that pub we found last night. What was it called?'

'The White Lion,' Mal said.

'Then we wouldn't have met these nice young ladies, would we?' his friend Andy said, sliding his arm oh so casually along the back of Bea's seat.

'No, but they had plenty of whisky.'

'That's what you think,' Kitty mumbled.

Len turned to look at her. 'What?'

'It was probably topped up with methylated

spirits coloured to look like whisky. They sell it to the servicemen when they're too drunk to tell the difference.'

Mal roared with laughter. 'Looks like you were had, pal! Imagine that, a Scotsman who can't tell his whisky!'

'You were drinking it, too!' Len snapped back, his face colouring. But after a moment, he smiled grudgingly, and soon they were all laughing.

They relaxed a little after that. They found out the young men were part of a Scottish Highland regiment sent down to London three days earlier.

'Although we can't tell you what we're doing,' Len said, tapping the side of his nose. 'It's all very hush-hush.'

Mal tried to make conversation with her, and Kitty did her best to join in, but she'd lost so much confidence that she had almost forgotten how to be young and carefree and flirtatious.

The dancing started, and Bea and Lily quickly made their way on to the dance floor with their partners, leaving Kitty with Mal.

'Is it my cologne?' he said. She looked round to see him watching her earnestly.

'I beg your pardon?'

'Only I've been sitting here trying to work out what it is you don't like about me, and I reckon that's what it must be. It certainly can't be any-thing else, because I'm perfect in every other way,' he said.

Kitty smiled in spite of herself. 'Oh, you think so, do you?'

'Of course. I mean, look at me.' He leaned back so she could get a better view. 'I'm a good catch, even if I do say so myself. I mean, I've got the looks, and the charm–'

'And the modesty!' Kitty laughed.

'And I'm a darn good dancer, too. D'you want to see?' He held out his hand to her. 'Come on, lass,' he urged. 'At least if we're dancing you don't have to try to make conversation with me.'

Kitty smiled. 'That's true.'

She had almost forgotten how much she loved dancing. She had certainly forgotten what it felt like to be in a man's arms. She was still too nervous to let herself go, but she liked the feeling of Mal's hand resting in the small of her back, firm and strong, guiding her around the floor.

'Relax,' he leaned forward to murmur in her ear, so close she could feel the warmth of his breath fanning against her face. 'You're supposed to be enjoying yourself, remember?'

The next moment the lilting waltz ended and the music picked up tempo. Kitty took a step back from Mal and started back towards their table, but he held on to her hand, drawing her back.

'You can't go now,' he said. 'We're just getting started.'

Kitty shook her head. Around her, the other couples were starting to jitterbug, jumping and whirling, bumping into her and ricocheting off again. 'I don't like this kind of dancing.'

'Have you ever tried it?'

'No, but–'

'Then you can't say you don't like it.'

'But I don't know how–' Kitty started to protest, but Mal reached out and grasped her other hand.

'I'll show you.'

The steps weren't as hard as she'd feared. Soon Kitty was jitterbugging with the others, jumping and spinning and laughing with delight. The music got faster and faster and she could hardly breathe as she spun round and round, the other couples a blur of moving colour around her.

Then, suddenly, Mal grasped her round the waist and swung her high in the air. Kitty let out a scream of laughter as she felt herself flying above the crowd. She could feel her skirt flying up too, but she was enjoying herself too much to care that she might be showing her drawers to the world.

The music stopped and Mal lowered her gently until her feet touched the floor. But he went on holding her, his hands circling her waist. Kitty was still laughing, too breathless to speak, so she didn't notice as Mal pulled her closer and reached up to push the hair back from her face.

By the time she'd reacted and pulled away from him to smooth her hair back over her temple, it was too late. Kitty saw the dawning horror in his eyes.

'Your face–' he started to say.

She didn't wait for him to finish his sentence. She was already stumbling off the dance floor. She heard Bea calling out to her as she fled, but she ignored her, fetching her coat and hurrying for the door.

Bea caught up with her halfway down the street.

'Kitty?' She grabbed her arm, swinging her round to face her. 'I saw what happened. Are you all right?'

'I'm fine.' Kitty dabbed at her face with her coat sleeve.

'You're not. I can see you've been crying.' Bea paused, then said, 'I'm sure he didn't mean anything by it. He was just – surprised, that's all.'

'Shocked, you mean?' Bea might try to pretend to make her feel better, but Kitty had seen the horror and disgust on his face.

'Don't be daft, it's not that bad.' Bea's gaze travelled up to Kitty's scar, now hidden behind the curtain of her hair. 'Honestly, you're the only one who thinks it looks ugly.'

I'm not the only one, Kitty thought. Her fiancé Alex had jilted her just before their wedding a year ago. He'd made all kinds of excuses about not being sure about what their future held with the war on, but Kitty knew the real reason was that he was repelled by her scarred face. He could hardly bear to look at her.

'Look, why don't you come back inside?' Bea said. 'I'm sure Mal didn't–'

Kitty shook her head. Nothing on earth would have convinced her to go back into that dance hall, not after what had just happened.

'I'm a bit tired,' she said. 'I'd like to go home.'

'Shall we come with you?' She could hear the reluctance, in Bea's voice.

'No, it's all right. You stay. I don't want to spoil your evening.'

'I don't mind, honestly,' Bea insisted. Then she added, 'Although I did promise poor Lily a good night out...'

Kitty pressed her lips together to stop herself smiling. Bea wasn't one to miss a night out, either. 'Then you'd best get back, hadn't you?'

Night was falling, and Kitty hurried home,

anxious to get there before it got too dark. It wasn't the blackout that made her nervous – after five years, she'd got used to finding her way in the pitch-dark streets, measuring her steps, her ears cocked for the sound of cars and bicycles. But the idea of being caught out in an air raid still terrified her. She had been running to the shelter when she'd been caught by white-hot shrapnel raining out of the sky. Even now, all this time later, she could still feel it searing into her skin.

'Is that you, love?' Florrie Jenkins called out as Kitty let herself in the back door twenty minutes later.

'Yes, Mum.' Kitty followed the sound of her voice. Her mother was in the kitchen, doing some mending while a man on the wireless gave advice to listeners about what they should be doing on their allotments.

'Where are Dad and Arthur?' she asked.

'It's Home Guard drill tonight. You know they never miss it.' Her mother looked up at her over the sock she was darning. 'You're early,' she said.

'Yes – I was tired, so I decided to come home.'

'But you had a nice time?'

Kitty read the anxiety in her mother's gaze. Florrie was so desperate for her to be happy, it was written all over her face.

'Yes,' she said, forcing a smile. 'I had a lovely time.'

'I am glad.' Her mother let out a sigh of relief. 'Why don't you sit down and tell me all about it?'

So Kitty sat down in the chair opposite her mother, and made up a tale about the wonderful night out she'd had, how she had laughed and talked and danced with a Scottish soldier called Mal. It was only half true, but as she talked, she could see her mother's face clearing, her worried frown turning into a look of happiness.

'That is good news,' she said, when Kitty had finished. 'You should get out more, you know. It would do you the world of good.'

Kitty lifted her hand to smooth down her hair. 'I will,' she said 'I promise.'

Chapter Seven

'It's not fair. They shouldn't make you do this.'

Helen stood at the mirror, fastening her starched collar. Behind her, she could see Clare's reflection as she sat on the edge of the bed. From the look of distress on her face, Clare seemed more upset about the situation than Helen was.

'I don't think I have much choice,' she said. 'You heard what Major Ellis said. There's a shortage of QAs, so I have to act as Sister for two wards.'

'Yes, I know. But POWs! And after what happened–'

'Don't,' Helen cut her off sharply. 'There's no point in going on about it. It's my duty and I simply have to get on with it.'

Clare's mouth pulled down at the corners, a sure sign she was offended. 'I was only trying to help–'

But you're not, are you? You're only making it worse by going on about it. Helen bit back the retort. She knew how sensitive Clare could be.

'I know,' she said. 'I just find it hard to talk about, that's all.'

Her words seemed to have the right effect. Clare's expression softened. 'At least we'll be working on the ward together some of the time,' she said. 'So I'll be there when you need to get away from – them.' Her face brightened. 'We can hide in the kitchen drinking tea, and if anyone from the POWs' ward comes looking for you, I can say you're busy...'

'I expect I will be busy, with two wards to look after,' Helen said.

'You know what I mean,' Clare said archly. 'I can hide you away so you never have to have anything to do with those awful men–'

'Is that a letter from home?' Helen interrupted her, desperate to change the subject.

Clare picked up the envelope lying next to her on the bed. 'Yes, it's from my brother.'

'The pilot?'

Clare nodded. 'He's having a very jolly time, by all accounts.' She paused for a moment, then said, 'There was a letter waiting for you, too. I took it out of your pigeon-hole.'

'Oh yes?' There was something about the way Clare said it that made Helen instantly wary.

'It's from France.'

Helen carried on adjusting her collar, conscious that her fingers were suddenly shaking.

'Don't you want to read it?' Clare asked.

'No,' Helen said.

Clare took the letter out of her pocket. Helen saw the thin blue envelope and her heart lurched painfully against her ribs. It took all her self-control not to tear it out of Clare's hands.

'It's the third one he's sent. You'd think he'd take the hint, wouldn't you?'

Helen smiled reluctantly. 'He would call it determination.'

Clare looked up at her. 'You sound as if you're glad he's still writing to you.' She held out the envelope. 'Are you sure you don't want to read it?'

Helen eyed the envelope for a moment, then turned away firmly. 'Throw it away,' she said.

'If that's what you want.'

No, she thought. Of course it isn't what I want. But it was the way things had to be. She had no choice in the matter, any more than she had a choice about working on a ward full of POWs.

As if she could read her thoughts, Clare said, 'You're right. I mean, suppose he ever found out...'

'How do I look?' Helen interrupted. She turned round to face her, smoothing down her uniform.

Luckily, her distraction worked. Clare beamed at her. 'Very smart, love.'

'That's something, anyway.' Helen checked her watch. 'Oh well, I'd better go. Wish me luck.'

Clare grimaced. 'Poor Helen. I reckon you're going to need it.'

'What if they can't speak English?'

Dora looked up from scrubbing rust stains from the cast-iron bath tub. It had been a long time since Wren ward had been occupied, and it was dusty, unloved and in need of a thorough clean.

'I beg your pardon?'

'They won't, will they? Speak English, I mean?

Not if they're German.' Miss Sloan stood over her, her cloth in her hand, frowning with concern.

'I suppose not.' Dora turned back to her scrubbing but she could hear Miss Sloan fidgeting behind her, a sure sign she was upset about something.

'Then how will we manage?' she wanted to know.

Dora gave up trying to work, sat back on her heels and massaged the back of her neck. Leonora Sloan had been fretting all day about one thing or another, and it was starting to give Dora a headache.

'Matron said they'll probably have an English-speaking officer to translate for them,' she said.

Miss Sloan pulled a face. 'Well, I'm not sure I like the sound of that,' she said.

'And I'm sure Sister Dawson will be able to understand them a bit. She's been in Europe with the QAs, after all,' Dora said.

'If she ever shows her face,' Miss Sloan said darkly.

Dora frowned. 'What do you mean?'

'We haven't seen much of her, have we? She's supposed to be in charge of the ward, but she's hardly ever here.'

'Sister Dawson has two wards to run. It's hardly surprising she's busy,' Dora defended her.

'If you ask me, she seems more interested in the other ward than this one,' Miss Sloan remarked.

'I'm sure that's not true.'

'I think it is. She seems like rather a cold fish to me.'

Dora confronted the VAD. 'Actually, Helen

Dawson is a good friend of mine. And she isn't cold at all,' she said. 'She's one of the most conscientious, compassionate nurses I've ever worked with.'

That shut her up. Miss Sloan's mouth took on a pinched look. 'Well, pardon me if I was speaking out of turn,' she muttered. She went back to her polishing, attacking a dull spot on the chrome tap with unnecessary force.

Before she could say any more, Kitty Jenkins appeared in the doorway.

'The linen order has arrived, Staff. Will you check it?'

'That's Sister's job, surely?'

'Sister Dawson has been called away to the other ward, Staff.'

Dora shot a sideways look at Miss Sloan. The VAD had her back turned, still polishing away at the taps, but the stiffness of her spine spoke volumes. 'I'll do it,' she said.

As she followed Kitty out of the room, Dora said, 'Thank heavens you rescued me. I think Miss Sloan and I were about to fall out.'

She smiled, but Kitty didn't smile back. She had been in a bad mood ever since they found out they were being moved to the POWs' ward the day before. Dora knew Kitty had been to see Matron, but she guessed from the girl's stony expression that her meeting with Miss Fox had not gone well.

She followed Kitty to the linen cupboard, where Arthur Jenkins was waiting, leaning on his trolley, looking bored. He was a tall, gangly young man, with a tousled mop of pale brown hair, and a cluster of angry spots along his jawline.

He saw Dora approaching and drummed his fingers impatiently on the handle of his trolley, but she calmly ignored him as she took the list from Kitty and started to count the sheets and pillow-cases.

'They're all there,' Arthur interrupted her rudely.

Dora sent him a cold look over the piece of paper. 'I'm sure they are, but it's my job to check them all the same.' She finished counting and ticked the piece of paper. Then she said to Kitty, 'Right, now we'll check them properly.'

Arthur sighed and looked ostentatiously at his watch, but Dora once again ignored him as she and Kitty unfurled the top sheet and inspected it.

'Are you sure this linen is new?' Dora asked.

'It's what the laundry sent up,' Arthur shrugged.

'It seems very worn. And look, there's a hole in this one.' She shook her head. 'No, this won't do at all.' Dora turned to Arthur. 'Take it back to the laundry and tell them we need more.'

'They're good enough for the Nazis, surely,' Arthur muttered under his breath.

Dora swung round on him. 'They're not good enough for me! I want you to return this lot, and to come back with something decent. Well? What are you waiting for?' she snapped, as Arthur glared mutinously at her.

'What's going on?' Helen Dawson approached them, her expression stern under her frilled white cap.

'It's this linen that the laundry has sent up, Sister,' Dora said. 'It's far too worn to put on the beds.'

'Let me see.' Helen inspected one of the pillow-cases. 'It seems quite acceptable to me,' she said, handing it back to Dora.

Dora stared at her. 'But it's nearly threadbare. Look at this hole–' She went to show her, but Helen waved her away.

'I'm sure it's the best that can be done,' she said. 'It might not be ideal, but we must be practical and make do with what we have.'

'But there was a new delivery last week!' Dora protested.

Helen didn't look at her. Turning to Kitty, she said, 'See the beds are made up stat, Nurse. The prisoners will be here shortly, and we've already wasted enough time.'

She turned and left them, her starched apron crackling as she walked briskly away.

'That's told you,' Arthur Jenkins muttered under his breath. He sounded so pleased with himself, Dora couldn't bear to look at him. She stared after Helen, her mouth open in stunned disbelief.

This wasn't like her. The Helen she used to know would never have accepted something as shoddy as threadbare sheets.

Perhaps Miss Sloan was right after all, she thought.

Chapter Eight

There were guards on the ward doors when Kitty returned from lunch later.

It gave her a start to see the two young men in British khaki combat uniform, lounging against the wall, their rifles at their sides.

As she approached, she heard one of them say to the other, 'Hello, who have we here?'

The other soldier turned to look at her, and Kitty stopped in her tracks. She could feel her heart hammering against her ribs, as if it might burst out of the bib of her apron.

Oh no. It couldn't be. Not him...

Mal looked as shocked as she was. For the briefest moment, his eyes flicked up to her temple, now covered by her starched linen cap.

He cleared his throat nervously. 'Afternoon, Nurse,' he greeted her, his face colouring.

Kitty ignored his greeting. 'What's going on?' she asked.

'We're here to guard the prisoners,' Mal explained. 'Make sure they don't try to make a run for it.'

So this was the top secret, hush-hush mission they'd been sent on. Kitty would have laughed, if she wasn't so embarrassed at seeing Mal again.

She glanced towards the double doors. 'Are they here already?'

Before they could reply, the doors flew open

76

and Miss Sloan appeared.

'Thank heavens you're here, Nurse Jenkins. We've just had a telephone call to say the ambulance has arrived. They're on their way.'

Len grinned. 'There's your answer!'

As Kitty turned to go, Mal said, 'Look, about last night–'

Kitty ignored him and hurried after Miss Sloan on to the ward. As the doors closed, she heard Len say, 'Well, that's a turn up for the books, eh pal? And there was you, thinking you'd never see her again!'

'Much good it'll do me, I reckon,' Mal muttered in reply.

Without thinking, Kitty smoothed down her sleeve to reassure herself her scar was covered up.

Miss Sloan was pacing up and down the empty ward, her hands clasped together. Wisps of greying hair escaped from under her cap.

'I don't know what to do,' she squawked. 'They'll be here any minute and Nurse Riley is still on her dinner break.'

'Where's Sister Dawson?' Kitty asked.

Miss Sloan rolled her eyes. 'Well, that's a good question! She was called away to the other ward yet again. I telephoned to let her know they were on their way but a rather rude young woman told me Sister was too busy to come. We're on our own!' Her voice quivered. 'Oh Nurse, what shall we do?'

The VAD's panic had an oddly calming effect on Kitty. She surveyed the two lines of beds down either side of the long ward, illuminated by shafts of sunlight from the tall windows. The beds were all made up, hot water bottles in each to air the sheets. The air was fragrant with the smell of polish and Lysol. The cupboards and kitchen and sluice room were all stocked and ready.

'There's nothing else we can do, is there?' she said. 'We just have to wait.'

They didn't have to wait long. Within a few minutes, the doors opened and the first of the POWs were brought in.

Kitty stood in the middle of the ward, Miss Sloan at her side, as the porters carried in stretchers.

'They're so young!' the VAD whispered. 'I didn't expect that, did you?'

'No,' Kitty said. She wasn't sure what she had been expecting. In her mind, the Germans were murderous fiends. But these were little more than boys, some of them seemed no older than Arthur. They looked sick with terror, staring around them fearfully, their grey-green uniforms worn and filthy.

Pity lurched inside Kitty at the forlorn sight, but she braced herself against it. Young and afraid as they were, they were still capable of shooting a gun, or wielding a bayonet, or letting loose a torpedo to sink a ship...

Arthur came through the double doors, holding on to the end of a stretcher. Even from the other end of the ward Kitty could see the taut resentment on his face.

'You there!' A man strode in behind him. He wore an officer's uniform, with high leather boots and a cap tucked under his arm. He was exactly what Kitty had imagined a German to look like:

tall, blond and autocratic-looking.

He tapped Arthur on the shoulder. 'Have a care!' he snapped, his perfect English bearing only the slightest trace of an accent. 'He is a patient, not a sack of potatoes.'

Kitty saw Arthur's body stiffen, and held her breath. *Please, Arthur, don't do anything daft,* she prayed silently.

Arthur swung round to confront him, but Kitty managed to snag his gaze. She gave him a small, desperate shake of her head. Her brother pursed his lips, but to her relief he turned away.

The man barely seemed to notice. He stood in the middle of the ward and looked around.

'Who is in charge here?' he demanded. He turned to face Kitty and Miss Sloan, who stared back at him silently. 'You two,' he said, looking down his long straight nose at them. 'Which one of you is the *Oberschwester* – the sister in charge of this ward?'

Kitty could feel Miss Sloan's expectant gaze on her. Arthur was also watching her.

She knew she shouldn't be intimidated by the man, that he was a prisoner like the others, but there was something about those cold blue eyes that unnerved her.

'Well?' he snapped. 'Don't you understand English? I am asking you a question.'

'Perhaps if you asked her politely, she might answer you.'

Kitty's knees sagged with relief as Nurse Riley appeared in the doorway.

The man swung round. 'Are you the *Oberschwester?*'

'I'm Nurse Riley, the senior staff nurse on this ward. And you are?'

He pulled himself up to his full height. He towered over Nurse Riley, but she didn't seem intimidated in the slightest.

'I am Major Karl Von Mundel. I have been put in charge of the ward.'

Nurse Riley folded her arms across her chest. 'Oh yes? And who told you that, then?'

'I beg your pardon?'

'Unless Matron tells us otherwise, I think you'll find Sister Dawson runs this ward, not you.'

Kitty saw the man's eyes narrow. Good for you, she silently encouraged Nurse Riley.

'And where is this – Sister Dawson?' He pronounced the name with contempt.

Dora looked at Kitty, who managed a slight shake of her head.

'She isn't here at the moment,' Dora said.

Major Von Mundel looked affronted. 'That is not correct. She should be here.'

'I expect she will be, when she's finished attending to her other patients.' Nurse Riley looked up at him. 'In the meantime, Nurse Jenkins and I will take care of these men and prepare them for the doctor's round.'

'There is no need for that,' he dismissed. 'I am a doctor, and I will be looking after the patients on this ward.'

Dora shook her head. 'Thank you, but we have our own doctors in this hospital.'

He stood a little straighter. 'But I am a qualified surgeon!'

'Well, I'm sure you can discuss it with Dr Abbott, but until I hear otherwise, he'll be the one I take orders from.'

How she stood up to him, Kitty had no idea. The major's icy stare would have frozen her to the spot.

But Nurse Riley had a stubborn streak. Once she decided to dig her heels in, there would be no budging her.

Major Von Mundel seemed to know when he was defeated. He stared at her for a moment, then muttered something under his breath in German and strode off.

'That's told him!' Miss Sloan whispered admiringly. 'Good for Nurse Riley. I reckon he knows when he's beaten, don't you?'

'Yes,' Kitty said. But as she watched the officer striding down the ward, she couldn't help thinking that he wouldn't stay beaten for long.

Chapter Nine

'Right, ducks, let's have your arm.'

The pale-haired boy shrank away from Dora, his terrified gaze fixed on the needle in her hand. His bony face was as white as the linen pillow.

'It's all right, I'm not going to hurt you–' Dora stopped, remembering herself. 'Oh, what am I saying? You can't understand a word, can you?' She pointed to the needle and then to his arm, smiling encouragingly to make him understand that she meant him no harm.

81

She looked at Major Von Mundel, standing at the end of the bed. He brusquely translated for her.

The boy hesitated for a moment.

'*Schnell!*' Von Mundel barked, making Dora jump. Trembling, the boy offered up his arm.

'Good lad.' As quickly as she could, Dora rolled up his sleeve, cleaned his skin and gave the injection before he could change his mind.

'You see?' she said, taking out the needle. 'That didn't hurt at all, did it?'

The boy looked down at his arm, then back at her. Dora read the look of bewildered disbelief in his eyes.

'Yes, that's it,' she said. 'All finished.' She put the needle down, then straightened his bedclothes. 'Let's make you a bit more comfortable, shall we?'

As she leaned across him, the boy looked up at her with a tremulous smile. '*Danke*,' he said.

'He said thank you,' Von Mundel muttered through clenched teeth.

At least someone's got some manners, Dora thought. She smiled back at the young man. 'You're very welcome, ducks. Now try to get some nice kip.' Seeing his blank look, she mimicked sleep.

The boy nodded and settled down happily against the pillows she had just plumped for him.

Dora stood for a moment, watching him. Poor kid, he was only fifteen, just a couple of years older than her own little brother Alfie.

The ward was full of boys like him. The night nurse told her they often woke up screaming in the night for their mothers. Dora had only been nursing them for a week, but she already felt protective of them.

She glanced around at Major Von Mundel's stony face. He was a different matter entirely.

As they emerged from the curtains, he said, 'When is the doctor coming?'

'I expect he'll be here shortly,' said Dora, suppressing her irritation.

'I'm worried about Schultz, bed three,' Von Mundel said. 'I believe he needs his medication changed.'

'I'm sure Dr Abbott knows what he's doing,' Dora said tightly.

'I hardly think so. Dr Abbott is barely more than a schoolboy,' Von Mundel snorted.

Dora didn't reply. Things were already sour enough between her and Major Von Mundel.

She really wished they hadn't got off to such a bad start. It was her fault for letting her temper run away with her at their first meeting. But he'd been so superior, all she'd wanted was to take him down a peg or two.

But now, a week later, she regretted it. Especially as they had to work so closely together in Helen's absence. More often than not, it was Dora who had to deal with Major Von Mundel. And she was the one who had to bear the brunt of his arrogance.

He was really only there to translate, but he couldn't resist interfering in other ways, too. Whenever Dora had to give an injection or administer medication, he would be standing there peering over her shoulder down that long, straight nose of his, questioning everything.

It might have been easier if Helen had been there, but she was often absent from the ward. Lorry-loads of wounded soldiers arrived every day, and Helen spent most of her time on the other ward with Dr Abbott.

Von Mundel followed Dora now as she made her way to the next bed, a sullen-looking young man with a fractured knee who had been brought in two days previously.

'Hello, ducks, how are you feeling today?' Dora greeted him. Behind her, Von Mundel let loose with a rapid volley of German that she was sure had nothing to do with what she'd said. The young man replied at length, and soon the pair of them were having what seemed to be a heated conversation back and forth over her head. From the frown on his face, Von Mundel didn't seem pleased about something.

Dora tried to get on with her job of checking the young man's splint. But before she could lay a hand on him, Von Mundel announced, 'This patient says he is in great pain. I suspect he has a *wundliegen*. A – a–' he searched for the English word. 'A sore,' he said finally. 'On his leg.'

Dora shook her head. 'Oh no, that can't be. Nurse Jenkins checked his splint yesterday. She would have noticed and done something about it if there had been any sign of a pressure sore.'

'You think so?' Von Mundel's brows rose above his cold blue eyes. 'Because I can see merely by looking at it that this splint is too tight.'

He was right, Dora thought. There did seem to be a lot more pressure on his leg than she would have liked. With a sinking heart, and aware of Von

Mundel watching her, she removed the young man's dressing.

Sure enough, there was a large, purplish bruise, the skin already broken from where the splint had rubbed against it.

Von Mundel inspected it over her shoulder. 'Your Nurse Jenkins is clearly not very observant,' he commented. 'Or perhaps she didn't care to notice it?'

Dora lifted her chin to look at him. 'Nurse Jenkins is extremely dedicated.'

'Like your *oberschwester?*' He looked around. 'Where is she, by the way?'

Dora ignored his remark. 'I'm sure it was a genuine mistake on Nurse Jenkins' part,' she insisted, blushing. 'But I'll have a word with her and make sure it doesn't happen again.'

'I do not think she will pay much attention to you!' Von Mundel gave a snort of contempt. 'It seems to me the nurses here do as they please, since the *oberschwester* is hardly ever here to discipline them.' He looked up and down the empty ward. 'Where are they now, Nurse Riley? I can't see them tending to the patients, can you?'

'I–' Dora opened and closed her mouth, lost for words. She gazed down at the festering sore on the young man's leg. She wanted to argue, but deep down she knew Major Von Mundel was right.

As soon as she had finished her duties, Dora hurried off to confront Kitty and Miss Sloan.

She found them in the sluice, cleaning bedpans. Dora could hear their merry laughter from halfway down the passage as she approached. Usually their chatter wouldn't have troubled her,

85

but now it made her burn with rage.

She threw open the door, so suddenly Miss Sloan dropped the bedpan she was polishing. It fell to the tiled floor with a noisy clatter.

'Oh, Nurse Riley, you startled me–' she started to say, but Dora cut across her.

'Why didn't you check bed six's splint yesterday?' she demanded, turning on Kitty.

'I did–'

'Well, you didn't do it properly. He has a splint sore.'

Kitty didn't look too surprised. 'I'm sorry, Staff. I'm sure it was all right yesterday.' She didn't meet Dora's gaze as she said it.

Dora shook her head. 'I don't understand it. It's one of the first things you're taught in training, to avoid unnecessary discomfort to patients...'

'I said I'm sorry!' Kitty blurted out. But there was an edge of insolence in her voice that got under Dora's skin.

'Sorry isn't good enough,' Dora said. 'I've just had Major Von Mundel tear me off a strip, and I didn't know where to put myself.'

'Oh, you mustn't let him upset you, my dear,' Miss Sloan said consolingly. 'He just loves to throw his weight about. But he's not even a real doctor, is he? Not one of ours, anyway.'

Dora stared at her, lost for words. The VAD must have seen the anger simmering in her eyes, because she took a step back.

'And why are you both skulking about in here, anyway?' Dora said.

'We were cleaning bedpans, Staff,' Kitty said, as Miss Sloan seemed to be struck dumb.

'Gossiping, more like!' Dora said. 'What if Matron had come to inspect the ward and found no nurses there? What if one of the patients needed something?' She saw Kitty's lip curl and her fragile hold on her temper gave way. 'I know you don't care much for these men, Jenkins–' Kitty opened her mouth to speak but Dora held up her hand to silence her, 'but you are still a nurse at this hospital and I won't have you treating patients in this way. You're not only letting yourself down, you're letting the rest of us down too–'

'What on earth is going on here?' Helen appeared in the doorway. 'I could hear the commotion halfway down the passage.' She looked from Dora to Kitty and back again. 'Well?'

'Nurse Jenkins failed to check a patient's splint properly, and now he has a sore,' Dora said, her gaze still fixed on Kitty.

Helen turned to Kitty. 'Is this true, Nurse Jenkins?'

'I did check it, Sister,' Kitty insisted. 'It was all right yesterday.'

'All right, my eye! Sores like that don't come up overnight,' Dora put in.

'It's all right, Nurse Riley, I will deal with this,' Helen said mildly. 'Jenkins, please make sure this doesn't happen again.'

'No, Sister.'

'I want you to go and treat the patient's wound with antiseptic powder, and then apply a dry aseptic dressing.'

'I've already done it,' Dora said sullenly.

'Thank you, Nurse Riley. Then I think it's all been taken care of.'

As Helen left the room, Dora caught the smug look on Kitty's face. She'd got away with it.

Furious, Dora followed Helen to her office.

'Yes?' Helen said, as Dora closed the door behind her. 'Was there something else you wanted?'

'Is that it?' Dora said, scarcely able to contain her anger.

Helen looked at her blankly. 'I don't understand–'

'Kitty Jenkins broke the rules and caused harm to a patient. She should be sent to Matron.'

'It was only a splint sore!'

'It doesn't matter. She should still be punished, to make sure it doesn't happen again.'

Helen's brown eyes flashed. 'Are you trying to tell me how to do my job, Nurse Riley?' she snapped.

Dora stared at her. In all the years she had known Helen, she had never known her to be anything but kind, gentle and unfailingly patient. She scarcely recognised the hard-faced young woman on the other side of the desk.

'As I said, it was an honest mistake, and I'm sure she's learned her lesson,' Helen said quietly.

'That's the trouble. I'm not sure if it was an honest mistake,' Dora said.

Helen frowned. 'What do you mean? You think Nurse Jenkins might be trying to harm the patients deliberately?'

'I don't know if I'd go that far,' Dora said. 'But I think she's neglecting her duties. She doesn't want to be here, you see.'

Helen gave a small, sad smile. 'Do any of us?' she said.

Dora looked at her. 'I don't know what you mean...'

Helen sat back in her seat. 'I saw a great many things while I was stationed abroad,' she began. 'Terrible, awful things. I learned to dislike the Germans for what they did and the destruction they wreaked, and the lives they ruined. If you'd witnessed half what I have...' her voice trailed off.

'Is that why you came home?' Dora asked.

Helen's gaze dropped to the paper lying on the desk in front of her. 'I couldn't bear it any more, so I put in for a transfer,' she said. She paused for a moment, then looked up at Dora. 'Surely you must feel the same?' she appealed. 'After what happened to your family?'

For a moment, Dora allowed all the thoughts she kept so carefully at bay to flood into her mind. Danny's death, the loss of her home, the constant fear she felt for Nick...There was so much tragedy; if she allowed herself to think about it too much, she would have gone mad.

'They're our patients,' she insisted. 'Whether we like it or not, we have a duty to look after them.'

'You wouldn't say that if–' Helen broke off.

'If what?' Dora pressed her.

'Nothing.' Helen gave her a sad smile. 'I just wonder what you'd do if your sense of duty was tested as mine has been. If it was, perhaps you might not be so quick to judge the rest of us.'

Chapter Ten

It was teatime on a warm late June evening, and for once Dora was due to go off duty early when the ward telephone rang to say another lorry-load of wounded prisoners was on its way up from the coast.

'It's all right, Staff, you get yourself home,' Miss Sloan insisted stoutly, her shoulders squaring. 'We'll hold the fort, won't we, Nurse Jenkins?'

Dora glanced at Kitty, who looked mutinous but said nothing.

'It's nice of you to offer, Miss Sloan, but I'm not sure you can,' Dora said. 'You'll be rushed off your feet in no time without help.'

'But you were so looking forward to spending time with your little ones...' Miss Sloan bit her lip, genuinely upset.

'It can't be helped.' Dora fastened the strings of her clean apron. 'Now then, how many did they say were coming?'

'At least twelve, I believe.' Miss Sloan's gaze travelled around the already overcrowded ward. 'But where will we put them all, Nurse?'

'That's a good question.' Dora paused for a moment, assessing the situation. She already had a rough idea where they might put the extra beds, but she couldn't do anything without orders from the ward sister. 'You'd best go and fetch Sister Dawson. She'll tell us what to do.'

Major Von Mundel had been hovering nearby, pretending to speak to a patient. But Dora knew he'd been listening to every word while she was on the telephone.

Now he approached her, his hands locked behind his back in his usual upright stance.

'Did I hear you say more patients are on their way?' he asked.

Dora nodded. 'They should be here in an hour, depending on the roads.'

Dr Von Mundel looked around, frowning, and Dora could tell he was thinking exactly the same as her. 'Where will you put them all?' he said.

'I'm sure we'll think of something.'

'And where is the *Oberschwester*? Absent as usual, I think?'

'I've sent for her.'

'Yes, but will you find her? Your Sister Dawson is elusive, like the Scarlet Pimpernel.'

Dora gritted her teeth. She didn't know which irritated her more, Helen's frequent absences or Von Mundel's delight in pointing them out to her.

She had tried to understand why Helen disliked working on the POWs' ward so much. But Dora had never known her friend to shrink from doing her duty, no matter how difficult it was for her.

She only hoped that Helen didn't let them down this time, when they desperately needed her help and guidance.

But her hopes sank five minutes later, when Miss Sloan returned to say that Sister Dawson had already gone off duty at five o'clock.

It's all right for some, she thought. By rights, she

91

should have gone off duty at five herself. By now, she should be giving her twins their tea and playing games with them.

'Typical,' Major Von Mundel muttered. 'Well, Nurse Riley, it looks as if you are in charge. Again,' he added. He smiled thinly, as if he was going to enjoy watching her make a mess of the situation.

Ignoring him, Dora turned to Kitty, and said, 'Jenkins, I want you to go and see Mr Hopkins, get him to send up some extra beds. And we'll need some orderlies to help us too, as many as he can spare.'

'And where do you intend to put all these extra beds?' Dr Von Mundel asked.

'I should think we could fit at least another four in here—'

'Out of the question!' Dr Von Mundel snapped. 'The men are already packed in as it is.'

'—and we can put another bed in each of the private rooms, so that's another three,' Dora went on, not listening. 'And three more can go in Sister's sitting room.'

Dr Von Mundel gave a snort of derision. 'Let's hope none of the men are infected, or it will spread like wildfire.'

Dora resisted the urge to tell him to shut up, and turned instead to Miss Sloan.

'Can you find some more bedlinen?' she said. 'Go down to the laundry and round to the other wards, and beg, steal or borrow whatever you can. It doesn't matter what state it's in. We'll mend the sheets ourselves if we have to!'

The next half-hour or so was a blur of activity, as the orderlies appeared with beds and mattresses.

Dora hurried up and down the ward, moving lockers and cupboards to make room for them.

One of the guards, the shorter and stockier of the pair, came to lend a hand. Dora noticed how he kept looking at Kitty. The poor young Scotsman had been watching her for over a week, but she never spoke to him, or even looked his way if she could help it.

'Thank you,' Dora said, as the guard lifted a heavy cupboard easily into place.

'That's all right, Nurse.' He straightened up, pushing his cap back to wipe the perspiration from his forehead.

'Although it wouldn't hurt him to lend a hand, would it? Especially since it's his lot we're doing it for.'

Dora looked at Dr Von Mundel, who stood at the far end of the ward, watching the proceedings with a look of icy disdain.

'You're right,' she said. 'It wouldn't hurt him at all.'

Shortly afterwards, Miss Sloan appeared with an armful of linen, and they rushed around making up all the beds and boiling up water for bottles. Miss Sloan and Kitty worked together, while Dora managed by herself. All the time she worked, she kept one ear cocked for the sound of the telephone, to say that the men had arrived.

She was busy making up a bed in one of the private rooms when the door opened behind her. Thinking it was Miss Sloan or Kitty, she said, 'Well, don't just stand there watching. Come and give me a hand, my back's killing me!'

'I should think so, Nurse Riley. What were you

taught in training about always making beds in pairs?'

The sound of the calm, authoritative voice sent a chill through her. Dora shot upright to see the Nightingale's matron, Kathleen Fox, standing in the doorway.

'I – I'm so sorry, Matron. I didn't know it was you,' she stammered, reaching up to tuck a stray curl of red hair into her cap.

'So I gathered.' Miss Fox looked around. 'I heard you were expecting more patients and I came to see how you were managing.'

'We're all right, Matron. Thank you.'

'Everything certainly seems under control.' She rubbed her hands together. 'Right, let's finish making this bed, shall we?'

'No!' Dora yelped out the word. 'I – I didn't mean you had to help–'

'Don't be silly, of course I want to help. It's all hands to the pump in a situation like this. Besides, it's a long time since I've made a bed,' she added, a small smile curving her lips. 'It might be nice to see if I still remember how to do it.'

Dora could feel the heat rising in her face, staining her cheeks a bright crimson as she stood opposite Matron, both of them working together to pull up and straighten the sheets before tucking them in. She didn't dare look up in case she met her eye.

I'll be in trouble for this, she thought. One way or another, I'll be in trouble.

It took less than a minute to make the bed, but it felt like forever. Afterwards, Miss Fox stood back to inspect her handiwork.

'Yes, well, as I said, it's been a long time since I made a bed,' she said, adjusting the turned-down sheet to the perfect fourteen inches. 'I don't know if it would bear a ward sister's scrutiny, do you?'

'I think it looks just right, Matron,' Dora mumbled, still too embarrassed to look at her.

'Perhaps you never lose the knack?' Miss Fox looked amused.

They returned to the main ward to find the extra beds in place and neatly made up.

'Where is Sister Dawson? I looked for her when I arrived, but I couldn't seem to find her...' Miss Fox's grey gaze scanned the ward.

Dora was suddenly aware of Major Von Mundel hovering in the corner of her vision, and prayed he wouldn't say anything.

'She had already gone off duty when we had the telephone call, Matron,' she explained, then added quickly, 'But as you can see, we've managed to cope.'

'Indeed you have.' Matron nodded her approval. 'Well done, Nurses.' Kitty stared down at her shoes while Miss Sloan turned pink with pleasure. Miss Fox turned to Dora. 'You will tell me if there is anything else I can do when the patients arrive, won't you?' she said.

'Yes, Matron.'

No sooner had Miss Fox gone than Major Von Mundel approached Dora. 'Did Matron say why Sister Dawson was not here?' he asked.

Dora frowned. 'Why should she? Sister Dawson was off duty.'

'And what about all the other times she is

absent from the ward?'

'What about them? Sister Dawson is very busy, she has another ward to look after. She can't help it if she's called away–'

Dr Von Mundel snorted impatiently. 'You are very loyal, Nurse Riley. But I fear your loyalty is misplaced. The *oberschwester* neglects her duties on this ward and should be reported to Matron.'

Dora stared at him, genuinely shocked. 'I couldn't do that!'

'Why not?'

'Because she's my friend.'

Dr Von Mundel looked puzzled. 'This is not a matter of friendship. Sister Dawson deserves to be reprimanded.'

'Yes, well, that might be the way you do things in your country, but not in mine. Where I come from friends are loyal to each other.'

His blue eyes were cold above his razor-sharp cheekbones. 'I do not see Sister Dawson being loyal to you, Nurse Riley.'

Chapter Eleven

The patients arrived shortly afterwards. According to their notes, they were part of a German unit who had surrendered to the Allies just outside Caen.

Looking at them, Dora could understand why they had given up. The men were exhausted and malnourished, their uniforms hanging off their thin frames. They were in a poor physical state, with infected wounds, broken bones and several bad coughs.

'I reckon they knew when they were beaten, eh Nurse?' Dr Abbott remarked, as they watched the men being brought in.

Dora glanced at Major Von Mundel, standing on the other side of the ward, his steely gaze fixed on the men. He gave no sign that he'd heard the doctor's comment, but Dora knew his keen ears missed nothing.

She didn't know why she should be so concerned about his feelings, when he clearly cared nothing for hers, but she wished Dr Abbott had kept his foolish remarks to himself.

But that was Jimmy Abbott all over. He was little more than a thoughtless boy, a fresh-faced young medical student who had suddenly found himself in his last year acting as both a physician and surgical registrar. If his onerous responsibilities weighed him down at all, he certainly never showed it. He was always larking about and playing practical jokes on the nurses.

A more different character from stern Major Von Mundel, Dora couldn't imagine. No wonder the pair didn't get on.

She could feel the Major's disapproval like an icy mist shrouding her as they started their rounds of the patients.

The worst injured was the unit's commanding officer, a lieutenant who had suffered a fractured femur. He had undergone an emergency operation at the field hospital in Caen, but he had lost a great deal of blood and was still unconscious.

'Well, if he hasn't woken up by now I don't suppose he ever will,' Dr Abbott said, scribbling on the man's notes. 'They should have taken his leg off, it might have saved his life.'

Out of the corner of her eye Dora saw Von Mundel wince.

'Should I have a nurse sit with him, just in case?' she ventured.

'It hardly seems worth wasting the poor girl's time.' Then Dr Abbott shrugged and added, 'But I don't suppose it would do any harm, would it? And you never know, miracles do happen.'

Once Dr Abbott had gone, Dora and Miss Sloan began the long round of settling the patients and making them comfortable. As she bathed, washed, shaved bristled chins and combed hair, Dora found the new patients were not as easy as the nervous boys she was used to dealing with. They were surly, rude and muttered comments under their breath that Dora knew must be insulting.

Teetering on the edge of exhaustion, it took all Dora's self-control to keep a smile pasted on her face.

'What's your name, love?' she asked one young man, who had been brought in with a gunshot wound to his groin. He stared blankly back at her through hostile blue eyes. He was slimly built and coldly handsome, his close-cropped hair as platinum blond as Jean Harlow's.

'*Wass is das? Ich verstehe nicht.*'

Dora waited for Major Von Mundel to translate as usual, but he remained silent and tight-lipped.

'What did he say?' she prompted.

'He says he can't understand you.' He turned

to the young man. *'Wie heißen sie?'*

Once again, the young man remained silent.

'Beantworte die Frage!' Von Mundel snapped at him through gritted teeth.

The young man sent the major a sly sideways look and mumbled something in response.

'He says his name is *Gefreiter* Felix Frost,' Major Von Mundel translated for him, his gaze still locked on the young man.

'Well, Felix, I'm going to clean you up and get you changed. You know – wash?' Dora picked up the flannel and mimed with it.

'Nein.' Felix shook his head.

'You don't have to worry, ducks, we don't mean you any harm. No one's going to hurt you,' she said.

The boy stared at her. *'Sie können mich nicht verletzen,'* he muttered. Dora couldn't understand what he was saying, but it sounded slightly threatening.

'Come on,' she said briskly. 'You've got to let us get you washed and changed. You'll feel better for it, I promise–'

She reached for him, but he batted her arm away, knocking her sideways.

'Holen Sie sich Ihre Hände weg von mir!' he snapped, his eyes blazing. *'Schmutzige Hure!'*

Suddenly, out of nowhere Dr Von Mundel lashed out and struck the young man, a blow that sent his head snapping backwards.

Dora cried out in shock as Felix put his hand up to touch the fresh cut on his lip. His face remained expressionless.

'He won't give you any more trouble,' Dr Von

Mundel said shortly. He pushed the curtains to one side and stepped through them. Dora abandoned her trolley, and followed him.

'What do you think you're doing?' Shock and anger took away her voice, so she could barely speak above a whisper.

Dr Von Mundel stared back at her blankly. 'He was being difficult, so I reprimanded him.'

'You hit him!'

'What else was I supposed to do, if he didn't follow orders? He is a soldier, Nurse Riley. Sometimes it is the only language they understand.'

'But—' Dora was so speechless with shock, she could barely manage to utter the words. 'How dare you!' she burst out finally.

'You didn't hear what he said to you.'

'No, but I can guess. And I'm sure I've had worse said to me.'

'Not by one of my men.' Von Mundel's high cheekbones were stained with angry colour. 'They should be grateful for the care they are receiving, not insolent towards you.' He jerked his head towards the curtains. 'As I said, he shouldn't give you any more trouble.'

He stalked off, leaving Dora to stare after him, stunned.

It was nearly nine o'clock, four hours after she should have gone off duty, when Dora was finally able to head home.

She was so weary she could barely set one foot in front of the other. But what made it worse was that she knew Walter and Winnie would be in bed by the time she got home. She had been so looking forward to spending time with them, but now all she could do was gaze at their sleeping heads tucked up in bed, the way she always did.

As Dora headed for the gates, she saw two figures coming towards her. A pair of young women, one tall, the other short and squat, their arms interlinked, laughing together.

Helen and her friend Clare.

Dr Von Mundel's words came back to Dora.

I do not see Sister Dawson being loyal to you, Nurse Riley.

He was right, she thought: Helen had abandoned her. Dora had done her best to make excuses for her friend, but the truth was that Helen always left her to cope on her own.

They were getting closer, their laughter ringing out, grating on her nerves. Dora felt her anger building up inside her, jangling like a bell in her head, and she knew she couldn't face Helen. She wasn't sure she could even speak to her without exploding. She pulled the collar of her cloak up around her ears and hurried past them, head down so they wouldn't notice her.

Chapter Twelve

The fractured femur was going to die. Dr Abbott had said so, and everyone knew it.

'He's lost so much blood, I don't suppose he'll wake up,' Nurse Riley had said. 'But it would be nice for someone to sit with him, just in case.'

Nice for who, Kitty wondered. Not for her, that was for sure. All she could think about was that she was missing her night out. She was supposed to be going up West with Bea and Lily after her shift finished. Bea had promised to get them into the American Red Cross Club in Curzon Street where she worked. It was supposed to be very swanky, and Kitty had been looking forward to it.

But if she wasn't waiting for them at the bus stop by half past nine on the dot, she knew they wouldn't bother to wait for her. Bea and her sister-in-law had become inseparable lately, and Kitty was beginning to feel like a spare part when they were out together. Especially as she had no interest in chasing men like they did.

But even though Kitty wasn't particularly interested in finding a boyfriend, she would still have rather been enjoying the plush surroundings of the Washington Club than sitting here, waiting for a stranger to wake up.

She glanced at her watch. It was just turned half past eight. There was still plenty of time, she told herself. With any luck, the night nurse would come on duty early and Kitty could leave her to look after the patient. She knew Nurse Riley wouldn't approve, but what she didn't know wouldn't hurt her.

'And you're not going to tell, are you?' she whispered to the man. He probably wouldn't live to tell any tales. As he lay in bed, curtained off from the other two beds in the private room, his breathing was already so shallow that Kitty had to lean close to check he was still alive.

She had done everything she could for him, any-

102

way. She had covered him with blankets and a hot water bottle to keep him warm and try to minimise shock. Now all she had to do was wait...

She picked up his notes and flicked through them idly, to pass the time.

His name was *Oberleutnant* Stefan Bauer, and he was the officer in charge of the captured unit. There was no age given, and no other details about his life. Just his army number and a bald list of medical details about him. He had sustained a serious fracture to the shaft of his right femur, with extensive damage to the surrounding muscles and connective tissue.

That was putting it mildly, Kitty thought. His right thigh was firmly encased in a Thomas' splint, but she could see the bones and muscles had been pulverised. It was a miracle he had made it to the field hospital, let alone all the way back to England.

But then, that craggy face looked as if it had already survived far more than it should have. Kitty studied him carefully. He was older than the other men, around thirty perhaps, or even older. He didn't have the pale colouring or the fine bone structure of his fellow Germans. His hair was darker, tawny in colour, and his features were coarse. His flattened nose looked as if it had been broken at least once, and the trace of a jagged scar ran down the left side from his temple to his jaw.

She touched her own face, close to her hairline. Unlike her, Stefan Bauer didn't try to hide his scars. He looked like a man who had fought his way through life.

Now he was facing a battle he couldn't win.

103

She almost felt sorry for him.

On the other side of the curtain, she heard the door to the private room open and checked her watch. It was only twenty to nine and blessed be, the night nurse had come on duty early. Smiling, Kitty stood up and pushed aside the curtain. But her smile died on her lips when she saw Mal standing in the doorway.

'I've come to say goodnight,' he said, looking down at the cap he was wringing between his hands. 'Len and I are going off duty now, and the other lads are taking over.'

Kitty nodded awkwardly. 'All right. See you in the morning.'

She started to retreat behind the curtains again, but Mal blurted out, 'Can I have a word before I go?'

A prickle of dread ran up Kitty's spine. Mal had tried to speak to her several times since he'd started doing sentry duty on the ward. So far, Kitty had managed to avoid him, but she could feel him watching her every day as she went about her duties, and she knew it was only a matter of time before he plucked up the courage to confront her again.

Kitty turned back to look at the man in the bed, as if he could somehow step in and protect her. But he went on sleeping deeply, his chest rising and falling.

'The night nurse will be here in a minute,' she said, glancing desperately past Mal towards the door.

'Then I'll be quick.' He took a deep breath. 'I just wanted to say I'm sorry.'

Kitty looked away so he couldn't see the colour scalding her cheeks. 'You've got no reason to apologise,' she mumbled.

'But I upset you.'

'You only did what everyone else does when they look at me.'

Out of the corner of her eye she saw him wince. He paused for a moment, then said, 'How – did it happen?'

'An air raid. I got hit by flying shrapnel.'

'I'm sorry.'

'Like I said, you've got no reason to apologise. Now, if you don't mind–'

'I'd still like to take you out one night.'

Kitty swung round to look at him. 'Why? Because you feel sorry for me?'

'No!'

'Because I don't need your pity, you know.'

'I know that. I want to take you out because I like you.'

Kitty looked at his face, so open and honest. He really did have a nice smile, she thought.

She shook her head. 'Thank you for the offer, but I don't want to go out with you,' she said.

He looked crestfallen. 'Why not?' Then he added, 'It *is* my cologne, isn't it?'

Kitty smiled in spite of herself. 'No.'

'Then why?'

'I–'

Behind her, the man in the bed let out a deep groan. Kitty immediately forgot all about Mal as she rushed to his side.

'Hello?' she said. 'Can you hear me?'

Stefan Bauer stirred, and his eyes flicked open,

giving sudden life to his mask-like face. They were deep set, brown flecked with ochre.

'*Wo bin ich?*' His voice was low and rough.

She had no idea what he was saying, but she tried to reply with something comforting. 'You're quite safe. You're in hospital.'

'Hospital?' He repeated the word slowly. His gaze focused on Kitty, as if seeing her for the first time.

'Hospital,' she repeated, pointing to her uniform.

Stefan Bauer let out a rough sigh, and his eyes flickered closed again.

'Is everything all right?' Mal stuck his head through the curtain.

'You're not supposed to be in here. Go away!' Kitty made to usher him out, but then a roar came from behind her. She turned round to see Stefan was suddenly awake and struggling to lever himself upright, his blazing gaze fixed on Mal.

'What are you doing? Get back into bed!' Kitty forgot about Mal and rushed to settle Stefan but he thrashed out wildly with his fists, catching her a glancing blow to the jaw that made her head ring. She stepped back, stunned.

'Oi! That's enough of that, pal!' Mal lunged forward, pinning him to the bed. Stefan fought back like a madman, his hands going around Mal's throat. Even with his injured leg, Stefan's brute strength seemed more than a match for Mal.

'Leave him alone!' Kitty cried, throwing himself between them. 'Let him go. He's injured!'

'He's a maniac!' Mal released him and staggered backwards. 'He went for you–'

'It's seeing you that's upset him,' Kitty said. 'You'd better go.'

'But I'm not leaving you with him—'

'I told you, you're the one agitating him.' She looked back at Stefan, who was staring at Mal as if he wanted to tear out his throat.

Mal took a step back. 'I'll hang about outside—' he started to say, but Kitty cut him off.

'Please go,' she said. 'Leave me alone to do my job.'

As soon as Mal had gone, the fight seemed to go out of the man. He collapsed against the pillows, breathing hard and wincing in pain. But at least he seemed calm for the moment.

'That's better,' she said. 'I'm surprised you haven't pulled your stitches out, carrying on like – ow!' A sudden pain shot through her pulsing jaw.

'I'm sorry.'

Kitty looked at the man in surprise. A couple of the other German soldiers spoke some English, but it never occurred to her that Stefan might be one of them. He seemed too rough, somehow. 'You speak English?'

He ignored the question. 'Your face...' His eyes were dark with concern. 'I'm sorry. It was an accident...'

'Oh, don't worry about me. I'll live.' Kitty opened and closed her mouth experimentally. It still clicked a bit, but the pain was subsiding. 'It's you I'm worried about.'

She picked up the thermometer from the trolley and went to put it in his mouth, but Stefan jerked his head away.

'I am in England?' he said slowly.

Kitty nodded. 'The Nightingale Hospital in Bethnal Green, London, to be exact.'

His brows lowered in a confused frown. Then he seemed to remember. 'We surrendered...' He looked round. 'Where are the others?'

'They're here, too. They're quite safe.'

'And Emil?' He turned urgent eyes to hers. 'Is Emil safe too?'

Kitty looked at him blankly. 'Emil?'

'I have to find him.' He struggled to sit up again, then collapsed backwards with a hiss of pain.

'Yes, well, I tried to warn you, didn't I?' Kitty said. 'You're not going anywhere with your leg in a splint. Now I'm going to have to check that dressing. It'll be a miracle if you haven't opened up those stitches...' She saw his desolate face and said, 'Look, I'll find out where your friend is.'

His eyes lit up with hope. 'You'll find Emil?'

Kitty nodded. 'I'll look at the list as soon as I've finished here–'

'Now.'

'I'll give the orders, thank you very much.' She advanced on him with the thermometer but he jerked his head away, his mouth an obstinate line.

'I see. It's like that, is it?' Kitty took a step back and looked down at her watch. Ten to nine. She knew she wasn't going to get anywhere with him unless she gave in, and she didn't have the time to mess about. 'All right, I'll do it now,' she sighed.

Miss Sloan was at the desk, tidying it up before the night nurse arrived.

'There you are, my dear,' she greeted Kitty. 'What on earth was all that fuss about? It sounded as if there was a murder going on in

108

there just now.'

'There nearly was.' Kitty scanned the desk. 'Have you seen the list of the patients that were just brought in?'

'Here it is.' Miss Sloan handed her the piece of paper. 'I do hope the night nurse arrives soon. I've arranged to go to a music recital with a friend, in aid of the Russian refugees...'

But Kitty had stopped listening as she scanned the names on the list.

Stefan seemed to be asleep when Kitty returned. But as soon as she crept through the curtains his eyes flicked open.

'Did you find him?' he said.

Kitty shook her head. 'I'm sorry, there's no one called Emil on the list.'

He turned his face away from her. 'He's dead, then,' he said in a flat voice.

'You never know, perhaps he was taken to another hospital.'

'No, he's dead. I saw his body on the ground when we surrendered. I just thought he might...' His voice trailed off.

'Was he a friend of yours?' Kitty asked. But the man had closed his eyes, his chest rising and falling in a deep rhythm that told her he was already asleep.

Kitty covered him up with a blanket and tip-toed away.

Chapter Thirteen

The night nurse arrived shortly afterwards, at nine o'clock. By the time Kitty had finished giving her report, it was nearly ten past. She quickly changed out of her uniform and hurried to the bus stop, just in time to see the number 15 bus disappearing down the road.

No doubt Bea and Lily were on it, she thought. Trust Bea to be punctual for once, on the very night Kitty needed her to be late!

She paused for a moment to get her breath back and work out her options. She could always follow them up West, she thought. There wouldn't be another bus that night, but if she ran all the way to the underground, and the trains were working properly, she might even catch them up before they reached Curzon Street.

But was it really worth the effort? After fourteen hours on her feet, the idea of going dancing didn't really appeal to her after all.

She didn't want to admit it to herself, but deep down she wasn't too disappointed that they had gone without her.

'Hello again.'

Kitty turned round at the sound of Mal's voice. He was leaning against a lamp post a few yards away, watching her.

'Fancy seeing you here,' he grinned.

Kitty narrowed her eyes. 'Are you following me?'

'No!' He laughed. 'I've got better things to do with my time, thanks very much. Or I thought I did,' he added, glancing at his watch. 'I was meant to be going up West with Len and Andy, but I reckon they must have gone off without me.'

'That makes two of us,' Kitty said.

'You mean your mates have abandoned you, too?'

'Looks like it.'

'So it's just us, then?'

She caught the hopeful look in his eye. 'I'm going home.'

His face fell. 'Aw, don't be a spoilsport. We could make a night of it.'

'No thanks.'

Mal frowned, 'So why don't you like me? You never got round to saying earlier.'

Kitty looked at him, leaning against the lamp post. He came across as so cocky and confident, but she could tell he wasn't like that at all underneath.

'It's not that I don't like you,' she said. 'I just don't want a boyfriend, that's all.'

'But you do like me?' he pounced on her words.

She smiled reluctantly. 'You're all right,' she conceded.

'All right! She says I'm all right!' Mal shouted out, startling an old woman who was shuffling past with her dog.

He scrambled up the lamp post and swung round it, his arm flung out dramatically. 'What a compliment!'

'Daft beggar!' Kitty shook her head. 'I'm going home.'

Mal jumped down from the lamp post, straight into her path. 'Can I walk you home?'

'No thanks, I can find my own way.'

'It's a bit dangerous in this blackout.'

'What are you on about? It's not even properly dark yet–' She stopped, every muscle in her body tensing.

'What is it?' Mal said.

'Can't you hear it?'

'Hear what?'

'The engines.' She tilted her head towards the sound. It was faint, scarcely more than a whisper on the air, but she could feel it more than hear it. 'There are planes coming.'

Mal listened for a moment. 'Sorry, love, I can't hear a–'

His words were drowned out by the insistent moan of the air raid siren, coming out of nowhere.

Kitty stood still, her blood freezing in her veins. But Mal didn't seem at all concerned.

'Looks like you were right,' he grinned. 'Oh well, I s'pose we'll have to take shelter until they go over.' He looked around. 'Which way to the nearest shelter?'

Kitty stared at him. She could see his mouth moving and she knew he was speaking, but she couldn't hear what he was saying over the crashing of her heart.

'Kitty?' He looked back at her, frowning. 'What's the matter? You've gone very pale.'

His words were drowned out by the sudden retort of the anti-aircraft guns in Victoria Park. Across the road, two buses had stopped and the passengers were making their way to the shelter.

Kitty froze, every muscle in her body turned to stone by the harsh sounds echoing around her. Somewhere in all the madness she felt Mal take her arm. 'Come on,' he said.

He took charge, and Kitty finally felt her feet moving as they followed the people thronging towards the shelter. But as they were crossing the road, the deep thrum of the plane engines grew louder. She risked a look over her shoulder and saw one of them, its sinister, long shape against the darkening sky.

Again she froze, staring up as the plane passed overhead. The drone of the engine seemed to fill her brain, shutting out everything else, mesmerising her...

And then, suddenly – silence. An ominous sound that sucked everything into it. Kitty caught the fearful looks on the faces of the people heading for the shelter and knew that, like her, they were counting the seconds before–

They all knew the blast was coming but it still caught them by surprise, shattering the silence and shaking the ground under their feet. The next moment a cloud of smoke and dust rose across the rooftops, drifting towards them.

'That was close!' someone said.

Another plane was coming, and everyone started to hurry, except Kitty, whose feet were welded to the pavement again. She might have stayed there if Mal hadn't picked her up and carried her down the steps to the shelter.

He dumped her on a long bench, beside a harassed-looking woman with a lot of crying children.

'You'll be safe here,' he promised.

113

Another explosion somewhere above them brought a shower of plaster dust down on them. The children cried louder, but their mother calmly handed out slices of bread and marge to silence them, a fixed smile on her face.

'Look, we're having a picnic,' she said, her voice falsely bright.

Mal started to take his hand away, but Kitty held on to it in panic.

'Where are you going? You can't leave me!'

He nodded back towards the steps. 'I've got to go and see if I can help.'

'But it's not safe!'

He grinned. 'I didn't know you cared.' He carefully extricated himself from her grasp. 'I'll be fine,' he said. 'I'll see you in the morning.'

Kitty couldn't watch him go. She stared instead at the thick film of dust that covered her shoes. Just a few minutes earlier, that dust might have been someone's home. Perhaps one of the people crammed in here, in this damp, gloomy shelter, would leave in a few hours only to find their house and everything they had was destroyed.

Another blast shook the walls of the shelter.

'Here.' Kitty felt a nudge in her ribs and looked round to see the woman next to her proffering a slice of bread and marge. 'I've got plenty to go round,' she smiled.

'Thank you.' Kitty took it.

'It'll be all right, you know,' the woman said. She had one of her children on her lap, hugging him tightly to her. 'I'll look after you. We'll see it out together.'

'Thank you.' Kitty took a bite of the bread. It

114

was hard and greyish brown in colour, and it stuck in her throat.

The woman smiled confidingly. 'He's very brave, isn't he? Your young man.'

'Yes,' Kitty said, without thinking. 'Yes, he is.'

Chapter Fourteen

Doodlebugs, everyone called them, as if giving them a cheery name would make them less terrifying.

It was a long night. The V-1s came over for hours, on and off. No sooner had the all-clear sounded and everyone relaxed than another air raid warning started up.

Dora and her family had debated going to the shelter, but there was hardly time between the raids.

'Besides,' Nanna Winnie sniffed, 'my old bones won't take another night in that damp shelter. If my number's up, then I'd rather go in my own bed, thank you very much.'

'No one's number is going to be up,' Dora's mother replied firmly, hugging little Mabel tighter into her lap. They had got the children out of bed, and now Walter and Winnie dozed in Dora's arms, warm and sleepy in their nightclothes. At least she'd got her wish to spend time with her children, although not in the way she would have wanted. 'Turn that wireless up, Alfie. *Saturday Night Theatre* will be starting soon.'

But even though they all pretended to be engrossed in the play, Dora knew that like her, her mother and grandmother were listening to each bomb as it droned overhead, their hearts stopping when the engine cut out, waiting for it to drop.

The only one who seemed to enjoy the air raid was Alfie, who peered up at the sky through a gap in the blackout curtain.

'It's funny, ain't it?' he remarked. 'Sometimes they come straight down like a stone, and other times they take ages, like a feather. Why do you think that is?'

'I don't know, do I?' his mother snapped. 'Now come away from that window before anyone sees the light.'

'The V-1s can't see us, they ain't got no pilots.'

'They might not be able to see us, but the ARP wardens can. I don't want them coming round here with a fine, thank you very much.'

Saturday Night Theatre ended, but Dora had stopped listening to it long before the end. Then it was *Evening Prayers,* followed by *Saturday Night at the Palais* with Harry Leader and his band.

Dora glanced at her nanna, moving slowly back and forth in her old rocking chair. Once her hands would have been busy with knitting or mending until late into the night, but now she couldn't see well enough by the lamplight to work. With nothing to distract her, she could only stare into the empty grate.

Her mother seemed just as preoccupied. Even though she tried to smile and tap her hands on her knee in time to the music, every now and then her troubled gaze would stray to the clock on the mantelpiece. Dora knew exactly what she was thinking.

'She'll be all right,' she said. 'Bea's a big girl, she can take care of herself. Besides, Lily's with her.'

'Yes, but what if...' Rose's voice trailed off, as if she couldn't allow herself to utter the terrible thoughts that tormented her. 'I'd just like her home safe,' she finished quietly.

'And she will be,' Dora said. 'But our Bea's got more sense than to try to get back with all this going on. I expect she and Lily have taken shelter somewhere until it's finished.'

'You're right, love. I'm just being daft, as usual.' Her mother nodded, but Dora could see she was still worried.

Finally, when the wireless ended at midnight, they all wearily took themselves off to bed. The twins didn't stir as Dora settled them in her double bed, but Mabel woke up.

'Where's Mum?' she wanted to know, rubbing her eyes sleepily.

'She'll be back soon, ducks.'

Mabel instantly snapped awake, her brown eyes wide and fearful. 'Where is she? Why hasn't she come home?'

A distant explosion rattled the windows in their frames. Mabel yelped with terror. 'I want my Mum!' she whined.

'Shh, you'll wake Walter and Winnie,' Dora whispered. But it was too late, they were already stirring.

Once awake, it didn't take long for them to catch on to their cousin's terror. Before long, all three of them were crying. Dora struggled to console them all, singing them songs and making up silly rhymes to distract them. Walter and Winnie joined in, but Lily's daughter remained sullen and watchful, her mouth turned down in an exact imitation of her mother.

Finally, Dora managed to settle them all in their beds. She cuddled down with her arms round the twins, finally giving in to the heavy weariness that engulfed her.

But no sooner had she fallen asleep than she was being woken up again by a tug on her sleeve.

'Auntie Dora!' She opened her eyes to find herself staring into Mabel's tearful face.

Dora struggled to sit up. 'What is it, love?'

'I've wet the bed.' Her lip trembled and a moment later she burst into noisy tears. Dora rushed to console her, fearful that she would wake the twins again.

'It's all right, love. It was an accident, there's no harm done.'

'Mum'll smack me.'

'She won't know.' Careful not to disturb the twins, Dora clambered out of bed. 'We'll sort it out,' she promised. 'Come on, let's get you washed and find you something clean to put on.'

Still bleary with sleep, she led Mabel through to the kitchen. She wasn't surprised to find the light on and her mother still up, wrapped in her dressing gown in Nanna's rocking chair.

'What's going on?' Rose asked.

'Just a little accident, that's all.'

Her mother looked from Dora to Mabel and back again, and understanding crossed her face.

She rose to her feet, wrapping her dressing

gown around herself. 'I'll strip the bed,' she said.

While her mother put the sheets to soak in the scullery sink, Dora washed Mabel down and found a fresh nightgown for her. Then she settled her down in her own bed, in between the twins.

'I want my mum!' Mabel wept, as Dora pulled the cover up around her. 'I wish she was here.'

'Believe me, so do I,' Dora murmured under her breath. Although the way she was feeling now, she would probably wring Lily Doyle's neck.

She returned to the kitchen to find her mother scrubbing at the mattress.

'I think I've got the worst of it off,' she said. 'It should be dry by tomorrow night if I put it out in the yard first thing. Lily will just have to sleep on the floor.'

Lily should be here, sorting this out instead of leaving it to us. Dora pressed her lips together to stop herself saying the words. She didn't want to remind her mother that Bea still hadn't come home.

'You should be in bed,' she said instead.

'Oh, it's hard for me to sleep these days. Especially with your nanna. She's so restless. And she has such terrible nightmares...'

'Nightmares?' Dora was shocked. She couldn't imagine her indomitable nanna losing sleep over anything.

'She thinks the house is falling down on her,' Rose said. 'She's been like it ever since we left Griffin Street.' She shook her head. 'It hit her hard, you know, losing her home like that.'

'I know,' Dora said heavily. It had been difficult for all of them, but Nanna Winnie felt it most keenly. Griffin Street had been her first home as

119

a young bride. To have it all destroyed like that, especially at her age, must have been nearly impossible to bear.

Her mother's gaze strayed back to the clock.

'Why don't you sleep in with Mabel and the twins?' Dora suggested. 'I'll take the chair for tonight.'

'Oh, but I couldn't. You've got to be up for work in the morning.'

'So have you. You've got a home to run and a family to look after, remember?' Dora looked at her mother's exhausted face. 'I'll be all right. Honestly, Mum, go to bed. You look all in.'

'But Bea–'

'I'll wait up for her,' Dora promised. *And I'll have a few words to say to her when she finally decides to come home,* she added silently.

It was nearly two in the morning when Dora woke up to the clatter of high heels coming down the basement steps. There was much scuffling about outside with the key, then a moment later Bea and Lily fell through the back door, giggling helplessly.

Dora got out of the armchair, stretching her aching limbs.

'What time do you call this?' she said.

Bea stuck her chin out. 'Why? Ain't you got a watch?'

Lily gave a muffled snort of laughter. Dora ignored her. The mingled smell of cheap scent and alcohol filled the room.

'Mum's been worried sick about you,' she said to Bea.

'Yes, well, we had to take shelter, didn't we?'

Bea replied defiantly. 'Or did you expect us to walk home with all those doodlebugs raining down on us?'

It was exactly what she'd told her mother, but that didn't stop Dora feeling annoyed.

She turned her attention to Lily, swaying slightly on her feet. 'And as for you,' she said. 'Your little girl's been crying for you half the night.'

At least she had the grace to look guilty at that. 'How is she?'

'She's settled now. Mum's with her. But she's wet the bed, so you've got nowhere to sleep tonight.' She knew she should have tried not to sound so pleased about it, but she couldn't help it.

'It's all right, Lil. You can bunk in with me tonight,' Bea offered, glaring at Dora.

'You shouldn't go gallivanting off and leave her, you know,' Dora said. 'You're her mum.'

'For your information, she hasn't been gallivanting,' Bea answered for her. 'She's got a job. Ain't you, Lil?' She stuck her arm through her sister-in-law's.

Dora stared at Lily. 'What's she talking about?'

'Bea's got me a job helping out at the Washington Club with her,' Lily replied with a touch of defiance.

'I see.' Dora folded her arms. 'So you'll be out like this every night, I s'pose?'

'So what?' Lily said defensively. 'You're always saying I should do some war work.'

'I can think of better things you could be doing for the war effort than emptying ash trays for American soldiers.'

'Oh, you mean like wiping German soldiers'

backsides?' Lily shot back.

Bea must have seen the look on Dora's face because she tugged her sister-in-law's arm and said, 'Come on, Lil. Let's not argue tonight. I'm too tired and she ain't worth it.'

As they walked away, Dora called after them, 'You'd better look in on Mabel before you go to bed. She's your kid, after all.'

'Take no notice,' she heard Bea mutter.

'Oh, I don't,' Lily replied haughtily. 'Dora Riley can act as high and mighty with me as she wants, but at least I know what side I'm on!'

Chapter Fifteen

The new patient was little more than a boy, pale, malnourished and blue about the lips. His racking cough shook his thin body so hard he could barely answer the questions Major Von Mundel asked.

Dr Abbott stood at the foot of the bed, flanked by Dora and Helen, and made a great show of checking his watch as he watched the pair conversing in rapid German.

'Oh, for heaven's sake! I only want to know his symptoms, not his entire ruddy life story!' He snatched up his stethoscope and stepped forward, nudging Major Von Mundel out of the way. 'Let me have a look at him. I'll soon tell you what's wrong!'

After a quick examination of the patient's chest, Dr Abbott declared that he was suffering from acute bronchitis.

'Rest in a semi-recumbent position, menthol inhalation, mustard poultices as needed,' he said, writing on the man's notes.

Behind them, Major Von Mundel cleared his throat.

'Excuse me, Herr Doctor?'

Dora looked up in surprise. The Major had never spoken up before during the doctor's round, although she had a feeling he had been tempted to do so several times in the past.

Dr Abbott was just as surprised. He peered at the officer over his spectacles. 'Yes? What is it?'

'I believe you may be mistaken in your diagnosis.'

Dr Abbott bristled. 'And what makes you think that?'

Dora could hear the hostility behind his words, but Von Mundel obviously couldn't. Either that, or he'd chosen to ignore it.

'The patient is complaining of a pain in his side when he lies down. There is also considerable effusion, breathlessness and cyanosis,' he said.

Dr Abbott's face flushed. 'It might have been helpful if you'd mentioned some of those symptoms earlier,' he muttered.

'Pardon me, Herr Doctor. I assumed you would be able to diagnose a case of pleurisy without my help.'

Dr Abbott's colour deepened. Dora and Helen exchanged uncomfortable looks.

'Very well,' he said, handing the notes back to Helen. 'We'll keep an eye on him. Restrict his diet to liquid feeds and I'll prescribe a diaphoretic for the fever–'

'He needs aspiration,' Major Von Mundel said curtly.

Dr Abbott's chin lifted. 'That really isn't necessary,' he dismissed. 'Most pleurisy cases recover on their own in a couple of weeks–'

'He'll be dead by then,' Major Von Mundel cut him off. 'The boy is drowning. Even you can see that?'

Even you. The words hung on the air between them. Dora could feel Dr Abbott's mortification as keenly as if it were her own.

'He needs to have the fluid removed from his lungs before it kills him,' the Major went on. He paused, then said, 'I could perform the procedure, if you are unable?'

It was the worst thing he could have said. Dr Abbott pulled himself up to his full height, his boyish face mottled with angry colour.

'May I remind you, Von Mundel, that this is my patient?' he said icily.

'Then I suggest you treat him, before it's too late,' the officer snapped back.

There was a long, tense silence. Dora held her breath as the two men stared at each other. Dr Abbott seemed to be trapped like a frightened rabbit in the glare of Von Mundel's cold blue gaze.

Then he broke away and turned to Helen. 'As I was saying, I will prescribe a diaphoretic–'

Without saying another word, Von Mundel turned on his heel and walked away.

He didn't return for the rest of the doctor's round. Dr Abbott's usually genial mood had also disappeared. He barely spoke a word to Dora or

124

Helen as they hurried round to each patient. He was rushing, but to Dora the round still seemed to last forever.

'Well!' she said to Helen, when Dr Abbott had finally gone. 'What did you think of that?'

'I thought it was utterly shocking,' Helen replied. 'How dare he try to tell Dr Abbott what to do! It's typical of the man's arrogance.'

Dora frowned. 'You don't think he might have a point?'

'No, I don't!' Helen looked aghast at the idea.

'But what if he's right? That boy could die.'

'I'm sure the doctor knows what he's doing,' Helen said primly.

'Yes, but Major—'

'Major Von Mundel is not a doctor at this hospital,' Helen cut her off sharply.

'He's a qualified surgeon.'

'How do you know that? You only have his word for it.'

'He seems to know what he's talking about. More than Dr Abbott, at any rate.'

Helen looked scandalised. 'How can you say that?'

'Because it's true. Oh, come on, Dawson!' Dora reasoned with her. 'You know as well as I do that Jimmy Abbott means well, but he was never the best medical student, and he's not the best doctor either.' She paused. 'Can't you talk to him? He might listen to you...'

'No, I could not!' Helen looked scandalised. 'It's not my job. And it's not yours, either,' she added, as Dora opened her mouth to protest. 'You should know better than to criticise a doctor, Nurse Riley.'

She went into her office and closed the door firmly on Dora, ending the conversation.

Dora stared at the door in frustration. It wasn't like Helen to be so stubborn. Dora knew very well that she would have spoken up if it meant saving a patient's life.

But not if the patient was a German.

The thought shocked her. It couldn't be true. Helen was too compassionate, too good a nurse, to make those kinds of distinctions. A life was a life, no matter where the person came from. The Helen she knew would never do such a thing.

Major Von Mundel was by the young man's bedside when Dora returned later. He looked at the mustard poultice she had prepared, but said nothing.

Dora couldn't look at him as she set about administering the poultice. She knew all too well how inadequate her efforts were, and it filled her with shame.

But she had to put on a brave face for her patient. *'Guten tag,* young man,' she greeted him brightly. *'Wie geht es ihnen heute?'*

'Mein Brust schmerzt, schwester.'

'He says his chest hurts,' Von Mundel translated for her tautly.

'Yes, well, I'm not surprised about that. But this might make you feel better. *Besser,'* she said. 'I think that's the word, isn't it?'

She could feel the Major's gaze on her as she worked.

'I didn't know you had started speaking German?' Von Mundel said.

'I wouldn't call it speaking!' Dora replied. 'But I got a dictionary out of the library and learnt a few words. I thought it might help the patients to settle down better?'

Von Mundel was silent for a moment. Then he said, 'Thank you.'

Dora shrugged it off. 'It's only a few words. Mind you, it caused a few raised eyebrows at the library. That lady behind the counter probably thinks I'm a spy now–'

'No,' he said, 'I mean thank you for what you said earlier. I heard you talking to the *oberschwester.*'

Dora blushed. 'Sister Dawson is in a difficult position,' she said. 'We can't go against doctor's orders. But I know she would help if she could...'

'Would she? I wonder.' Von Mundel sent her a shrewd look. 'But thank you, Nurse Riley. I appreciate you trying.'

Dora glanced at the young man in the bed. Just as she had known, the mustard poultice did nothing for him. He still struggled for breath, his lips blue with the lack of oxygen in his blood. 'I just want him to get better.'

Major Von Mundel sighed. 'Sadly, Nurse Riley, I do not think that will happen,' he said.

Oberleutnant Stefan Bauer was fully awake and propped up in bed when Kitty went into his room to check his splint. His skin still had a greyish pallor where he'd lost so much blood, but, he didn't look like a man who'd had a brush with death.

Kitty pushed her wash trolley to his bedside and pulled the curtains around his bed.

'Good morning,' she greeted him. 'How are you feeling today?'

'When can I leave?'

His blunt question took her aback. Kitty stared at him. He looked back at her, his brown gaze frank and direct.

'Well, I don't know,' she said, reaching for the thermometer. 'You'll have to ask the doctor–'

'I'm asking you.'

Kitty blinked at him. He was so rude, she almost snapped back at him. But there was something about the look in his eyes that stopped her.

She thought about it for a moment. 'We'll have to keep a close eye on you for the next couple of weeks, make sure your wound doesn't get infected. And then you'll have to stay in this splint until your bones have knitted together...'

'And how long will that take?' he interrupted her impatiently.

'I don't know. A month or so, I suppose.'

'And then I can go?'

'Oh no. After that you'll have to wear a walking calliper for at least four months, to strengthen your leg–'

'Four months!' He looked aghast. 'No, it is not possible. I can't stay here that long.'

His arrogance irked her. 'You're a prisoner. You don't have any choice,' she reminded him tartly. 'Besides, you're lucky to be alive. Everyone thought you were going to die.'

His mouth curled at that, but Kitty could tell from the look in his eyes that she'd startled him.

He remained silent as she checked his temperature and pulse rate, and noted the figures on his chart. It was only when she picked up the bottle of methylated spirits that he shied away from her.

'What are you doing?' he demanded.

'Checking your splint, what does it look like?' She pressed a swab to the open bottle and tipped it. 'I have to keep your skin dry to stop pressure sores.'

'I can do it myself,' he muttered, holding on to the bed-clothes to cover himself.

'I don't think you can, the state you're in,' Kitty said briskly. 'Look at you, you can hardly move. Now come on, don't be a baby. I've seen it all before, you know—'

'Not you!' he snapped. He nodded towards Miss Sloan, 'Get her to do it. The old woman.'

For a moment they glared at each other. Stefan Bauer's rugged face was a mask of stubbornness, his jaw set rigid. He looked so like a petulant child, Kitty almost laughed.

'Very well,' she sighed, putting down the swab. 'I'll ask her. But I don't think she'd appreciate you calling her old!'

Luckily Leonora Sloan didn't mind taking over. 'Poor man, I daresay he's embarrassed at being vulnerable in front of a pretty young thing like you,' she said, as they did the beds together later.

'He doesn't strike me as the vulnerable type,' Kitty said.

'No, he doesn't, does he?' Miss Sloan looked thoughtful. 'I heard Major Von Mundel discussing him with one of the other soldiers earlier on. He's quite the hero, from what I understand.'

'Oh?'

'Oh yes. All his men look up to him, apparently. I gather he was quite a commander.'

'Well, he needn't think he's going to be giving the orders around here!' Kitty said firmly.

Mal was on the doors with his friend Len as usual when Kitty went off for her break later. She could barely manage an embarrassed nod as she slid past.

'Oh dear, pal. Looks like you're in her bad books again!' Len chuckled. 'What have you done this time?'

Kitty kept her eyes glued to the floor as she scuttled away. She knew Mal deserved more after the way he'd looked after her the previous evening, but she was too mortified to speak to him. What must he think of her? She could feel herself burning with shame whenever she remembered the pathetic way she'd clung to him and begged him not to leave her.

She had a quick cup of tea and a much needed sit-down, but as she emerged from the basement canteen fifteen minutes later, she saw Mal waiting for her.

Panic seized her. 'I'm not supposed to speak to you while I'm on duty,' she hissed, keeping her eyes averted. 'If Matron sees–'

'I just wanted to see if you got home all right last night,' Mal interrupted her. 'You seemed in such a state when I left...'

A blush scalded her face. 'I spent the night in the shelter,' she mumbled.

'Were you all right? I wanted to come back and check on you, but a bomb went off and they closed the road.'

Her eyes flew to his, forgetting the rules for a minute. 'Are you all right?'

'Oh yes, I'm right as rain. But it brought a house down. There was a family trapped inside. We managed to get the three kids out, but their mum...'

'Don't,' Kitty shuddered. 'It's too awful.' She shook her head. 'You must think I'm soft, making such a fuss when there are people like that suffering far worse.'

'I don't think you're soft at all.'

The intensity of his gaze embarrassed her. She cleared her throat, suddenly nervous.

'Thank you, anyway,' she said

As she went to walk away, he called after her, 'If you really want to thank me you could go out with me sometime.'

She smiled. 'You never give up, do you?'

'You know what they say. Faint heart never won fair lady.'

Kitty opened her mouth to refuse, then shocked herself by saying, 'All right, then.'

He looked even more shocked than she was. 'You will? When?'

She thought about it. 'I'll let you know when I've next got the evening off, if you like.'

'All right. I'll look forward to it.'

'Me too.'

His look of utter surprise made her smile all the way back to the ward.

Chapter Sixteen

By the end of the week, the young pleurisy patient had died.

Kitty helped Nurse Riley perform last offices. The senior nurse was in a strange mood as they stripped the bed ready for the laying out. It was always sad to lose a patient, but Dora Riley seemed to be taking this one's death very hard indeed. Kitty could hear the catch in her voice as she recited a final prayer at his bedside.

They went through their duties quickly, and in silence. The young man was washed, his short fair hair combed and his nails trimmed.

'What shall we dress him in?' Kitty asked, when they'd finished. 'I suppose it will have to be his prison uniform–'

'No!' Dora looked up from the label she was filling in. 'Go and find some clean clothes. I'm sure we must have some spare from the old emergency ward. I won't let him be buried a prisoner. It ain't right.'

Kitty looked at her in surprise. The staff nurse's mouth was an obstinate line, but Kitty could swear there were tears in her eyes.

They managed to find some clothes for him, then wrapped him in a sheet. As Dora stitched the shroud in place, Kitty cleared his belongings from the bedside locker.

There were a couple of photographs, one of a

pretty young girl who must have been his sweetheart, and another of a smiling family. There was also a silver St Christopher, and a tiny, battered Bible.

'He must have kept this in his pocket the whole time.' The tissue-thin pages whispered as she flicked through them, the tiny print incomprehensible to her. 'It's funny, isn't it, to think of them reading the same Bible as us?'

'Why is it so strange?' Dora said sharply. 'They're no different from us. They've got wives and mothers and sisters, just like everyone else. People who want them to come home...'

Kitty looked at the St Christopher, glinting on the end of its chain. Her mum had given Raymond one just like it for his twenty-first birthday, a few weeks before he joined the navy.

'What shall I do with this?' she asked. 'It looks valuable.'

Dora looked up at it, and for a moment she seemed lost in thought. Then she said, 'I'll pass it on to Sister Dawson. She can keep it locked in her office with the rest of his possessions until it can be sent back to his family.'

Helen was in her office as usual. She looked up as Dora came in.

'Yes? What is it?'

Dora put the box down on her desk in front of her. 'Helmut Gruber's belongings. The boy with pleurisy?' she said, as Helen looked blank. 'He died this morning.'

'Oh yes. Of course.' Helen blushed.

'I wasn't sure what to do with them,' Dora went

on. 'I'm sure his family would want them back, but I don't know how we'd go about sending them...'

'I'll ask Matron.' Helen stared at the box in front of her. Was that guilt on her face, Dora wondered. If it was, she deserved it.

Her better judgement told her to walk away. But she couldn't stop herself speaking.

'He didn't have to die,' she blurted out. 'If Dr Abbott had only listened to Major Von Mundel...'

'People make mistakes,' Helen muttered. 'Besides, there was nothing we could do about it.'

'You could have done something. You could have made Dr Abbott listen.'

The words were out before Dora could stop herself. Helen's head shot up, their eyes meeting. 'That's not true!' she said. 'You know as well as I do that it's not our place to argue with a doctor—'

'That's never stopped you in the past, has it? I've seen you stand up to a doctor if you thought it was in the interests of a patient. I bet you would have said something if Helmut Gruber had been an RAF pilot, or a British soldier. But just because he was a German, you think his life doesn't matter!'

Helen's gaze dropped away from hers. 'That's not true,' she murmured.

'Isn't it? You've shown no concern for the POWs so far, from what I can see. You're rarely on the ward, and when you are you might as well not be there for all the interest you take. You don't like the Germans, do you?'

'Do you?' Helen flashed back.

For a moment, Dora heard her sister-in-law Lily's voice in her head, taunting her.

At least I know what side I'm on.

'It doesn't matter what I think of them,' she said. 'They're still my patients, and I treat them just the same as anyone else who needs my care.'

'Yes, well, perhaps that's not so easy for the rest of us,' Helen muttered.

Dora stared at her. Helen didn't meet her eye. She gazed down at her hands, lacing and unlacing on the desk in front of her. 'Why not?'

'Let's just say I have my reasons.'

'What reasons?'

Helen was silent for a moment, her attention still fixed on her hands. Her long fingers were raw and bitten at the tips, Dora noticed.

'I was attacked by a POW,' she said at last.

Dora froze. 'When?'

'A few weeks ago. While I was working in a field hospital near Tobruk.' Once again Helen paused for a moment, and Dora could see her fighting for control of her emotions. 'A unit of Germans had been brought in. Only a couple of serious injuries, but most of them starving and exhausted. They were only supposed to stay for one night, until they could be shipped off...' She took a deep, steadying breath. 'I was on night duty, on my own. I was supposed to be sitting with an unconscious patient, but one of the Germans starting carrying on, demanding attention. When I refused, he smashed a glass on his nightstand and tried to push it into my face.' Her voice was flat, matter of fact, with only the barest hint of a tremor.

'Oh, Helen!'

'It's all right, I wasn't badly hurt. He didn't cut me or anything, but he did sprain my wrist where

135

he twisted it up behind my back.' She rubbed her arm under her thick calico sleeve. 'It was more the shock than anything,' she said. 'After that night, I found I couldn't do it any more. I kept having nightmares, you see ... so they sent me home.'

'And now you're here, nursing POWs?' Dora said.

Helen looked up at her, her brown eyes full of appeal. 'Now do you understand why I've found it so hard? I know I have to do it, but every time I hear their voices, I just freeze...'

'Oh, Helen.' Dora stared at her friend's wretched face. Why hadn't she realised the truth before? 'Can't you speak to your commanding officer? Surely if she understood the situation–'

'She already knows. Why do you think I was transferred back to England?' Helen was rueful. 'Major Ellis already thinks it's more than enough that I've been allowed to come home.'

She gave Dora a sad smile. 'I'm sorry that I haven't been pulling my weight,' she said. 'But I've just found it so difficult...'

'Of course.' Dora's anger evaporated, replaced by concern for her friend. 'And I'm sorry I lost my temper with you.'

'No, you're right,' Helen said bracingly. 'I need to pull myself together and remember my duty.' She gave Dora a brave smile. 'I'm going to start pulling my weight on this ward from now on.'

'You don't have to, you know. I'm sure we can manage...'

'No, I must. As Major Ellis would say, I need to buck up!'

That night there was news of another raid over Germany. According to the BBC, the Allies had rained more bombs over Berlin.

'Good thing, too!' Kitty's father beamed with satisfaction as they sat around the table for tea. 'About time those Germans got a taste of their own medicine, after everything they put us through over the past few years.' He rubbed his hands together. 'We've got 'em on the run now, all right!'

'I just wish it would all stop,' her mother said quietly as she dished out the vegetable pie.

'I don't!' Arthur joined in. 'Not until I get my chance to have a go, anyway.'

Kitty looked at her mother's stricken face across the table. Suddenly a picture came into her mind of another mother, sitting at her own family's table worrying about her son, not knowing that his Bible and St Christopher would soon be making their way home to her.

'Not eating, love?' Her mother looked anxious as Kitty pushed her plate away.

She shook her head. 'Sorry, Mum, I think I've lost my appetite,' she said.

Chapter Seventeen

In early August the fair came to Hackney Marshes, and Bea decided that they should all go.

'I'll bring my new boyfriend Hank,' she said. 'And you can bring Mal.'

'I'm not sure about that,' Kitty said. 'Can't we keep it just us girls?'

'Where's the fun in that?' Bea pouted. 'Go on, it'll be a lark. And I've been dying for you to meet Hank.'

Kitty was keen to meet him, too. Bea had been going on for ages about the handsome GI she'd met at the Washington Club. To listen to her, anyone would think he was Cary Grant, Clark Gable and Spencer Tracy combined, with a dash of Tyrone Power thrown in for good measure.

But when Kitty saw Hank, she realised that for once her friend hadn't been exaggerating.

'Isn't he divine?' Bea sighed, as they watched the men compete on the coconut shy. 'So good-looking. Don't you think he's good-looking, Kitty?'

'He's very handsome.' No one could argue with that. Hank was a tall, broad-shouldered giant of a man, with slicked black hair, dark eyes and a devilish smile. He dwarfed Mal as they stood together at the shy, aiming wooden balls at the coconuts. Bea had already warned Kitty not to expect her boyfriend to win her anything, since Hank was the best shot in his unit, and captain of the baseball team.

'And charming, too. Such good manners, not at all like the British men. No offence, of course,' she added with a giggle. 'I mean, your Mal seems very nice.'

'He is,' Kitty said.

She watched the two of them, side by side. Mal might not have Hank's movie star looks, but he was sweet and funny, and he made her laugh. Somehow without even knowing it, their one night out together had stretched into another, and now they had been courting for nearly a month.

'I thought you said he was a good shot?' Lily mocked, as Hank aimed another ball wide and it hit the sacking backcloth with a whump. Mal patted his shoulder in consolation.

Bea ignored her. 'Did I tell you he's rich?' she went on to Kitty. 'His family owns a farm in Texas–'

'So he says,' Lily mumbled through a mouth full of chocolate. The best part of the day had been Hank arriving with a big box of candy, as he called it.

'Anyway, they have miles and miles of land, and pots of money,' Bea continued. She sighed happily. 'I think I'm in love!'

Lily choked on her chocolate and started coughing until tears streamed down her face. 'In love?' she spluttered. 'Gawd, Bea, you've only known him five minutes!'

'That doesn't matter,' Bea said primly, digging in her bag and handing her sister-in-law a handkerchief. 'It doesn't matter if I've known him a week or ten years; once you meet The One you just know. Ain't that right, Kit?'

'Don't ask me,' Kitty shrugged.

Bea twisted round to face her. 'You mean you don't feel like that about Mal?'

'Don't be daft, I hardly know him.'

'Quite right,' Lily said. 'You ought to listen to your mate, Bea Doyle. She's got her head screwed on, unlike you.' She helped herself to another chocolate from the box. Bea scowled at her sister-in-law.

'I can't help it if he's swept me off my feet, can I? All I know is I'd follow Hank to the ends of the earth if he asked me.'

'I don't know if I'd follow Mal to the ends of the earth,' Kitty said, gazing over at him as he consoled Hank over another missed shot.

'That's because you're afraid,' Bea told her confidently. 'After what happened with Alex, you're worried about giving your heart to another man in case he breaks it.'

'Am I?' Kitty frowned.

Bea patted her arm. 'Trust me, love, Mal is the one for you. Anyone can see that.'

Just at that moment, Mal and Hank returned. Hank was empty-handed, while Mal had his arms full of a big stuffed teddy.

'For you,' he said, placing it reverently in Kitty's arms. 'He's called Monty.'

'Thank you.' She glanced over at Bea, whose face was like thunder.

'Sorry, sweetheart,' Hank said. 'I guess the best man won.'

'Everyone knows the coconut shy is a fix,' she said, her mouth a tight line. She turned to Lily. 'I hope you haven't eaten all the Turkish Delights?' she said, snatching the box out of her hands. 'You know they're my favourites.'

As they walked away, Mal reached for Kitty's hand. 'What were you girls gossiping about? You looked like you were having a good old chinwag.'

'Oh, nothing.' Kitty hugged Monty tightly under her arm.

Perhaps Bea was right, she thought. Perhaps her heartbreak over Alex had made her wary

140

about falling in love again.

Or perhaps she just didn't want to look too far into the future because she didn't know what it might hold. Whatever the reason, all she knew was that she was happy with Mal, and that was enough for now.

Her mother had just finished doing the ironing when Kitty returned home shortly before tea. She appeared in the kitchen doorway as Kitty was shrugging off her coat.

'Is Mal not with you?' Florrie Jenkins looked disappointed. 'I was going to ask if he wanted to stay for tea.'

'He had to report back for duty.'

'What a shame, I was looking forward to seeing him. You'll have to invite him round again soon.' She smiled at the teddy in her daughter's arms. 'Who's this, then?'

'His name's Monty. Mal won him for me at the fair.'

'Monty, eh? After the hero of Alamein, I s'pose?' Kitty nodded. 'Did you have a nice time at the fair?'

Of course her mother wanted to hear all about her day out. Kitty followed her to the kitchen and gave her all the details as they folded the ironing together.

'That Bea Doyle always was a fast little piece,' Florrie said, shaking her head.

'She reckons she's dead serious with this American.'

'I dunno what her mother would say about it.' Florrie folded up a shirt and added it to the pile. 'Although I suppose if he's half as nice as your

141

young man, she won't have much to complain about.'

'You like Mal, don't you?' Kitty said.

Her mother smiled. 'Oh, yes. And your dad approves, too. We wouldn't mind welcoming him into the family.'

'Mum!'

'What? It's the next step, isn't it, getting engaged.'

'But I scarcely know him.'

'Oh, I know it's early days. But I'd love to see you happily married.'

'We'll see, shall we?' Kitty picked up the pile of ironing. 'Do you want me to take this lot upstairs?'

'Thank you, love. They'll all be home soon and I need to get the tea on.'

It gave Kitty a jolt to walk into Arthur's room. Once he'd shared it with Raymond, but their father had dismantled the bed after their brother was killed. He talked about selling it, but Kitty knew he kept it in the shed on his allotment. He couldn't bear to see it, but no one could bring themselves to get rid of it, either.

Even with the bed gone, Arthur hadn't tried to spread out his possessions to make the room look more lived in. There was still a space on one side of the room where the bed had been, still half the wardrobe empty where Raymond's clothes had hung.

Kitty hung up Arthur's shirts to fill the space, but she knew he would only push them all to one side again. Even after more than a year, he was still waiting for his brother to return.

She closed the wardrobe door. Arthur's Home

Guard uniform hung on the back of it, ready for drill practice that evening. He was so proud to be a member of the Local Defence Volunteers, had joined up as soon as he turned sixteen. He and their father never missed a night's duty. He even kept a photograph of himself in his uniform on his chest of drawers, next to another framed photograph of Raymond in his Royal Navy uniform.

As Kitty turned to look at it, something else caught her eye. There, beside the photographs, a familiar looking object lay glinting.

Kitty went over to look. But no sooner had she registered what it was and where she had seen it than Arthur's voice came from behind her, sharp and angry.

'What are you looking at?'

He stood in the doorway, white-lipped with tension.

'Put that down,' he hissed.

Kitty held up the St Christopher. 'Where did you get it?'

'It's mine.'

Kitty looked at the tiny silver figure dangling on the end of the chain. She would have known it anywhere. 'It belonged to that patient – the one who died.' She stared at him in shock. 'You took it from Sister's office, didn't you?'

She expected him to deny it, but his chin lifted defiantly. 'What if I did? It's not as if he needs it any more, is it?' he sneered.

Was this really Arthur speaking? Kitty barely recognised him. 'But Arthur, that's stealing. You have to put it back.'

'Why should I?'

'Because it's wrong. And you'll get into trouble if you're caught.'

'I took it ages ago and haven't got caught so far, have I?'

Kitty's mouth fell open. 'You mean you've done it before?'

'Once or twice,' he shrugged. 'But so has everyone else,' he insisted. 'Billy Parsons is always helping himself from the prisoners' lockers. No one ever reports it.' He nodded at the St Christopher in her hand. 'He reckons that's solid silver. Should be able to get a few bob for it at the pop shop.'

For a moment Kitty couldn't speak. This couldn't be happening, she told herself. Her little brother might be a fool to himself sometimes, but he was no thief.

And yet here he was, bragging about it as if it was nothing.

'And what about when Sister finds out it's stolen?' she said.

'Oh, she won't even notice it's missing. She hasn't bothered to send the box of his belongings back, so that shows how much she cares. They're prisoners, Kitty,' he said, seeing her face. 'No one cares about them. And I'm not going to get into any trouble. Not if you don't say anything?' He sent her a long look.

'Of course I wouldn't. But not for your sake,' Kitty added. 'Mum's had enough worry, she doesn't need any more.' She looked at the charm dangling from her hand. 'But this has got to go back.'

'No!' Arthur made to snatch it, but Kitty held it out of his grasp.

144

'I mean it, Arthur. It doesn't feel right, having it in the house.'

'It won't be here for much longer. I'll take it to the pawn shop first thing—'

'No, you won't. I'm taking it back when I go on duty.'

'But it's mine!'

'It doesn't belong to you, Arthur.' Kitty shook her head. 'I don't understand you, I really don't. What on earth possessed you to take it in the first place?'

'I told you, everyone—'

'That's no excuse, Arthur Jenkins, and you know it! Those porters get up to all sorts of tricks, but I've never known you to join in, let alone to steal. Our mum and dad certainly didn't bring you up that way.'

Arthur was mutinously silent for a moment. Then he suddenly blurted out, 'I did it for Ray.'

Kitty turned to face him. 'You what?'

'I wanted to get back at them for what they did.'

Kitty sighed. 'And you think Ray would want you to turn into a thief?' she said.

'I had to do something!' His face was mottled with angry colour. 'I can't stand it, Kit. I can't stand having to run around after them like we're their servants or something, knowing what they did to our brother ... and I don't know how you stand it either,' he muttered.

'I do it because it's my job, just like it is yours.'

'Are you sure about that?' Arthur glared at her. 'Because it seems to me you're taking their side.' His gaze fixed on the St Christopher in her hand.

'If you think that, then you're even dafter than I

145

thought!' Kitty closed her fist around the charm. 'I'm just trying to keep us both out of trouble,' she said quietly.

As she turned away, Arthur said, 'So how will you return it?'

'I don't know, I haven't thought about it. I suppose I'll have to find a way to put it back in Sister's office.'

'And what if you get caught? They'll think you nicked it.'

She looked at him calmly. 'That's a chance I'll have to take, isn't it?'

Chapter Eighteen

The charm was burning a hole in Kitty's pocket when she went on duty the following morning. She felt sure everyone must be able to see the guilt written all over her face.

She had hoped to be able to sneak the charm back into Sister's office without anyone noticing, but unfortunately for her, this was one of the rare mornings when Sister Dawson was present on the ward. She spent most of the morning shut away in her office, so there was no chance for Kitty to creep in. She only hoped Sister hadn't chosen this morning to return the young soldier's belongings.

As she waited for her chance, Kitty could barely concentrate on her tasks. She made poultices too hot, forgot to wrap hot water bottles so they scalded patients' feet, and mixed up the morning urine samples so the results were all wrong. Her hands were shaking so much she managed to spill a cup of tea that was meant for Stefan Bauer all over herself.

'Really, Nurse Jenkins,' Dora Riley scolded. 'I don't know what's wrong with you this morning. I wonder if you stayed too late at the fair last night?'

'Sorry, Staff.'

'Now get yourself cleaned up, and fetch Miss Sloan to help you change the patient's bed. These sheets will have to be soaked before they go down to the laundry.'

'Yes, Staff. Sorry, Staff.' Kitty glanced at Stefan Bauer. He watched her with narrowed eyes but said nothing.

Finally, just as Kitty had given up all hope, Sister Dawson was called away to an emergency on the other ward. Shortly afterwards, Nurse Riley went off for her midday break.

'Now, make sure you don't cause any more havoc while I'm away,' she warned Kitty.

'I'll do my best, Staff.'

Her anxiety must have shown on her face because Dora Riley frowned and said, 'Are you sure you're feeling all right? You're very pale.'

'I'm quite well, Staff,' Kitty said, although her stomach was churning.

Dora didn't look convinced. 'We'll see how you are when I get back,' she said. 'If you're still looking peaky I'll send you straight to sick bay.'

Finally, after what seemed like a lifetime, she left. But before Kitty could sneak off to Sister's office, Miss Sloan caught her.

'Where are you going? We've got all the instruments to clean, remember, and you're not leaving me alone with that steriliser. You know I can't manage it by myself. Nasty, hissing, spitting thing. I swear it has a grudge against me.'

'I won't be a minute. I've just got to put something in Sister's office.'

'Well, don't leave me too long,' Miss Sloan warned.

The door to Sister's office was open. Kitty glanced around before she went inside. In the private room opposite, two of the young men were discussing something in German while Stefan lay silently between them, his eyes half closed.

Kitty squared her shoulders and went into Sister's office, trying to look as if she belonged there.

She closed the door behind her and started searching hurriedly for the box. It wasn't on any of the shelves. Her heart racing, she searched through Sister's desk, terrified that at any moment the door would be flung open and she would be caught red-handed.

Finally, she found the box in the bottom drawer, under some papers. Kitty's hands were shaking so much she could scarcely manage to get the lid off.

For a moment Kitty paused, looking at the young man's belongings. There was little to show for his life, just a couple of letters and family photographs. Guilt stung her. How could Arthur have done something so cruel?

She quickly laid the St Christopher back in the box and was trying to get the lid on the box when she heard Sister's voice in the corridor.

Kitty froze, every nerve and muscle suddenly

paralysed by fear. She knew she should move, or hide, but all she could do was stand there, listening to Sister's footsteps coming up the corridor towards her.

She stared at the doorknob, turning slowly. Another moment and everything would be over...

Then, suddenly, she heard Stefan's voice.

'*Oberschwester?* May I speak to you for a moment?'

Kitty's heart was in her throat, stopping her breath. A second later, the doorknob stopped turning.

'Yes? What is it?' Sister Dawson said with a faint note of irritation.

The sound of her footsteps moving away from the door galvanised Kitty into life. She quickly put the lid on the box and stuffed it back in the drawer.

She hurried to the door, opened it a crack and looked out. Sister Dawson was in the private room opposite, her back to the door, standing at Stefan's bedside. Kitty quietly closed the door to Sister's office and scuttled off down the passageway. She was so busy looking over her shoulder she didn't see Miss Sloan until she had slammed straight into her.

'There you are!' the VAD boomed at her. 'Well might you look guilty, Nurse, leaving me alone with that wretched steriliser.'

'I'm sorry,' Kitty said. 'I'll help you now–'

'No need.' Miss Sloan looked huffy. 'I did it all by myself. And I have the scars to prove it. But you'll have to do it next time,' she warned.

'I will,' Kitty promised. She was so relieved and

grateful, she would have sterilised every instrument in the hospital.

'Jenkins?' Sister Dawson's voice rang out behind her. 'Come here, will you?'

Every sinew in Kitty's body instantly stiffened. Had she spoken too soon?

But Sister Dawson was summoning her into the private room.

'This patient has been complaining of pain,' she said, pointing at Stefan. 'I've adjusted the straps on his splint and I can't find any sign of a sore, but I want you to treat it just in case.'

'Yes, Sister.'

Kitty returned with the trolley, and set about working a strip of soaped bandage around the metal rings. She didn't look at Stefan as she worked, but she was aware of him watching her.

'Did you manage to accomplish your mission?' he said in a low voice.

Kitty paused for a fraction of a second, then carried on. 'I don't know what you mean,' she muttered.

'In Sister's office? I saw you creeping in there earlier on.'

Kitty managed a light laugh. 'I really don't know what you're talking about,' she said. 'I wasn't creeping anywhere. I had a laundry order for her to sign, that's all–'

'Ah,' he said. 'A laundry order. I thought you might be returning the trinket your brother stole last week.'

Kitty felt the colour draining from her face, leaving her light-headed.

'That is your brother, isn't it? The tall, thin

boy?' Stefan went on.

Kitty stared at him, then at Felix and Hans on either side of him. Hans was sleeping, but Felix was wide awake, writing a letter.

'They can't understand what I'm saying,' Stefan said, an amused smile curving his lips. 'Your secret is safe with me, *Fraülein*.'

Kitty quickly finished what she was doing and darted off. She knew it would make her look guilty but she was too flustered to think clearly.

She would have liked to avoid him for the rest of the day, but a couple of hours later she was sent back to the private room to adjust Stefan's splint again.

Hans, the young man in the bed next to Stefan, was thrashing restlessly under his covers, sobbing and shaking in his sleep. Neither Stefan nor Felix seemed to be paying him any attention.

'A bad dream,' Stefan said. 'He has them from time to time.'

Kitty looked at him. 'Should I do something?'

Stefan shook his head. 'He will go back to sleep soon.'

'Does this happen often?'

'Most nights,' Stefan shrugged. 'But now he has started to have them during the day, too.' He looked at Hans. 'I am not surprised. He has seen too much for his young age.'

Kitty saw the flicker of sympathy in his hard eyes. It was the first real emotion she had ever seen in him.

Felix, the young man with the gunshot wound, muttered something. Stefan growled back at him. Felix made another remark, lay down and pulled the covers up over his head, shutting them all out. Kitty didn't understand any of what was said, but she gathered there was no love lost between the two men.

A moment later, Hans' panic seemed to subside, and he sank back to sleep.

'You see?' Stefan said.

Their eyes met briefly. Kitty looked away first. 'It's time to move you,' she said.

As she bent over his bed, Kitty could feel her body prickling with sweat inside her heavy uniform. She kept her movements stiff, afraid if she moved too close he would see the sheen of perspiration on her brow.

But in spite of her efforts, she had the feeling he was aware of her discomfort. Nothing seemed to get past Stefan Bauer's keen eye.

She knew she had to say something, to clear the air between them. She took a deep breath. 'What happened earlier–'

'It's none of my business,' Stefan said flatly.

'Yes, but I just wanted you to know Arthur – my brother – he's not really a thief–' He sent her a long look but said nothing. 'He's just got these ideas in his head...'

'*Fraülein*, you don't have to tell me anything. I understand all about brothers and their foolish ideas,' Stefan murmured.

Kitty was curious. 'You have a brother?'

A brief look of pain crossed his face, quickly masked. 'I did,' he said. 'But Emil is dead now.'

Emil. Kitty knew she'd heard the name before, but she couldn't think where.

'I just don't want you to think badly of Arthur,'

152

Kitty pleaded. 'When he took that St Christopher – he did it for our brother Raymond.'

Stefan frowned. 'I do not understand? You have another brother?'

'I did. But he was killed in the North Atlantic.'

Stefan was silent for a moment. 'So he thought that by stealing a dead boy's belongings he would be getting revenge for his brother's death, is that what you are saying?'

Kitty felt herself blushing. 'I know it sounds daft–'

'Yes,' he said. 'It does.'

'You won't tell anyone?' She hated herself for asking the question, but she had to know.

Stefan shrugged. 'What is there to tell? It's over now.'

'Yes, but–'

His eyes met hers. '*Nein, Fraülein,* I am not one to give away other people's secrets,' he said wearily. 'I have too many of my own.'

Chapter Nineteen

'It is worrying, I must admit.'

Dora sent Dr Abbott a sideways look. Things must be bad indeed if even he was looking troubled.

They were gathered in Sister's office, although as usual Helen had absented herself to deal with a new admission on the other ward. It was left to Dora to deal with Dr Abbott. He had come to see

Stefan Bauer, the patient with the fractured femur. After more than a month in a splint, the X-rays had shown that the broken bones in his leg had still not knitted together.

'I would have expected to see some kind of union by now,' Dr Abbott was saying with a frown. 'The man seems to be in good health otherwise, so there's no reason for those bones not to heal. And you're certain the limb has been kept perfectly immobile in all this time?' he said to Dora.

She bristled at the implied criticism. 'His splint has been checked every day, Doctor.'

'Yes. Yes, of course.' Dr Abbott looked thoughtful. 'Well, I suppose it's possible that there may have been some kind of infection early on, leading to loss of bone. After all, we have no idea what happened when the fracture was set at the field hospital.'

It was a statement, not a question. Dora remained silent, her fingers locked behind her back. Out of the corner of her eye, she could see Major Von Mundel's impassive face, listening carefully to every word.

'Will he need another operation, Doctor?' she ventured.

Dr Abbott shook his head. 'I don't think that will be necessary,' he said. 'Let's just wait and see, shall we? You never know, sometimes bones can take ages to mend, and then all of a sudden–'

'You are not going to operate?' Major Von Mundel interrupted him.

Dr Abbott barely glanced at him, addressing himself to Dora. 'As I said, we should wait and see.'

'Wait and see.' Major Von Mundel repeated the words slowly and carefully, as if feeling the weight of each one.

Dora read his meaning. *Wait and see.* Just like they had with the poor young man who'd died of pleurisy.

Dr Abbott turned to look at him at last. 'You sound as if you disagree?'

Von Mundel stared straight back at him. 'As you have made perfectly clear, Herr Doctor, my opinion counts for nothing. So perhaps you will excuse me?' He nodded briefly to Dora and then left.

Dora watched him striding off down the ward. Over the past few weeks she had come to understand his body language. His tall, straight spine was stiff with suppressed rage and frustration.

But Dr Abbott remained clueless. 'What's wrong with him, I wonder?' he said.

Dora was just about to shake her head and plead ignorance, but then she stopped herself. 'I reckon he thinks you should operate,' she said.

'Yes, well, as he said himself, his opinion counts for nothing.'

Dora stared at Jimmy Abbott, with his sleep-ruffled hair and faded brown stain on the lapel of his white coat. She couldn't help seeing him through Major Von Mundel's eyes. 'He is an experienced surgeon,' she said quietly.

'He's a prisoner!' Dr Abbott retorted. 'And no matter how much he might throw his weight about on this ward, he has no real authority in this hospital.'

'I think he knows that, Doctor.'

'Well, he'd do well to remember it!' Dr Abbott looked petulant 'Anyway, about this fractured femur... I want to start him on a daily course of passive hyperaemia, along with calcium, para-thyroid and vitamin therapy. Let's see if we can't stimulate those wretched bones to start mending, shall we?'

Dora pushed herself to get on with her chores for the rest of the morning, giving enemas and injections, checking temperatures and pulses, preparing poultices and massaging liniment into limbs. In between, she served tea and made beds, handed out bedpans, and scrubbed the bathrooms from top to bottom.

Meanwhile, Major Von Mundel couldn't seem to find anything useful to do. He paced up and down the ward, snapping at the nurses and upsetting everyone.

Miss Sloan was particularly put out about it. 'I don't understand it,' she complained to Dora as they polished the bathroom taps. 'The Major is usually very civil to me. A cold fish, but always polite.'

'I expect he's got a lot on his mind,' Dora replied.

At four o'clock, she went for her tea break in the kitchen. She brewed a pot of tea, and as an after-thought, poured a cup for Major Von Mundel too.

She found him sitting just outside the double doors, in a waiting area that had once been re-served for the patients' families when it was an ordinary surgical ward. It was away from the main ward, but still within sight of the guards on the doors.

Major Von Mundel sat on one of the hard chairs, leaning forward, his elbows propped on his knees. His fingers were steepled in front of his face, and for a moment Dora thought he might be praying, until she realised he was simply deep in thought.

He looked up sharply as she approached, his lip curling when he saw the teacup in her hands.

"What is this?'

'Tea? I thought you might like a cup?'

'Tea? Is that your cure for everything?'

'Well, I won't deny it's got me through a few hard times!' Dora said.

His eyes narrowed and Dora steeled herself, sensing he was about to lash out. But to her surprise his mouth was curved in a slight smile.

'I beg your pardon, Nurse Riley,' he said curtly. 'It is wrong of me to take my frustration out on you. None of this is your fault.' He paused. 'I just find the situation very – difficult, that is all.'

'I know,' Dora said.

She put the cup down on the table in front of him and turned to leave.

'Please,' Major Von Mundel said. 'You will sit with me for a moment, yes?'

Dora looked around. She was on her break, after all. And there was no one to reprimand her, as Helen was still on the other ward.

And the poor Major looked as if he needed to talk to someone.

'Maybe I will take the weight off my feet for a minute,' she said, sitting herself down in the chair opposite his.

But Major Von Mundel didn't seem to be in the

157

mood for talking. The silence stretched awkwardly between them, and Dora began to wish she had escaped back to the kitchen while she'd had a chance.

'Dr Abbott is a good doctor, you know,' she said, to fill the silence. 'I know it might not seem like it to you, but–'

'On the contrary, I'm sure he is. Or he will be, one day,' Major Von Mundel said. 'But he lacks experience. He would benefit from proper guidance.'

'That's hardly his fault. All the experienced doctors have been sent off to Europe.'

'I know that, Nurse Riley. But Dr Abbott is very young to be given so much responsibility. I'm certain he feels it also, but he is afraid to admit it because he doesn't wish to appear foolish.'

Dora considered his words. 'I daresay you're right,' she conceded.

'But there can be no room for pride when a patient's future is in the balance.' Major Von Mundel went on. 'Stefan Bauer needs an operation to remove the disease from his bones, otherwise the healthy tissue will not grow and he will not walk again. Surely that is more important than a doctor's pride?' Dora saw the appeal in his eyes but said nothing. She didn't know the words to say to make it right. 'It is so difficult for me, to see so clearly what must be done, and yet not to be allowed to do it,' Major Von Mundel went on. He held up his hands. 'It is like having these tied behind my back.'

She nodded. 'It is such a waste.'

He looked surprised. 'You agree with me?'

'Why not? You're right, we could do with your

158

experience.'

'And you're not afraid I would go mad with a scalpel and kill everyone?' There was a note of bitter irony in his voice.

'I've always believed doctors are dedicated to saving lives, no matter where they come from.'

Major Von Mundel sighed. 'Let's hope your Dr Abbott sees it that way, Nurse Riley.'

Chapter Twenty

That night Kitty went out with Mal to watch the new John Wayne film at the Rialto. But the harder she tried to concentrate on the story, the more her thoughts seemed to slide away.

'What did you reckon to it?' Mal asked later, when they stepped out into the damp, drizzly night.

'I enjoyed it.' Kitty prayed he wouldn't ask her about the plot, since she couldn't remember the first thing about it.

'You might have enjoyed it more if you'd actually watched it!' Mal sent her a sideways look. 'I saw you, Kitty, you were miles away. I hope you weren't daydreaming about another man?' he teased.

Kitty looked away so he wouldn't see her blushing. 'As a matter of fact, I was thinking about a patient at the hospital.'

'Oh well, that's charming! So it's not just another man you're thinking about, it's also a German!'

'It's not like that. I've just found out this patient probably won't walk again.'

She still felt the sadness like a heavy weight in the pit of her stomach. Poor Stefan Bauer still knew nothing of his fate. Kitty couldn't imagine how he would react when he found out. All his energies had been focused on getting out of the hospital, and now...

Mal frowned. 'And what's that got to do with you?'

'Nothing, I suppose. I just feel sorry for him.'

'You shouldn't waste your pity on a German,' Mal dismissed.

'He's still a patient.'

Mal pulled a face. 'Well, I wouldn't worry about him, anyway,' he said. 'He'll be well looked after, I'm sure. He'll probably have a cushy time at the POW camp, since he won't be sent out on any work party. I wouldn't mind being able to sit out the rest of the war in comfort!' he laughed.

Kitty turned on him. 'You don't understand, do you? He won't walk again for the rest of his life, not just the war!'

'All right, you don't have to shout at me!' Mal retreated into a hurt silence. As they made their way home, Kitty felt the weight of his sullen mood and knew she would have to apologise. This was their first night out together in ages, and she didn't want it to end in an argument.

'I'm sorry,' she said. 'I shouldn't have gone on about it and let it spoil our evening.'

Mal sent her a sheepish look. 'I'm sorry too,' he said. 'I know you're only thinking about him because you care.' He smiled ruefully. 'I can't help it if I'm a jealous fool, can I?'

'What have you got to be jealous about?'

'You!' He slid his arm around her shoulders. 'You forget, I'm guarding that ward every day. I see the way those men look at you.'

'Come off it!' Kitty laughed. 'Who'd look at me?'

'Any man with eyes in his head.' Mal turned to face her, reaching up to brush her carefully arranged hair back from her face. Kitty automatically flinched away but he trapped her chin between his hands, holding her fast.

'Why do you always have to hide away?' he said softly. 'You're beautiful, Kitty Jenkins.'

'Stop it,' she ducked her head. 'You're making fun of me.'

'I'm not. I mean it, I think you're the most beautiful girl in the world.' He leaned in to kiss her gently on the lips. 'There,' he said, lifting his head from hers. 'I bet you weren't thinking of another man then, were you?'

'No,' she admitted, smiling.

He slid his arm around her shoulders again, pulling her close to him.

'You know your problem, Kitty? You take on too much. I mean, it's all well and good you looking after your patients. I admire you for caring for them, I really do. I bet there aren't many who'd think so much about the Germans, especially after what they did to your family–' He paused for a moment. 'But you shouldn't worry about them too much. They're not worth it, Kitty. You've got to remember who's really important to you, and think about them, instead.'

'I suppose you're right.'

'No suppose about it. I am right,' Mal said.

He did have a point, Kitty thought as they walked home. It was one thing to look after the POWs while she was on duty, but she shouldn't be thinking about them or anyone else while she was out with her boyfriend. This was supposed to be their time together, and they got precious little of it as it was.

But in spite of Kitty's good intentions, Stefan Bauer was the first one on her mind when she woke up the following morning. She reported for duty with a heavy heart, dreading what was to come.

Nurse Riley briefed her on the treatment he was to receive – daily passive hyperaemia, faradic stimulation, regular massage and exposure to the sun. Everything they could imagine, apart from surgery.

Kitty would have liked to ask why they weren't operating on him, but she was far too junior to ask such a question, and Nurse Riley's grim expression was too forbidding.

Instead she asked the question that had been playing on her mind all night. 'Does he know yet, Staff?'

Dora shook her head. 'Dr Abbott thinks it might be better for him if he doesn't find out just yet, not until we've given these other treatments a try. And for heaven's sake, girl, try to smile,' she warned Kitty. 'That long face of yours would make anyone lose the will to live!'

'Yes, Staff.' Kitty obligingly forced her mouth up at the corners, but her heart was still heavy when she went in to see Stefan later.

Hans was moaning in his sleep again, his head thrashing from side to side, the muscles in his face clenched in a horrible grimace.

She looked at Stefan. 'Another bad dream?'

He nodded, his expression grim. 'He hardy slept last night.' He paused, then added, 'The men came to question him yesterday.'

The men from the government had taken to visiting every week or so. They would question the new patients, sometimes in Sister's office or behind the curtains if they were too ill to be moved. They would ask them about their beliefs and their Nazi sympathies, then process them accordingly. Those most dedicated to the Nazi cause would have a black cloth patch sewn on their clothes, those with no sympathies would get a white patch, and the rest would have a grey one.

'They haven't questioned you yet?' she said.

'Not yet. But my time will come.'

'What will you tell them?'

She heard the smile in his voice, even with her back turned. 'You want to know if I am a true Nazi, *Fraülein?*'

'It's nothing to do with me, I'm sure,' Kitty replied huffily.

'*Nein,* I suppose not. You detest us all, I think.' Before she could respond, he went on, 'but in case you want to know, I have no interest in this war. I just want this damn leg of mine to heal so I can go home, if I still have a home to go to when all this is over,' he added bitterly.

'Do you have family in Germany?' Kitty asked.

'I don't come from Germany.'

Kitty swung round, frowning. 'But I thought—'

163

'I am German, but my home is – was – in Serbia. When Germany went to war, we were conscripted into the army with everyone else.'

'You didn't want to fight?'

'I am a German, it is my duty.' But there was no passion behind his words, Kitty noticed. Not like Felix or a few of the other men, who made no secret of their hatred for Britain, and treated Kitty and the other nurses with barely concealed contempt.

'As to your other question – I have no family. Not since my brother died.' He turned his attention to the rubber bandage she was unrolling. 'What is this?'

'It's a new treatment we're trying.'

'And will it do any good?'

'The doctor thinks so.'

'But it won't make me walk again, will it?'

Kitty's head shot up, panic flaring through her. 'Who told you–?'

Too late she realised the truth. Stefan's mouth twisted. 'You did,' he said. 'Oh, do not look so alarmed, *Fraülein*. I am not a fool. I saw how the doctor looked at those X-rays yesterday.'

Kitty chewed her lip. 'You weren't supposed to know.'

'Then I thank you for your honesty at least.'

She looked down at the length of India-rubber bandage in her hands. It seemed almost absurd that such a flimsy, insubstantial thing might help him. 'There are still a lot of treatments we could try–'

'Of course.' He spoke with such quiet resignation, Kitty could almost feel her heart breaking apart inside her chest.

She looked at Stefan, the pride in his tilted chin as he tried to face his fate. Something inside her clicked.

'You will walk again,' she said.

He sent her a sharp, puzzled look. 'What makes you so sure?'

'Because you want to do it. And I want you to do it.'

'And why should you care?'

Mal's words suddenly came into her mind. *You shouldn't waste your pity on a German.*

'Because I'm a nurse and it's my job to care,' she said. Then she added, 'and because you didn't tell anyone about Arthur.'

He shook his head. 'I told you, I know how to keep a secret.' His gaze moved to the bandage in her hands. 'Do you really think I might walk again?' he said.

She hoped for once her emotions weren't written so clearly on her face. 'I think you could do anything, if you set your mind to it,' she said.

For once his smile reached his eyes, warmth kindling in their brown depths. 'Perhaps you are right,' he said.

Chapter Twenty-One

December 1944

'I daresay this'll be my last Christmas.'

Dora exchanged a quick, knowing smile with her mother across the kitchen table. Nanna Winnie's annual lament was as much a part of the festive season as the King's Speech on the wireless.

It was a rainy Sunday afternoon in the middle of December, and Rose had dug out the box of old Christmas decorations to see if they would do for another year. Walter, Winnie and Mabel were helping sort through them at one end of the table, while Bea permed Lily's hair at the other.

'Here we go again!' Dora's mother sighed, rolling her eyes to the heavens.

'I mean it,' Nanna Winnie said. 'I won't live to see another one.'

Walter looked up at Dora, his eyes wide. 'Is Nanna going to die, Mum?' he whispered.

'Take no notice, love,' Dora's mother answered for her. 'She says the same thing every year.'

'It's being so cheerful as keeps her going!' Dora grinned. 'Ain't that right, Nanna?'

'You can be as cheeky as you like,' Nanna scowled back. 'But you mark my words. One of these days, I'll be right.'

'Well, let's hope it ain't this Christmas.' Rose held up a tangle of tattered paper chain. 'I reckon this lot has seen better days, don't you?'

'I know the feeling,' Nanna moaned, massaging her knee. 'This damp weather does terrible things to my arthritis.'

'Put that blanket over you to stay warm,' Dora called over to her. 'I'll give your legs a rub later.'

'Thank you, ducks. It's nice to have someone useful about the place.' Nanna glared at Bea and Lily.

'I was thinking,' Dora said, as she helped her mother untangle the paper chain. 'Why don't we invite old Mrs Price for Christmas? I don't like to think of her all on her own in Griffin Street.'

'Good idea,' her mother agreed. 'It can't be very cheerful for her, living by herself with all those bombed-out houses around her. I'll pop down and see her.'

'I could go,' Dora offered. 'I said I'd stop and have a cup of tea with her this week.' She liked to keep an eye on the old lady.

Bea pulled a face. 'Does she have to come?' she asked. 'I wanted to invite Hank for Christmas dinner.'

Dora and her mother looked at each other. They'd heard a great deal about the mysterious GI over the past few months, but they had never been allowed to meet him.

'I just thought it would be nice for him,' Bea answered their unspoken question. 'He's such a long way from home, he deserves a few home comforts.'

'I dunno about home comforts!' Rose smiled. 'If this Christmas is anything like the last one well be lucky if we can find a rabbit and some veg off the allotment for our Christmas dinner.'

'Oh, that's all right,' Bea said carelessly. 'I expect he'll bring extra rations with him.'

Mabel's eyes gleamed greedily. 'Will there be chocolate?'

'And sweets?' Little Winnie chimed in.

'Of course,' Bea shrugged. 'Hank can get his hands on anything he wants.'

'Including you,' Lily muttered, then yelped with pain as Bea tugged hard on her hair.

'Oh, sorry. Did I wind that curl too tight?' Bea's face was the picture of innocence.

'I'm not sure I like the idea of a Yank here for Christmas,' Nanna declared. 'And if he does come, I ain't going to be putting the flags out. He'll have to take us as he finds us. And you needn't think I'm putting my teeth in for him, neither,' she said, glaring round at them all.

'Ooh no, Nanna. We'd never think that,' Dora smiled. 'We know you only get them out on special occasions.'

'I don't think I can even remember the last time she put them in...' Rose paused, trying to think.

'I think it was the Coronation,' Dora said.

'No, it was the day the king came to visit the East End,' her mother corrected her. 'Do you remember, she put them in just in case His Majesty dropped round for a cup of tea?'

'You two can laugh, but there's nothing wrong with showing a bit of respect!' Nanna folded her arms across her bosom. 'And just so you all know, I ain't putting them in again until the day we win this war!'

'Let's hope that won't be too long,' Rose

sighed. 'It'll be lovely to have everyone round the table again for Christmas, just like the old days.'

They all fell silent for a moment, and Dora could tell they were all thinking the same thing, about their loved ones far from home. Her brother Peter and sister Josie, and of course her darling Nick. She thought of all the Christmases they'd spent together in the past, and how she'd taken it for granted that they would always be there. If they were spared, she knew she would never take them for granted again.

'So can I invite Hank for Christmas?' Bea broke the silence.

'Why not?' Rose said. 'The more the merrier, I reckon. Don't you, Dora?'

'I'll say. That's what we could all do with, a good old knees-up this Christmas. We've all been too miserable for too long.'

Of course it would never be the same without Nick there to share it with her. But she'd made a promise to keep her chin up, and she meant to stick to it.

'Besides,' Rose smiled at Bea, 'you've been courting for a while now. It's about time we met this young man of yours.'

'Sounds like it's serious?' Dora said.

Bea looked unusually coy. 'It might be.'

'Pearl Saunders' eldest girl has just got married to an American,' Rose said.

'You mean she had to get married. She's nearly four months gone!' Lily put in sourly.

'At least he's done the decent thing,' Rose said. 'Although I hope you won't end up like that, Bea,' she added sternly.

Bea shook her head. 'I ain't daft.'

'I dunno about that,' Lily mumbled.

Bea turned on her. 'And you can shut up, Lily Doyle. Just because you don't like Hank.'

'I didn't say that, did I? I just think you should be careful, that's all. He's a bit too much of a charmer, if you ask me.'

'You're just jealous.'

'What have I got to be jealous about? I'm a married woman, in case you'd forgotten.'

'I ain't forgotten, but I reckon you do sometimes!'

Lily gasped. 'You take that back, Bea Doyle!'

'Only if you take back what you said about Hank!'

'I was only speaking the truth!'

'Then you can do your own bloody hair!' Bea upended the box of curlers on to the floor and stormed off.

Lily turned to Dora and her mother, her face innocent. 'I was only speaking the truth,' she repeated.

They watched as Lily got down on her hands and knees to pick up the scattered curlers. 'I hope they're not like this on Christmas Day!' Rose sighed.

'I pity poor Hank if they are.' Dora finished untangling the paper chain. 'There. What do you think?'

No sooner had she held it up than it fell apart in her hands.

Dora looked at the decoration, then at her mother. The next minute they both burst out laughing.

'Let's hope it ain't a sign of things to come!' Rose Doyle said.

It wasn't just at home that the Christmas festivities were starting.

With the V-2 attacks happening all over the south coast, the hospital committee had decided that the countryside was no safer than London any more, so many of the patients were being transported back to the Nightingale.

It gladdened Dora's heart to see the Green Line buses arriving instead of taking people away. Every day, more wards opened up, and some of her old friends returned. There were still several military wards and many QAs around, but when Dora looked around the canteen now she could see as many blue Nightingale uniforms as she could Queen Alexandra's scarlet and grey.

And with the return of the Nightingale came Christmas. All over the hospital, paper garlands started festooning the wards and passageways. Fairy lights decorated the gloomy basement canteen, and miracle of miracles, Mr Hopkins managed to get hold of a Christmas tree for the first time in two years. It stood proudly outside the battered front entrance to the hospital, next to the wooden notice that Matron had put up during the Blitz, proudly declaring that the bomb-damaged Nightingale Hospital was 'Even More Open For Business Than Usual!'

It brought a lump to Dora's throat to see the tree there. Her mum had talked about signs, and perhaps this really was a sign that things were finally getting back to normal at last. They had a long way

171

to go – half the hospital buildings were still in desperate need of repair – but somehow the Christmas tree seemed like a little beacon of hope.

She was sure she wasn't the only one who had caught the festive spirit. Walking around the hospital, she was often met by smiling QAs and porters cheerily humming Christmas carols.

The only place not touched by Christmas magic was the POWs' ward. The pale green walls remained resolutely bare and unadorned, a stark contrast to the rest of the hospital. There wasn't even a sprig of holly to brighten the place up.

Major Von Mundel must've noticed it too. One morning after Dr Abbott had finished his round, the Major asked Helen if there were any decorations available for them to brighten up the ward.

'Just a few odd pieces would do,' he'd said. 'And the men would be happy to put them up themselves, to spare you the trouble.'

'What a lovely idea,' Dora smiled. 'I was just thinking we could do with some paper chains in here. What do you think, Sister Dawson?'

Helen was tight-lipped. 'I'm not sure if there are any decorations left over,' she said.

'Oh, but there must be, surely?' Dora said. 'We used to have boxes and boxes full in the basement.'

'I think they were taken down to the country with everything else.'

'Yes, but surely they must have come back with everything else? I could go down to the basement and look–'

'That won't be necessary,' Helen cut her off. 'I'll get Mr Hopkins to look. There are more im-

172

portant jobs for you to do than search for Christmas decorations, Nurse Riley!'

She was smiling when she said it, but Dora could see the glint of steel in her eyes.

She went about her work and thought no more about it, until two days later when she was on her way back from taking a patient to theatre, and heard shrieks of laughter coming from one of the military wards.

She peeped around the door, only to see Helen and Clare decorating an enormous Christmas tree.

'Where did you get that?'

Helen stopped dead, a bauble dangling from her fingers. She had the grace to look guilty, Dora noticed.

'Mr Hopkins managed to get it for us as a special treat for our soldiers,' Clare said. 'It's even bigger than the one outside, don't you think?'

'It looks like it.' Dora gazed up at it.

'Between you and me, I think he's got rather a soft spot for Dawson,' Clare went on. 'I think he'd do anything to please her.'

'It's a pity he couldn't find any extra decorations for the POWs' ward, in that case.' Dora sent Helen a steady look. 'Or perhaps you didn't bother to ask him?' she suggested.

Helen was silent. Clare looked from one to the other.

'What's going on?' she wanted to know. 'Helen? What is she talking about?'

'It's nothing,' Helen said quietly. She turned away, reaching up to hook the bauble on a branch.

'She was supposed to be finding some decorations for the POWs' ward,' Dora explained to Clare.

'I've changed my mind,' Helen said quietly. 'I've decided you are not to use any of the hospital decorations for the prisoners' ward.'

'I should think not!' Clare said. 'What an awful idea. As if they deserve anything!'

Dora ignored her, addressing herself instead to Helen's turned back.

'Why?' she said. 'Why won't you let them have their decorations? It's not too much to ask–'

'Oh, for heaven's sake, why do you think?' Clare cut in. 'They're prisoners, Riley!'

Once again, Dora ignored Clare's prattling. 'Or is it because of what happened to you?' she asked Helen.

Helen said nothing. She reached for a piece of tinsel and draped it over a branch, but Dora could see her hands shaking.

'Because if that is the reason, I don't think it's right,' Dora said. 'I know, you were upset by what happened to you, but you've got to get over it.' She saw her friend's spine stiffen, but she carried on, 'You can't let it affect your life like this, Helen. And you certainly can't let it affect your work–'

'Be quiet,' Clare said. 'Can't you see you're up-setting her?'

'But she needs to hear it.' Dora turned back to Helen. 'This is not like you. You're not spiteful or vindictive. I know you've been through a bad time, but was it really so terrible that you want to take it out on those boys?'

'Shut up!' Dora jumped in shock as Helen swung round to face her. 'How dare you speak to

174

me like that? You have no idea what–'

She stopped speaking abruptly. Her face was so twisted with anger and spite, Dora barely recognised her.

'Dawson–' she started to say, but Helen held up her hand to silence her.

'It's Sister Dawson to you!' she snapped.

'What–'

'You may have forgotten your place, Riley, but I am your superior, and I will not allow you to speak to me like that. Do you understand?'

'But–'

'I said, do you understand?'

Dora caught Clare's smirking expression out of the corner of her eye.

'Yes,' she muttered.

'Yes, Sister Dawson,' Helen corrected her, spitting out each word.

Dora's cheeks scalded with shame. 'Yes, Sister Dawson.'

Helen drew herself up to her full height. 'Very well,' she said. 'Go back to your work, Nurse Riley. I don't want to hear any more about this, do I make myself clear?'

'Yes, Sister.'

Dora was still shaking with shock when she returned to the POWs' ward. She couldn't stop playing the scene over and over in her head. It wasn't so much what Helen had said as the way she'd said it. Dora didn't think she had ever seen her friend so furious.

But Dora was furious too. She was furious that Helen had humiliated her in front of a ward full of patients, and furious that her friend was being so spiteful and unfair. Most of all, she was furious that the POWs were being punished for it.

Well, we'll see about that, she thought. Helen might think she'd had the last word and the matter was settled, but as far as Dora was concerned, it wasn't over. Not by a long chalk.

Chapter Twenty-Two

Dora avoided Helen for the rest of the day. When they did have to speak, she was respectful and polite, but Helen could feel the wall between them. She began to wish she had not spoken so harshly to her friend.

'You did the right thing,' Clare assured her as they walked back to the QAs' home through the cold December rain after their duty was over. 'She can't be allowed to speak to you like that. You have to make sure she knows who is in charge. If you ask me, you've been far too soft with her, and now she's taking advantage.'

'But it wasn't all her fault,' Helen reasoned. 'She doesn't understand–'

'That doesn't matter. You don't have to explain anything to her. You're her superior, and she should follow your orders, whether she understands the reason or not.'

Then you really don't know Dora Riley, Helen thought. She smiled in spite of herself to think of all the times her friend had defied a ward sister to help someone, or to stand up for what she believed was right.

'Besides,' Clare went on, her nose in the air, 'I really don't know why she cares so much about those wretched Germans, anyway. It's not as if they give a damn about her.'

'That's just the way she is. She cares about everyone.'

Clare sent her a scathing look. 'Now you sound as if you're defending her!' she accused. 'Honestly, Helen, I do wish you'd make up your mind!'

'I'm not defending her, honestly.'

'I should think not,' Clare said. 'Because if you ask me, Dora Riley seems to care more about the prisoners than she does about your feelings. And that's not a true friend, is it?'

'No,' Helen said quietly.

The QAs were being billeted in what had once been the sisters' home. When she stepped through the doors, Helen always expected to see Sister Parker searching for her spectacles, or to smell Sister Wren's cloying scent, or to hear Sister Blake practising her musical scales. The sisters' home held so many memories for her. It was here that she'd started to rebuild her life after the death of her husband Charlie. And it was while living here that she had fallen in love with handsome Casualty doctor David McKay.

She was standing in the doorway, shaking the rain off her umbrella, when she saw the thin blue envelope poking out of her pigeon-hole on the other side of the hall. The sight of it startled her, and for a moment she wondered if she'd somehow conjured David through her thoughts.

Clare saw it too. She sent Helen a sideways

look. 'He's still writing to you, I see.'

Helen set down her umbrella in the stand by the door. She walked over to the pigeon-holes and reached for the letter, but she couldn't bring herself to touch it.

'Aren't you going to take it?' Clare's voice had an edge of impatience behind it. 'Honestly, Helen, it's just a letter. It can't hurt you.' She sighed. 'Here, let me–'

She made a move towards it, but Helen snatched the letter out of the pigeon-hole before her friend could take it.

Once it was in her hand, she stared down at it, at a loss as to what to do next.

'Are you going to read it?' Clare asked.

'I – don't know.'

'You're better off throwing it away, just like the others,' Clare said. 'No point in upsetting yourself, is there?'

Helen shook her head, her gaze still fixed on the blue envelope in her hand. The sight of David's handwriting made her heart contract painfully in her chest. How often had she teased him about that scrawl when they worked together...?

'I don't even know why he's still writing to you,' Clare was still speaking. 'You've told him you don't want anything to do with him, and yet he's still pestering you. If you ask me, it's just selfish–' She held out her hand. 'Here, give it to me. I'll throw it away for you.'

Clare tried to take the letter, but Helen tightened her grip on it. 'No,' she said.

'You want to read it, don't you?' Clare accused. 'Oh, Helen, are you sure that's a good idea? You'll only upset yourself.'

'I don't know what I want to do.'

'Then let me help you.'

Before Helen could react, Clare snatched the letter from her.

'Give that back.' Helen held out her hand, but Clare held it out of her reach.

'No,' she said.

'But it's my letter, and I want it.'

'Why? I told you, you'll only upset yourself.'

Helen stared into Clare's face. She was so sure she was right, she reminded Helen of Dora. Why was she surrounded by people who insisted they knew what was best for her?

'Give me the letter,' she said quietly.

'But–'

'Give me the letter, Clare!' Helen raised her voice. Her hand shook with anger as she held it out to her. 'For heaven's sake, why do you always have to interfere?'

She could have bitten off her tongue as soon as she saw Clare's face darken.

Clare slapped the letter back into Helen's hand. 'It's all right, you don't have to lose your temper,' she muttered in a hurt voice. 'I was only trying to help.'

Helen was instantly contrite. 'I know. I'm sorry. Here,' she tried to hand the letter back. 'You take it. You're right, I shouldn't read it–'

Clare shook her head. 'Oh no, I don't want it. Heaven forbid I should interfere!'

Helen sighed. 'You know I didn't mean that–' she tried to say, but Clare was already walking away from her. 'Where are you going?' Helen called after her. 'I thought we were going to the officers' mess together?'

'I'd rather be alone, if you don't mind.'

Helen watched her go, and felt wretched. She seemed to be pushing all her friends away. First Dora, then Clare.

And David...

She looked at the letter in her hands. She'd pushed him away, too.

Clare didn't return to their room with her. She would be sulking in the common room until Helen had apologised enough.

Helen put the letter on her nightstand. She couldn't take her eyes off it as she changed out of her uniform.

She should have let Clare take it, just as she had all the others. Her friend was right, it would do her no good to read it.

Besides, she already knew what David would say. His letter would be beseeching, bewildered, trying to understand what had happened, begging her for another chance...

Poor David. She wished she could explain why she no longer wanted him, but she knew she never could.

She was in bed when Clare returned much later that evening. She didn't speak, but Helen could feel the silent resentment radiating from her. By the time she woke the following morning, Clare had left without her.

Helen wondered how long it would go on this time. It never did to upset Clare. She could sulk for days and days following the slightest disagreement.

It was always better to get it over with and apologise, even if Helen didn't feel as if she was really in the wrong.

She found Clare eating breakfast by herself in the hospital canteen.

Helen set her tray down beside her. 'May I join you?' she asked.

Clare didn't reply. She nibbled on a slice of bread and marge, staring ahead in wounded silence.

She still didn't speak as they made their way up to the ward together. Helen pushed down her annoyance. Part of her wanted to walk away and leave her to sulk, but she desperately needed a friend, and Clare was the only person she had left. She was also the only one who truly understood how she felt.

Helen took a deep breath. 'I'm sorry,' she said.

Clare went on walking, not meeting Helen's eye. But just as Helen was beginning to think she would never speak to her again, she suddenly said, 'I only wanted to help.'

'I know,' Helen said humbly.

'You shouldn't push me away, you know. You need me.'

Helen nodded. 'You've been a good friend to me, Clare. I don't know what I would have done without you.'

It was the right thing to say. To Helen's relief, Clare suddenly smiled and linked arms with her.

'You can trust me, you know,' she said.

'I know that.'

'I'm your friend. I only have your best interests at heart... Helen?' Clare's voice sharpened. 'Are you listening to me?'

But Helen had stopped dead. They were outside the POWs' ward, and something had caught her attention.

'What is it?' Clare said.

Helen pointed to the glass in the double doors, too shocked to speak.

Clare craned her neck to look, and a slow, malicious smile spread across her face.

'Oh no,' she said. 'She's gone too far this time!'

Helen pushed open the double doors and marched to the ward, Clare at her heels.

She could barely comprehend the scene in front of her. The ward looked like a factory production line. Men in grey prison uniforms sat around the table in the middle of the ward, tearing strips of newspaper then passing them down the table for others to loop and glue them into long strings. The men who couldn't get out of bed were folding sheets of newspaper into paper lanterns and fastening them on to strings. Major Von Mundel strode from bed to bed, supervising their work.

And there, in the middle of it, was Dora Riley. She was on top of a ladder, looping the newspaper chains over the light fittings, watched by Miss Sloan and Kitty Jenkins, their arms full of more paper chains. The walls were already festooned with them.

Helen stared around her. She could feel herself trembling with rage.

'What is the meaning of this?' she said.

Kitty Jenkins jumped to attention, dropping the

paper chain, which fell into a rustling pile at her feet.

Helen fixed her gaze on Dora, still perched on top of the ladder. 'I thought I said there were to be no decorations on this ward?' she said.

Dora slowly descended until she and Helen were face-to-face. 'Actually, Sister Dawson, you said we weren't to use any of the hospital's decorations. You didn't say anything about making them ourselves.'

Helen stared into Dora's freckled face. Her smile was pleasant and polite, but there was a glint of defiance in her green eyes.

'You shouldn't use newspaper,' Clare butted in. 'It's needed for salvage.'

'I know that,' Dora replied. 'We're only using the old stuff we've been allowed to keep as firelighters.' She turned to Helen. 'It looks good, don't you reckon?'

Helen caught the hint of challenge in her voice. She was doing it deliberately to humiliate her, she thought. She could feel all the men watching her keenly, waiting to see what she would do.

'Take them down,' she said.

Dora frowned. 'Why? What's the harm in putting up a few decorations?'

'I said take them down! That's an order, Nurse Riley!'

They were almost toe-to-toe. Dora was a head shorter than Helen, but she looked up at her defiantly. 'No,' she said.

Helen heard Clare gasp behind her. The men had stopped what they were doing and were openly staring.

She turned to Kitty Jenkins and Miss Sloan. 'Take them down,' she snapped.

They looked at each other. Neither of them moved.

'You must admit Sister, they do cheer the place up,' Miss Sloan said in appeal.

Helen stared at them all, standing shoulder-to-shoulder. She was so incensed she could barely breathe.

'Very well, I'll take them down myself!' she snapped.

Before she knew what she was doing, she was ripping the chains down from the walls in a frenzy. She heard Clare call out to her but she didn't stop to listen, her head filled with hot, red rage.

It was only when the decorations lay in a tattered pile at her feet that she stopped and looked round, breathing hard. A circle of faces – the patients, Major Von Mundel, Clare, Dora and the other nurses – all stared back at her with concern and incomprehension.

She looked down at the ruined paper chains and shame washed over her at her loss of control. Oh God, what was she thinking?

'Helen?'

Dora whispered her name. She was staring at her, a worried look on her face. Behind her, everyone in the silent ward was watching Helen in utter dismay.

Helen drew herself up to her full height. 'Report to Matron,' she said. She turned to Miss Sloan and Kitty. 'All of you.'

Kitty looked distraught. Dora squared her shoulders. 'It's not their fault,' she said. 'If anyone should take the blame, it's me.'

Helen stared at her. *Oh, believe me, I do blame you,* she thought.

'Report to Matron,' she repeated. 'Or are you going to defy me again?'

They trailed out of the ward. Kitty and Miss Sloan had their heads down, but Dora kept her defiant gaze fixed on Helen.

'Look at her!' Clare laughed bitterly. 'Who does she think she is, Joan of Arc?'

Helen ignored her, and stormed out of the ward. As she went, she could feel a tide of silently accusing gazes sweeping over her.

After what had happened, she didn't think she could ever bear to set foot in there again.

The men applauded Dora when she returned to the ward with Kitty and Miss Sloan half an hour later.

'Listen to them!' Miss Sloan smiled, her face flushed with excitement. 'Talk about hail the conquering heroes!'

'That's all very well, but we've still been docked a day's pay and a day's holiday,' Kitty said. 'Not to mention getting a right telling-off from Matron.'

Dora sent her a sideways look. The girl was still trembling from the blistering reprimand they'd received. Poor Kitty, she didn't deserve it. Dora wished she could have spared her.

By contrast, Miss Sloan seemed quite invigorated by it all.

'I haven't done anything this daring since I joined the Suffrage Movement,' she declared. 'It's made me feel quite giddy.'

'Yes, well, don't go chaining yourselves to any bed-frames, will you?' Dora said.

At least that drew a reluctant smile from Kitty. 'I'd like to see that,' she murmured.

'I must say, I can't believe that Sister Dawson would be quite so vindictive,' Miss Sloan went on. 'She seemed like such a dear girl.'

'You're right,' Dora agreed. The Helen she knew would never have behaved so spitefully. Something was very wrong, Dora was sure of it. She wondered if parting from David McKay had hurt her worse than she was letting on.

'Look out, here comes trouble!' Kitty said. Dora turned to see Major Von Mundel striding down the ward towards them.

'Nurse Riley,' he addressed her in a tight-lipped voice. 'You have returned, I see. We – that is, the men – were concerned about you.' Then, before Dora could reply, he went on, 'The fire has gone out again. Perhaps you could do something about it?'

'I'll see to it myself, Major.'

'Thank you, Nurse Riley.' He paused, then added, 'the men would also like to express their appreciation for your efforts on their behalf.'

He spun on his heel and walked off.

'Is that all the thanks we get?' Kitty muttered.

'Oh, I don't know.' Dora watched him striding down the ward, his head held high. 'Coming from him that's high praise indeed.'

Chapter Twenty-Three

After nearly four months, Kitty Jenkins could only marvel at Stefan Bauer's tenacity. He never gave up.

It had become almost like an unspoken pact between them, to prove everyone wrong. No one else believed that the bones in Stefan's leg would ever mend enough for him to walk again. But Kitty had been determined to give him the chance. She had dedicated herself as much as she could to his daily treatments, and Stefan had submitted to the rubber bandages and the electric currents and the endless, painful massage without a word of complaint.

And finally, all their hard work began to pay off. After a few weeks, the X-rays showed that his shattered femur was beginning to knit together. Within a month it was strong enough for him to start walking with the calliper.

Every day Stefan would push himself, at first dragging his wasted, useless leg up and down the ward, for hours on end if Kitty would allow it, until sweat stood out on his brow and the powerful muscles in his arms quivered with exhaustion.

'Surely that's enough?' Kitty would say. But Stefan would only shake his head, his teeth gritted in determination.

'Once more,' he would insist. 'Just once more, *Fraülein,* and then I promise I will go back to bed

187

like a good boy.'

And Kitty would always relent, because no matter how much she might complain about the extra work he caused her, she secretly admired his grit and wanted him to walk on his own as badly as he did.

Dr Abbott was grudgingly impressed when he saw the progress Stefan had made.

'You've done very well, Nurse Jenkins. I must say you've made a terrific effort, far more than I could have expected.'

Kitty had glanced at Stefan, his broad chest heaving with exertion. There was no word of praise for his Herculean efforts.

I'm not the one hauling myself up and down the ward until my muscles scream in pain, she wanted to say. But she knew better than to speak up to a doctor.

She watched Stefan now, serving tea to the other patients. He liked to make himself useful now he was up and about. He helped with the meals, read letters to the patients, and even did a couple of odd jobs about the ward.

'I dunno what we ever did without you!' Dora Riley would say to him. But Stefan always gruffly shrugged off her thanks, just as he shrugged off the other prisoners' attempts at friendship. Popular as he was, he seemed determined to remain a lone wolf.

As if he could sense her watching him, Stefan suddenly looked up and their eyes met for a moment along the length of the ward.

'Still at it, mate?' Mal called over from his sentry position by the double doors, breaking the moment. Kitty turned away guiltily. She was only watching her patient, making sure he didn't exert himself too much, she told herself.

'That's enough for today,' she called out.

'Just a few more minutes.'

'You've already done more than enough. If you carry on your muscles might get too tired–'

But one look at his determined expression, and she knew it was no use arguing with him.

'A few more minutes, *Fraülein*. Please.'

The word caught her by surprise. Stefan Bauer maintained an air of studied indifference and rarely pleaded for anything. For a moment she caught the look of appeal in his eyes, but then his mask came down again.

'I will finish what I am doing,' he stated firmly. He turned away from her and started down the middle of the ward, carefully carrying a cup in one hand, the other leaning heavily on a walking stick, his powerful shoulders taut with effort beneath his grey prison pyjamas.

Kitty had watched him so many times she could almost feel every step as if she were doing it herself. So when she saw his injured leg trailing slightly, she started towards him.

But she was too late. Stefan tried to drag his leg forward, but his weight was suddenly all wrong, throwing him off balance. Kitty could only watch helplessly as he stumbled forward, the cup falling from his hand as he crashed down heavily like a felled tree in the middle of the ward.

The other men sat up straighter in bed, leaning forward, all of them concerned. As Kitty hurried to help him, she heard Mal and Len laughing over by the doors.

She sent them a sharp glare and bent down to help Stefan, but he shrugged her off.

'I can manage,' he insisted gruffly.

'Just let me–'

'I said I can manage!' he roared. Kitty stepped back. She could feel the humiliation burning in him as he struggled to his feet.

It took him a long time, but Kitty knew better than to interfere. When he was finally standing again, she said, 'I'll get you a wheelchair–'

Stefan fixed his grim gaze on the other end of the ward.

'I'll manage,' he said.

Kitty looked from Stefan to the double doors, where Mal and Len lounged, still grinning.

'All right,' she agreed quietly.

This time she walked at his side. She didn't touch him or look at him, but she was aware of him out of the corner of her eye. She could hear him grunting with effort with every slow, excruciating step, and she willed him on silently, urging him to succeed for the sake of his pride.

By the time he reached the doors the sweat was pouring down his face. But when he turned to her, there was no mistaking the grim satisfaction in his smile.

'You did it!' Without thinking, she reached for him. She didn't even realise what she'd done until Stefan looked down at her hand resting on his arm, then back up at her.

She didn't hear Mal approaching until he spoke up.

'It's nearly six o'clock,' he said shortly. 'We'll be

late for the film.'

'I'll be there in a minute,' Kitty replied out of the corner of her mouth, keeping a wary eye out for Sister Dawson.

'But you're supposed to be off duty at six,' Mal reminded her stubbornly. 'Surely you've already given up more than enough of your time?' He shot Stefan a dirty look.

'I won't be long.'

He frowned. 'I'll meet you downstairs,' he muttered. 'But don't be too late. I don't want to miss the start of the film.'

'Your friend does not like to be kept waiting, I think,' Stefan observed, as Mal stomped off.

'He'll just have to be patient,' Kitty replied primly. 'Now, let's get you into bed–'

He shook his head. 'Let one of the other nurses do it,' he said. 'You must meet your friend.'

'He can wait–'

'Indeed, he cannot, *Fraülein*.' Stefan's mouth twisted. 'That much is obvious, even to me.'

Mal was waiting for her at the hospital gates when Kitty came off duty a quarter of an hour later. She could tell straight away he was in a bad mood from the scowl on his face.

'You took your time,' were his first words as he checked his watch. 'We'll miss the first film if we don't hurry.'

'It doesn't matter–'

'It does to me!' He set off, striding down the road. Kitty hurried after him. She knew he was expecting her to apologise, but she was too angry herself.

'You know you're not supposed to talk to me

when I'm on duty,' she said. 'Sister would have a fit if she caught you.'

Mal glanced at her, his face like thunder. 'Oh, so you can't spare a word for your boyfriend but it's all right for you to flirt with that German, is it?' he said.

It was such an absurd thing to say, Kitty laughed with astonishment. 'I wasn't flirting with him!'

'Weren't you? That's what it looked like to me. Pawing him and batting your eyelashes at him, just because he managed to put one foot in front of the other. I'd like to know what your precious Sister would have to say about that!'

Kitty stared at him. She wasn't sure he was even serious until she saw his petulant frown. 'He's a patient, Mal. I was just trying to help him.'

'Are you sure that's all there is to it? You seem very friendly,' he said bitterly.

Suddenly it dawned on her. 'Surely you're not jealous?'

'I don't know what I'm supposed to think,' he mumbled. 'You spend so much time with him. You're always with him, walking up and down that ward.'

'It's my job,' Kitty said. 'I want him to walk again.'

'Why? You don't owe him anything.'

'I think I do.'

His frown deepened. 'How do you work that out?'

Kitty hesitated. Stefan had told her his story as they walked up and down the ward together. Over the past few months, he had told her a lot about his life in Serbia, how he and his younger brother

192

Emil had grown up in an orphanage with no one but the other to rely on. He told her how the Nazis had taken over his country and how he had watched his brother become seduced by them until Stefan felt he had lost him forever.

He had also told her about the day Emil died.

'Do you know how he came to be wounded?' she asked Mal now.

'No,' he shrugged. 'And I can't say I care much, either.'

'Well, you should. He was badly beaten by Allied soldiers. Then they drove their truck over him as he lay injured.'

Mal looked appalled. But then his chin lifted. 'Well, I daresay he asked for it,' he said.

'How? His unit had already surrendered. All he was trying to do was defend his brother after the soldiers shot him.' She looked at Mal. 'They put him up against a wall and used him for target practice, Mal. Our boys.'

Mal stared back at her, and Kitty could see the tide of emotions flowing across his face.

'He's lying,' he said finally. 'I don't believe a word he says, and you shouldn't either if you've got any sense.' He sneered at her. 'Our lads wouldn't do that.'

'How do you know?' Kitty said. 'How do you know our side aren't just as cruel as the Germans?'

'Because I've fought alongside them!' Mal shot back. 'I've seen some of my best friends killed right beside me. And I know that for every wounded German there are British men who have suffered far worse. Like your own brother.'

Kitty lowered her gaze. 'Don't you think I

193

know that?'

'Do you? I wonder.' He sent her a reproachful look. 'Sometimes I wonder if you know whose side you're on any more, Kitty Jenkins.'

'How can you say that?'

'It's true. I see you with those prisoners, laughing and joking. Now I've got nothing against any of them personally, but I know that if things had been different none of them would have hesitated to put a bullet in my head or a bayonet in my belly. Including your friend Stefan. And I would have done the same to him.'

'Don't,' Kitty shuddered.

'Why not? That's just the way war is, Kitty. Like I said, for every German with a sad story to tell, there are half a dozen of our lads with an even worse one. So if I were you, I shouldn't waste my pity on the Germans. If you want to feel sorry for anyone, it should be your own side.'

'I see it's the old troll's turn to put you to bed tonight?'

Felix's voice was mocking. Stefan quickly glanced at Miss Sloan, forgetting she couldn't understand a word the young soldier was saying. But she smiled back at him, blissfully unaware as she pulled the covers up over him.

'What a pity for you, *Oberleutnant*, that it isn't your girlfriend,' Felix went on. 'I know how you look forward to saying goodnight to her,' he taunted.

Stefan ignored him. He had heard the young *Gefreiter's* comments too often to be affected by them any longer. Instead he made a point of smiling sweetly to Miss Sloan and thanking her in English for her care, knowing how much it would irritate Felix.

Miss Sloan blushed. 'Oh, you're welcome, young man,' she beamed back. She turned to Felix, but her smile faded when he glared back at her with a hostile, icy gaze.

As soon as Miss Sloan had gone, Felix turned on Stefan. 'You are a disgrace to your uniform,' he hissed. 'Look at you, fraternising with the enemy.'

'Miss Sloan is hardly the enemy,' Stefan mocked. 'She is an elderly lady who teaches music.'

Felix ignored him. 'You are a disgrace,' he repeated. 'I do not understand how you made it to the rank of *Oberleutnant*.'

'By following orders, just like you,' Stefan replied.

Two bright spots of angry colour stained Felix's high cheekbones. Stefan had no animosity towards the young man. He reminded him of Emil, just a child who had been given a gun and a uniform and brainwashed into believing that the whole world outside the Fatherland was his enemy. If Emil had lived, he would have been as proud of the black patch on his prison garb as Felix was.

Stefan looked at him, sitting upright in his bed, his eyes cold and watchful. 'You can stop fighting, you know,' he said wearily. 'The war is over. For us, anyway.'

'Never!' Felix spat out the word. 'I will never be like you, *Oberleutnant*, rolling over on your back like a dog to have its belly scratched.'

Stefan sighed. 'Very well, if you want to make life difficult for yourself, then so be it. I am only giving you my advice.'

'I don't need your advice!' Felix's eyes blazed with icy fire. 'Do you think I want to be like you? I will never make a fool of myself the way you do, falling in love with that ugly nurse!'

Stefan froze. 'What are you talking about?'

A slow smile of satisfaction spread across Felix's face. 'Oh, I see I have touched a nerve,' he smirked. 'Did you think it was a secret, *Oberleutnant?* Did you think no one would be able to see you had feelings for her?' His tone was almost pitying. 'I see it very clearly. And I am sure she does, too. But perhaps you would make a good pair,' he mused. 'You, a cripple, and her, so scarred and hideous...'

'I maybe crippled, but at least I can still satisfy a woman!' Stefan lashed out.

Felix paled, his mouth a tight, angry line. They all knew about the gunshot injury to his groin, but none of them ever talked about it in front of him.

It was a cruel, unworthy blow, but Stefan didn't care.

Felix retreated into wounded silence and was mercifully quiet for the rest of the evening. But he had already lit a fire, and his words burned away steadily in Stefan's mind.

He had given too much of himself away. If a dolt like Felix could see it, then who else could see what a fool he had made of himself?

He lay back against the pillows, staring up at the ceiling in the darkness, longing for sleep but knowing it would never come.

How had it come to this? He had never intended for any of it to happen. Ever since their mother died and their father abandoned them in the orphanage so he could go off and marry again, Stefan had gone through all his life keeping the rest of the world at arm's-length. He hid behind a mask of indifference, never allowing anyone the power to hurt him. It was how he had survived growing up, how he had made a life for himself and Emil, and it was how he meant to get through the war.

He could never have imagined in his worst nightmares that he would ever allow someone like Kitty to penetrate his defences. And yet somehow it had happened. And now he felt more exposed and vulnerable than he ever had in his life, even when he was lying wounded on the ground at the point of a British soldier's gun, convinced he was going to die.

Did she know? he wondered. Stefan rubbed the clammy sweat from his brow. Perhaps she knew, and she pitied him.

He would far rather be hated than pitied, he thought.

Chapter Twenty-Four

It was a freezing cold Christmas Eve, and Dora arrived on the ward just before seven in the morning to find the place in darkness and the patients shivering in their beds while the night nurse struggled to set the fire in the cold grate.

'It's not my fault!' She jumped guiltily to her feet when she saw Dora, rolling down her sleeves. Dora tried not to notice the ash she brushed on to her starched cuffs. 'A V-2 came down on the other side of Victoria Park last night, so Sister sent me down to Casualty to help out, and then I came back and it had gone out–' Her breath curled in the icy air. 'I did my best,' she finished lamely.

'Let me have a go.' Dora unfastened her cuffs and put them in her pocket, then rolled up her sleeves. She knelt down in front of the grate. 'There's a knack to it.' She took the long twist of newspaper from the nurse's frozen fingers. 'You have to coax it a bit, like this...'

Finally, after several failed attempts, the fire started to kindle. 'There.' Dora sat back on her heels. 'That should do it. I don't suppose there's any extra coal in the bucket?'

The nurse shook her head. 'There's not much more than dust, and Mr Hopkins said we're lucky to get that.'

'Mr Hopkins could give Ebeneezer Scrooge a run for his money.' Dora stood up and brushed down her uniform. 'Well, that should keep us going for a while, at least.' She looked around the ward. 'Have the patients had their morning tea?'

'Not yet, Staff.' The night nurse looked close to tears, her face smudged with coal dust. 'I'm all behind this morning.'

'Never mind, I'll give you a hand.' Dora refastened her cuffs. 'A nice hot drink might help warm them up. With any luck, they won't notice the fire.'

The men might not have noticed, but Major

198

Von Mundel did. He arrived that morning with the new guard shift, striding on to the ward as if he owned the place as usual, his hands clasped behind his back. He stopped in front of the ward fire, frowning.

'Before you say anything, I've just got it lit again,' Dora said, hurrying past him to deliver another cup of tea to a patient. 'You wait and see, it'll be as warm as toast in a minute.'

Ignoring his sceptical look, she swept off back to the kitchen to fetch some more tea. Kitty and Miss Sloan arrived and immediately began helping her.

'I see the Major is in one of his moods this morning,' Miss Sloan observed as she set teacups on a tray.

Dora smiled. 'Don't worry, Miss S. I've got a surprise for him later that should put a smile on his face.'

Miss Sloan's brows rose. 'Oh yes? What's that?'

'I put it in here this morning.' Dora went to the kitchen cupboard and opened it to show them.

'Chocolate!' Miss Sloan gave a cry of pleasure while Kitty just gawped.

'And there's a bottle of whisky, too. Real whisky,' she added, seeing the look of dismay on Kitty's face.

'But where did you get it, my dear?' Miss Sloan wanted to know.

'Bea's boyfriend,' Kitty answered for her.

'That's right,' Dora said. 'Bea's always bringing stuff home, so I've just been saving my share up. I thought it'd be a nice treat for everyone.' She grinned. 'Sometimes it's handy, having a GI in the family.'

'It's a very nice thought, my dear. Best not tell Sister, though,' Miss Sloan said, shooting a wary glance towards the kitchen door.

'It's all right, she's not on duty until one,' Dora said.

'Just as well,' Kitty said. 'She'd have a fit.'

'Then it'll have to be our secret. Now come on, let's finish serving the tea, then after breakfast we'll hand out the chocolate.'

It was a shame, Dora thought. The Helen she'd once known would have delighted in such a nice surprise. The ward sisters usually bought gifts to cheer up the patients at Christmas, and Helen's were always very thoughtful.

But the Helen she had once known seemed to have gone forever. Her experiences abroad had hardened her, turned her into a person Dora barely recognised, and certainly didn't like.

The men's faces were a picture when she and the other nurses handed out pieces of chocolate and a nip of whisky to each man. Dora saw amazement, disbelief and then finally joy as they realised that their gifts were real. They toasted Dora, the nurses and each other, with the whisky, and soon there was quite a party atmosphere as they chatted and laughed amongst themselves.

Major Von Mundel stood in the middle of the ward, his glass of whisky untouched in his hand, surveying it all through narrowed eyes. His expression was unreadable.

'Look at him,' Kitty whispered. 'You'd think he'd crack a smile at Christmas, wouldn't you?'

'It's hard to tell what he's thinking, isn't it?'

Miss Sloan said. 'He's quite inscrutable.'

'Miserable, I'd call it!'

Dora approached him. 'What's wrong, Major?' she asked. 'Don't you approve?'

'It is not that. I am just – surprised, I think.' He turned to look at her. 'This kindness is un-expected.'

For a second their eyes met. Dora looked away sharply. 'Yes, well, you've got to do something special at Christmas, ain't you? I'm sorry it's a day early, but I ain't going to be on duty on Christmas Day, so–'

'*Nein,* this is correct. In Germany it is tradi-tional to give gifts on Christmas Eve.'

'Fancy that. I reckon my kids would like that. They're always too excited to wait until Christ-mas Day.'

He regarded her with those unreadable blue eyes. 'You have children, Nurse Riley?'

She nodded. 'Twins – a boy and a girl.'

'Twins?' His brows rose. 'And how old are they?'

'They turned seven this summer.'

He looked away, his gaze raking the line of beds. 'It will be nice for you to spend Christmas with your family, I think.'

Dora lifted her chin. 'Yes, but we're not a proper family until their dad comes home.'

'*Nein,*' Major Von Mundel said heavily. 'I under-stand.' He paused for a moment, then said, 'I also have two children, a boy and a girl.'

Dora looked at him sharply. 'I didn't know... I never thought–'

'You didn't think I had a family?' His mouth curved in a mirthless smile. 'Like you, we all have

201

loved ones, Nurse Riley.'

'Yes. Yes, of course.' She stared down into the amber depths of her glass. Of course she knew that. The men were always showing her photographs of their sweethearts, their mothers, their wives and children. But Major Von Mundel was different. He never talked about his family, so she had assumed he didn't have one.

Looking at him, standing there so proud and tall in his grey prison uniform, it was hard to imagine he had a life outside the war at all.

'How old are your children?' she asked.

'Adel is twelve, and Gerte is eight.'

'How long is it since you've seen them?'

His lips tightened. 'My daughter was three years old when I left.'

Dora saw the emotion he was doing his best to conceal, and her heart went out to him. At least Nick had managed to spend a few days with Walter and Winnie last Christmas.

Without Helen's lowering presence, there were high spirits on the ward for the rest of the morning. The men laughed and joked, played cards and wrote letters home. Then someone started up a rousing chorus of a German song. Miss Sloan clapped along, but Dora was glad she didn't understand the words, because she was sure it wasn't suitable for a genteel music teacher's ears.

'You should save your voices for the carol singing later,' she said, over the din.

'Carol singing?' Major Von Mundel queried.

'The nurses go round all the wards singing Christmas carols and everyone joins in,' Dora explained. Then a thought struck her, and she said, 'Do you have Christmas carols in Germany?'

Major Von Mundel's chin lifted and he stared down his long nose at her in the way he always did when she had said something absurd. 'Of course we have Christmas carols!'

'Some of the most beautiful songs come from Germany and Austria,' Miss Sloan put in. Then she started to sing in her high, warbling voice, '*Stille nacht, Heilige nacht...*'

'"Silent Night",' Dora said. 'That's one of my favourites.'

'It's even more beautiful in German,' Miss Sloan said. 'Isn't that right, Major?'

'It is very beautiful,' Von Mundel agreed. Dora glanced at him. His face was expressionless, but she had heard the emotion that clogged his voice.

'Wait until we come round this evening,' she said. 'The nurses all turn their cloaks inside out so the red lining is showing, and we carry candles in jars to light our way. It's lovely, it really is.'

'It sounds most – charming,' Major Von Mundel said stiffly. 'I shall look forward to it, Nurse Riley.'

The fun and games soon stopped when Helen came on duty after lunch. She prowled the ward with a sour, forbidding expression, running her finger over bedframes and locker tops, speaking only to point out a water jug that hadn't been refilled, or a sheet not turned down the correct fourteen inches.

The men sat up in their beds, watching her with fearful eyes. They hadn't forgotten her wild temper over the Christmas decorations.

Helen hadn't forgotten it either. She never

looked at Dora, and barely spoke to her except to bark an order at her.

Thankfully, in the middle of the afternoon Clare arrived to summon Helen to an emergency on the military ward. Dora was shocked at how relieved she felt when her friend had gone. The men seemed to feel it too, although they kept shooting wary looks at the door, waiting tensely for her to come back.

But she still hadn't returned by the time the evening meal was served. Afterwards, Kitty and Dora went to join the other nurses for the carol singing. Miss Sloan remained on the ward with Major Von Mundel.

'Have a wonderful time, won't you?' she said. 'We're looking forward to hearing you when you come to visit us.'

The other nurses were gathered around the foot of the staircase in the main hospital entrance, a sea of scarlet cloaks.

'There you are,' Clare said. 'We were going to start without you.'

I bet you were, Dora thought. She glanced at Helen, her face like stone. 'Well, we're here now.' She lit her candle and placed it carefully in the jar one of the nurses had given her.

Helen cleared her throat. 'We'll start on the top floor, with the medical wards,' she announced. 'Then we'll visit the surgical wards, and the Casualty department, and finish with the three military wards–'

'Three?' Dora said. 'Don't you mean four?'

The other nurses exchanged wary looks. A couple of them started to shuffle their feet. Dora suddenly knew what was coming, even before Helen spoke up and said, 'We've been discussing it and we've decided not to include the POWs' ward.'

'Why not?'

Once again, they all exchanged looks. 'It doesn't seem right,' one of the other nurses said quietly.

'My boyfriend is away in France, and I don't want to be singing to Germans,' another piped up.

Dora turned on her. 'My husband is away in France, too,' she said, staring hard until the other girl looked away.

She let her gaze travel from one to the other, searching their faces. 'Honestly, I thought better of you all,' she said. 'We're supposed to be helping people, ain't we?'

'Only our own kind,' Clare muttered.

Dora shot her a filthy look. 'These men ain't monsters. They're just boys, no more than children some of them. They're a long way from home, missing their families just like everyone else in this rotten war!'

There was a long, uncomfortable silence. 'She's got a point,' one of the nurses started to say, but Clare silenced her.

'We all agreed,' she said. 'Anyway, it's decided now.'

'In that case, you can count me out.' Dora blew out the candle and set her jar down.

'And me,' Kitty said.

'Don't be like that–'

'I mean it. If my patients can't enjoy the carols, then neither will I.'

The other nurses all looked to Helen, who glared at Dora. 'I'm sorry you won't be joining us,' she said quietly.

The men all looked up expectantly when Dora walked back in to the ward, Kitty trailing behind her.

Miss Sloan came forward to greet them, her smile fading. 'Where is everyone, Nurse Riley?' she asked, looking behind them towards the doors. 'Are they on their way?'

'They are not coming,' Major Von Mundel said behind her. 'They do not want to entertain Germans. That is correct, is it not, Nurse Riley?'

Dora couldn't look at him. She shook her head, too upset to speak.

Major Von Mundel gave a resigned sigh. 'It is as I thought,' he said. 'When you first talked of the idea I had my doubts that it would happen.'

He turned away, but Miss Sloan went on staring at them, her eyes full of hurt. 'You mean ... but how could they?' Her mouth quavered. 'For heaven's sake, it's Christmas. To deny someone the gift of music at this time ... it's too cruel.' She shook her head.

'I know,' Dora said helplessly. 'But what I can we do about it?'

'I'll tell you what we can do about it, Nurse Riley.' Miss Sloan stood up straighter, squaring her shoulders. 'We will not allow ourselves to be defeated. If no one will sing Christmas carols for us, then – we'll sing our own!'

Dora frowned. 'I'm not sure about that–' but then she caught the fire blazing in Miss Sloan's eyes and felt her own blood ignite. 'Why not?' she said. 'You're right, why shouldn't we sing our own?' She turned to Major Von Mundel. 'Major, could you ask them to sing for us?'

Major Von Mundel opened his mouth to protest, but he must also have seen the determined look in Miss Sloan's eyes. He turned to the men and spoke rapidly to them in German.

There was a ripple of muttered conversation up and down the line of beds, then they turned back to face Major Von Mundel. The oldest of the men, a weighty man in his forties, cleared his throat and started to sing in a powerful tenor voice.

'*Stille Nacht, Heilige Nacht, Alles schläft; einsam wacht...*'

Gradually other voices joined in, until the air was filled with the joyful, beautiful sound of men singing.

'*Nur das traute hochheilige Paar ... Holder Knabe im lockigen Haar, Schlaf in himmlischer Ruh ... Schlaf in himmlischer Ruh...*'

A lump of emotion rose in Dora's throat. 'That was lovely–' she started to say, but then from somewhere in the distance came an answering cry.

'Silent Night, Holy Night... All is calm, all is bright...'

She and Kitty looked at each other. 'The other nurses,' Kitty said. 'They must have decided to come after all...'

'No, my dear. Those are men's voices.' Miss Sloan cocked her head to listen. 'It's coming from over there, the other end of the passageway.'

'The other military ward,' Dora said. She turned to Major Von Mundel. 'Can you make them sing again?' she asked.

Major Von Mundel nodded to the men, who started to sing. Soon the two languages were swelling and mingling in one joyful, perfectly harmonious chorus.

Miss Sloan turned to Dora, her face rapt. 'Isn't it beautiful?' she cried.

Dora nodded, tears stinging her eyes. 'It is,' she said.

Then Kitty nudged her. 'Nurse Riley?' she whispered.

Dora followed her gaze to the doors, where the other nurses were standing, their faces lit by the candles flickering in their jars. They were singing too, caught up in the wonderful sound. The war and all its woes seemed to be forgotten in a moment of pure joy.

All except for Helen, who stood, stony faced, her lips pressed together, her eyes full of spite.

Chapter Twenty-Five

'What do you mean, you don't want to get up?'

Stefan turned his head away so he wouldn't have to see Kitty Jenkins standing at the end of his bed, the calliper in her hand. How he'd come to hate that damn thing over the past few months!

'It's Christmas morning,' he muttered.

'Yes, but you haven't been out of bed in two days,' Kitty said. 'It's not like you. You won't get better if you don't put weight on that leg, you know.'

She was trying to encourage him, but this morning her cheerfulness only grated on him.

'Please, *Fraülein,* do not waste any more time on me,' he said. 'There are other patients who need you more than I do.'

'But I want to help you,' she said plaintively. 'We've worked so hard...'

He saw the hurt in her eyes and felt his treacherous heart melt.

Seeing her face, so open and filled with trust, Stefan realised that he could easily fall in love with her. Perhaps he was already in love with her. He had never been in love, so he couldn't tell. But he knew how it would end if he allowed himself to submit to his feelings.

He should never have let his guard down. But he was like a dog, starved and beaten throughout its life, who had suddenly been exposed to kindness and a gentle hand. It was only natural that he would want more.

But he couldn't allow it to happen. It was wrong and it was dangerous. Cruel as he was, Felix had made him realise how reckless he had been to let his guard down, and now it had to end. Better to cut himself free now than to live with the lingering pain.

She was still holding the calliper out to him. Stefan looked at it, then back at her. 'Why?' he asked.

She frowned. 'What do you mean?'

'It is a simple question, *Fraülein.* Why do you want to help me? I know how much you and your family dislike the Germans, and with good cause. Surely you would rather I was in my grave than on my feet?'

Kitty opened her mouth, then closed it again. 'You're not like the rest of them–' she started to say.

'Why? Why am I not?' He saw her flinch at his harsh tone, but he couldn't help it. Suddenly her answer was very important to him.

Kitty was silent for a moment, searching for an answer. 'Well ... you're not from Germany, for a start–'

'No, but I am still a German. I am an officer in the German army.'

'But they made you join up. You said so...'

'Perhaps, but I still fought for them. I killed for them.' He saw her flinch but he knew he had to say it, to push a final wedge between them, to destroy any lingering shred of feelings they might have for each other. 'I have killed a great many men, *Fraü-lein*. Young men, like your brother–'

'No!' she cut him off.

'You do not want to believe me. I can see you wish to think well of me, but I promise you there is nothing here.' He leaned forward, placing his hand over his heart.

'Why – why are you saying this?'

'Because I want you to see me for what I truly am. A killer, who does not deserve your help, or your sympathy.'

She was hurt and bewildered, he could see it in her eyes. He was hurt too, but he had to do it. He had to put space between them, for both their sakes.

'And so I said to him, I don't mind if I do!'

Everyone around the table laughed. Even Kitty's mother managed a quiet chuckle.

'You are a card, Malcolm. Isn't he, Kitty?'

Kitty looked up from her reverie to find everyone looking expectantly at her. 'Yes,' she smiled a fraction too late. 'Yes, he is.'

Mal grinned. 'Poor Kitty, I expect she's already heard all my jokes. Starting to repeat myself, aren't I, love?'

Kitty smiled again, but her thoughts were elsewhere.

She should be happy, she thought. It was Christmas Day, she had a few hours off duty and her mother had cooked a lovely dinner for them all. But instead her heart lay like a stone inside her chest.

She couldn't stop thinking about Stefan Bauer and the way he had spoken to her that morning. She had never seen him so low or so angry before. The lost, desperate look on his face haunted her.

'Are you all right, love?' Kitty looked up to see her mother frowning anxiously from across the table.

'I'm fine, Mum. Just a bit tired, that's all.'

Her father pointed his fork at her, his mouth full of stuffed mutton. 'They work you too hard at that hospital.'

'Aye, you're right there, Mr Jenkins,' Mal agreed. 'She takes on too much. You should see her, running about all the time. I don't know how she does it.' He smiled admiringly at her across the table.

'It wouldn't be so bad if it was our boys she was nursing,' her father snorted angrily. 'But looking after the enemy... It's a disgrace, that's what it is.

211

After what they've done to our brave boys...' He shook his head.

I have killed a great many men, Fraülein. Young men, like your brother. The words came into Kitty's head.

'What are we supposed to do, let them die?' she asked.

'Why not?' Her father glared back. 'The only good German is a dead German, as far as I'm concerned.'

'Hear, hear,' Arthur chimed in.

'And what about our boys who are over there?' Kitty asked. 'Would you like the same thing to happen to them?'

She saw her father's red, speechless face and knew she'd gone too far. Horace Jenkins always had the last word in everything.

Her mother must have noticed too, because she jumped in quickly.

'Has everyone had enough? There's plenty more veg, if anyone wants any...?' She seized the serving dish and started to pass it round, a desperate look on her face. 'No? Are you sure? I'll go and fetch the pudding, then.'

The moment of tension passed, and soon everyone was tucking into the Christmas pudding and praising it to the skies.

'I'm glad you like it,' Florrie Jenkins blushed with pleasure. 'I got the recipe off *Kitchen Front*. It's made with carrots. I know it's not how we'd usually have it, but it's not too bad.'

'It's delicious, Mrs Jenkins,' Mal said. 'Better than we'd ever get in the NAAFI, let me tell you. And it's so nice to spend Christmas with a family, with mine being so far away in Scotland.'

'Well, I hope you'll look on us as your family too, Malcolm,' her mother beamed.

'Oh, I do.' Mal reached for Kitty's hand under the table.

'Perhaps we soon will be family?' her father said.

'Dad!' Kitty felt her face scalding with colour, but Mal just chuckled.

'You never know, Mr Jenkins!' he said with a wink.

They all laughed, but Kitty could only stare down at her plate, mortified, until thankfully Arthur changed the subject back to the war. The Allies were finally driving the Germans back from the ground they had gained in Belgium two weeks earlier, and soon the men were discussing what their next move should be.

For once Kitty was glad of the war talk, because it meant that she could allow her thoughts to wander off. And it wasn't long before they drifted back to Stefan Bauer.

No matter how hard she tried, Kitty couldn't work out why Stefan's attitude had changed so much. After driving himself so hard for so long, why had he suddenly decided he didn't want her help? It was such a shame, and such a waste of effort. And it was so unlike him to give up, too. Stefan Bauer was a fighter, anyone could see that. Kitty had seen him almost weeping in pain, but still he refused to give up. So why throw in the towel now, when he was so close?

There had to be a reason, she thought. But she couldn't imagine what it might be.

The men's discussion was still going on as Kitty and her mother cleared away the dishes.

'Listen to them,' her mother said affectionately, 'putting the world to rights as usual.'

'I dunno what they'll find to talk about when the war's over,' Kitty agreed, scraping the leftovers into the pig bin.

'I'll be glad when it is over,' her mother said quietly. 'I daresay you will be too, won't you, love? What will they do with the German prisoners, I wonder?'

'Send them home, I suppose.' Kitty was surprised at the pang she felt. Six months ago the idea of nursing German prisoners of war had filled her with revulsion. But now she had learned that they weren't monsters, but flesh and blood just like herself.

And then there was Stefan. The thought of him leaving England and her never seeing him again filled her with a surge of unexpected panic.

What was wrong with her, she wondered.

There was a burst of laughter around the table in the next room. Florrie Jenkins beamed.

'It's so nice to have Malcolm here,' she said. 'He's been such a tonic to us all, especially Arthur. I think he's missed having an older brother to look up to.' She turned to Kitty. 'And I'm glad you've found yourself a nice young man, too. You deserve someone who'll take care of you. Malcolm's a good man. He loves you.'

Before Kitty could reply, Arthur appeared in the doorway.

'Dad says to come in, because the King's Speech is starting soon,' he announced.

After they'd listened to His Majesty on the wireless, they played cards. Kitty could feel Mal's restlessness as he sat beside her, playing round after round of gin rummy and whist.

She sensed he was agitated about something, but she didn't know what.

Her mother's words came back to her. *He's a good man ... he loves you.*

But do I love him? Kitty wondered. She remembered the way Bea had described how her heart skipped and her knees went weak whenever she saw Hank. Kitty couldn't say she'd ever felt like that about Mal.

But perhaps that wasn't love. Perhaps what Bea felt was something out of the movies and the penny romances, and real love was slower and steadier, like the feelings she had for Mal?

She looked at her mother and father, sitting companionably across the table from each other. She couldn't imagine them going weak-kneed about each other, yet they had been married for more than twenty-five years.

Then she glanced at her brother. Her mother was right, Mal was a good influence on Arthur. He hadn't got into any trouble since Mal had taken him under his wing.

Soon five o'clock came, and Mal had to return to duty. He asked Kitty to walk with him to the corner of the road.

It was already dark outside, and a thick frost glittered on the pavement in the dim light of the street lamps. When they reached the corner, Kitty gave him a quick peck on the cheek and went to hurry away, but Mal reached for her, pulling her back into his arms.

'Don't I get a proper Christmas kiss?' he said.

Kitty laughed, but she wasn't laughing a moment later when Mal's mouth came down hard on hers. She put her hands up to his shoulders and tried to push him away, but it only seemed to excite him more. He pushed her back against the wall, his tongue invading her mouth in a rough, obscene way while his hips pressed into hers.

She finally managed to break free, gasping for air. 'What was that for?'

He leered at her, his eyes glittering in the darkness. 'My Christmas present. Did you like it?'

She touched her bruised lips. 'No.'

'Go on, you loved it,' he smirked.

She pulled away from him, straightening her clothes. 'I – I have to go.'

'When will I see you again?' he called after her.

'I don't know... I'll have to wait and see when Sister gives me an evening off.'

'You do that, and I'll take you somewhere nice. Up West, maybe, to one of those posh restaurants.'

'You don't have to do that.'

'I want to. I want it to be special. You just get yourself dolled up, Kitty Jenkins!'

She didn't look back as she walked down the street on shaky legs.

Chapter Twenty-Six

Hank the Yank was every bit as impressive as Bea had made him out to be.

It was as if a movie star had suddenly stepped from the screen of the local picture house to join them for Christmas dinner. Dora couldn't take her eyes off the handsome GI sitting opposite her at the dinner table, and she knew she wasn't the only one. Even Nanna seemed taken with him. She didn't say much, but Dora noticed she'd slipped out and put her teeth in just before they sat down to eat.

Hank's glamorous presence seemed to fill the tiny kitchen. Everything about him was polished, from his uniform – so much smarter than the rough serge their boys wore – to his disarming smile, slicked back hair and smooth charm.

His manners were perfect. He'd arrived bearing gifts for them all: nylons, sweets, cigarettes and so much food her mother nearly fainted at the sight of it. He lavished praise on the Christmas dinner as if he'd never tasted anything so delicious. He flirted with Nanna and even made old Mrs Price blush with his compliments. He did magic tricks that left the children open-mouthed with wonder, and answered Alfie's endless questions about guns and bombs and battles with endless patience.

And yet there was something about him Dora didn't like. She didn't know why she had taken against him when he was trying so hard to fit in, but he seemed almost too good to be true.

Not that anyone else seemed to notice as they all fluttered around him like moths around a shining light. Bea sat beside him, preening herself with pride. She kept sending him admiring sideways looks, as if she couldn't quite believe her luck.

The only one who didn't seem to be falling for Hank's charm was Lily. She sat at the far end of the table, scowling down at her plate and ignoring Mabel's demands for attention.

'Trust her to be in one of her moods on Christmas Day!' Nanna muttered to Dora.

When Dora got up to fetch the Christmas pudding, Lily immediately offered to help her.

'Well, I never! Talk about a Christmas miracle,' Nanna Winnie said as Lily jumped up from her chair. 'I never thought I'd see the day that girl lifted a finger in this house.'

Lily practically shoved Dora into the scullery, pulling the curtain closed behind them.

'I can't stand it!' she said, putting her hands to her temples. 'I had to get away before I burst and said something!'

'About what?' Dora frowned.

'Him!' Lily jerked her head towards the kitchen. 'Mr sodding Perfect in there.'

'He does seem a bit full of himself—'

'Full of himself? Did you hear him going on about the dinner? It was only a bit of mutton, not the Last Supper!'

Dora smiled as she lifted the pudding from the pan. 'He was only being polite, I s'pose.'

'He's a liar,' Lily declared flatly. 'And Bea's falling for it. She's going to make a fool of herself, you mark my words.' She shook her head. 'I've tried telling her, but she won't listen. She reckons they're love's young dream.'

'Well, he does seem very fond of her–'

'That's what they're all like!' Lily raised her voice, then glanced over her shoulder towards the kitchen and lowered it again. 'I've seen them at that club, the way they talk to the British girls,' she hissed. 'They're all over them, buying them presents and promising them the earth, until they get what they want. And then you don't see them for dust.'

Dora placed the pudding on a plate and started to unwrap it from its steaming shroud. 'I'm sure if he's that bad, Bea will find out soon enough,' she said.

'If it's not too late by then.' Lily looked gloomy.

'What's that supposed to mean?' Dora asked, although she already knew the answer.

'One of the girls at the club was courting a GI. He told her he loved her, promised he'd marry her and take her to America to live. Until she ended up in the family way.' Her face was bitter. 'He didn't want to know her then. Turns out he's already got a wife and a couple of kids waiting for him back home.'

Dora stopped. 'You don't think Hank's married?'

'I don't know what to think,' Lily said.

Dora went back to unwrapping the pudding. 'Bea's got more sense than that,' she said.

'Has she?' Lily sent her a long look. 'You know what she's like, Dora. She gets carried away. You've got to talk to her,' she urged. 'Make her see sense.'

'Me!' Dora laughed. 'I don't think she'll listen to me.'

'But you've got to try,' Lily pleaded. 'He's no good for her, Dora. Anyone can see that.'

Dora looked at her sister-in-law's beseeching face. It was rare for Lily to spare a thought for anyone but herself, but for once she seemed genuinely concerned. She was good friends with Bea, so perhaps she knew something Dora didn't...

'Where's that puddin'?' Nanna called out from the kitchen. 'Bleedin' hell, it'll be Easter by the time you get it dished up!'

Dora watched her younger sister carefully across the table as she handed round the dishes of Christmas pudding. Bea appeared so happy, and from the besotted looks they gave each other, it seemed as if Hank was genuinely fond of her. Lily must have got it wrong, she thought.

'Be careful,' Rose Doyle warned the younger children. 'There's a silver threepence in the pudding. Make sure you don't swallow it.'

'I've got it!' Bea dug about in her pudding with her spoon and produced the coin.

'That means you'll have good luck,' her mother beamed.

'You'll have to make a wish,' Dora said.

Bea closed her eyes. 'I wish I could go to America,' she announced.

Dora glanced at Hank. His smile didn't waver, but she thought she saw a look of panic in his eyes. Or was she imagining it, after what Lily had said?

'Oh, Auntie Bea! It won't come true if you tell everyone,' Mabel giggled.

'It won't come true anyway,' Lily muttered darkly, prodding at her pudding.

Bea turned to her. 'What did you say?'

'You heard.'

They glared at each other down the length of the table. Then Bea tossed her red curls and said, 'You're just jealous, Lily Doyle!'

Lily gasped. 'Jealous? Of you? Don't make me laugh!'

'What's that supposed to mean?'

'Look in the mirror, then you'll find out!'

'You bloody little cat!'

'Now girls, don't start,' Rose pleaded. 'What will our guest think of us?'

Dora looked at Hank again. He was staring down at his plate with a frozen expression on his face. He looked as if he wished himself a million miles away.

'Mum's right,' she said. 'We're having a nice dinner. Don't spoil it.'

There was a knock on the door. 'Now who's that, I wonder?' Rose said.

'Probably one of the neighbours, complaining about the racket,' Nanna said.

'It's not like the neighbours to use the front door.' Rose stood up to answer it.

As soon as she'd gone, Dora turned to Bea. 'Behave yourself,' she warned. 'Mum's gone to a lot of trouble over this dinner, the least you can do is try to be civil.'

Bea shot a look down the length of the table. 'Tell her, she started it,' she muttered.

'I'm telling both of you.' Dora turned from one to the other. 'If I hear one more word out of either of you–'

She stopped, realising no one was listening to her. All eyes were fixed on the door behind her.

Dora turned slowly. Her mother stood in the doorway, her face deathly white. 'Mum? What is it?'

And then she saw the telegram in her mother's hand, and her heart sank like a stone in her chest.

Somewhere in the back of her mind, she heard Lily whimper, 'It's Peter, ain't it?' But her mother's gaze was fixed on her.

'I'm so sorry, love,' she whispered.

Chapter Twenty-Seven

Dora Riley was late for duty on Boxing Day morning.

Karl Von Mundel arrived at half past six with the guards, expecting to see Nurse Riley already there, helping to serve the breakfasts as usual. But instead he found a harassed-looking night nurse handing out cups of tea and slices of bread and marge.

'Where is Nurse Riley?' he asked, looking up and down the ward. 'She is usually early.'

'I know!' The night nurse rolled her eyes heavenwards. 'I've got used to her helping me. But she's not supposed to be on duty until seven o'clock, so I can't really complain. By the way, I need you to speak to a new patient. He was brought in during the night and I think he's

222

feeling a bit lost, poor chap.'

Von Mundel followed her to the young man's bedside. It was another gunshot wound, this time badly infected. He translated for the boy, trying to put him at his ease, but all the time his eyes were fixed on the door, waiting for Dora.

He was not usually a man given to nerves, but this morning he had to admit to a flutter of apprehension about what he was about to do. It had seemed like a good idea at the camp, but now he was here, his confidence deserted him.

What if he had misjudged the situation? Nurse Riley had always seemed friendly towards him, but their relationship had never gone beyond the professional. What if he was overstepping some kind of boundary? He had no wish to embarrass her, especially after she had shown his men so much kindness.

But at the same time, he felt foolishly excited at the thought of what he was about to do. He could just imagine her reaction when she saw the gift he had brought her, the smile spreading across her freckled face, lighting up her green eyes. She was no beauty, but when she smiled it transformed her.

The guards had looked askance at the box when they searched him that morning, and for a moment Von Mundel didn't think he would be allowed to bring it. But when they'd seen what was inside and he'd explained what it was for, they'd relented and agreed it was a nice thing to do for Nurse Riley.

'Got a soft spot for her, have you?' the soldier called Mal teased.

Von Mundel could only stare at him, shocked at the suggestion. He had only ever had eyes for his darling Liesl, ever since they were young. He had never even considered looking at another woman in that way.

No, thankfully he was not attracted to Dora Riley. It would have only embarrassed them both if he was, especially as he knew she was as devoted to her husband as he would always be to Liesl.

But he liked her. He looked forward to seeing her every day, hearing her ready laugh echoing down the ward. Everyone liked and respected Dora, because she had a kind word for everyone. Not that she took any nonsense from anyone, especially not him. Her plain-speaking attitude had taken Von Mundel aback at first, but now he respected her for it. She was direct, but never cruel.

And she stood up for what she believed in, even if it meant risking herself to do it. Von Mundel didn't think he would ever forget the way she had stood up to Sister Dawson over the Christmas decorations and the carol singing. It had meant a great deal to the men, and to him. He hadn't expected much of the English nurses when he'd first arrived, but Dora Riley had surprised him.

He had missed her yesterday. It had been a long and tiresome day with Sister Dawson, who made no secret of her dislike for him and the patients. Von Mundel had allowed his thoughts to drift towards Dora, wondering what she was doing and whether she was enjoying her Christmas with her family. It had been so long since he'd enjoyed a family Christmas, he envied her.

The double doors opened just before seven, and

he looked around sharply. But it was only Nurse Jenkins, closely followed by Miss Sloan. The older woman was breathless as usual, wrapped up in a bundle of coats and scarves. She had told him she cycled several miles in to work every morning, from a village in a place called Essex, where she taught music. It seemed very curious to him that a music teacher would want to nurse in a hospital, but Miss Sloan had insisted she wanted to 'do her bit'.

'Where is Nurse Riley?' he asked, trying not to betray his anxiety. 'Is she not coming today?'

'Oh yes, she's supposed to be here,' Nurse Jenkins replied, looking round. 'That's odd, she's usually early.'

But neither of them seemed to think much about it as they went about their work, taking bedpans round to the patients, washing them and making their beds.

Some of the patients were in great pain, waiting for the doctor to do his rounds. They needed more medication than the doctor prescribed, but until Dr Abbott visited them they had to go on suffering.

It was frustrating, Von Mundel thought. Outside in the courtyard, a working party of German POWs were being used to help rebuild the crumbling hospital buildings. Yet he was not allowed to use his skills where they were badly needed.

He was trying to console the patient who had been brought in overnight when Dora Riley arrived. For once she was not smiling, he noticed. He hoped something hadn't happened to upset her.

He fought the urge to rush up to her. Instead he waited until she had taken off her cloak, then greeted her with his usual curt nod.

'*Guten morgen*, Nurse Riley.'

Usually she would reply in her mangled cockney German. Her accent was dire, and he would always wince at it, and that would make her smile. It was a little joke between them that was played out every morning.

But this morning she merely gave him a nod and muttered, 'Good morning.'

He felt a stab of disappointment. 'Did you have a pleasant Christmas?' he asked.

She gave him a small, distracted smile, then turned away to speak to Nurse Jenkins, leaving him standing in the middle of the ward.

Von Mundel watched her. He had been so looking forward to seeing her, had pictured exactly how it would be. But she barely seemed to be able to look at him, let alone speak.

He followed her over to the new patient's bedside. She was reading his chart.

'He needs something for his pain.' Annoyance made him speak more sharply than he should, but Dora Riley scarcely seemed to notice.

'I'm sure Dr Abbott will prescribe something when he does his rounds,' she said, not looking up from the chart.

'And when will that be? Is he supposed to suffer because your Dr Abbott cannot get out of bed?'

He saw the angry flush flood her face. 'If it wasn't for our Dr Abbott, most of these men would be dead by now!' she snapped back. Handing the chart to Nurse Jenkins, she stalked off to the next bed, leaving him standing open-mouthed once more.

It was the same for the rest of the day. Dora Riley moved like an automaton, going through her duties but barely speaking or looking at anyone. Von Mundel could scarcely believe it. Was this really the same young woman who had been so cheerful on Christmas Eve?

The men noticed it, too.

'What has happened to *Schwester* Riley, Major?' they asked over and over again. 'Is she ill?'

'*Ich weiss es nicht.* I don't know,' was the only reply Von Mundel could give them. But he was worried. Something was definitely wrong, he knew that much. Something very bad must have happened to take the smile off Nurse Riley's face.

Her mind was elsewhere, he could see. It was evident later that day, when he discovered she had failed to check a patient's TPRs.

'I did,' she insisted when Von Mundel pointed out her mistake. 'I remember doing it.'

'Well, you did not record it on the chart,' he said.

She turned on him. 'You're not supposed to be looking at the patients' charts,' she reminded him. 'Their treatment is no concern of yours.'

'Their welfare is my concern,' he shot back angrily. 'And if you are not doing your job properly–'

'I don't answer to you!' Dora's lips were white with anger.

Von Mundel could only stare at her in astonishment. He was used to Sister Dawson putting him in his place, but never Nurse Riley. He liked to think she had come to value his assistance and expertise. But now here she was, behaving as if he was nothing, just another lowly prisoner to be scorned.

'Perhaps I should speak to Matron?' he said.

'If that's what you want.'

Once again, she walked away from him. Von Mundel looked around to see Miss Sloan and Nurse Jenkins watching the scene, open-mouthed. When they saw him watching them, they scurried away, their heads down. They seemed as embarrassed as he felt.

He had no intention of reporting Dora Riley, but he was angry and disappointed. She was always the one person he could trust, but overnight she had changed, neglecting patients and acting as if she didn't care.

But he could not shake off the feeling that all was not well with her. Something had happened to upset her, and he wanted to find out what.

He had his chance that evening, just before he was taken back to the POW camp for the night. Miss Sloan had already gone off duty at teatime, and Nurse Jenkins was helping *Oberleutnant* Bauer with his exercises before the night nurse arrived.

Dora was in Sister's office. Von Mundel could see her through the half-open door, sitting at the desk, staring blankly down at the report in front of her. The pen was in her hand, but she didn't seem able to write anything.

He rapped on the door and went inside. Dora looked up, and for a moment he saw the unguarded anguish on her face before the mask came down again.

'Major,' she said coldly.

'I am leaving now, Nurse Riley. But before I go, I have something I wish to give you.'

She frowned as he produced the box and placed it on the desk between them. 'What's this?'

'Open it, and you will see.'

He watched her face carefully as she opened the box. Her expression didn't change as she took out the wooden boat and placed it on the desk in front of her. Then she took out the animals, lions and elephants, monkeys and giraffes, all perfectly carved. Von Mundel's heart swelled with pride at the craftsmanship that had gone into them.

'The prisoners at the camp made them, to pass the time,' he explained, feeling suddenly shy. 'I thought you would like them – for your children?'

She looked at the tiny bear in her palm. 'They're beautiful,' she said flatly.

Von Mundel looked at her face, devoid of emotion, and all his joy seeped out of him. He had been looking forward to this moment, anticipating her pleasure. But there was nothing.

He swallowed down his disappointment. 'Very well, then,' he said shortly. 'I will leave you to your work–'

As he turned to leave, she suddenly blurted out, 'I had a telegram.'

Von Mundel turned, his blood cold in his veins. He knew what that meant only too well. 'A telegram?'

She slid it out from behind the bib of her apron and pushed it across the desk towards him. The poor girl had been carrying it around with her all day. It must have felt as heavy as a stone against her heart.

He hesitated, then picked it up. But he hardly needed to read the words. He had sent too many of them in his time.

He put it back down on the desk, and watched as Nurse Riley folded it as carefully as if it was a love letter, then slipped it back into the bib of her apron.

'It came yesterday,' she said.

'I am sorry.' He was painfully aware of how inadequate the words were.

Why did it have to come on Christmas Day? News like that was always painful, but to come on Christmas Day seemed like a very cruel blow.

'But surely you should not be here?' he said.

'That's what my mum said. But I didn't want to stay at home. I didn't want time to think...'

As if anything would stop her doing that. It was all the poor girl had been doing all day, he could tell. He felt wretched for the way he'd spoken to her. But at the same time he felt honoured that she had shared her secret with him. Nurse Riley did not express her feelings to everyone.

'I might as well be here, making myself useful,' she said. 'Although I don't think I've been much use to anyone today, have I?'

Her little rueful smile nearly broke his heart. He fought the urge to reach for her.

'I am sorry,' he repeated.

Her chin lifted. 'It says missing, presumed dead,' she said. 'That means there's still hope, doesn't it?'

She was looking up at him, searching for the faintest glimmer of light in the darkness. He couldn't bring himself to take that away from her. 'There is always hope, Nurse Riley,' he said.

'That's what I thought.' She nodded, her face brave. 'I know Nick, he'll find his way home to us. He wouldn't leave me and the kids, he promised...'

Her voice choked, and the next moment she was crying. Without thinking, Von Mundel went to her, kneeling by her side to wrap his arms around her. He expected her to resist but she buried her face in his chest and cried.

Von Mundel cradled her against his heart, feeling her sobs shake her body, breathing in her clean scent of starch and soap. All the time he thought of his precious Liesl. He had been hundreds of miles away in France when he found out she had been killed by the RAF bombing their city. All he'd wanted to do was to run, to be with his children, to hold and comfort them the way he was comforting Dora now.

He felt the hot tears sliding down his own cheeks. How he wished he could have held Liesl one more time like this.

A sound outside startled him from his reverie. He looked up to see a flash of movement through the half-open door, followed by the sound of footsteps hurrying away.

Nurse Riley sat bolt upright. 'What was that?'

'I don't know. Perhaps the night nurse...' Von Mundel went to the door and looked out. There was no sign of anyone in the empty ward. The night nurse had not yet come on duty.

By the time he turned back, Nurse Riley had recovered herself.

'I'm sorry,' she said, brushing down her apron so he couldn't see her blushing face. 'What must you think of me?'

He gazed at her for a moment. 'I think you are a courageous woman, Nurse Riley.'

Her blush deepened. 'I don't feel very courageous at the moment,' she confessed, staring at the ground.

'Nevertheless, I know you will be strong for your children and for your husband.'

Nurse Riley allowed herself to look up at him, and he saw her shoulders straightening as she mentally rallied herself.

'Yes,' she said firmly. 'Yes, I will. Thank you, Major.'

She left, and it was only then Von Mundel realised the toys were still lying on the desk, untouched and forgotten.

Chapter Twenty-Eight

'Guess who I saw last night, canoodling with a German?'

Kitty paused, her powder puff halfway to her face.

'What's this?' Her father lowered his newspaper, frowning over the top of it. 'I hope it wasn't you, Kitty?'

'As if our Kitty would do such a thing!' her mother answered for her over the busy click of her knitting needles. 'Besides, she's already got a nice boyfriend, haven't you, love?'

Kitty stared at her reflection in the cracked glass of her compact. A pair of guilty eyes looked back at her.

'Do you want to know who it is, or don't you?' Arthur demanded impatiently. 'All right then, I'll tell you,' he went on without waiting for an answer. 'It was that Nurse Riley.'

Kitty stared at him. 'What are you talking about?' she said. 'That's nonsense.'

'I saw her,' Arthur insisted. 'Mr Hopkins sent me up to the ward to collect the soiled dressings, and as I was going past Sister's office I saw her and that German officer – you know, the one who's always throwing his weight around, looking down his nose at everyone?'

'Major Von Mundel?'

'That's the one. They were kissing!'

Kitty shook her head. 'You're making it up!'

'All right, they might not have been kissing,' Arthur conceded. 'But he had his arms round her, and they looked very friendly. There's definitely something going on there,' he said.

Kitty went back to powdering her face. 'I still don't believe it,' she said flatly.

'I'm just telling you what I saw, that's all.'

'Nurse Riley wouldn't do something like that. She's a respectable married woman. And you'd better not go spreading rumours like that, Arthur Jenkins,' she warned him.

'I know what I saw,' Arthur insisted stubbornly.

'And there's plenty of so-called respectable married women that do carry on while their husbands are away,' her mother put in.

'Carrying on is one thing,' her father declared. 'But carrying on with a German...' His mouth curled. 'Any woman who would do that is nothing

233

better than a prostitute and a traitor to her country.'

'Horace, please!' Florrie Jenkins protested mildly. 'Don't use language like that in this house.'

'I'm only speaking the truth,' her husband said, clamping his pipe between his lips as he went back to reading his newspaper.

Kitty studied her face in the mirror of her compact as she pressed powder into her temple. She felt sure her guilt was written there for everyone to see, as clearly as the scarred flesh she was doing her best to cover.

Not that she had done anything wrong. She had barely spoken to Stefan since Christmas Day. But whenever she was near him, Kitty could feel the attraction crackling between them, so hot and fierce she was astonished no one else had noticed it.

Even now, thinking about him brought a warm flush to her cheeks that her powder did nothing to disguise.

She closed her compact with a snap, shutting off the thought. It did her no good to allow herself to think about him. Stefan had no interest in her, he'd made that very clear, and even if he did, it was foolish to imagine they might have any future together.

She glanced at her father puffing on his pipe and harrumphing at something he'd read in the newspaper, the balding top of his head just visible above its pages. Imagine if she introduced Stefan to him! He would turn her out of the house in a minute.

She shuddered at the thought.

'You look nice, dear. Are you going out with Mal tonight?' Her mother's voice interrupted her reverie.

'Yes.' Kitty delved her lipstick tube with the end of her finger to get the last remaining corner of colour, and dabbed it on her lips. 'He's taking me to the West End for dinner.'

'Up West, eh? That sounds fancy. Is it a special occasion?'

'I don't think so,' Kitty shrugged. 'I think he just felt like splashing out, that's all. I told him I didn't want anything too posh, but he insisted.'

'Did he, now?' Her mother sent her an inscrutable look.

'He's a nice chap,' her father put in. He lowered his newspaper and pointed the end of his pipe in her direction. 'You want to keep hold of him, Kitty.'

Kitty looked away on the pretence of putting on her shoes. The truth was, this was going to be her last night out with Mal.

Her father was right, he was a nice chap. But she wasn't in love with him, and it wasn't fair to keep stringing him along, especially when she knew she had feelings for someone else. Even if she had no future with Stefan, she didn't feel as if she could make a future with Mal, either.

She knew it was going to be difficult to tell him, even worse as Mal was splashing out on a posh dinner. She'd begged him to change their plans for dinner, but typical Mal, he hadn't listened.

'I want to make it special for you,' he'd insisted, adding to her guilt.

As they travelled up West on the Tube later, Kitty

reflected on her decision. How could she possibly end their romance when he'd gone to so much trouble for her? Bea would say she had lost her marbles. Mal obviously loved her, and she was a fool not to appreciate him.

She glanced sideways at him, sitting beside her, his hand resting in hers. Her mother was right, he was a good man. Most girls would be only too happy to be courting someone like him.

You're going to end up an old maid, Kitty Jenkins, she thought. But even that didn't seem as bad as spending the rest of her life with the wrong man.

Mal had booked a table at a swanky restaurant just off Piccadilly. It looked like a palace, with crystal chandeliers, gilt chairs and snowy white linen. As they made their way to the table, Kitty felt out of place among all the fur coats and posh accents.

'I don't know why we had to come here,' she whispered. 'I would have been just as happy at the Lyons Corner House.'

'Only the best for my girl,' Mal said.

Kitty cringed. Why did he have to be so nice to her, tonight of all nights? It was almost as if he knew what was coming, and he wanted to make her feel as bad as possible.

But there was no sign of any malice in his honest, open face as he smiled at her across the table over their meal. He was so pleased with himself for bringing her here, Kitty thought, her heart contracting with pity. She couldn't possibly end it now, not like this, after he'd gone to so much trouble for her. Surely one more night wouldn't hurt? She could tell him tomorrow, or the next day. Tonight would be too cruel...

And then she saw him reach into his pocket and draw out a small, leather-covered box.

'Kitty...' he started to say, reaching for her hand. Panic flooded through her. She wanted to run, but her legs had turned to jelly.

'No.' Her mouth formed the word, but no sound came out. Mal wasn't listening anyway. He had shifted out of his seat and was down on one knee.

'I love you, Kitty Jenkins,' he said, his gaze fixed on hers. 'Will you do me the great honour of becoming my wife?'

Everyone was staring at them, all heads turned in their direction. Kitty suddenly felt hot and dizzy. She stared down at her hand, still trapped in his.

The moment went on and on, as if they had all been frozen in time.

'Say something, for Gawd's sake!' Mal laughed uneasily. 'I'm getting cramp down here!'

Kitty looked at him, his smile fixed as he gazed at her. She had a sudden vision of her life unrolling, her mother smiling and excited as she helped her plan the wedding, her father proudly walking her down the aisle, their misery over Raymond forgotten at last.

Just say yes, a small voice inside her head said. *Just say yes and you'll make everyone happy.*

Except herself.

'Kitty?' She saw the realisation dawning in Mal's eyes before she opened her mouth to speak.

'I'm sorry,' she whispered.

Still no one moved. Murmurs started to ripple

around the room as word spread of what had happened. Someone laughed out loud. All the while, Mal stayed where he was, on one knee, one hand holding hers, the other holding the engagement ring, as still as a statue.

'You can stay there as long as you like, old chap. She still isn't going to say yes!' a toffee-nosed voice called out from the back of the room. Kitty felt Mal's humiliation as keenly if it were her own.

The only way she could spare him was to leave. She slipped her hand from his lifeless grasp and reached for her bag. 'I – I'll make my own way home,' she murmured.

Chapter Twenty-Nine

It was a cold, rainy night. The dim light from the street lamps was reflected on the wet streets as Kitty turned up the collar of her coat and hurried down Piccadilly towards the underground station, desperate to put as much distance as she could between her and what had just happened.

Poor Mal. She couldn't forget the picture of him kneeling there, holding up that engagement ring, his expression turning from hopeful to bewildered and forlorn as everyone looked on. She wondered if she should have stayed, but she would only have prolonged his humiliation, and her own.

She remembered her mother's inscrutable look and wondered if she'd guessed what was to come. Kitty wished she had warned her. Then perhaps she could have saved them all some embarrassment.

Now her mother was probably waiting for her at home, expecting to hear her happy news, to see her daughter's sparkling new engagement ring and share her excitement. No doubt she had already started to make plans for the wedding, Kitty thought.

Her heart sank. That was two people she had upset and disappointed. How could she be so selfish?

She was halfway up Piccadilly, just level with the Ritz Hotel, when Mal caught up with her. She heard his footsteps behind her, but before she could turn to face him he'd grabbed her arm, spinning her round.

'What was that all about?' he demanded. His blazing, angry face terrified her. 'How dare you humiliate me like that? Making me look a fool in front of all those people!'

'I didn't know you were going to propose, did I?'

'Why the hell did you think I'd brought you all the way here? I told you I wanted to make it special.'

Kitty looked down at his hands, gripping her arms. 'What was I supposed to do?'

'You were supposed to say yes!'

'I'm sorry.'

'Sorry isn't good enough. I deserve an explanation, at least.' He thrust his face close to hers, his fingers biting into her flesh through her coat. 'Why don't you want to marry me? Is there someone else, is that it?'

'Let me go, you're hurting me–'

'Not until you give me a reason!'

She forced herself to look at him. 'I don't love you,' she said.

He flinched as if she'd struck him. 'But all this time we've been together ... I thought you liked me–'

'I do like you,' she said. 'But that's not enough, is it? You deserve more than I can give you...'

His chin lifted. 'You're right about that. I could do a lot better than you!'

She saw the defiant anger in his eyes. He was lashing out, trying to hurt her. The least Kitty could do was allow him his pride.

'Then I hope you find someone,' she said quietly.

She disentangled herself from his grip and started to walk away.

'You won't find anyone else, you know,' Mal called after her. Kitty ignored him and went on walking. 'Not with that big ugly scar of yours!'

She stopped in her tracks, her hand going up automatically to her temple.

'You can cover it up, but you can't hide it,' Mal's sneering voice came from behind her. 'Everyone knows how ugly you are. Do you really think anyone else would ever want you? Even your first fiancé couldn't stand the sight of you. I only went on with you in the first place because I felt sorry for you,' he went on, jeering softly. 'And I thought you'd be easy. I mean, it's not like you'd get a lot of offers looking like that, is it?'

He doesn't mean it, he's just trying to hurt you, Kitty told herself. But his words went straight to her heart.

'I reckon you've done me a favour,' Mal called after her. 'I could get someone prettier than you, Kitty Jenkins. Someone who doesn't make me feel sick to look at her!'

Swallowing down her pain and humiliation, she called back, 'You'd better start looking then, hadn't you?'

She started to walk away again, but she heard his footsteps pounding on the wet street behind her.

'You don't walk away from me! Not until I say so!'

He grabbed a handful of hair, yanking her backwards. She screamed with pain. 'Let me go!'

'No chance. I've spent a lot of money on you, and I want my money's worth!' He pulled her into a narrow alleyway until the darkness swallowed them both. Kitty's heart hammered against her ribs, fighting to escape from her chest. She fought against him, clawing and scratching, but he was too strong for her. He pinned her against the wall, his hands going inside her coat, roaming roughly over her body.

'At least I don't have to wait for the wedding night, since there isn't going to be one!' Mal's voice was harsh, his breath hot against her ear. The next moment his mouth was on her neck, devouring her. At the same time, he ripped at the front of her dress, popping the buttons.

At the mouth of the alleyway people walked by, going about their business and enjoying their evening. Kitty could hear their voices just a few yards away. Surely they could see her? But then she realised that if they looked at all, all they would see was a young soldier and his sweetheart enjoying a kiss and cuddle.

But it was more than that. This was like a fight to the death. She barely recognised Mal any more. He was like a savage, mouth and tongue and teeth and hands tearing at her, invading her, careless of anything but getting what he wanted. Kitty tried to scream but his hand clamped over her mouth, pushing her back with such force her head banged against the brickwork. For a moment her vision clouded and the world shimmered in front of her. She felt her knees buckle as Mal started to push her to the ground.

Then she heard a sound from the end of the alley. Lost in all the hubbub of busy Piccadilly at night, she somehow managed to pick out a voice she knew.

Her sense of self-preservation reasserted itself. She managed to twist her arm free, clawing with her nails down the side of his face. Mal released his grip over her mouth for a second, just long enough for her to turn her head away and scream out with every bit of strength she had left.

'Bea! Help!'

For a moment nothing happened. Mal had her pinned to the ground but he tensed, waiting like a cat poised to spring away at the first sign of danger.

Then, suddenly, two figures appeared silhouetted in the mouth of the alleyway, and she heard Bea's voice calling out tentatively, 'Kitty? Is that you?'

Mal was on his feet in a second, straightening his clothes. Kitty lay sprawled at his feet, too weak and afraid to move.

'Tidy yourself up!' she heard Mal hiss. She tried to pull her dress down as Bea's footsteps echoed down the alleyway, with Hank following closely behind.

'Evening,' Mal greeted them, his voice falsely bright. 'Fancy seeing you here.'

But Bea didn't look at him. Her gaze was fixed on Kitty.

'Would someone mind telling me what's going on?' she said.

Most of the family were in bed by the time they got to Bea's house, so there wasn't a crowd of people to witness Kitty's humiliation. Only Dora Riley and her mother were still up, waiting for Bea to come home.

Thankfully, neither of them asked too many questions. Dora silently set about cleaning the graze on the back of Kitty's head, while Rose Doyle sat at the other end of the kitchen table, sewing the buttons back on Kitty's dress.

'You should go to the police,' she said to Kitty. 'The lad ought to be reported for what he did.'

But Kitty was adamant. 'I don't want to make a fuss,' she said. 'It would only upset Mum and Dad if they knew, and they've been through enough already. You won't tell Mum, will you?' she pleaded.

'Bless you, love, of course I won't. We know how to keep a secret, don't we, Dora?'

Dora said nothing. Kitty couldn't see her face as she stood behind her, dabbing gentian violet on her grazed scalp.

She suddenly remembered what Arthur had

said about Nurse Riley and Major Von Mundel. Was Dora keeping a secret of her own?

'I dread to think what would have happened if Hank and I hadn't been passing,' Bea said.

'Don't,' Kitty shuddered, pulling Bea's old dressing gown tighter around her. The same thought kept running through her head, all the way home. It had seemed nothing short of a miracle when she had heard her friend's familiar voice.

'You don't think he would've–'

'I don't know, and I don't want to think about it.' It was bad enough that she could still smell him on her skin. She couldn't wait to get home and scrub herself clean.

Even the nip of brandy Dora had given her couldn't take away the taste of him from inside her mouth. 'I don't know how I'm going to face him at the hospital after this,' she said.

'It's him who should be ashamed to show his face,' Dora muttered.

'Perhaps he won't show his face,' Bea said. 'Especially not after the pasting Hank gave him. You should have seen him, Dora,' she said proudly. 'I thought he was going to break Mal's jaw.'

'He sounds a real hero.'

'Oh, he was.' Bea preened herself. She didn't seem to notice the heavy irony in her sister's voice, but Kitty did.

Dora finished cleaning Kitty's wound and put the stopper back in the bottle. 'There, that should be all right.'

'And I've finished these buttons,' Rose Doyle put in, shaking out Kitty's dress. 'One was missing, but I've been through my box and I think I've managed to match it.'

'That's smashing, Mrs Doyle. Thank you.' Kitty gave her a grateful smile.

'It's the least we could do, love.' Rose rested her hand on Kitty's shoulder. 'Now, are you sure you don't want to stop the night? I could make you a bed up down here, by the fire–'

'Thank you, but I'd best get home. Dad goes mad if I'm not home by eleven.'

'Just as you like.' Rose gave her shoulder a final squeeze, then headed off to bed. Dora went too, leaving Bea and Kitty alone to talk.

'So you're not going to tell your mum and dad, then?' Bea said.

Kitty shook her head. 'Like I said, they've been through enough worry.' She picked up Bea's hand mirror from the table and inspected her face. At least all the bruises were on her arms and body. With any luck her parents wouldn't notice anything.

She put on the dress Bea's mum had just mended for her. The fabric seemed to smell of Mal, too. It had once been one of her favourites, but Kitty knew she would never wear it again.

'I just don't understand what made him do it,' Bea mused. 'He always seemed so nice. To turn like that–'

'I suppose I must have hurt his pride when I turned down his proposal,' Kitty said.

Bea gawped at her. 'He proposed?' Kitty nodded. 'You didn't tell me that! When? What happened?'

She listened avidly, her chin propped on her

hands, as Kitty told her the full story of that evening. She could see the growing astonishment on Bea's face.

'And you turned him down after he went to all that trouble?' she said, when Kitty had finished.

'Yes, and I'm glad I did now I've seen what he's really like.' She had felt sorry for him at first, but not any more.

'Yes, I suppose we've seen a different side to him,' Bea conceded. 'But to think, you've had two proposals and I'm still waiting for one!'

Kitty saw her friend's mouth turn down at the corners and she knew she was thinking about Hank.

'I'm sure you and Hank will end up together,' she tried to console her.

Bea shrugged. 'Oh yes, I'm sure we will,' she agreed, inspecting her nails. 'After all, he's met the family and they love him, so it's only a matter of time–'

She sounded so self-assured, Kitty envied her. She could never imagine her family loving Stefan.

They would rather I married a vicious bully like Mal than a German, she thought bitterly.

'You're lucky,' she said quietly.

'I know.' Bea looked pleased with herself. 'But I still don't understand why you turned Mal down. All right, I know he turned out to be a nasty piece of work. But I thought you were keen on him?' She smiled. 'Or have you got another man tucked away somewhere that I don't know about?'

'Don't be daft.' Kitty looked away quickly, so Bea couldn't see her blushing face. But she'd underestimated how sharp her friend could be.

Bea stared at her. 'You do! There's someone else, isn't there?'

'No,' Kitty muttered.

'Don't you dare lie to me, Kitty Jenkins, I know you too well. Who is he? Do I know him?'

'No–' Kitty said. She could have bitten off her tongue when she saw Bea's triumphant expression.

'So there is someone? I knew it! Come on, spill the beans.'

'I can't tell you.'

'Why not? Is he married? Oh Kitty, please tell me he hasn't got a wife tucked away somewhere.'

Kitty shook her head. 'No, he isn't married.'

'Then why can't you–' Bea broke off, realisation dawning. 'Oh my God. He's a German, isn't he? One of your patients?'

Kitty looked down at her hands. She knew she was better not telling anyone her secret. But there was another part of her that wanted to talk about him, to say his name out loud just once...

'Well, there is someone I like...' she admitted slowly.

'I knew it!' Bea's eyes gleamed with excitement. 'Oh, this is so romantic. It's just like Romeo and Juliet, isn't it? You're a dark horse, Kitty Jenkins! Tell me all about him, I want to hear everything.'

'First you must swear not to tell anyone,' Kitty warned.

Bea drew her finger across her mouth. 'My lips are sealed,' she promised.

Chapter Thirty

The wooden ark was still on the desk in Sister's office, where Dora had abandoned it. Someone had lined up the tiny carved animals two by two. They snaked across the surface of the desk, waiting to board the miniature gangplank.

Dora picked up the monkey and held it up by its long curling tail. She hadn't really taken in how beautifully made it was, from its cleverly curved feet to its cheeky little face. Someone had taken a great deal of care over it.

She was sorry she hadn't thanked Major Von Mundel properly for the thoughtful gift. She had never expected such kindness from him.

And not just for the toys, either.

A flush rose in her cheeks at the thought of how she'd behaved. It was so unlike her, she had shocked herself. She was a tough East End girl, she kept her feelings to herself. Even at home, in front of her own family, she pasted a grim smile on her face and insisted she was coping. And thankfully no one questioned her, even though she was sure none of them believed it.

But here, in front of Major Von Mundel of all people, she had allowed herself to break down and give in to the horrible, bottomless despair she had been holding in ever since that wretched telegram arrived.

It seemed incredible when she thought about it.

Dora never allowed anyone to see her cry, and yet she had sobbed like a child in a stranger's arms.

Or perhaps it was because he was a stranger that she had felt she could allow her grief to spill out? She barely knew him, and he expected nothing of her. She didn't have to put on a front for him the way she had to for her mother, or her children.

'I thought you had forgotten about them?'

She swung round at the sound of Major Von Mundel's voice. He stood in the doorway, watching her. Looking at that haughty, high-cheekboned face and those icy blue eyes, Dora wondered how she had ever succumbed to her moment of madness. He was the last person in the world she would have imagined she would seek solace from.

And yet...

She looked back at the monkey in her hand, aware that she was blushing furiously.

'They're smashing,' she said. 'I'm sorry I never got the chance to thank you last night.'

'Oh, it is nothing.' He brushed it off lightly. 'The men pass the time by making toys and trinkets from the scraps they are given at the camp. I am glad they will have a good home.' He stepped forward and picked up the lion.

'But perhaps your daughter might have preferred something a little less fierce. *Eine Puppe*, perhaps? A doll?'

Dora smiled. 'You wouldn't say that if you met my Winnie! She's a real tomboy, always getting into mischief. She takes after her–' She stopped, her mouth shutting like a trap to hold in the word.

She fixed her gaze on the monkey, praying that Major Von Mundel wouldn't ask her any more.

249

She could feel the tears clogging her throat and knew she couldn't trust herself to speak without crying again.

Thankfully Major Von Mundel seemed to understand.

'The reason I came to find you, Nurse Riley, is *Gefreiter* Gruber – the gunshot wound that was admitted two nights ago? I have just spoken to him and he still seems to be in great pain.'

'Is he? I noticed when I read his chart this morning that Dr Abbott had increased his medication. I'll mention it to Sister Dawson when we do the drugs round.'

'I would be most grateful if you could. But I was wondering, if he is in so much pain, perhaps his wound is infected?'

'I'll go and check it now.'

'Thank you, Nurse Riley.' He gave her one of his rare smiles. Looking at him, Dora wondered if he was as embarrassed about the previous evening as she was.

She started to put the wooden animals back into the ark. 'I'll put these up on the shelf, so they won't get lost,' she said.

'Allow me,' Major Von Mundel said, stepping in to help her.

'It's all right, I can manage–'

They were both holding on to the toy, their fingers touching, when the door swung open and Helen walked in.

She looked from one to the other, her expression icy. 'What is going on here?'

'Pardon me, *Oberschwester*, I was just leaving.' Major Von Mundel turned back to Dora. 'You will attend to the matter we discussed, Nurse Riley?'

'Yes. I'll see to it straight away.'

'Thank you.' He turned back to Helen, gave her a curt nod, then left.

Helen looked at the door, then at Dora. 'What was that all about?'

'The patient in bed eight is complaining of pain. I promised the Major I'd check the wound for infection.'

'And you jump to do his bidding, I suppose?' Helen's brows rose. 'Since when does Major Von Mundel give the orders around here?'

'He doesn't,' Dora said. 'But if a patient is in pain–'

'What's that?' Helen cut her off, staring at the wooden toy in Dora's hands.

'It's a Noah's Ark. Major Von Mundel thought I might like it for the twins. The POWs made it – isn't it beautiful?' She held up the boat to show her, but Helen hardly looked at it.

'So he's bringing you presents now, is he?' she said in a low voice.

Dora frowned. 'What's that supposed to mean?'

'Nothing. It doesn't matter,' Helen dismissed it with a shake of her head. 'I want you to prepare a patient for discharge.'

'Oh? Which patient is that?'

Helen consulted the piece of paper in her hands. 'Stefan Bauer. He's being transferred to the camp later today.'

Dora's first thought was Kitty Jenkins. She wasn't due on duty until that afternoon. She would be so disappointed if she missed the chance to say goodbye, after all the hard work she'd put in helping him to recover.

'Surely he's not ready to be discharged, Sister?' she said. 'He still hasn't got all the movement back in his leg yet–'

'He can walk, can't he?'

'Well yes, but–'

'Then he's well enough to leave. Dr Abbott doesn't believe it serves any useful purpose keeping him here when he's unlikely to recover fully, and I agree with him,' Helen said tartly.

'He certainly won't recover if he's sent to the POW camp,' Dora murmured.

'That's none of our concern.' Helen frowned. 'Really, you must stop yourself getting so close to these people. They can't be trusted.'

Dora gazed down at the toy in her hands. 'You make them sound like wild animals.'

'Perhaps that's what they are.'

The cold way she said it shocked Dora. And then there was that bleak look in her eyes. It was the look of someone haunted by a memory she could never escape.

Something began to stir in Dora's mind, a dark memory of her own she had kept long buried.

'Helen–' she started to say, but Helen cut her off.

'At any rate, you should stay away from Major Von Mundel,' she said briskly.

'But why?' Dora stared at her. 'He brought a toy for my children. He's been very kind to me–'

'How kind?'

Something in her tone made Dora's hackles rise. 'What do you mean?'

'He brings you presents, you run to do his bidding the moment he snaps his fingers, and as for all that nonsense over the Christmas decorations–'

'That was for the patients!'

'And then I walk in to my office and find you practically holding hands!' Helen went on, ignoring her. 'Tell me, what am I supposed to think?'

It was as if someone had thrown a bucket of icy water over her, shocking her so much she forgot how to breathe.

'You don't think I would do something like that–'

'No, of course I don't,' Helen said impatiently. 'But you need to be careful, Dora. You don't know how it looks to other people. You know how they like to gossip. I'd hate for anything to get back to Nick...'

'I have no idea what I said,' Helen told Clare later. 'All I did was try to give her some friendly advice. I never expected her to react like that.'

'Did she lose her temper?' Clare leaned forward, her eyes eager for details. 'I bet she did, didn't she? I knew as soon as I saw her she'd be trouble. It's the red hair. They just can't control themselves–'

'No, she didn't. That's the odd thing.' Helen knew better than anyone that Dora had a quick temper. But if anything she'd almost seen the emotion draining from her, along with all the colour in her face, leaving a deathly, unnerving stillness. 'She just walked out,' she said.

'And you haven't seen her since?' Clare asked.

'I haven't been back to the ward since then.' A new load of patients had been brought in to the military ward shortly afterwards, and Helen had been busy settling them in.

She had to admit she was rather relieved of the chance to escape. She sensed Dora was like a steaming kettle, about to explode.

'At any rate, she is off duty this afternoon,' she said. 'With any luck I can avoid her until then, give her a chance to calm down.'

'I don't know why you should be afraid of her,' Clare said with asperity. 'You're the ward sister, after all. Besides, you were only giving her some friendly advice.'

'Perhaps I shouldn't have interfered,' Helen said.

'Or maybe she has a guilty conscience?' Clare suggested. 'Perhaps you touched a nerve and she didn't like it?'

'Oh no, I don't think so,' Helen shook her head. 'Dora would never do anything like that. She's devoted to Nick.'

'Well, something's got her stirred up,' Clare said. She patted Helen's arm. 'You did all you could, love. If she can't see that then she's even more foolish than I think she is.'

But Helen was still troubled when she returned to the POWs' ward after lunch. Dora had already gone, and Helen didn't know whether to be relieved or apprehensive. It might have been better if they'd had a chance to clear the air, she thought.

She had just returned to her office when Major Von Mundel strode in without knocking.

'What did you say to Nurse Riley?' he demanded.

Helen looked up sharply. She was about to reprimand him when she saw the look of tight-lipped anger on his face. 'I don't know what you're talking about,' she said.

'I think you do, *Oberschwester*. What did you say to make her so upset?'

Helen rallied, her chin lifting. 'If you must know, I told her I was worried about her getting too involved with you. I reminded her she was a married woman, and–'

'You said what?'

Helen straightened her shoulders. 'Don't you dare take that tone with me–'

'*Oberschwester*, you do know that Nurse Riley's husband is dead?'

Now it was Helen's turn to feel the blood draining from her in an icy rush to her feet. 'What?'

'He is missing, presumed dead. The telegram arrived on Christmas Day.'

'But I don't understand – why didn't she tell me?' she stammered.

Major Von Mundel sent her a chilling look. 'Perhaps, *Oberschwester*, she no longer considers you a friend. And I wouldn't blame her for that, would you?'

Chapter Thirty-One

Mal was in his usual place by the double doors when Kitty arrived for work just after lunch. For once his friend Len wasn't with him.

Anxiety gnawed at the pit of Kitty's stomach and it was all she could do to push her feet in his direction. She had been dreading coming face-to-face with him after what had happened.

'You've got nothing to be embarrassed about,' Bea had told her the previous night. 'He should be the one who's ashamed, not you.'

She was right, Kitty thought, lifting her head as she approached him. As she drew nearer, she could see the sheepish look on Mal's battered face. Kitty forced herself to meet his eye, and was pleased when he looked away.

He was in a bad way. One eye was almost closed up and shrouded in bruises, and she could see the tracks of her nails down his swollen jaw.

As she moved towards him he said, 'Had a good look? This is all your fault!'

She gasped at the unfairness, but said nothing. He was trying to goad her, but she had already made up her mind not to speak to him.

'You didn't have to bring your mate into it, y'know,' he went on in an injured tone. 'I wouldn't have hurt you. I was only having a bit of fun.'

Kitty stared at him. Without the dark alley to hide him, he seemed smaller, less threatening.

Her silence seemed to unnerve him. As she went to move past him, he mumbled, 'Anyway, I'm sorry, if that's what you want to hear.'

'That's big of you.' The words were out before Kitty could stop them.

'I mean it.' His eyes were downcast. 'I've had time to think about it, and I know I was wrong. So if you'd just give me another chance...?'

Kitty was so amazed she nearly laughed out loud. 'I don't know how you can even ask me that.'

'Why? We had a good time together, didn't we?

And you know I love you–'

'You've got a funny way of showing it. Besides, why would you ever want me, when you can do so much better?'

He had the grace to look embarrassed, colour flooding his face, mingling with the deep red of his battered jaw.

'I didn't mean what I said. I was angry...' He looked up at her, his eyes appealing. 'I wouldn't have said those terrible things if I didn't think so much about you–'

He actually believed his twisted reasoning, Kitty thought. He'd insulted her, and abused her, and terrified her in a dark alley, and she was supposed to forgive him because it showed he cared.

'Come on, Kitty,' he coaxed. 'I do like you, you know I do...'

She looked him up and down. 'No thanks,' she said curtly. 'You might not think you can do better, but I know I can.'

She could see his mood changing before her eyes. She saw his face go taut with anger and she stepped away from him, terrified that he was going to hurt her again.

'Fine,' he bit out. 'Suit yourself. But I'm going to tell everyone I finished it with you!'

Suddenly she realised why he had taken the trouble to apologise, why he was so desperate to win her back. It was nothing to do with his feelings for her, it was because he didn't want to be seen to lose. Everyone was probably mocking him because even the girl with the scarred face didn't want him.

He was so pathetic, he was barely worth her time.

'Say what you like,' she threw over her shoulder as she walked away. 'I don't care any more.'

She felt surprisingly calm as she went to the cloakroom to hang up her cape. She had dreaded seeing Mal again, but now she felt stronger for it.

The first person she saw when she stepped on to the ward was Miss Sloan.

'Oh, thank goodness you're here, my dear,' she sighed, wringing her hands. 'It's been the most dreadful morning.'

'Why? What's happened?'

'I think Nurse Riley and Sister Dawson must have had a falling out. Nurse Riley didn't speak to a soul until she went off duty, and now Sister Dawson's just as bad.'

Kitty looked down the ward, her heart sinking. She dreaded Sister being on the ward at the best of times. Her permanently dark mood seemed to hang like a cloud over them all.

'Speak of the devil...' Miss Sloan looked past Kitty's shoulder to where Sister Dawson was approaching.

'There you are, Nurse Jenkins.' She made a great show of consulting the watch on her apron, even though Kitty knew she was a few minutes early. 'Here is your work list for this afternoon...'

Kitty waited patiently as Sister Dawson went through the list, explaining all the jobs she had to do. It was only when she'd finished that Sister said as an afterthought, 'Oh yes, and the fractured femur is being discharged today. Make sure he's prepared, will you? And pack up his belongings for him, if he has any.'

'You mean Stefan Bauer?'

258

One look at Sister Dawson's frown and Kitty knew she had overstepped the mark. Kitty pressed her lips together to stop herself saying any more. Over Sister's shoulder, she could see Miss Sloan's look of dismay.

'It's such a shame, isn't it?' Miss Sloan whispered later, when they were washing bedpans in the sluice. 'I've developed rather a soft spot for that young man, haven't you?'

'No more than any other patient,' Kitty said crisply. 'Anyway, it's a good thing he's leaving,' she went on, her head down, rinsing a pan under the tap. 'It means he's recovered.'

'I suppose that's one way of looking at it,' Miss Sloan said, although it was plain from her expression that she did not agree. 'And that's entirely down to you, my dear,' she added. 'You've worked so hard to get him back on his feet. I wouldn't be surprised if you received a commendation from Matron for your efforts, too.'

As if a commendation from Matron would make up for the wretchedness she felt, Kitty thought as she headed back down the ward later. Hearing that Stefan was leaving had been like a punch in her stomach, and she'd carried the pain with her all day.

She had known it was bound to happen. But somehow she had managed to turn her mind away from the prospect.

She passed the door of his room several times as she went about her duties, and each time she had to stop herself going in to him. She was terribly torn. Part of her wanted to shut him out, to pretend he had already gone. Another part wanted to be with him for as long as she still could.

In the end, Sister Dawson gave her no choice.

'Haven't you seen to the fractured femur yet, Jenkins?' she said, waving his discharge paper in her face. 'Attend to it, stat. The porter will be coming up to collect him in an hour.'

Stefan was sitting up in bed, talking to Hans in German. Felix Frost lay in his bed in the corner, reading a letter.

Stefan looked up when she came in, pushing her trolley of wash things. Kitty could see at once the wary look in his eyes. He seemed to be bracing himself.

'I suppose you've heard the good news, *Fraülein?*' he said.

Kitty nodded. 'That's why I'm here, to get you smartened up before you leave.'

She was aware of Felix watching them keenly from the next bed. She knew he spoke no English, but she still had the uneasy feeling he understood everything that was going on. She pulled the curtains around the bed, shutting him out.

As usual, Stefan insisted on washing himself. Neither of them spoke as she watched him shaving, mesmerised by the long, smooth strokes of the razor on his chin. The clock on the wall ticked away, ponderously measuring out the minutes. Soon Stefan would be gone, and it would be too late to tell him how she felt.

Kitty pressed her lips together to stop herself blurting out something foolish. Stefan plainly didn't care about her, so she couldn't allow herself to care either.

'Do you know which camp they're sending you

to?' she asked, for something to say.

He shook his head. 'But what does it matter?' He dipped the razor in the bowl of water, rinsing off the soap. 'I am still a prisoner wherever I am.'

'I thought perhaps I could write to you.'

His eyes met hers in the mirror. Kitty's mouth went dry, and she found herself longing for him to say the words she could not. 'I do not think that is a good idea, *Fraulein*,' he said.

As he finished washing, Kitty turned her attention to clearing out his locker. Stefan had brought few belongings with him. Other than his prison uniform, there was just a tattered photograph of him with his brother Emil, both of them grinning into the camera. Stefan had shown it to her reluctantly once, when she'd asked about Emil.

She looked more closely at the photograph. She barely recognised Stefan as the smiling, carefree young man in the photograph.

Stefan glanced over her shoulder then turned away. 'Throw it away,' he said. 'I do not need it any more.'

'Oh, but you can't!' Kitty protested. 'Surely you'll want to take it with you?'

Stefan took the photograph from her. He studied it for a moment, then suddenly thrust it back into her hands. 'What is the point of holding on to memories? We must leave the past where it belongs.'

After he'd finished washing, Kitty retreated to the other side of the curtains while Stefan changed into his POW uniform. Once again, Felix stopped reading his letter and watched her with interest, his head cocked to one side, like a cat might watch a mouse. He called out something in German to Stefan, and got a terse reply in return that brought a nasty smile to his face.

The curtains parted and Stefan emerged. It gave Kitty a shock to see him dressed in his uniform.

'Well, I suppose this is goodbye,' he said gruffly.

'Yes, I suppose it is.'

'I doubt if our paths will cross again.'

A lump rose in her throat. 'No,' she said.

For a moment she thought she saw a flicker of emotion in those dark russet eyes. 'Thank you–' he started to say, but she held up her hand to stop him.

'I was only doing my job.'

'Were you?' His sudden, searching look took her by surprise, and for a moment she thought he was going to say something.

But at that moment Arthur arrived, pushing an empty wheelchair, flanked by a guard Kitty didn't recognise.

'Time to go,' he said.

Stefan's gaze dropped to the wheelchair. He shook his head. '*Nein*, I will not use it.'

'You ain't got a choice, mate,' Arthur said nastily.

Stefan glared at him. 'I said I will walk out of here on my own two feet, and that is what I will do,' he growled.

Arthur's ears turned pink, and Kitty could tell he was going to lose his temper.

'It's all right, Arthur. Let him walk if he wants to.'

'But–' Her brother opened his mouth to argue, but the guard stepped in.

'I don't care if he wants to go on horseback, as

long as we get going,' he said.

Stefan turned back to Kitty. '*Auf Wiedersehen, Fraülein,*' he said solemnly. 'I wish you well.'

'You too, *Oberleutnant* Bauer.'

And then he was gone. Kitty forced herself to watch him, walking tall and straight, barely needing the calliper's help. Utterly determined to the end. She watched until the hot tears blurred her vision and she couldn't see any more.

Chapter Thirty-Two

Dora had managed to calm herself down by the time she went to visit Mrs Price in Griffin Street that night.

'Thank you for coming round, my dear,' the old lady said as Dora let herself in the back door. 'I wasn't sure I'd be seeing you, after everything that's happened.'

Dora looked at her in surprise. It took her a moment to remember that Mrs Price had been sitting at their table enjoying Christmas dinner when the telegraph arrived.

'I promised I'd drop in, didn't I?' Dora handed her a dish, carefully wrapped in cloth. 'Mum made some potato pie and she had some left over, so she wondered if you'd like it?'

'Oh, that's very kind of her. She's a diamond, your mum.'

Mrs Price paused, and Dora felt a pang of dread, knowing what question was coming next.

'I'll put the kettle on, shall I?' she said quickly, hoping to divert the old lady's attention.

'No need, it's just brewed. You sit down and take the weight off your feet while I pour it. I reckon you've done enough running around after people today.'

Dora sat down in one of the old armchairs flanking the fireplace and tried to warm her hands at the feeble fire spluttering in the grate. Timmy the cat appeared and wound himself around her legs.

'I don't suppose you've had any more news?' Mrs Price asked, as she carried the tray over.

Dora's heart sank at the question. 'I won't know anything until I get a letter.'

'No, of course. I should have remembered that.' Mrs Price set the tray down between them. 'I hope you don't have to wait too long. I remember what it was like, waiting for news about our boys...' Her gaze strayed to the mantelpiece, where a photograph of Philip and Eric Price smiled down at them. They looked so proud in their uniforms.

Dora concentrated on stroking Timmy's scrawny neck. She wished Mrs Price wouldn't talk about it as if Nick was already dead. 'Missing,' the telegram had said, and Dora clung to that word like a lifeline. While he was only missing, there was still hope, even if no one else seemed to believe it.

Timmy sprang into her lap, nudging her hand.

Mrs Price looked pleased. 'You've made a friend there,' she said, handing her a cup of tea. 'You should be honoured. Timmy's very particular about people.'

'It's taken a while for him to get used to me,' Dora said, running her hand down his back. She could feel the knobbly bones of his spine through his thin ginger fur. 'I remember when Nick and I first came to feed him, it took so long to find–' She stopped abruptly. The memory was like a fragment of broken glass, too sharp-edged and painful to hold for long.

She lifted her cup to her lips. The tea was hot and scalded her mouth, but at least she could hide her downcast face behind it.

Mrs Price leaned over and patted her knee. 'It will get easier, love,' she promised. 'I know it doesn't seem like it at the moment, but it will.'

But I don't want it to get easier, Dora thought as she headed home later. Because then she'd have to accept he was gone, and she couldn't do that.

Missing. She wouldn't allow herself to think further than that. She would rather deal with the pain of not knowing, no matter how jagged and spiky it felt, than to try to find some peace without him.

While Nick was only missing, there was still a shred of light and hope. And that was all Dora had to keep her going.

She stayed with Mrs Price for another half an hour, then headed home.

As usual, she could hear voices coming from the kitchen as she climbed the stairs to the top part of the house where the Doyles lived. But her mother's voice sounded slightly strained, the way it always did when she was putting on airs and graces.

No sooner had she opened the door than Rose Doyle pounced on her.

'There you are!' Her smile was fixed as she dried

her hands on her pinny. 'Why didn't you tell us you were expecting a visitor?'

Dora frowned. 'Who?'

'She wasn't expecting me, Mrs Doyle.'

Rose stood aside, giving Dora a clear view of the kitchen. Helen Dawson knelt on the rug in front of the fire, playing with the twins and Mabel as if it was the most normal thing in the world for her to be there.

She looked up, and their eyes met. 'Hello, Dora,' she said.

'Helen's been teaching us draughts, but we keep beating her!' Walter crowed to his mother.

Dora ignored her son, her gaze still fixed on Helen. Laughing, with her long dark hair falling about her face, she looked more like the girl Dora had once known.

'What do you want?' she asked.

Helen sat back on her heels. 'You left a package in my office. I thought I'd bring it round–' She nodded towards the box on the table. It was the one Von Mundel had brought her two days before.

'It's a surprise,' Winnie put in. 'Can we open it, Mum?'

'I didn't give it to the children,' Helen said quietly. 'I thought you'd want to do that.'

'Can we open it, Mum? Can we?' The twins were on their feet, clamouring around her.

'I suppose so.'

She watched them opening the box, taking out the ark and oohing and aahing over each of the little wooden animals.

'Ain't it smashing, Mum?' Walter said. 'Look, it's got lions and elephants and monkeys and everything!' He held one of the tiny beasts up for her to look at.

'It's lovely, ducks,' Dora said without enthusiasm. She had so looked forward to giving the children their present, but somehow having Helen here had taken all the joy from her.

'There are enough little monkeys in this house, I reckon!' Rose stepped forward, ruffling Walter's hair. 'Come on, kids, let's take your toy into the bedroom, and leave your mum to talk to her friend, shall we?' She gathered up the wooden animals and ushered the children out of the room. 'You too, Mum,' she said to Nanna Winnie, who sat in her old rocking chair, watching Dora and Helen keenly.

'I'm all right where I am, ta.' Nanna looked at Dora, smacking her toothless gums in anticipation of a good old argument.

'Mum!' Rose shot her a warning glance.

Nanna sighed. 'Oh, all right, then. If I must.' She raised herself out of her chair with a loud groan. 'I always miss the fun,' she muttered, as she shambled off.

And then they were alone. Helen got to her feet, brushing her skirt down. 'I can't believe how much the children have grown,' she said. 'They were just babies the last time I saw them. And this house is new, too.' She looked around her. 'You've made it look really homely–'

'What do you want, Helen?' Dora cut her off. 'I know you didn't just come to bring the children their toy, especially since you don't approve of them having it.'

Helen looked shamefaced. 'You're right,' she

said. Then she lifted her gaze to meet Dora's. 'Why didn't you tell me about Nick?' she asked.

The question startled Dora. Now it was her turn to look away. 'You didn't give me a chance,' she said. 'You were too busy accusing me of carrying on with Major Von Mundel!' Her voice caught. Even now, her anger nearly choked her.

Helen's face coloured. 'I'm sorry,' she said. 'I should never have said those things. It was very wrong of me–'

'You were only saying what you believed.'

'I don't,' Helen said quickly. 'I know you'd never– I'm so sorry,' she repeated miserably.

'Then there's nothing more to say, is there?' The twins' clothes were hanging on a clothes horse around the fire to dry. Dora picked a vest up and started to fold it. All the while, she could feel Helen standing behind her.

'Have they told you what happened?' she asked.

Dora shook her head. She picked up another vest and folded it, adding it to the pile.

'Is there anything I can do?'

'No thanks.'

Helen stepped forward. 'Let me help with that–' She went to pick up another vest from the clothes horse, but Dora snatched it out of her hands.

'I don't need any help, thanks,' she snapped.

Helen drew back. Dora could sense her helplessness, but she was too hurt and angry to be forgiving.

'I wish you'd told me,' Helen said. 'I'm your friend...'

'Are you?'

That startled her. Helen stared at her for a

moment, her face crumpling. 'Please don't be like this,' she begged.

'How do you expect me to be?'

'I just want to help you!'

'And I've just told you, I don't need your help.' Dora finished folding the clothes. 'Now, if you don't mind–'

She picked up the pile and started towards the bedroom.

'That's your trouble, Dora Riley,' Helen said behind her. 'You never admit when you need help.' Dora stopped, turning slowly to face her. 'You're too proud,' Helen went on. 'You keep everything locked away, tell everyone you can manage when you can't.' She stepped towards her, holding out her hand. 'I'm only trying to be a friend to you–'

'You're not my friend. Not any more!'

The words exploded out of her. Helen looked stunned. 'You don't mean that,' she whispered.

'Yes, I do.' Dora turned on her. 'You've changed, Helen. You're not the girl I used to know.'

'That's not true–'

'Isn't it? The Helen I knew was kind and gentle, not cruel like you. She would never have torn down Christmas decorations out of spite, or refused to sing a carol to cheer up a sick patient!'

Helen flinched. 'Things have been difficult for me – since I came back to England,' she said quietly.

'You reckon I don't know that?' Dora dumped the pile of clothes on Nanna's chair and advanced towards Helen. 'You tell me I'm too proud, that I keep everything locked away, but you're every bit as bad as me, Helen Dawson. The only trouble is,

269

you can't hide it as well as I can.'

Helen's eyes widened, huge, dark pools in her pale face. 'I – I don't know what you mean,' she stammered. 'I haven't hidden anything–'

'Really?' Dora folded her arms across her chest. 'Then why don't you tell me the truth about what happened to you in Africa?'

Chapter Thirty-Three

Helen looked at the ground. 'I told you what happened. I was attacked.'

'And what else?'

'I – I don't know what you're talking about.'

'I've watched you. I've seen how you flinch whenever one of the prisoners comes near you, or even speaks to you. You can't bear to touch them–'

'Are you surprised, after what happened to me?' Helen said sharply.

'What did happen to you, Helen? That's what I want to know. Because it must have been more than you're telling everyone.'

Dora held her gaze, silently urging her to tell the truth. Helen stared back at her for a moment, then she looked away.

'I can't stay here and listen to this–' She started to gather up her coat and belongings, her movements agitated.

'He raped you, didn't he?'

Helen froze, her hands raised to put on her hat.

For a moment Dora caught the anguish in her gaze before her mask came down again.

'Really, Dora, I wish you–'

'Does anyone else know?' Dora interrupted her. 'Does David–'

'No!' Helen's mouth slammed shut as if she would have snatched the word back from the air if she could. But it was too late.

Her shoulders slumped in defeat. 'No,' she said, more quietly. 'No, he doesn't know.'

For a moment neither of them moved. Helen stood, still in her coat and hat, a forlorn statue in the middle of the kitchen.

Dora went to the cupboard and found the bottle of brandy on the top shelf that Hank had brought them at Christmas. No one touched the stuff, but her mother had kept it 'for emergencies'.

She got out two glasses and poured a splash of brandy into each of them, then handed one to Helen.

'I think you'd better sit down and tell me all about it,' she said.

It took a long time for Helen to tell her story. Dora waited patiently, sitting opposite her in Nanna's rocking chair. She understood how difficult it was for Helen to find the words and say them out loud for the first time.

She didn't give him a name. He was a prisoner of war, she said, an educated German officer who acted as a translator on the ward.

Dora thought of Major Von Mundel. No wonder Helen despised him so much.

'We trusted him,' Helen said. 'He was allowed to wander at will around the ward, he played cards with the men, helped us serve the meals. He was almost like one of us.' She swallowed hard. 'I thought of him more like a friend than as a prisoner – we all did,' she said. 'He would even keep me company while I was on nights. We'd sit and talk, and he'd tell me all about his family, and I'd tell him about mine, and about David...' Her hand shook as she raised her glass to her lips. 'The other girls teased me he had a soft spot for me. But I didn't take any notice,' she whispered. 'I just thought he was harmless. And then he started to leave me letters, and presents.' Her gaze strayed to the box on the table which had contained the wooden ark. 'I'd come on duty and find a little posy of flowers on the desk, or some poetry he'd written. The other girls thought it was sweet, but I didn't like it.'

'What did you do?' Dora asked.

'I told him it had to stop. I told him I liked him as a friend, but I was engaged to David, and I didn't want him to get the wrong idea.'

'And what did he say to that?'

'Nothing.' Helen took another gulp of brandy. 'He seemed to accept it. The presents and letters stopped, and we went back to the way things were. Or so I thought. But looking back, I suppose there was something odd about him. He would watch me when the doctors were there. If I laughed with them, or even spoke to one of them for too long, it would put him in a bad mood for the rest of the day.' She looked up at Dora, imploring for her understanding. 'I didn't realise it at the time, or I would have done something about it. It was only after–' She broke off, staring down at the glass she cradled in her hands.

'What happened?' Dora asked softly.

It took a long time for Helen to reply. Dora watched her friend staring into space. She looked as if she was a million miles away, but Dora could see the pain flickering in her eyes as she relived what had happened to her. She was fighting to put it into words, Dora could tell.

It had all started, she explained finally, with a party at the officers' mess. Helen had had a good time, drinking and laughing with her friends, but she had gone home early with a headache.

'I went back to the hospital compound to ask the night nurse for some aspirin,' she said. 'He was waiting for me by the perimeter fence. He asked me if I'd had a good evening.' She shook her head. 'Even then, I didn't think anything of it. I thought he was just being polite. I even started to tell him about the evening, but then – I don't know ... he changed...' Her face was bleak, remembering. 'He told me he'd been watching the officers' mess all night, that he'd seen me talking to other men. Then he hit me.' Her voice was devoid of emotion. 'I was so shocked, I didn't even react. He went berserk. He called me terrible names, told me I was a whore and I deserved to be treated like one. Then he hit me again and knocked me to the ground...'

She raised her glass to her lips but didn't drink. Her eyes stared unseeingly ahead of her, as if she was watching the scene all over again.

'I didn't even try to fight him off,' she whispered. 'I don't know why I didn't. I just lay there until it was over, like I was dead...' She shook her head.

'There was else nothing you could do.'

'Yes, but to just let it happen like that ... I feel so ashamed... It's what you should do, isn't it? Everyone fights back...'

I didn't. Dora's hands tightened around her glass. Her stepfather had forced himself on her for years, and she had stopped fighting back. Kicking and clawing and scratching only prolonged the agony and gave him power. In the end she just lay there and forced her mind to float free, detaching herself from what was happening to her body.

She wondered if she should speak up, tell her story. Perhaps it would make Helen feel better to know she wasn't alone. But when she opened her mouth to speak, the words wouldn't come.

'What happened then?' was all she could say.

'Nothing. He stood up, got dressed and walked away, as if nothing had happened. I just lay there for a while, and then I went back to the nurses' quarters.'

'You didn't tell anyone.' It was more of a statement than a question.

Helen shook her head. 'I was too ashamed. And I didn't want to admit it had really happened, either. I thought if I didn't tell anyone, it wasn't really true...' She took a deep breath. 'But then Clare came home from the party and found me in the shower, scrubbing myself. I was crying, and my skin was raw, but I still couldn't get clean...' Her voice hitched. 'She helped me. She dried me off and dressed me as if I was a child, and then she made me tell her the whole story.'

She lifted her eyes to meet Dora's. 'I know you don't like her, but she saved my life. She looked after me. She was the one who made up the story about me being attacked. I had the bruises to prove it, after all.' She put her hand up to her face. 'Clare came with me to see the commander the following morning, and she did all the talking, and managed to get me transferred back to England. I don't know what would have happened if it wasn't for her. I think I might have just crawled away into the desert and died...'

'What about him?' Dora said.

Helen shuddered. 'I couldn't report for duty – I just couldn't face him – but Clare said he was laughing and joking, and making tea for the nurses, as if nothing had happened. I started to think I was going mad, as if I'd imagined it all.' She put down her glass and wrapped her arms around herself, as if to make herself as small as possible. 'I couldn't stay there. He might have been able to pretend that nothing had happened, but I couldn't.'

'And then you came home and they put you on the POWs' ward,' Dora said.

'Now do you see?' Helen's eyes were dark, pleading for her understanding. 'I can't bear to be near them. Every time I hear their voices or their laughter, it just reminds me...' She looked at Dora. 'And then there's him,' she said dully.

'Major Von Mundel?'

She winced at the sound of his name. 'I don't trust him,' she said. 'I watch you with him, and I keep thinking what if–'

'He wouldn't,' Dora said. 'He isn't like that.'

'That's how I felt, until–' Helen fell silent, but her look spoke volumes.

Dora drained her glass. 'And you've never told anyone else about this?' she said, changing the subject. Helen shook her head. 'Not even David?'

'No!' Helen looked dismayed. 'I could never tell him. I'd die of shame if he knew.'

'But surely he must know sometime?' She looked at Helen's stricken face, and suddenly the truth dawned. How could she have not seen it before? 'You've left him,' she said.

Helen looked down at her hands, knotted in her lap. 'It seemed like the best way,' she said quietly.

Dora stared at her friend, her heart tugging with pity for her. Poor Helen. Just when she'd finally found love again, fate stepped in and took it away from her. 'What did you tell him?'

'The same as I've been telling everyone else. That I felt we'd drifted apart and I'd stopped loving him.'

'But you haven't?'

Helen looked up, her eyes wretched. 'What do you think?'

'And how did he take it?'

'Not very well.' Her mouth twisted. 'He's been bombarding me with letters ever since, begging me to take him back, to give him another chance. It breaks my heart,' she sighed.

'Then wouldn't it be easier to tell him the truth? I'm sure he'd understand...'

'It would never be the same between us. It couldn't be.' Helen shook her head, her dark hair tumbling around her face. 'No matter what he said, I'd know he'd always be wondering about what happened to me. And besides, what man would want a woman who was damaged goods?'

Dora lowered her gaze. She was not one to judge. She had never told Nick what she had gone through with her stepfather, either. It was the memory of what Alf Doyle had done to her that had almost kept her and Nick apart forever.

But somehow her love for him had allowed her to conquer her fear and shame. She wished the same thing could happen to her friend.

'You won't tell him, will you?' Helen was staring at her, imploring her.

Dora shook her head. 'He won't hear it from me.'

'Are you sure? I couldn't bear it if he knew...'

'I can keep a secret, Helen.' God knows, she'd been keeping enough of her own.

Helen gave her a shaky smile. 'I know. I should never have doubted you. And I should have told you what had happened. But I didn't want to talk about it, and Clare thought it would be best if we kept it between us, so—'

I bet she did, Dora thought. It explained the proprietorial way Clare acted over Helen, always trying to shut Dora out. Helen never seemed to notice it, but Dora did.

But then she remembered how Clare had helped Helen, and how she had been such a good friend to her when she needed one. She really had no right to criticise, she decided.

'Do you forgive me?' Helen's voice broke in to her thoughts. Dora frowned.

'What for?'

'For the way I've behaved. I know I haven't been a good friend to you—'

'I haven't been a good friend to you, either.'

Perhaps if she had been a better friend she might have noticed Helen's anguish sooner.

Helen gave her a tentative smile. 'Perhaps we can make up for it now?'

'I hope so.'

Helen held up her empty glass for a toast. 'To friendship.'

Dora clashed her glass against Helen's. 'And no more secrets,' she said.

Chapter Thirty-Four

February 1945

'Well, look who it is!'

Kitty didn't pay any attention to Arthur's comment as they walked through the hospital gates together. She was used to her brother making derogatory remarks about the POW work party whenever he saw them. Ever since Christmas, a lorry-load of a dozen or so prisoners and their guards arrived each morning to work on rebuilding the hospital.

Kitty had ceased to notice them over the two months they had been working there, but Arthur never failed to stop and hurl abuse their way.

She was about to tell him to shut up, when his next comment stopped her in her tracks.

'It is him, isn't it? That one with the gammy leg?' Arthur peered closer, his mouth curling. 'It is him! I'd know that arrogant face of his anywhere.'

278

Kitty turned to look properly at the men toiling among the tumbledown outbuildings, their slate-coloured uniforms blending with the grey chill of the February morning.

She picked out Stefan straight away, heading across the weed-strewn waste ground, a hod of bricks resting on his shoulder. Only the slightest trace of a limp gave away that he had once been injured.

Her heart leapt in her chest and she had to press her lips together to stop herself crying out his name.

'It is him, isn't it?' Arthur said.

'Is it? I can't tell.' Kitty managed an indifferent shrug. 'Come on, we'll be late.' She started to walk away, but her legs had turned to jelly beneath her.

She was a fool to think she had forgotten about Stefan Bauer. She had done her best to push him to the back of her mind because she had no choice. But he was always there, lingering on the edge of her thoughts.

To her shame, she had even held on to the photograph of him and his brother that he had told her to throw away. She kept it at the bottom of her jewellery box and refused to allow herself to look at it, but it was a comfort to know it was there.

And now he was here, right in front of her, and it felt as if all her dreams and all her worst nightmares had come true at once.

Kitty waited until Arthur had gone off to the porters' lodge and she had reached the steps of the main hospital building before she risked another look back over her shoulder at him. He was stooped over, unloading bricks from the hod. As she watched him, he suddenly straightened up. He took his cap off and raked his hand through his brown hair, scanning the horizon.

He caught sight of her and Kitty's heart stopped in her chest, waiting for him to recognise her. She smiled, her hand half raised, ready to wave when he looked her way. But his gaze slid straight past her before he went back to his work.

Kitty lowered her hand, fighting down her bitter disappointment. All this time, she had imagined that Stefan might be pining for her the way she was for him. But it had been nearly two months now. He probably didn't even remember her.

She was watching him, Stefan knew. He was aware of her from the moment she had walked in through the hospital gates with her brother. He had tracked her out of the corner of his eye as they walked up the drive together. She had said good-bye to her brother at the porters' lodge and then continued alone towards the main hospital building.

Only when he thought it was safe had Stefan finally allowed himself to look up. And there she was, staring straight back at him.

He saw her smile, her hand lifting, ready to wave. And he'd also seen her disappointment when he looked away. But he wasn't ready. He'd spent the past two months putting his heart back together, pretending he didn't care. He didn't want it broken again.

Too late, he thought grimly. His fragile defences had shattered into a million pieces the moment he

280

saw her smile.

Coming back to the hospital had been a mistake, just as he'd known it would be. When the *Lagerführer* had declared him fit enough to be sent out in one of the work parties, Stefan had prayed he would be assigned to one of the farms that dotted the flat Essex countryside around the camp.

Even when he was sent off to rebuild broken-down houses in Shoreditch, he had no complaints. The work was hard but the sun shone and Stefan enjoyed being outside after the confines of the POW camp.

Then, this morning, the *Lagerführer* had announced he was being taken off the job and sent to the Nightingale instead.

And just to make matters worse, the weather had turned, from bright sunshine to leaden skies, heavy with the promise of snow. The prisoners' uniforms were barely enough to keep out the savage cold as a biting wind blew in across the empty ground.

Stefan found himself thinking about Kitty again. He was surprised she had recognised him. He thought she would have forgotten about him. He had assumed she would be engaged to her soldier by now.

'Bauer! Back to work!' the foreman called out to him, shaking him out of his reverie. 'Lazy bugger, I hope I ain't going to have trouble with you?'

Stefan gave him a mock salute and went off to load up the hod with bricks. It was a joke between them; the foreman knew him well as a workhorse. He could get ten hours of labour out of him with no complaint.

Not like the boy beside him. He was a skinny lad, sixteen years old at the most. He looked scared out of his wits. And by the haphazard way he was loading up the hod, he wasn't used to hard manual labour, either.

Stefan watched him with amusement for a while, dropping single bricks on to the hod in a random fashion, then cautiously testing its weight.

'The foreman will expect you to carry more than that,' he said to him in German. 'Here, let me show you.' He picked his way across the stony ground towards him. 'You lay them on two at a time, you see? Then these two in the opposite direction, until the hod is full.'

The young man watched him, his expression apprehensive.

'You haven't done this before, have you?' Stefan said kindly. The boy shook his head.

'I was planting crops on a farm, but the *Lagerführer* said I must come here.' He jumped at the sound of laughter from the men laying bricks on the other side of the site.

'Don't worry, you'll soon get used to it,' Stefan said, clapping him on the shoulder. He could feel the lad's bones under the rough fabric of his uniform. There wasn't an ounce of flesh on him. 'They're a good bunch on the building sites. They'll make fun of you, but it's all in good fun. The guards are all right, too. They don't mind us having a laugh and a joke, and sometimes they'll even give us a cigarette if they can spare one.'

He looked down at the young man's hands, blue and scabbed with chilblains. 'Don't you have any gloves?'

'*Nein.*'

Stefan sighed, took off his own pair and handed them to him. The boy started to refuse, but Stefan insisted.

'Come,' he said. 'Before the foreman starts shouting again.'

He picked up the hod he had just filled and hefted it on to his shoulder. His back ached and the weakened muscles in his injured leg felt like twisted, burning ropes under his skin as he stumbled over the uneven ground to where the other men were laying bricks. He was aware of the young man struggling behind him, his puny frame buckling under the weight of the hod.

But at least he had heart. He didn't give up all morning, even though he was clearly finding it hard.

At noon, they sat down on upturned buckets to eat their lunch. Stefan sat with the boy, Gunther, and shared a cigarette the guard had given him.

'You see?' he said. 'It isn't so bad, is it?'

'I suppose not,' Gunther agreed cautiously. He looked around. 'What is this place?'

'It is a hospital. Where we're sitting now – it used to be the building where the offices were. And over there–' he pointed. 'That was where the nurses used to live until the Luftwaffe bombed it all.'

Gunther frowned at him, curious. 'How do you know so much about it?'

Stefan opened his mouth, then closed it again. He couldn't even say Kitty's name. 'I was a patient here,' he said briefly. 'One of the nurses told me.'

It was starting to rain as they returned to work. It lashed Stefan's face like a thousand icy knives but he didn't break his pace as he hauled the bricks across the site. The work was tedious, and his back and leg were complaining, but he welcomed the cold and the pain as it helped take his mind off Kitty. He kept his gaze fixed on the churned mud under his boots, never allowing himself to look up at the hospital buildings in case he saw her.

He had delivered a load of bricks and was halfway across the site for another when he heard a scream that made him swing round. The other men had dropped their tools and were running back towards the site.

'Get back to work, all of you!' the foreman shouted, as the guards raised their weapons, all their earlier friendliness forgotten.

Stefan hung back, his eyes narrowed, watching the scene. Then he saw why the men were running. They were clustered around a figure on the ground. It was young Gunther.

He dropped his hod and hurried towards them, pushing his way through the other men to where the boy lay lifeless.

'What happened?' he demanded.

'It – it was an accident,' one of the other men explained. 'He slipped in the mud ... the bricks fell on him...'

Stefan leaned over the boy, slapping his face. It was as white as wax, but for the rivulets of crimson blood running down his temple. 'Gunther? Wake up!'

To his utter relief, the boy's eyes fluttered open. He looked panic-stricken when he saw the ring of faces above him. 'Wh ... what–'

'You dropped a brick on your head, you little fool!' Stefan turned to the other men. 'Stand back, all of you. Give the boy some air.'

The men muttered, but they recognised the authority in his tone and stepped away.

Gunther struggled to sit up, but Stefan pushed him gently back, cradling his head. 'No, don't get up. Rest there for a moment.' He could feel warm stickiness flowing on to his hand.

The foreman pushed his way to his side. 'How is he?' he asked.

'He needs a doctor.'

'He's in the right place for that, at least,' the man said grimly. He conferred with the guards for a moment, then said, 'We'll get someone to take him. But you'll have to go with him,' he added to Stefan.

Panic surged through him. 'Me? Why?'

'You're his friend, ain't you? Besides, you're the only one speaks English and German.'

'He's not my friend. I don't have any friends–' Stefan started to say stubbornly. Then he looked into Gunther's eyes, so terrified and appealing. 'Very well,' he muttered.

'Good.' The foreman straightened up, rubbing his hands together as if he was already washing his hands of the whole matter. 'The guard says there's a ward set aside for POWs. You can take him there.'

Kitty thought she was seeing a ghost when Stefan appeared on the ward.

Nurse Riley had already told them to expect a head injury, so she wasn't surprised when two porters arrived, carrying a stretcher. What did shock her was Stefan following behind, flanked by guards.

Their eyes met, and he looked away sharply.

Nurse Riley stepped in and took charge, asking Stefan questions about what had happened, whether the patient was conscious, whether the bleeding had come from the wound or from his ears. Stefan answered her briefly, his gaze still fixed on the ground.

'Will he be all right?' he asked quietly.

'We'll take him down to theatre so the doctor can dress his wound. Don't worry, from what you say it doesn't sound too serious, but we have to make sure.' She turned to Kitty. 'Could you wash and prepare the patient for surgery–' she started to say, then she glanced at Stefan and changed her mind. 'On second thoughts, I'll do it. You take the *Oberleutnant* to the bathroom and help clean him up.'

Kitty looked at Stefan in dismay. It was the first time she'd noticed his hands were covered in blood.

She took Stefan to the bathroom and waited in silence as he washed the blood from his hands at the basin. She stood by the door, as far away as she could from the basin, but the room still felt stiflingly small.

He had his back turned to her and she allowed her gaze to linger on him, travelling up his tall frame to admire the breadth of his shoulders under his grey prison uniform. It was only when she reached the back of his shorn head that she realised that he was watching her in the mirror.

She dropped her gaze to her shoes, black against the white tiled floor.

'How are you?' she said.

'Good, thank you.' His voice was clipped, as if every word had escaped from between closed lips.

'And your leg?'

He shrugged. 'Still holding me up.'

'You seem to be walking well, at any rate?'

She watched him rubbing the hard green soap over his hands. They were like strangers. Once they could have chatted easily, but now each word seemed to be an effort.

'Do you like it – at the camp?' she asked.

His mouth twisted at the question. 'They treat me well enough.'

He was trying to be polite, but Kitty could see from the tension in his face and body that he didn't want to speak to her. She should stop trying, she thought. Keep what was left of her dignity.

And yet she couldn't. She had a few precious moments left with him, and she had to make the most of them.

'I was surprised to see you here,' she started again. 'Everyone misses you, especially Hans. I don't think he gets on very well with Felix!' She smiled.

He didn't respond. He finished rinsing his hands and reached for the towel. Kitty picked it up and handed it to him, and their hands brushed.

Stefan snatched his hand back as if he'd been burnt. 'I am ready to go now,' he said shortly.

Sister Riley was coming up the passage towards them as they left the bathroom.

'Ah, there you are,' she said. 'I was just coming

to find you. Your friend has gone down to theatre now. Once his wound has been dressed, we'll probably keep him in overnight, just to make sure everything is all right.'

Stefan nodded. *'Danke,* Nurse Riley. I will inform the *Lagerführer.'*

Nurse Riley turned to Kitty. 'Jenkins, perhaps you would escort the *Oberleutnant* out?'

Kitty caught her meaningful look. Nurse Riley obviously thought she was being kind, allowing them to have some more time together. She couldn't have been more wrong.

They walked the length of the ward in silence, both staring straight ahead, keeping as far apart as they could, to where the guards were waiting.

'You can take the prisoner away now,' Kitty said shortly. Then she turned on her heel and walked up the ward, forcing herself not to look back.

Chapter Thirty-Five

Dora had actually started to convince herself that the telegram had been a mistake when the letter finally came from Nick's commanding officer, Colonel Matthews.

It was a nice letter, embarrassed and apologetic. Dora let her eyes skim over it, trying not to take in the details. She didn't want to know how her husband's unit had met surprise enemy resistance in Belgium, or about the heavy shelling that had taken place, or that many men had been killed or captured. Nor did she want to know that Nick's name wasn't on the list of prisoners of war the Germans had sent to Allied command.

It didn't matter to Dora that in the colonel's opinion Nick had died a hero, or that he was a good man, sadly missed by the rest of his unit. Nor did she particularly care about the officer's deep sympathy, or his ardent wish that she should find some comfort in Almighty God during her sad time.

All she cared about was that, in spite of all the colonel's flowery words, her husband would not be coming home.

'I'm so sorry,' Helen said, when Dora showed her the letter. She had gone to her office in the military ward and handed it over without speaking.

'I don't suppose they could have made a mistake?' Dora said. 'I bet it happens all the time, doesn't it? People get lost, forgotten about ... just because he's not on a list it doesn't mean he's–' She stopped, unable to say the word.

'I suppose it's possible,' Helen said gently, but Dora could see from her friend's eyes that she didn't believe it, any more than her mother, or her grandmother, or anyone else in her family believed it.

She stared at the letter, wanting to rip it into a thousand pieces. That wretched piece of paper spelled the end of her last hope.

'You shouldn't be here,' Helen said. 'Why don't you take the rest of the day off? I'll inform Matron–'

'No,' Dora said quickly. 'I don't want her to

know. I couldn't bear it if anyone made a fuss–'

It was bad enough at home, with everyone creeping around her and speaking to her as if she were an invalid. Dora knew they were only trying to be kind, but all she wanted to do was to be left to carry on.

'Does anyone else on the ward know?' Helen asked.

Dora shook her head. 'Only Major Von Mundel. I know what you're thinking,' she added, seeing Helen's face change, 'but he's been very good to me. He cares.'

Helen's mouth pursed with disapproval. Over the past two months, she had been doing her best to overcome her dislike for the POWs, but she still couldn't bring herself to trust Major Von Mundel.

'At least let me change the rota so you can go off duty early,' she said.

'There's no need, honestly. I'd rather keep myself busy–'

'That's an order, Nurse Riley!' Helen cut her off, then smiled. 'Look, I've got this evening off too. Why don't we go out for tea? My treat. We could take Walter and Winnie, too. They'd like that, wouldn't they?'

'I'm sure they would,' Dora agreed. 'They've been asking when their Auntie Helen is coming round to play again.'

'That's settled, then.' Helen sat back in her chair. 'I'll meet you at five and we'll go somewhere nice.'

Just at that moment Clare came breezing in. Her face fell when she saw Dora.

'Oh, I beg your pardon,' she said tightly. 'I didn't realise you were here.'

'I was just going,' Dora said.

'Oh, please don't leave on my account. I'm sure I wouldn't want to break up the party.' Clare passed a piece of paper to Helen. 'The linen order,' she said.

'Thank you.' As Helen signed it, Clare's gaze fell on Dora's letter, still lying on the desk. 'What's this?'

Dora snatched it out of her hands. 'It's mine.' She folded it up and put it back in her pocket, then left before Clare could ask any more questions.

'Was it something I said?' Clare asked, after the door had banged shut.

She smiled archly, but Helen's expression was grave as she looked back at her. 'That letter was from her husband's commanding officer, explaining how he died.'

'Oh!' Clare was taken aback. 'I'm sorry.'

Helen said nothing as she handed her the linen order then returned to her work. Clare stood her ground, staring at the top of Helen's white cap. How dare she dismiss her like that, as if she was a probationer! They were supposed to be best friends.

This was all Dora Riley's doing, she thought darkly. Helen was never as friendly after she had spent time with her.

Helen looked up at her. 'Was that all?'

'For now, yes,' Clare replied, wounded. She walked to the door, then said, 'What time shall we meet this evening? The pictures?' she prompted, when Helen frowned. 'It's Friday night, remember?'

'Oh yes, of course.' Helen's face twisted, and Clare knew with a sinking heart what was coming. 'I'm afraid I'll have to cancel.'

Now it was Clare's turn to frown. 'Are you on duty until nine? I'm sure it said on the rota you finished at five–'

She saw Helen's brows pucker, and wondered if she'd gone too far. But she liked to make a note of Helen's shifts, so she could plan their time together.

'I do,' she said. 'But I've arranged to go out for tea with Dora and her children tonight.'

'But we always go to the pictures on a Friday night!' Clare blurted out.

'I know, but this is important. My friend has just had some bad news, she needs some company. You do understand that, don't you?'

What about me? Clare wanted to shout. She was supposed to be Helen's friend, too. Why didn't her feelings count for anything?

But she could see Helen frowning, and she didn't want to appear selfish, so she smiled and said, 'Of course.'

'You could come to tea with us,' Helen said. She didn't look too enthusiastic about the idea.

'No, thank you.' Clare fought to keep the hurt out of her voice. 'You know what they say. Three's a crowd.'

Helen sighed. 'Don't be like that–'

Clare could see her patience wearing thin, so she said, 'I mean it, you go and have a nice time with your friend.' She emphasised the word. 'She needs you, not me.'

Helen didn't seem to notice her sarcasm, or if

she did, she chose to ignore it. 'We can go to the pictures next week, if you like,' she said.

Don't do me any favours, will you? Clare thought sourly.

She managed to keep her feelings to herself that night as she watched Helen getting ready to go out. She tried not to think about how usually it would have been the two of them getting dressed up and drawing stocking lines up the back of each other's legs with eye pencil.

She was afraid she had already allowed her resentment to creep out too much. She didn't want to put Helen off. So she sat on her bed, making a big show of writing a letter while Helen did her hair in the mirror.

'Are you sure you don't want to come out with us?' Helen asked. She felt guilty, Clare thought with satisfaction.

'No, thank you. I need to finish this letter. My parents have been complaining for weeks that I never write to them.'

Helen smiled. 'It's a good thing you're not going out, in that case.'

'Yes, it is.' Clare kept her own smile carefully fixed in place. 'Have a lovely time, won't you? And remember to give Riley my regards.'

'I will.'

Clare waited tensely until Helen had gone. It was only when the door had closed behind her that she threw her pen in rage. It hit the wall, spattering blue ink down the plasterwork.

After everything she'd done, this was the way Helen treated her! She had supported her through thick and thin, only to be cast aside as soon as

293

Dora Riley came along.

She abandoned the letter she was writing. She had lied to Helen; her parents wouldn't give a damn whether she wrote to them or not. They had forgotten about her the minute she left home to sign up with the QAs. They had four other children to think about. Her older sisters were married with children, and her two younger brothers were in the air force. Clare was the forgotten middle child, thirty years old, unmarried and childless. She could have disappeared and no one would have noticed.

Clare, the one no one wanted. The girl who was doomed to be cast aside.

She tried so hard to make friends. At school, during her hospital training, in the QAs. But somehow all the girls seemed to pal up and leave her out. She didn't understand why, although she had once heard one of the QAs describe her mockingly as being 'like a pathetic puppy, always bounding about, trying to please'.

And then Helen came along. Clare couldn't believe her luck when they were assigned to the same room. Helen was quite the most beautiful, graceful creature Clare had ever met. And she was kind, too. They weren't exactly friends, but at least she didn't treat Clare with the same disdain as the other girls.

Perhaps they would never have become real friends if Clare hadn't found her that night, sobbing in the shower. She had only come home early from the party in the officers' mess because everyone was ignoring her as usual. She was on her way to bed when she heard a sound coming from the bathroom. She had discovered Helen cowering in a cubicle, scalding hot water streaming over her, scrubbing her skin raw with a hard brush.

From that moment, Clare had become Helen's best friend, her protector and her confidante. She took complete charge of the situation, and Helen was happy to allow her to do it. Her confidence was gone, and she needed someone to look after her. For the first time in her life, Clare felt needed and important.

And then Dora Riley had come along and ruined everything.

It was obvious from the start that she and Helen had a special bond. Clare had seen the spark that came into Helen's eyes when she first saw her. Even when the two of them fell out – much to Clare's delight – she could still see the life starting to flow back into her friend. She knew it was only a matter of time before she lost her forever.

And now it had happened.

The worst thing was, Helen had confided in Dora, told her the secret that had bound her and Clare together. Now Dora knew, Clare was no longer special. Helen had already started to spend more time with Dora. It was only a matter of time before Clare was cast aside completely.

And she couldn't say a word against the wretched girl because of her dead husband. Now all Helen seemed to think about was how she could help Dora. She had even begun to rise above her own unhappiness for the sake of her friend.

Clare thought about them, off together without her. True, Helen had invited her, but Clare knew she didn't really want her to come. And Dora certainly wouldn't want her to be there; she had made her dislike of her all too obvious.

Clare had even thought about inventing a dead sweetheart of her own, someone from her past, to try to win back Helen's attention. But she wasn't sure if she could carry off the lie. Dora would see through it, even if Helen didn't. She was as sharp as a tack, that one. And so common, too. How someone as refined as Helen had ever become friends with a vulgar girl like her was a mystery to Clare.

She wished Helen would come to her senses and realise how awful Dora was. Then perhaps she would remember what a loyal friend Clare had been, how she had stood by her, how she had never betrayed her. Clare doubted if Dora would ever be as worthy of her trust as she was...

And then it came to her. She would prove how untrustworthy Dora could be, and then Helen would come crawling back to her.

She screwed up the letter to her parents. They would never bother to read it anyway. Then she pulled out a new sheet of writing paper, rescued her pen, and began to compose a new letter...

Chapter Thirty-Six

'Careful, Bauer,' the foreman called out. 'You'll do yourself an injury if you carry on like that!'

Stefan ignored him as he trudged across the site, the hod of bricks braced on his shoulders. He knew the foreman couldn't believe his luck, finding a worker as willing as him. He toiled tirelessly, from the time they climbed off the lorry just after dawn, until it collected them at dusk to return to camp. No hod was too heavy, no work too back-breaking. He hauled bricks, mixed mortar and cleared rubble, working like a machine and rarely taking a break.

He knew the other prisoners resented him for making them look bad, but he didn't do it to please anyone, least of all their captors.

He did it to forget.

Not that it worked. No matter how exhausted he was when he went to bed, he knew when his head touched the hard, flat pillow he would be immediately haunted by the vision of Kitty Jenkins.

He knew he'd done the right thing. She had a good life ahead of her, and he had no right to get in the way. What could he promise her, apart from an uncertain future? Kitty deserved more than he could ever give her.

Anyway, he kept telling himself, he wasn't the kind of man to need encumbrances in his life. Loving someone brought pain, it made him vulnerable. He was better off alone.

But deep down he knew it was too late for that. He had already fallen in love with Kitty Jenkins, and he was already suffering a world of pain. And he'd hurt Kitty, too. The look of sadness in her eyes when he'd rejected her would stay with him for the rest of his life. He had set out to spare her pain, and instead he'd caused her more.

The best thing he could do now was to stay out of her life, he thought grimly as he hauled another load of bricks across the site. The sooner this building was finished, the sooner he could leave this wretched hospital and never see her again.

'Gunther!' Stefan was mixing mortar when he heard the foreman's shout. He looked up to see the young man stumbling towards them, his expression sheepish, his head swathed in dressing. Mal, Kitty's cocky-looking boyfriend, was with him.

'You lazy devil! It's about time you showed up for work!' The foreman slapped him on his skinny shoulder.

'No work for this one,' Mal said in the gruff accent Stefan found so hard to understand. 'He's got to go back to the camp and rest for a couple of days. We've come down to wait for the lorry.'

Mal left Gunther with the foreman and strolled over to chat to one of the guards a few yards away from where Stefan was working.

Stefan kept his head down, trying not to be seen. But he couldn't help overhearing their conversation as they smoked a cigarette. Mal was telling the guard about a girl he'd met the previous night.

'You should have seen her,' he was saying. 'She was gorgeous. Blonde, blue eyes – and her figure...' He described a shape in the air with his hands. 'I'm telling you, she'd give Betty Grable a run for her money!'

'I thought you were courting that little nurse?' the other guard said. 'What was her name? Kitty something–'

'Oh, her.' Mal was dismissive. 'No, I threw that one over a few weeks ago.'

Stefan stopped, his head cocked to listen.

'Oh, aye? Last I heard, you were planning to get engaged.'

'No, pal, you've got it wrong. You think I'd marry that? She wasn't much of a looker.' Mal paused to take a drag on his cigarette. 'No, I was just messing about with her until something better came along.'

Stefan burned with fury. His hands tightened on the shaft of his spade as if it was Mal's neck.

'Anyway, I'm a free agent now,' Mal went on airily. 'And there are plenty of lonely lasses in London...'

The other guard muttered something Stefan couldn't hear, and Mal laughed out loud. 'Oh aye, pal. And I'll tell you something else – I won't be wasting my time with any more frightened little virgins, either. Give me a girl who likes a good time!'

The lorry rumbled up the drive towards them. Mal stubbed out his cigarette, bade his friend goodbye and called Gunther over. Stefan turned his back as he passed, but Mal didn't spare him a glance as he strode off towards the waiting vehicle.

His friend watched him go. 'He's a bloody liar,' Stefan heard him tell the other guard. 'The way I heard it, he popped the question and she turned him down.'

'Serves him right,' the other guard joined in. 'I've always thought he was a bit too full of himself.'

'Bloody shortarse Scotsman. Anyone would think he was God's gift to women!'

'Bauer! Hurry up with that mortar, or it'll be set by the time you've finished,' the foreman interrupted.

Stefan went back to his work, but his thoughts were in turmoil.

Kitty had turned Mal down.

What did it matter? It made no difference to him. They still couldn't be together. Everything he'd told himself still stood. He could give her nothing, promise her nothing except unhappiness and uncertainty.

And his love.

But that wasn't enough, was it? It wasn't enough to part her from her family, to cause painful rifts with the people she cared about. He couldn't put her in that position, make her choose...

But she had already chosen. She did that when she turned down Mal's proposal.

It was too late for him, anyway. He'd had a chance to tell her how he felt before he left the hospital, and he had been too cowardly to take it. Then fate had brought him back to her, and still he hadn't grasped his chance.

Fate would never be so kind again.

'Poor Gunther,' one of the other men said. 'I wonder if he'll ever be back?'

'They'll probably send him back to the farm. He won't be able to get himself injured there,' another said.

'Knowing Gunther's luck, he'll probably step on a rake!'

'Or get attacked by a bull!'

'He was lucky, anyway,' another man said. 'I wouldn't mind a couple of days in a nice comfortable hospital bed.'

Stefan looked at the spade he was holding, and an idea began to stir in the back of his mind.

Fate might not help him again, but perhaps he could help himself.

As bad luck would have it, Kitty was the only nurse on the ward when Stefan Bauer arrived, his hand wrapped in a filthy rag.

'Managed to slice it open on the edge of a spade, daft beggar!' the guard explained with a grin. 'Could you take a look at it for him, Nurse?'

Kitty couldn't bring herself to look at Stefan as she peeled off the rag and examined his wound.

'It ain't too bad, is it, Nurse? Only I reckon the foreman would have something to say about it if he lost another worker!' the guard grinned.

Kitty forced a smile back. 'I'll clean it and then we'll see. It might need a couple of stitches but I think we should be able to save it.'

'Did you hear that, mate? You'll still be able to mix that mortar.' As she pulled the curtains around them, the guard winked at Kitty and said, 'I might as well nip outside and have a smoke, since you're likely to be here a while.'

'Oh, but–' Kitty started to say, but the guard interrupted her.

'Don't worry, miss, I shouldn't think he'll give you any trouble.'

If only you knew. Kitty held herself rigid as the guard sauntered away, pulling the curtains closed behind him, shutting them both in.

She quickly set about cleaning the wound, working in silence, aware of Stefan watching her every move. She prayed he wouldn't notice how clammy her hands were.

'It will not need stitches, I think.' He broke the

silence. 'It is not a deep cut.'

'No.'

There was a long pause, then he said, 'Your hands are shaking, *Fraülein.*' He sounded amused.

Kitty said nothing as she continued to dab at his hand. He had the coarse skin and calloused palms of a labourer, but his fingers were long and almost delicate, like a musician's.

'Aren't you going to ask me how I did it?' he asked.

'It's none of my business,' she muttered.

'I did it for you.'

That shocked her. She looked up sharply. 'What? You mean, you did this deliberately?'

'It was the only way I could see you again.'

Their eyes met.

'I – I don't understand,' she said, confused. 'The last time we met, you acted as if you barely knew me.'

'I wanted you to forget me.' This time it was Stefan who looked away. 'I knew how you felt, and I didn't want you to waste your love on me.'

'Then why are you here now?'

His broad shoulders lifted in a helpless shrug. 'Because I couldn't stay away.'

Kitty finished cleaning the wound and covered it with gauze, then began to apply the dressing. All the while, she fought to push down the hope that rose in her chest. She had been through too much disappointment to allow herself to trust again.

'So you do – have feelings for me?' she asked, her gaze fixed on the dressing as she wound it carefully around his hand.

He sighed. 'Ah yes, *Fraülein.* Although how I

wish I didn't, for both our sakes.'

Pain jabbed at her. She could feel him backing away again, slipping through her fingers. 'What do you mean?'

'Because there can be no future for us.' His voice was husky. 'How can there be, when I am a prisoner?'

'You won't be a prisoner forever.'

'No. But even if I was a free man, we could never be together. What would your family say? Could you ever tell them about me?'

She looked away. 'I might—'

Stefan gave an impatient snort. 'You are lying to yourself, *Fraülein*. They would never accept me. They would be angry, they would cast you out—'

'I don't care!'

'Yes, you do. You care very much.' He shook his head. 'I can't ask you to do it, to give up your life for me—'

'You're not asking me to do anything. I want to do it.'

'*Nein*—'

'Why not?'

'Then why did you come back?' she snapped, jumping to her feet. 'Why did you come here and raise my hopes, make me think you cared—'

'I do care!'

'You don't! If you really loved me, you wouldn't be talking like this. You wouldn't be telling me why we can't be together—'

She didn't manage to finish her sentence before Stefan had shot to his feet and was kissing her. Kitty was too shocked to react at first as he grabbed her around the waist, lifting her feet off the ground so his mouth could meet hers.

By the time she'd realised what was happening she was back on the floor. He was still holding on to her.

'Can you not see I am afraid?' he whispered. 'I do not know how to love, *Fraülein*. What if I can't?'

Kitty looked up at him. His eyes were dark with raw pain and longing.

'I think you already do,' she said.

Chapter Thirty-Seven

March 1945

There was a wooden train waiting for Dora when she arrived on duty that morning. It sat on the desk in the middle of the ward, three carriages lined up precisely behind it, attached with string. In each carriage sat a tiny doll, one with yellow wool hair, one with black and one with red, all dressed in white.

'They are good, yes?' Dora was admiring the yellow-haired doll when Major Von Mundel came up behind her.

'They're smashing,' Dora agreed.

'Very ingenious, I think, as they have no tools to make them.' Major Von Mundel picked up the red-haired doll. 'This man used a piece of iron from his bed to carve the wood, and sewed their dresses with a needle made from the opener of a tin of sardines. Their dresses were an old *taschen-tuch* – a handkerchief? It makes them look like angels, I think.'

'Very clever, I'm sure. But what are they for?'

'They are for you, Nurse Riley. For your children.' He looked shyly pleased with himself, like a bashful schoolboy. 'And there are many more, if they like them...'

'You don't have to keep giving me presents!'

'I want to.'

Dora looked at the red-haired doll in his hand, and Helen's warning came into her mind. 'Please, Nurse Riley?' He held out the doll to her. 'I would like to think I was helping your children, as I cannot help my own.'

Dora saw his forlorn expression and hated herself for even thinking about what Helen had said.

'Tell you what,' she said. 'Why don't I give these toys to the WVS? They have a shop where they sell things to raise money for our POWs. They'd love these, I'll bet.'

His expression stiffened. 'As you wish.'

'I think it would be a good idea, don't you? Then other children could enjoy them, too.' She silently pleaded with him for understanding.

He looked at her for a moment, then nodded. 'I think it would be a good idea, Nurse Riley,' he agreed. 'And perhaps I could bring more toys and other things that the men have made?'

'I'm sure they'd appreciate it.'

Major Von Mundel considered it. 'It is fitting, I think, that our prisoners of war will be helping yours.'

'I never thought of it like that,' Dora smiled.

'But now you mention it, I suppose it is.'

They were interrupted by Arthur Jenkins, coming into the ward shoving a wheelchair ahead of him.

'You've got a prisoner wants taking down to theatre,' he muttered.

Dora opened her mouth to reply, but Major Von Mundel got in first. 'How dare you address a nurse in that way? Have some respect!' he hissed.

Colour rose in Arthur's face. He stared back at the Major with utter loathing. Dora sensed a fight brewing, and stepped in quickly.

'We have a patient, yes,' she said. 'Come with me.'

She led the way to where the man was waiting to be taken down for his hernia operation.

'Be careful with him,' she warned, as Arthur helped him roughly into the wheelchair.

He ignored her. But as they were making their way down to theatre, Arthur suddenly asked, 'I don't s'pose there's any more word on your husband, is there, Nurse Riley?'

His words stopped Dora in her tracks. Nick's loss was like a broken limb. As long as she didn't test it, she could manage. But as soon as she put any weight on it, the pain shot through her, taking her breath away.

'No,' she said quietly.

'He's definitely gone, then?'

Dora clenched her hands into fists at her sides, bracing herself. A month after the letter arrived, she had given up hoping for a miracle.

'Only some of the lads were talking about him just the other day,' Arthur went on, seemingly oblivious to her pain. 'I didn't know him myself, of course – he'd signed up before I started working here – but Mr Hopkins was telling us what a good fellow he was when he worked here. Salt of the earth, he said. And you know, Mr Hopkins doesn't say that about everyone.'

He was just being nice, Dora told herself. He wasn't to know that every word he said was like a knife blade slashing at her.

'Anyway, the lads were wondering if they should do something in his memory. I mean, you shouldn't forget a man who died for his country, should you?' His gaze met hers. 'What do you think, Nurse Riley?'

Mercifully, they had reached the doors to the theatre block, where Theatre Sister was waiting for them. Dora quickly left the patient with her, and hurried back to the ward.

Arthur didn't mean anything by it, she kept telling herself. But there was something about the keen way he had watched her that made her think he knew exactly the effect his words were having.

As if she needed anyone to remind her how much she missed Nick. He was on her mind every single minute of the day. Her grief would have consumed her, driven her mad if she'd let it. But in order to function, to get through her day without breaking down, she had learned to subdue her thoughts of him. By pushing them down, she could be the person everyone expected her to be, competent and cheerful, a dutiful nurse and a good mother to her children.

But they were still there, lurking beneath the surface, like dark, dense weeds on a pond bed. As

Dora skimmed along, she could feel the tendrils reaching up to her, ready to twine around her and drag her down.

It didn't take much to bring him to her mind. Hearing his name, or a favourite song, or a voice that sounded like his, or seeing a flash of a dark curly head in the middle of a busy street, and she would feel those tendrils grasping at her, pulling her into the murky depths.

Fortunately she was kept busy all day. Several new patients arrived on the ward, and there were charts to be written up, beds to be made, temperatures and pulses to be taken, and endless enemas and aperients and dressings and drips to be done. Arthur went back and forth with the other patients, fetching and carrying. Dora could feel him watching her, but luckily he said no more about Nick.

It wasn't until later that afternoon that she remembered the toys Major Von Mundel had given her that morning.

'I'll take them down to the canteen while I'm on my tea break,' she said to Miss Sloan. 'I'm sure the ladies from the WVS will be able to pass them on.'

'Oh, but they've already gone, my dear,' Miss Sloan said. 'Young Arthur took them just now. I thought you'd told him to do it?'

'No,' Dora frowned. 'No, I didn't.'

Miss Sloan looked crestfallen. 'Oh dear, have I done something wrong?'

Dora shook her head. 'But I think someone else has,' she muttered.

Arthur tossed the wooden engine into the fiery

maw of the stoke hole and smiled as he watched it burn.

He tried to imagine the Nazi who'd made it, labouring away on a piece of scrap wood for hours. What a waste of time, he sneered.

He picked up the next doll. It had bright red hair, like Dora Riley.

Wouldn't she be furious when she found out what he'd done? But by then it would be too late.

He was glad, thinking about how upset she would be. It served her right, the way she kowtowed to the Germans. Especially that arrogant swine Von Mundel. She let him swan around as if he owned the place.

And we all know why, he thought, skimming the red-haired doll into the stoke hole. It crackled as it burned, sending out a shower of bright sparks.

The door opened behind him, and he heard footsteps on the stairs. Then Dora Riley's voice coming out of the darkness.

'Arthur Jenkins? Are you down here?'

Arthur calmly turned back to the fire and tipped the rest of the contents of the box on to the flames. Dora Riley didn't frighten him. Besides, he was ready for her.

'There you are,' Dora approached him. 'Didn't you hear me calling to–' Her gaze fell to the empty box in his hands. 'Where are the toys?'

Arthur didn't reply. He went on staring into the flames of the stoke hole. The way they danced was almost mesmerising, he could watch it all day.

Behind him, Dora let out a cry. She grabbed a pair of tongs and tried to pull the toys out. But all she could save was a single doll, burnt to a blackened stump but for its stupidly smiling face.

Arthur could hardly keep from smiling himself to look at it.

'Who told you to take those toys?' Dora demanded, turning on him.

He composed his features into a picture of innocence. 'I – found the box and thought it was rubbish, Nurse.'

'You're lying. You knew very well what it was. You did this on purpose!'

'Why would I do a thing like that, Nurse?'

Dora stared at him angrily, her face flickering with light from the flames. 'Those toys were meant for the WVS shop, to raise money for our prisoners of war.'

That shook him a little, but he rallied. 'We don't need anything from the Germans!'

'Tell that to the poor POWs who'll go without now!' Dora threw down the tongs. 'You should be ashamed of yourself, Arthur Jenkins!'

'You're the one who should be ashamed of yourself!'

She was walking away from him when he said it. She turned back slowly.

'What's that supposed to mean?'

Arthur looked at her. 'It's a disgrace, that's what it is. And your poor husband not even cold in the ground.'

Dora advanced towards him. The look on her face made Arthur quake, but he stood his ground.

'What are you talking about?'

'You and that German, carrying on. And you needn't deny it, 'cos I saw the two of you at Christmas. He had his arms round you.' He saw the colour drain from Dora Riley's face, her freckles standing out livid against the whiteness of her skin. 'You make me sick,' he said. 'While your husband was fighting and dying for his country, you were kissing and cuddling with a Nazi–'

The slap came out of nowhere, sending his head flying backwards and nearly knocking him off balance. Arthur recovered himself, his hand going to his stinging cheek. His ears were ringing so hard he could barely hear what Dora was saying to him. He could only see her mouth moving and the flash of fury in her eyes.

'–and if I hear you've been spreading filthy lies about me, Arthur Jenkins, you'll get worse than that!' were her final angry words. Then she stormed out.

Arthur heard her footsteps stomping up the basement stairs, and then the door slammed above him, so hard it echoed around the brick walls. He kept his hand pressed to his cheek. Her blow had hurt, but the wound to his pride was worse.

He kicked out angrily at the blackened doll she had dropped at his feet.

Well, she'd done it now, he thought.

Dora stood outside the basement door, gulping in the cold, fresh air. It was a blustery day, and the wind whipped at her cap, nearly tearing it from her head. But Dora barely noticed, she was so consumed with anger and disgust.

How could anyone think that she would ever...

Her mind recoiled from the thought. She couldn't even put it into words, it was so horrible.

And yet Arthur had seen her with his own eyes, caught in a single moment of weakness. It might not have been what he thought it was, but Dora still burned with shame over it. She should never have let her guard down, allowed herself to be vulnerable.

Was Arthur right? Had she betrayed Nick?

She looked around, panicking that she barely recognised the landscape around her. She had spent nearly ten years of her life here, and yet suddenly the hospital buildings all seemed strange to her, as if the world had shifted on its axis.

She hated herself, but she hated Arthur more. How dare he cast a stain on her marriage and sour Nick's memory?

But then, perhaps she only had herself to blame. Hadn't Helen tried to warn her about getting too close to the Germans? But as usual Dora had decided she knew best, and now she was suffering the consequences.

Helen was right, she should never have made friends with Major Von Mundel.

Somehow she managed to gather herself enough to go back to the ward. She kept her head down, not wanting to meet anyone's eye, sure that her guilt was written for everyone to see.

'Nurse Riley?' Dora jumped at the sound of her name. She looked up to see Helen standing at the door to her office. 'Could you come in here, please? There's someone to see you.'

Dora hurried up the ward, her mind racing. 'Someone to see me, Sister? But who—'

The words died in her throat when she saw her brother Alfie sitting in the chair opposite Helen's

312

desk. He looked so out of place in the neat office, with his scruffy brown hair, grubby hands and trousers barely meeting his boots.

Dora saw her brother's look of distress, and suddenly all her other worries vanished.

'Alfie, what is it?' Her heart pushed its way up to her throat, nearly choking her. 'Is it Nanna–?'

He shook his head. 'It's Auntie Lily. She's run away from home!'

Chapter Thirty-Eight

'Hank. My Hank.'

Kitty handed over another handkerchief, helpless to do anything else. Bea had been sobbing at the kitchen table for over an hour. She was like a bottomless pit of grief.

From what Kitty could make out between Bea's hysterics, Lily Doyle had packed her bags and done a flit, taking her little daughter with her. According to the note she'd left, she'd run off with Bea's boyfriend Hank.

'They've fallen in love, so she reckons,' Bea said, her face puffy with crying. 'Turns out they've been seeing each other behind my back all this time. Sneaky little bitch! And after I was so good to her, taking her out because I was worried she was lonely. Letting her play gooseberry with me and Hank, when all the time she was making eyes at him behind my back, planning to steal him away from me!'

313

It takes two, Kitty thought. But she knew better than to say anything. The last thing she wanted was for Bea to start crying again.

'Do you know where they've gone?'

'No, and I don't care, either. They can go to hell for all I care. She'd better not come near me again if she knows what's good for her!'

'It's funny, she always used to be so against him,' Kitty said. 'I didn't think she liked him at all.'

'That just goes to show what an underhand cow she is, doesn't it?' Bea said. 'She was trying to put me off him because she wanted him for herself.'

Kitty watched her blowing her nose noisily. 'Perhaps it's for the best you found out what he was really like now, before it was too late?' she said.

Bea glared at her, her eyes red and swollen. 'It's already too late, can't you tell? My heart's broken and I don't think I'll ever get over it. We were supposed to be going to America to start a new life. Now he'll be taking her instead of me. It's not fair!'

She started howling again. Kitty's mother came into the kitchen.

'Would you like a cup of tea, dear?' she whispered.

Bea sniffed back her tears. 'Haven't you got anything stronger?'

Florrie Jenkins looked anxious. 'Well, no...'

'Then it will have to be tea,' Bea said. 'With plenty of sugar, for the shock.'

'We haven't got any sugar,' Florrie said to Kitty as she helped her make the tea in the scullery. 'Will that be all right?'

'It'll have to be.'

'How long do you think she's going to stay?' her mother asked. 'Only I've got to get your dad's tea on.'

Kitty shot a grim look over her shoulder towards the kitchen. 'Who knows?' Bea looked as if she was there for the duration, slumped over the kitchen table, her sodden handkerchief pressed to her face.

'She makes me sick,' Bea muttered, as Kitty pushed the teacup in front of her. Her mother had taken refuge with her crocheting in the parlour. 'To look at her, you'd think butter wouldn't melt. Always whining about how sad and lonely she was, making us all feel sorry for her. And all the time she was laughing at me, letting me make a fool of myself!'

'I'm sure it wasn't like that–' Kitty started to say, but Bea cut her off.

'Excuse me, allow me to know about my own sister-in-law!' She shook her head. 'I don't know what my poor brother will say when he finds out his wife's run off – ugh, what is this?' She took a sip of her tea and made a face. 'I thought I said plenty of sugar?'

'We haven't got any. You'll have to do without.'

'I suppose it'll have to do,' Bea said gloomily. She took another sip and grimaced. 'I suppose that's something else that will have to change. Hank used to bring all those extra rations round. Now she'll be the one getting all the chocolates and the nylons!'

Kitty looked away. She knew it wasn't supposed to be funny, but she couldn't help smiling at her friend's remark. Only Bea could think of stockings at a time like this.

It was too much to hope that Bea wouldn't notice. 'Well, I'm glad someone's laughing!' she snapped, her voice heavy with sarcasm. 'You could be more sympathetic, Kitty Jenkins. I am broken-hearted, after all.'

'I'm sorry. I am, honestly.' Kitty bit her lip. If Bea started crying again she might never leave.

'Anyway, she'll get what's coming to her,' Bea said, crumpling her handkerchief into a ball in her fist. 'I'm going to write to Peter and tell him all about it. You wait till he hears what she's been doing!'

'Are you sure that's a good idea?' Kitty said. 'How do you think he's going to feel, getting a letter like that? Especially when he's so far away.'

'Yes, well, he's got to know sometime, hasn't he?'

Bea looked so self-righteous, Kitty felt like reminding her who it was who'd led Lily astray in the first place. But once again, she held her tongue.

'Anyway, I've got to do something,' Bea said. 'They can't just be allowed to treat me like this and get away with it. I know,' she went on, her face brightening. 'I'll pretend I'm pregnant. That'll scare him!'

'But you don't know where he is.'

Bea's face fell. 'You're right,' she mumbled, downcast. 'I don't know what I can do, in that case.'

She looked so defeated, Kitty's heart went out to her. 'You're better off just forgetting all about him,' she said.

Bea turned on her. 'That's easy for you to say.

You've never been in love.' Then, before Kitty could reply, she went on, 'But you're right, I shouldn't stay in moping. I'm a free agent now, I might as well go out and enjoy myself.' She grinned at Kitty. 'What do you say? We'll get dolled up, put on our glad rags and go out on the town. You never know, we might meet a couple of nice boys.'

'I can't do that,' Kitty said.

Bea frowned. 'Why not?'

'You know why,' Kitty lowered her voice. 'I already have a sweetheart.'

'Who?' Bea looked puzzled for a moment, then her face cleared. 'Oh, you mean the German?'

'Shh!' Kitty shot a wary look towards the kitchen door.

'Keep your voice down. I don't want Mum to hear.'

'Yes, but that's not real, is it?' Bea was dismissive.

Kitty bristled. 'I don't know what you mean.'

'I mean it's not as if he's really your sweetheart. He can't take you dancing or anything, can he? You never even see him.'

'Yes, I do. I see him every morning when I go to work, and every evening when I head home. And sometimes, if we're lucky, we can pass letters to each other.'

She lived for Stefan's letters. He might have found it hard to speak about his feelings for her, but his love flowed through his words on paper.

'So you wave to each other and pass notes? How daring!' Bea laughed scornfully.

Kitty felt the heat rising in her face. 'It might not seem like much to you, but Stefan could get

317

locked up or even shot if we were found out,' she defended herself. 'And when the war's over, we'll be together properly,' she added.

Bea looked pitying. 'Don't be daft. Once the war's over he'll go home and forget all about you.'

'No, he won't!'

'Well, he's hardly going to stay here, is he?'

Kitty lifted her chin. 'Then I'll go with him. What?' she said, as Bea laughed. 'What's wrong with following my heart? It wasn't such a daft idea when you thought you were going to America with Hank–'

She saw her friend's face crumple and shut up abruptly. 'I'm sorry, Bea,' she started to say. 'I didn't mean–'

'It's all right.' Bea was tight-lipped, the picture of injured dignity. 'It's time I was going home, anyway.'

'Stay, please,' Kitty begged. 'Have some tea with us. I'm sure Mum wouldn't mind–'

'I'd rather be on my own, thank you.' Bea gathered up her coat and hat. As she reached the door, she turned, her lips pursing. 'You might think you're very clever, Kitty Jenkins, but let me tell you this. Men are all the same, wherever they come from. And sooner or later this Stefan of yours is going to break your heart, just like Hank broke mine!'

The more she thought about it, the more Bea was convinced she was right. Kitty might fancy she was in love with this Stefan, but Bea knew better. She could see her friend was riding for a very painful fall.

She pondered the matter as she walked home. Poor Kitty, she had always been so unlucky in love. First her fiancé Alex had jilted her, then Mal had turned out to be a bad lot.

And now Stefan was going to let her down, too.

She crossed Victoria Park, her coat collar turned up against the blustery spring weather. She barely recognised the place where she had played as a child. It was now transformed into a patchwork of allotments, with a battery of anti-aircraft guns where the rose garden had once stood.

In fact she scarcely recognised much of Bethnal Green these days. So many of the streets she had known had been flattened in the Blitz, its residents moved on. An air of sadness and loss hung like a mist over the streets that had once been vibrant with market stalls and costermongers, and bicycle vendors selling their wares.

Bea wouldn't have been sad to leave it. Of course she wouldn't have wanted to leave her family, but she had outgrown the East End and she'd been ready to move on to her big adventure in America, as a GI bride.

But that wouldn't happen now. Despair stabbed her like a knife plunging in to her heart.

It wouldn't happen to Kitty Jenkins, either. Bea could see it coming a mile off, but Kitty was so naive and so besotted she couldn't see further than the end of her nose. She was convinced that somehow a miracle was going to happen, and that she and Stefan were going to be together forever, that he was going to whisk her off to his country.

And of course, nothing Bea could say would convince her otherwise.

But what must it be like, she wondered, to have a man so in love with you he would be prepared to be shot for your sake? A man who would injure himself just to be able to spend a few minutes with you?

Bea pushed the thought angrily from her mind. She wasn't jealous, and she wasn't trying to hurt her friend, either. She only wanted Kitty to be realistic, to avoid the heartache that she was suffering.

Stefan was going to hurt her, Bea was sure of it. Her friend had already fallen for him, she could see it in the way Kitty's face lit up whenever she talked about him. And the longer it went on, the deeper she fell, and the more it would hurt when it finally ended.

Devoted or not, Kitty was wasting her time with Stefan, Bea decided. And while she was with him, she would never find anyone more suitable. She needed to be saved from herself.

And as her best friend, Bea had to be the one to help her.

Chapter Thirty-Nine

It was the end of another hard day's labour. The men had downed tools and were gathering in the warm spring sunshine of the late afternoon, waiting for the lorry to arrive to take them back to camp.

Stefan paused to wipe the perspiration off his brow with his sleeve. He could smell the sour odour of sweat coming off the coarse fabric of his uniform. He would be glad when today was finally over. Every muscle in his body was groaning in protest. His leg, though getting stronger, had nearly failed him a couple of times, buckling under the weight of the heavy bricks he carried.

He was desperate for a cigarette.

He squinted towards the hospital building. He knew Kitty had already gone home for the evening, but habit still made him look for her.

That was when he saw the two men coming towards them. He recognised Mal's stocky form in his green uniform, but there was someone else with him. A tall, skinny figure in a brown coat–

Arthur Jenkins.

One of the guards stood a few yards away, smoking a cigarette. Stefan felt his hackles rise, every sense on alert, as Mal approached the man and spoke to him.

'Hey, *Oberleutnant!* We will play cards tonight, yes?' one of the other prisoners called over to him, but all Stefan's attention was fixed on the conversation between Mal and the guard.

Something was happening. He didn't like it.

He saw the guard glance his way, frowning. Arthur, meanwhile, kept his gaze fixed on the ground, kicking at a loose stone with the toe of his boot, his hands thrust deep in his pockets.

The lorry arrived, rumbling into the yard. The men automatically started to move towards it in a huddle, like sheep, herded by the other guard.

'Come on, then, let's get going. You too, Bauer.'

Stefan looked back at Mal. Their eyes met, and he saw the utter loathing written on the other man's face.

He started to move towards the lorry, but the other guard called him back.

'Just a minute, Bauer.'

The first guard was beckoning him over.

'What's going on?' The guard near the lorry looked wary. 'Chalky–'

'Just got a bit of business needs sorting out.' The guard beckoned him again. 'There's someone here wants a word with you.'

Stefan stood his ground. He knew what was coming, but he wasn't going to make it easy for them.

'They can come to me,' he said. He tried to tense his muscles, to prepare himself.

'Get over here, Bauer. That's an order!' the guard barked.

'No, it's all right.' Mal put his hand up. 'We can chat to him over there, if that's what he wants. Eh, Arthur, lad?'

He was smiling as he strolled over, his tone friendly.

Disarmed, Stefan lowered his guard, just for a second–

Mal's fist flashed out without warning and hit him square in the face. Stefan heard the sickening crunch of his nose before he felt it. He staggered backwards, but managed to stay on his feet.

'That's for messing about with my girl,' Mal growled.

Behind him, Stefan could hear shouting behind him from the other men in the lorry, calling out in protest, but he didn't turn round.

He put his hand up briefly to his face. Sticky

blood flowed over his fingers. Out of the corner of his eye, he saw Arthur Jenkins turn pale.

'Your girl?' he said. 'That's not what I heard.'

'You heard wrong then, didn't you?'

Stefan took a step towards him. 'I heard about what happened that night in the alleyway, too,' he grated. 'You're lucky I don't kill you.'

'Alleyway?' Arthur echoed nervously. 'What alleyway?'

'You mean he hasn't told you?' Stefan mocked.

'It's nothing,' Mal dismissed. 'He's lying, can't you tell?'

'You're the liar, my friend. And a coward, too. You think you'd have the nerve to face me if it was just the two of us here?'

Mal lashed out and punched him again, a low blow that caught him in the stomach and knocked the breath out of him. Stefan's treacherous legs buckled and he sank to his knees.

He looked over to where the guard stood with his back to them, staring out across the horizon, a cigarette clamped in his mouth.

Mal turned to Arthur. 'Go on,' he said. 'It's your turn.'

Arthur hung back, chewing his lip. He looked like a lanky, overgrown child.

'Go on!' Mal gave him a shove. 'This is what you wanted, isn't it? Revenge? This was all your idea, remember?'

Stefan looked up as Arthur's shadow fell over him.

'I am sorry,' he tried to speak through swollen, bloody lips. 'I know you are angry, and I do not blame you. But I love her. We never meant to hurt anyone, we just want to be together—'

'Shut up!' Arthur's boot lashed out and caught him hard in the side of his head. 'Shut up, you Nazi scum!'

'That's it,' Mal hissed. 'This is your chance. Do it for Kitty. Do it for your brother—'

Suddenly all hell was unleashed. Stefan curled into a ball and tried to protect himself as Arthur went berserk, kicking him again and again. His head, his back, his arms and legs – the blows came thick and fast.

Somewhere behind him, the other prisoners were roaring, trying to break out of the lorry. Then Stefan heard the guard shouting, 'That's enough, you two! We'll have the bloody MPs after us for this! Get out of here, and take that sodding maniac with you!'

The sound of running footsteps receded into the distance. But still Stefan didn't move. He was in so much pain, he was afraid to uncurl himself in case his body opened up and his guts spilled out.

'Well, this is a ruddy mess,' one of the guards said.

'I wasn't to know, was I?' the other defended himself. 'He just asked for a favour, that's all. A couple of minutes with him, for messing with his girl.'

Stefan squinted up through a blur of blood at their worried faces, staring down at him.

'What shall we do now?' one of them asked.

'We'll say there was a fight—'

'And they'll believe that, will they? When no one else has a scratch on them?'

'Then we'll just have to think of something

324

else!' the guard said, exasperated. 'Come on, let's get him to the hospital before he croaks on us.'

They hauled him roughly to his feet, supporting him on either side. Stefan tried to stand up but his feet scrabbled uselessly underneath him, trying to find solid ground.

'I'm sorry, mate,' the guard whispered to him. 'It was nothing personal. I was just doing a favour for a friend. You do understand that, don't you?' His face swam into view, his expression anxious. 'You won't say anything, will you, pal?'

Oberleutnant Bauer was in a terrible state, but no one seemed to be able to explain why.

It was a fight, so the guards said.

'And where is the other man?' Major Von Mundel asked, looking around him. 'Surely you do not expect me to believe that the *Oberleutnant* did not hit back?'

The guards said nothing. They stood like a pair of schoolboys who'd been caught out in a prank, shuffling their feet and not meeting his eye. It was all Von Mundel could do not to lash out and strike them down himself.

'It was a fight,' one of them insisted again.

'But not a fair one, I think.' He fought to contain his rage. 'What happened? Did you tie his hands behind his back and use him as a punchbag? Is that what you call a fight?'

The guards looked at each other, shamefaced.

'You have not heard the last of this,' he hissed. 'I will report both of you for negligence at the very least!'

Not that Stefan Bauer was any more forthcom-

325

ing. He maintained a stiff silence, his swollen, bloodied lips pressed together despite Von Mundel's best efforts to get him to speak.

'Who did this to you? Don't you want them punished?' he railed at him in frustration. But Stefan merely stared straight ahead of him, his eyes barely visible amid the puffed, bruised flesh.

'It is a disgrace,' Von Mundel muttered to Nurse Riley as she cleaned Stefan up. 'The man is lucky to be alive, after what they did to him.'

'The doctor says there are no broken bones,' Nurse Riley replied briskly. 'They're mainly cuts and bruises.'

'How can you tell? He will need to be kept in for observation, to be sure there are no internal injuries–'

'No!' Finally Stefan spoke up, the word torn from deep in his throat.

'Now, don't upset yourself,' Dora hurried to reassure him. 'Dr Abbott will decide what's to be done with you when he does his rounds later.' She sent Von Mundel an unfriendly glance over her shoulder. 'Perhaps you could leave us alone?' she said.

Von Mundel stiffened. 'But I need to be here!'

'Why? The *Oberleutnant* speaks perfect English, so we don't need you to translate. I'm sure you could be more useful elsewhere.'

Major Von Mundel stared at her, stung. Her face was bland and smiling, but he was being dismissed and they both knew it.

'Very well,' he said stiffly.

He retreated to the other end of the ward and watched her, dabbing at the man's wounds with antiseptic swabs. She had been in an odd mood all day. There had been no friendly greeting that morning, and if he didn't know better he would think she was trying to avoid him.

He saw her talking to Stefan Bauer, their heads close together, and he knew the soldier would be confiding in her. Nurse Riley had a way of getting people to open up and talk to her.

He waited for her by the sluice, pouncing on her as she returned from dressing Stefan's wounds.

'Well?' he said. 'What did he say to you?'

She frowned up at him. 'I think that's between me and my patient, don't you?'

'Did he tell you who beat him?'

'No, he didn't.'

She was lying, he could tell. He knew her well enough to read her face by now. But there was something about the way she looked at him, the expression in her green eyes, that stopped him asking any more.

There was a reason for her silence, he thought. He was disappointed that she didn't trust him enough to share it.

'Very well,' he said stiffly. 'Then it will have to remain a mystery.'

'Yes, it will. Was that all you wanted?'

There it was again, that bland smile. Had he done something to offend her?

He wished he could ask her what it was, but all he did was nod and say, 'Yes. For now.' Then, as she walked away, he called after her, 'Did they like the toys?'

He saw her freeze, her back still turned to him. 'I beg your pardon?'

327

'The WVS? I wondered if they liked the toys? I was speaking to the men at the camp and they were very pleased that their efforts might help British prisoners–'

Dora half turned to face him and he saw the blush burning in her face. 'I'm afraid they were destroyed,' she mumbled.

'Destroyed? How?'

'One of the porters found them and took them down to the stoke hole by mistake.'

There it was again, that hitch in her voice that told him she was lying.

'It was no accident, was it, Nurse Riley?'

Dora turned to face him. 'No,' she said quietly.

Once again, he read her face. Those downcast eyes, the set of her mouth – she was upset, more than she should be over a few toys.

'There is something else,' he said.

She glanced up at him, and he caught the quick flash of dismay. 'No,' she muttered.

'Yes, there is. You are lying, just as you were about not knowing who attacked the *Oberleutnant.* What is it, Nurse Riley?'

She was silent for a long time. Then she said, 'There's been talk...'

'Talk? What kind of talk?'

Dora couldn't meet his eye. 'About you and me.'

He almost laughed. 'But that is absurd!'

'I know, but someone saw us – at Christmas...'

She was blushing furiously, and he could feel his own colour rising. 'I see,' he said gravely. 'And who is this person spreading these rumours?'

'It doesn't matter.'

'Is it the *Oberschwester?* I know she disapproves

328

of me–'

'No, it isn't. Please,' Dora begged him, 'don't say any more. It's over. I spoke to him, and–'

'Him?' Von Mundel cut her off. 'So it is a man? Who is it, Nurse Riley? I want to know. I have a right to know if someone is speaking ill of me.'

Dora lowered her gaze. 'Arthur Jenkins,' she mumbled.

'Who?' It took Von Mundel a moment to place the name. 'You mean the porter?' He frowned. He was aware of the boy skulking sullenly around the ward from time to time, but other than that he had never paid him much notice before.

And then another thought struck him. 'Was he the one who burned the toys?'

Dora nodded. 'But I've dealt with it,' she said hastily. 'Honestly, I've talked to him and I've warned him to stop.'

'But that is not good enough!' Von Mundel could feel an angry pulse beating in his temple. 'He should not be allowed to get away with this. I will deal with him–'

'And then what will happen?' Dora said. 'You're a prisoner, Major. If you so much as raise your voice to Arthur Jenkins you're the one who'll end up getting punished.'

Von Mundel stared at her in frustration. She was right. He was just like poor Stefan Bauer, unable to fight back.

'Please,' Dora begged. 'I just want to forget all about it, let it die down. Will you do that?'

He looked at her imploring face and let out a sigh. 'Very well,' he said. 'If that's what you want, Nurse Riley.'

He only hoped she wasn't as good at reading his expression as he was at reading hers.

The pain medication Dr Abbott prescribed was enough to knock out an elephant, but not Stefan Bauer. It took all Dora's efforts to stop him getting out of bed. When she turned her back on him to attend to another patient, he was half-dressed and ready to leave by the time she had finished.

'Why do I have to stay when I am perfectly well?' he grumbled as Dora ushered him back into bed.

She looked at him, his teeth gritted, perspiration standing out on his brow. He might be trying to pretend he wasn't in pain, but the sick, greyish pallor of his skin told her otherwise.

'You don't look perfectly well to me,' she said. 'Besides, I've already told you. The doctor wants to keep an eye on you for the next couple of days, just to make sure there's no internal damage we don't know about.' She pulled the covers up around him. 'Now, please stay in bed. I have enough to do without chasing you round the ward all evening.'

Stefan folded his arms across his face, his expression mutinous. Dora sighed. 'This is all because of Nurse Jenkins, isn't it?'

He looked up at her sharply. 'She told you?'

'I guessed a long time ago.' Dora smiled. 'I know you don't want to worry her, but believe me, she's seen you in a worse state than this.'

'This is different,' he muttered. 'I don't want her to know—'

'—You don't want her to know what a cowardly little swine her brother is?' Dora finished for him.

Stefan's stubbled chin lifted. 'I cannot blame him,' he said. 'He was only trying to protect his sister. I would have done the same to defend my family.'

Would you? Dora thought. She doubted it. If Stefan had a problem with someone she had a feeling he would face them man to man, not kick them when they were defenceless.

But that was Arthur Jenkins all over. A nasty little coward.

Stefan, on the other hand, reminded her of her Nick. She smiled. 'You sound like a true East End boy.'

His battered face was wistful. 'If only that was true, Nurse Riley. Then perhaps we would not be in this mess.'

Chapter Forty

Kitty was shocked to see Stefan on the ward when she reported for duty early the following morning. Nurse Riley warned her he was in a bad way before she saw him.

'The swelling has gone down, but he still has some nasty cuts and bruises,' she said. 'Dr Abbott has kept him in for observation, but so far there's no sign of permanent damage.'

But nothing could have prepared Kitty for the sight of Stefan lying there, his face half swaddled in dressings, blackish purple bruises blossoming around his eyes.

A lump rose in her throat. 'What happened to you?' she whispered.

He turned his head to look at her. 'Your brother knows about us.'

Kitty reeled. 'Arthur did this?'

'And your friend Mal.'

Kitty looked towards the double doors. Luckily for Mal, he wasn't on duty. Arthur had taken the day off too, complaining of a stomach ache. Now she understood why.

'I'll kill them,' she muttered.

'Don't you think there's been enough of that?' Stefan reached for her hand. 'It's you I'm worried about. Your brother will tell your father, I think.'

'I don't care,' Kitty said. 'He had to know sometime.'

'Yes, but not like this.' Stefan paused. 'Will he punish you?'

'I don't know.' An image of her father that morning, flying into another of his pointless rages over a burnt piece of toast, and her mother quietly weeping in the scullery, came into her mind.

Stefan seemed to read her thoughts. 'It would have been better if you and I had never met,' he said grimly.

'How can you say that?'

'Because then you might have married a nice English boy, and your family would have been happy.'

'But I wouldn't have been happy.'

He tried to smile, then flinched with pain. 'And are you happy now?'

'Yes,' she replied, without hesitation. And it was true. She didn't know why, she certainly had no right to be. All the simple things that other couples took for granted were forbidden to her. She didn't know if she would ever be able to walk down the street with him, much less go dancing or even hold hands.

Perhaps they wouldn't even have a future. Perhaps their romance was doomed from the start.

But all she knew was that she was happy just knowing that he loved her now, with all his heart. And she loved him.

And she would gladly do it all over again.

His hand found hers, their fingers touching on top of the bedcovers. 'I am afraid for you, *liebling*. I only wish I could be there with you when you talk to your father. I feel so useless–' He sighed with frustration.

'I don't think you being there would help at all.' Kitty saw his worried frown and smiled. 'It'll be all right,' she said. 'I'll talk to him tonight. I'm sure it won't be that bad. I mean, what's the worst he can do?'

Poor Kitty, Dora thought as she watched them from the other end of the ward. She had really set herself up for trouble when she fell in love with Stefan Bauer.

Kitty's wretched brother had a lot to answer for, one way or another. Dora hadn't been surprised when she'd found out Arthur had decided not to show his face today. It was too much to hope that his guilty conscience was troubling him. Fools like Arthur Jenkins were so convinced they were right, they could never see any way but their own.

She saw Kitty's hand brush against Stefan's,

and turned away. It was just as well Helen didn't come on duty until eight. She would never have tolerated such behaviour.

After helping Kitty and Miss Sloan with clearing away the breakfast dishes, making beds and dealing with bedpans, one of Dora's first jobs that morning was to prepare one of the new patients for surgery.

'Right then,' she said brightly, pushing aside the curtains. 'Let's get you all spruced up ready for – oh!' She started at the sight of Major Von Mundel at the man's bedside. 'I'm sorry. I didn't know you were here.'

He shot to his feet. 'Pardon me, Nurse Riley. I was explaining to *Geimeiner* Hassel what his operation involved.'

'Oh well, you carry on.'

'*Nein*, I have finished now. I will leave you to your work.' He nodded briefly to the young man then hurried off, closing the curtains behind him. It was only when he'd gone that Dora realised they hadn't looked each other in the eye once.

It was so sad, she thought. Once they might have smiled, exchanged some pleasantries, but now there was nothing but awkwardness between them. She had lost a good friend in Major Von Mundel.

Another reason to thank Arthur Jenkins, she thought bitterly.

By the time Dora had finished preparing the patient, Helen had come on duty.

All the nurses immediately stopped what they were doing and stood to attention, but Helen swept past without looking at any of them. Dora

334

caught her friend's tight-lipped expression and was instantly wary.

Something had happened, she was sure of it.

Helen wore the same grim look as they gathered around the ward table for morning prayers. She stared down at her hands as Dora passed on the night nurse's report, then did her rounds and handed out the work lists with barely a word.

'Someone's in a good mood!' Miss Sloan observed as they dispersed to get on with their duties.

'It's going to be a bad day for us,' Kitty agreed.

But Dora was more concerned about her friend. Helen looked close to tears throughout the morning as she accompanied first Dr Abbott and then Matron on their rounds. Every time Dora tried to speak to her, she was met with a blank stare and a cold, terse reply.

By lunchtime, she could stand it no longer. Just before she went on her break, Dora knocked on the door to Helen's office.

'Come in.'

Helen looked up, her smile fading when she saw Dora standing before her. 'Yes?' she said.

All morning, Dora had been mentally rehearsing ways she could approach Helen. But when she opened her mouth, all she could blurt out was, 'Have I done something wrong?'

Helen put down her pen and glared at her. 'You have to ask me that question?'

Dora was taken aback. 'I don't know what you're talking about–'

'Oh, I think you do!'

A picture of Major Von Mundel flashed into

335

Dora's mind. Helen must have heard the rumours that Arthur Jenkins had been spreading, she thought.

'I had a letter this morning,' Helen said, tight-lipped. 'From David.'

'Oh.' Relief flooded through Dora, followed by confusion. 'But what's that got to do with me?'

Helen gave a mirthless laugh. 'Nothing. But that didn't stop you poking your nose in, did it? And after everything I said to you–'

Dora frowned. 'You're not making sense.'

'He knows, Dora. He knows everything – about what happened.'

'But how?'

Helen sighed. 'Don't play the innocent with me. We both know you wrote to him.'

'Me?' Dora echoed in disbelief. 'But I didn't–'

'I don't want to hear it!' Helen waved her hand, dismissing her. 'I don't want to hear your excuses. For God's sake, why couldn't you just mind your own business? I told you I didn't want him to know, and yet you took it upon yourself to write to him. Why, Dora? Why would you do that to me?'

'Now just a minute–' Dora gathered herself. 'I didn't write to David.'

'But you signed it!'

'I'm telling you, it wasn't me.'

'Then who was it?'

'I don't know, do I? But anyone could put my name on a letter.'

'But you and Clare are the only ones who know.'

'Then perhaps you should ask her,' Dora said.

Helen stared at her in disbelief. 'Are you suggesting Clare wrote a letter to David, pretending it was from you?'

'Why not? I reckon it's just the sort of sneaky thing she'd do.'

'Sneaky! That's rich, coming from you. Clare's kept my secret for months. Why would she suddenly take it into her head to write to David after all this time?'

'As I said, you'd better ask her that,' Dora said. 'All I know is I didn't write that letter. I made you a promise and I would never break my word. You do believe me, don't you?'

The long look Helen gave her spoke volumes. 'I don't know what to think any more,' she murmured.

Dora stiffened. 'Then we ain't got anything more to say to each other,' she said. 'I may be a lot of things, Helen, but I ain't a liar. And I keep secrets, too.'

She turned to leave. As she reached the door, she heard Helen say her name, but she was too proud to look back.

Chapter Forty-One

Kitty didn't know what to expect when she got home that evening.

Her heart was racing in her chest as she let herself in the back door. Her mother was at the stove, making cocoa. When she looked up, Kitty could see she'd been crying.

Florrie Jenkins turned off the gas and turned to

Kitty, wiping her hands on her pinny.

'Oh Kitty love,' she whispered. 'What have you done?'

Before Kitty could reply, her father's voice rose from the parlour. 'Is that her?'

Kitty looked at her mother's fearful face. 'Yes, Dad.'

'Come in here, girl.'

Fear dried Kitty's throat, but she managed a smile for her mother.

'Here goes,' she whispered. 'Wish me luck, won't you?'

Her mother put her hand on her arm. 'Try not to upset him, won't you?' she begged.

'I think it's a bit late for that, don't you, Mum?'

Her father was sitting in his favourite moquette armchair. His face was impassive but the restless tapping of his fingers on the arm of the chair gave away his agitation. Kitty looked down at his hand and realised that he had almost worn away the fabric over the years.

Arthur sat in the armchair opposite, wearing the same stern, self-righteous expression as his father.

Kitty turned to her brother in disgust. 'I'm surprised you've got the nerve to show your face, after what you did.'

Arthur turned red. 'I only did what was right,' he muttered. 'Which is more than I can say for you–'

'Be quiet, Arthur,' her father ordered. 'Kitty, sit down.' He nodded towards the hard wooden chairs around the table.

She lifted her chin, determined not to be intimidated. 'I'd rather stand, if you don't mind–'

'I said sit down!' His voice rose.

338

'Do as he says, love. Please?' She hadn't realised her mother had crept into the room behind her. Kitty took one look at her imploring face and pulled out a chair.

Her father paused for a moment. He stared down at his fingers tapping on the arm of the chair and Kitty could see him trying to compose himself.

Finally, he said, 'So what's all this our Arthur's been telling us about you carrying on with some German?'

Kitty looked from her mother's anxious face to Arthur's sullen expression. Finally, she allowed herself to look at her father.

She took a deep, steadying breath. 'It's true,' she said.

'You see?' Arthur piped up. 'I told you, didn't I?'

'I told you to be quiet, Arthur!' Horace Jenkins growled, his gaze fixed on Kitty. His face was unreadable.

'It's not what you think,' she started to explain. 'Stefan isn't–'

Her father held up his hand, silencing her. 'I don't want to hear it,' he said. 'I won't have his name spoken in this house.'

'How could you?' her mother whispered. 'A German–'

'Do you think I wanted it to happen?' Kitty said. 'He didn't want it either, but we couldn't help it. We just fell in love–' She saw her father flinch. 'I know this is difficult for you, but if you could just meet him, you'd know he isn't like–'

'I don't want to meet him!' Her father turned on her, coldly furious. 'You think I'd have a German

339

in this house, after what happened to Raymond?'

'Stefan didn't kill Raymond–'

'I told you, I don't want to hear his name! I don't care what he's like, either.' He shook his head. 'I can't understand you, Kitty. You know what the Germans did to us...' His voice cracked, betraying his pain. 'They destroyed this family.'

'And we destroyed his,' Kitty said. 'His brother was killed, shot dead by Allied troops. Our boys, Dad–'

'They deserved it,' Arthur said.

'They were surrendering!' Kitty shot back. She turned to her father. 'They're no different from us, Dad. They have homes, and families. They are good and bad, just like we are–'

'Enough of this!' Her father slammed his hand down on the arm of his chair, startling her into silence. 'I won't hear any more.' He rose from his chair. 'You're to have nothing more to do with him, Kitty. And that's my final word.'

'No!'

'I'll write to the camp, have him moved some-where else. Somewhere far away–'

'You can't do that. He'll be in trouble if they find out.'

'Serves him right for taking advantage of Eng-lish girls, doesn't it?'

'He didn't take advantage of me. I love him.'

She saw her father jump from his chair and lunge at her, his face livid. But the ringing slap still caught her by surprise.

'How dare you?' he hissed. 'How dare you speak like that in this house! I won't have it, d'you hear me? I won't have my daughter talking like a slut!'

Kitty put her hand up to her stinging cheek. 'A slut? Is that what you think I am?' Her father looked away, his face rigid. 'I s'pose you'd rather I was like Bea Doyle, running after GIs? I s'pose you'd rather I went dancing up West, and getting up to all sorts for a pair of nylons. It wouldn't matter what I did, would it, as long as they were on our side! But to fall in love with one man, a good, decent man, whose only crime is to be born in the wrong country – well, that makes me a whore!'

Her father swung round to face her, his eyes bulging with fury. Kitty flinched back, but refused to be cowed.

'Go on, slap me again if it makes you feel better,' she taunted him. 'You can hit me all you like but it won't change the way I feel. I love Stefan, and I want to be with him.'

'Not while you're under my roof, you won't.'

Kitty stared at him, shocked. 'Are you turning me out of the house?'

'If that's what it takes to bring you to your senses.'

Kitty stared at him. 'All right,' she said. 'If that's what you want, I'll move out.'

'No!' Her mother came to life. 'We don't want you to go, do we, Father? Tell her she mustn't go.'

Horace Jenkins folded his arms across his chest. 'She's over twenty-one, she can do as she likes.'

'Horace!'

'She's made her choice, Florrie.'

'I'll go and pack my things,' Kitty said quietly.

She was still reeling later as she emptied her chest of drawers on to the bed. She knew her father would be angry, but she'd never imagined

341

he would put her out on the street.

The door opened, and her heart leapt, thinking it might be her father. But it was only Arthur.

'Dad told me to fetch this for you–' He dumped a battered old suitcase on the bed.

'Thank you.'

Arthur hesitated for a moment, and Kitty could tell he was trying to work out what to say to her. But instead he ducked his head and left the room, banging the door behind him.

Kitty stared at the suitcase, tears filling her eyes. She hadn't seen it since she was a child, and her dad had taken them all for a week in Margate. She remembered her excitement as he hauled the suitcase on to the train, chiding her mother for packing so much.

'Did you have to bring the kitchen sink, woman?' he'd said. But it was a good-natured complaint, because that was what her father was like before his anger and bitterness consumed him. And her mother had just laughed, because that was what she did before her fear and misery consumed her. And Kitty had sat with her brothers, craning their necks, each of them competing to see who could be the first to see the sea...

She dashed away a tear at the sound of the soft knock on the door. Her mother crept into the room, and Kitty could see she'd been crying too.

'Don't go, Kitty,' she pleaded.

'What choice have I got?'

'But this is your home.'

'Not any more. He's made that very clear.' She glanced at the door.

'You know what your father's like. But he cares

for you, love. He just finds it hard to show it, that's all.'

Kitty looked at her mother. 'When are you going to stop making excuses for him, Mum? He's a bully.'

Florrie Jenkins winced. 'He loves you,' she insisted. 'You're his little girl. He just finds it very difficult to think that you'd–' She looked up at Kitty imploringly. 'Couldn't you just forget about this man?' she begged.

Kitty shook her head. 'I can't.'

'But what if he's moved away? Your dad reckons he's going to report him–'

'Then I'll go with him.'

Her mother stared at her. 'You wouldn't!'

'I would.' She hadn't realised it until she'd said it. 'We belong together, Mum,' she said simply.

Her mother stared at her wonderingly. 'You really love him, don't you?'

'Yes.'

'Enough to give up everything for him?'

'If I have to.'

Her mother watched her in silence as she finished her packing. 'Where will you go?' she asked quietly.

'I'll get a place at the nurses' home. They've just reopened it, so I'm sure they'll be able to fit me in.'

Fresh tears filled her mother's eyes. 'Can't you just do as your father says?'

Kitty shook her head. 'Not any more, Mum.'

She fastened the catches on the suitcase and hauled it off the bed. 'There,' she said: 'I think I've got everything I need.' She turned to her mother,

343

and for the first time she felt her resolve give way. Once she walked out of this house she would never be back.

Her mother seemed to share her thoughts. 'I always thought you'd leave this house as a bride,' she said.

'So did I.'

Florrie hugged her, wrapping her arms around her tightly, as if she couldn't bear to let her go. 'You will come back and visit, won't you?'

'Of course,' Kitty said.

'And you never know, your dad might change his mind one day?'

'You never know,' Kitty smiled. But they both knew that her father would never back down.

Chapter Forty-Two

The evening after his eighteenth birthday, Arthur Jenkins sat alone in the public bar of the Crown and Anchor, and got drunk.

'Steady on, kid,' the landlord warned, as he downed another pint. 'That's strong stuff if you're not used to it.'

'I ain't a kid!' Arthur slammed the glass down defiantly on the bar. 'Another one,' he said.

The landlord locked eyes with him for a moment, then reached for the glass. 'All right, as it's your birthday. But that's the last. Your father will have my guts for garters if I send you home drunk.'

The beer tasted bitter and disgusting, and Arthur had to force himself to glug it down, but it made his head swim and took the jagged edge off his misery, and that was what he needed.

Today was supposed to be the best day of his life, but a doctor had ruined it with a single stroke of his pen.

Grade D. Unfit for military service.

He drained his glass with a grimace and tried to order another, but the landlord was busy polishing glasses at the other end of the bar and refused to meet his eye. Arthur knew he should leave, but he stayed on the stool at the bar, staring into his empty glass. He had nowhere else to go.

He was completely lost.

He didn't know what the other lads at the porters' lodge would say. For years, Arthur had been planning for it, talking about the day he could finally enlist. After D-Day, they had teased him that the war would be over by the time he'd signed up, but Mr Hopkins had stuck up for him.

'Leave the lad alone, at least he wants to go and do his duty,' he'd said.

Now he would have to go back and face them all. The humiliation was almost too crushing to bear.

And then there was his father. Arthur's stomach churned, rising into his throat, at the thought of facing him.

It had all been so different yesterday. His mother had made him a cake with chocolate for icing, and his dad had brought his old service revolver down from the top of the wardrobe where he'd kept it for nearly thirty years.

'Just think, son,' he'd said. 'In a few weeks

345

you'll have one of these to call your own.'

He'd let him hold it, and shown him how it worked, but his mum had got upset and begged him to put it away. But before he had, his father had clapped him on the shoulder.

'My son, the soldier,' he'd said, pride shining out of his eyes. It was the same pride Arthur saw every time his father talked about Raymond.

How would he ever feel proud of Arthur now, with his weak chest and flat feet and bad eyes?

He pushed the glass across the bar. 'I'll have another.'

'Oh no, you won't,' the landlord said, snatching the empty glass. 'Go home, Arthur. Your mum will be worried about you.'

'I told you, I ain't a kid!'

'Then stop behaving like one.' The landlord glanced up at the clock on the wall. 'It's nearly ten o'clock. You dad will be in for his usual in a minute. Do you want him to find you like this?'

He was right, Arthur thought. He'd forgotten his father was working the evening shifts on the buses this week. At least if he got home soon, he could go to bed and not have to face him.

There were voices coming from the kitchen when he let himself in. Arthur tensed, worried that his father had changed his mind and come home early. But then he realised one of the voices was Kitty's.

She was sitting at the kitchen table with her mother. She jumped up guiltily when Arthur walked in, then relaxed.

'Oh, it's only you. I thought it was Dad, come back early.'

Arthur looked away as he shrugged off his coat. It wasn't his fault she was banished from the house, he told himself. His father gave her a choice, and she took it.

'What are you doing here?' he asked.

'I came to bring you a present.' She handed him the parcel, wrapped in brown paper. 'Happy birthday, Arthur.'

'Go on, then. Open it,' his mother prompted as he stared at the parcel in his sister's hands. The paper was soft and criss-crossed with lines where it had been used over and over again. He couldn't remember the last time he had seen a new sheet of wrapping paper.

Arthur took the parcel and unwrapped it. Inside was a knitted scarf in the red and white colours of Clapton Orient, his favourite football team.

'It took me ages to make,' Kitty said. 'You do like it, don't you?'

Arthur stared at the scarf in his hands, unable to speak. Guilt choked him.

'Here, try it on.' Kitty took the scarf out of his hands and went to wind it round his neck. As she stepped towards him, she suddenly sniffed and said, 'Have you been drinking?'

'I daresay he's been celebrating, haven't you, son?' His mother smiled. She rose from her seat. 'I'll go and make you a cup of tea.'

As she headed for the scullery, Kitty said, 'Mum told me you'd been to enlist. I bet you couldn't wait, could you?' He didn't reply. 'So go on, then. Where are they sending you?'

Still he couldn't speak. His tongue felt glued to the roof of his mouth.

347

'Oh dear, you don't look very happy about it,' Kitty smiled. 'Don't tell me you're digging latrines–'

He thrust the piece of paper into her hand. Kitty looked down at it. 'What's this?'

'See for yourself.'

He couldn't look at her as she scanned the paper. He expected her to laugh at him, but all she said was, 'Oh, Arthur. I'm sorry.'

Her sympathy stung him. After everything he'd done to her, Kitty still cared about him.

'Aren't you going to tell me it serves me right?' he said in a choked voice.

'Why should I?' Kitty sounded genuinely bemused. 'I know you had your heart set on signing up.'

'I tried to tell them that, but they wouldn't listen to me.' Finally, Arthur could open his heart to someone. 'What am I going to tell Dad?'

'Just tell him the truth.'

'But he'll be so disappointed. He'll think I'm a failure.'

'It's not your fault, Arthur.'

'But he was so looking forward to seeing me in uniform–'

Their mother returned, carrying the tea tray. 'Here we are,' she smiled.

Kitty looked at the clock. 'Sorry, Mum, I'll have to go,' she said regretfully. 'Dad will be home in a minute. I don't want him to catch me here.'

Florrie Jenkins looked crestfallen. 'I suppose not.' She set down the tray. 'I'll see you again soon, won't I, love?'

'I'll try to come round tomorrow night. But I

348

don't finish until nine, so we might only have a little while.'

Arthur watched them embrace, guilt flooding through him. It wasn't his fault, he told himself again. That German had broken up his family, not him.

He managed to avoid his father that night, and the following morning. But he couldn't avoid the lads at work.

They were all sympathetic, and Mr Hopkins put his hand on his shoulder and said, 'Never mind, lad. You did your best.' But Arthur could see the disappointment in his eyes as he said it.

His best wasn't good enough. He had failed.

And if the head porter could be upset about it, how much worse would his own father feel?

It was a long day. Arthur's head ached, and the drink he'd had the night before sloshed queasily around in his belly. Once he had to rush off to be sick on his way to taking a patient to theatre.

It was a relief when nine o'clock came. He was about to go off duty when a written message came down to the porters' lodge, asking him to come up to the POWs' ward.

'Can't someone else go?' Arthur begged. 'I'm just knocking off.'

Mr Hopkins shook his head. 'It's asking for you particularly. Perhaps it's that sister of yours? If it is, kindly tell her to telephone in future and speak to me, instead of sending down notes.' He waved the scrap of paper. 'I'm letting it go this once, but in future I'll be putting these in the bin, where they belong.'

Arthur plodded up to the POWs' ward, but Kitty

was nowhere to be found. Sister Dawson wasn't there, as usual, and Nurse Riley was in Sister's office, going through some paperwork with the night nurse. The lights in the ward had already been turned down and the lamps shaded with green cloth, casting a sickly glow.

Arthur was just about to leave when Major Von Mundel appeared. 'Ah, Herr Jenkins. If you are looking for your sister, I believe she is in the bathroom.'

Arthur glared at the man in dislike. Usually he would have ignored him as if he hadn't spoken. But it was late and he was too tired to argue. He also wanted to get home and go to bed before his dad came off his shift. It was cowardly, but he still hadn't worked out how he was going to break the news to him.

He went into the first bathroom and looked around, but there was no sign of Kitty. Arthur sighed with annoyance. Someone was playing silly beggars, and he had neither the time nor the patience for it.

He went into the second bathroom. 'Kitty?' he called out. He went to look round the door, when suddenly he felt a hand at his back, shoving him roughly into the room. A second later the door closed behind him.

Arthur swung round to find himself staring into the coldly smiling face of Major Von Mundel.

'Thank you for coming,' he said. 'I wasn't sure you would receive my note.'

Arthur looked around in panic. 'Where's Kitty?'

'Your sister went off duty ten minutes ago, Herr Jenkins. Or may I call you Arthur?'

He could feel his heart thudding in his throat. 'What's the matter?' Major Von Mundel taunted him softly. 'Have you lost your courage without your friends to back you up?'

Arthur elbowed past him and tried to make a break for the door, but Major Von Mundel was too quick for him. Like lightning, he grabbed Arthur's arm and yanked it up behind his back, slamming him into the wall.

'Please don't try to run, Arthur. Believe me, there are many men outside who would like to do far worse to you than I would. You see, you are not the only one with friends.' He pushed Arthur harder into the wall. The tiles were cold and hard against his cheek. *'Oberleutnant* Bauer has friends, too. And so does Nurse Riley.'

He leaned forward, his voice menacing in its softness. 'You have been spreading lies about her. She is a good woman, and she does not deserve to be treated like that. Do you understand? Do you?' He shook him so hard, Arthur felt his stomach rising in protest.

'I'm going to be – sick,' he gasped.

Major Von Mundel released him abruptly. Arthur barely made it to the toilet. He hung over the bowl, gasping and retching. All the time he could feel Major Von Mundel standing over him, watching him.

'You stink,' he said in disgust. 'Look at you. You are not a man. You are a disgrace.' He leaned over. 'Never, ever speak of Nurse Riley again, or I will kill you. Do you understand?' he hissed.

Suddenly the door opened and Dora Riley came in. 'What's going on?' she demanded.

'I am afraid poor Arthur here was taken ill. I was helping him,' Major Von Mundel replied.

'Is that right?'

Arthur sat back on his heels and wiped his face with his sleeve but said nothing.

Dora looked from one to the other. 'How are you feeling now?' she asked Arthur.

'I am sure he will be fine,' Major Von Mundel answered for him. 'All he needs is some fresh air.'

Dora's eyes narrowed. 'Are you sure there's nothing going on?'

Arthur looked again at Von Mundel. His eyes were as clear and cold as ice.

'Nothing,' he mumbled.

As he walked the length of the ward, Arthur could feel the eyes of every man following him. From somewhere in the gloom came a whisper in German, then the sound of muffled laughter.

He burned with humiliation. They could laugh, he thought. But he would make them all sorry.

Especially that arrogant bastard Von Mundel. More than anyone, he would pay for his humiliation.

Chapter Forty-Three

By Good Friday, everyone knew the war was drawing to a close. Almost a week earlier, Field Marshal Montgomery's army had crossed the Rhine. Now the Americans were closing in on the Ruhr, the Russians were crossing into Austria, and the Polish flag flew once again over Danzig. It looked as if the Germans had started to move out of Holland, too.

Everyone seemed in a light-hearted mood except Dora, as she stood at her window, watching the dawn rise over the scarred rooftops of Bethnal Green.

Nothing else mattered, because today should have been Nick's thirtieth birthday.

'Happy birthday, love,' she murmured, looking up into the sky, as heavy and grey as a bundle of dirty washing.

The twins slumbered on in the big bed, curved around the warm, rumpled space where their mother had lain a few minutes earlier. She had promised to help them make their dad a birthday card when she came off duty that afternoon.

'Can we send it to him?' Walter had asked the previous evening.

'No, we should keep it for when he comes home. That's a better idea, ain't it, Mum?' Winnie put in. 'Then we can watch him open it.'

A lump rose in Dora's throat and she glanced at her mother, who sat in tight-lipped silence.

'You've got to tell them sometime,' Rose had said later, as they washed up in the scullery.

'I will,' Dora said, drying a dish. 'But not yet.'

'What if they hear it from someone else? They're old enough to understand, you know. And you'd be surprised what kids take in–'

'I'll tell them when I'm ready, all right?'

Dora saw her mother flinch, and wished she hadn't been so sharp. Rose was only talking sense, as usual. And Dora had tried to sit the children down and tell them their father was dead. But every time she stopped herself before she managed to say the words.

She pressed her face closer to the window, feeling the cool glass against her forehead.

Let's face it, Dora Riley. You're not ready to admit it to yourself, let alone anyone else, she thought.

It wasn't fair. The world should have stopped on the day he died. It had stopped for her. But the rest of the world went on relentlessly, every night turning into day, and every day a series of hours to be got through and endured.

Dora did a good job of masking her feelings. She got up, washed, dressed, ate and went to work. She carried out her duties, chatting, smiling and offering comfort where it was needed. At home, she helped with the housework, looked after her children and gave every appearance that she was coping with her husband's loss.

It was only at night, when the whole house was asleep and the children were tucked in on either side of her, that she allowed herself to cry for Nick. Sometimes she would cry herself to sleep. At other times, she would lie awake all night, tortured by thoughts of him.

Everyone else might be celebrating the Great Advance of the Allies across Europe. But it meant nothing to Dora.

Because even when it was over, Nick still wouldn't be coming home.

But as usual she managed to put a smile on her face on the ward when they listened to the BBC news. Miss Sloan and Kitty gathered around the wireless, and Major Von Mundel joined them, translating for the rest of the men.

The latest news was that Hitler had ordered that German towns and factories be destroyed, leaving nothing for the Allies to capture. Dora looked at Major Von Mundel's grim expression as he translated, and wondered if he was thinking about his children.

She tried to talk to him afterwards, but Miss Sloan approached him, asking him to translate a patient's letter from home. Dora saw the relief on his face, and understood. They both needed something to occupy their minds today.

She was in the kitchen, preparing some beef tea for a patient with anaemia, when Helen Dawson appeared. In her hands was a small brown paper package.

'Riley, can you spare a moment?' she asked.

Dora was surprised. Ever since their argument a few days ago, they had been avoiding each other.

'What is it, Sister?' she asked.

'I've brought you this–' She put the package down and stepped back quickly, as if it were an unexploded incendiary she had just placed on the kitchen table.

Mystified, Dora opened the box. Inside was a small jam sponge cake, dusted with icing sugar.

'I – don't understand–'

'My mother sent it to me,' Helen said. 'I thought you might like it – as it's a special occasion?'

Dora looked at her sharply. She'd remembered. When everyone else seemed to want to forget about Nick and skim over his memory, Helen understood how important it was for Dora to keep him alive in her thoughts, at least.

Helen gave her a nervous little smile. 'I still remember Charlie's birthday too,' she said. 'Just because he's gone, it doesn't mean—'

'Thank you.' Dora cut her off. 'That's very kind of you.'

For a moment they looked at each other, bound by the understanding of what it was like to lose the love of their lives.

Then Dora pulled herself together and said, 'Never mind about standing here admiring it. Shall we have a slice?'

Helen looked wary. 'Are you sure you want to share it with me?'

'Don't you want any?'

'Well, yes, but—'

Dora read the message in her friend's eyes. The cake was a peace offering, and she was waiting to see if she would be forgiven.

'That's settled, then. It's nearly time for my morning break, anyway. I'll just take this beef tea out to the patient while you fetch a knife. And we'll keep some for Miss Sloan and Nurse Jenkins and Major Von Mundel, too.'

She looked at Helen as she said his name, but her friend's expression was neutral, giving nothing away.

When Dora returned, Helen held out the knife to her. 'You do it,' she said. 'You have to make a wish.'

Dora's mouth twisted. 'But it ain't my birthday!'

'That doesn't matter. It's still a birthday cake, so I'm sure it counts.'

Dora took the knife from Helen and closed her eyes as she pushed the blade into the cake. There was only one wish she made. It was the same wish she made every night.

Afterwards, they sat in the kitchen, eating cake and discussing the news. Dora was aware of the tension in the air between them, but at least they were speaking, and that was something.

Then Helen said, 'I've written to David.'

Dora stiffened, instantly wary. 'Oh yes?'

Helen chased some crumbs around her plate with her fork. 'I thought I should. I felt I needed to explain what had happened, rather than him hearing it from someone else.' She glanced up at Dora from under her lashes. 'I've had time to think about it, and I've decided it was the right thing to do. He deserved to know the truth.'

'I agree,' Dora said. 'But I didn't tell him.'

'It doesn't matter. I'm telling you I forgive you.'

'And I'm telling you I didn't do it!'

Helen sighed and put down her fork. 'Must we argue about this again? It doesn't matter what you did–'

'It does matter!' Dora insisted. 'It matters that you don't believe me. I'm not a liar, Helen.'

'I'm not calling you a liar–'

'Yes, you are!' Dora pushed the cake away. 'And you can take this. I don't want it.'

'Now you're being silly–'

'I'm not. We can't be friends if you don't think I'm telling you the truth.'

Their eyes locked across the table for a moment. Then Helen stood up, pushing back her chair. 'Very well,' she said. 'I've tried to talk to you, but you don't want to listen.'

Dora glared at the cake in front of her. 'Don't

forget to take this with you.'

'I bought it for you. For Nick.'

'Well, I don't want it.' She didn't lift her gaze, but she could feel Helen staring at her.

'You know your trouble, Dora Riley? You're too stubborn for your own good.'

'I might be, but I don't tell lies!' Dora threw back at her as she left the room.

She stared back at the cake, furious. It had been such a lovely moment, and Helen had ruined it.

She was too busy to notice Helen for the rest of the morning. A patient came back from theatre, and Kitty went to sit with him, then two more were taken down. Dora went with them. By the time she returned, Helen had gone off to the military ward.

She was probably telling Clare all about it, Dora thought sourly.

She and Miss Sloan served up the midday meal together, then Dora went off to the kitchen to put the kettle on.

'She heard the door open behind her, and looked over her shoulder to see Arthur Jenkins loitering in the doorway, looking as sullen as ever.

'You're a bit early to collect the dishes, ain't you?' she said, turning back to the sink. 'I don't think the patients have finished eating yet–'

'I'm looking for Von Mundel.'

'That's Major Von Mundel to you,' Dora corrected him. She filled the urn with water and switched it on. 'What do you want him for, anyway?'

'That's between him and me.'

'You cheeky little–' Dora turned to scold him,

which was when she saw the gun in his hand.

It was so unreal, she felt surprisingly calm. Keeping her eyes fixed on the gun, she said, 'Why don't you put that down and go back to the porters' lodge before you disturb the patients?'

'Not until I've seen him.' She barely recognised Arthur. His eyes were red-rimmed, staring out of a livid white face. He looked sick with fear.

She glanced at the door, mentally assessing the situation. Miss Sloan was busy serving the meal; Kitty was still sitting with the post-operative patient. The guards were at the far end of the ward. Even if she screamed, she doubted they would reach her before Arthur pulled the trigger.

'I'm sure we can sort this out, if you just put the gun down,' she said quietly.

The gun shook in Arthur's hand. 'You don't understand. He humiliated me!'

'I'm sorry, love. I'm sure he didn't mean–'

'He did!' Arthur's voice rose. 'You weren't there, you didn't see what he did to me... But you would defend him, wouldn't you? Sticking up for your lover! You're just as bad as he is!'

He levelled the gun at her. Dora took a step backwards, colliding with the table. All she could think about were her babies, and the wish she'd made just a couple of hours ago when she'd cut the cake.

She had wished that she could be with Nick.

'Arthur, please,' she whispered.

'Leave her alone,' a voice bit out. 'Your argument is with me, not her.'

Dora looked up sharply. She had been so focused on the gun, she hadn't noticed Major

Von Mundel in the doorway.

Neither had Arthur. He swung round wildly, pointing the barrel at the major's chest.

'Put it down, please!' Dora begged, but the Major merely sneered.

'Do not worry, Nurse Riley. He is too much of a coward to pull the trigger.'

'You want to bet?' Arthur said, raising the barrel to the Major's head. He had to grasp it in both hands to stop it shaking. 'I'll do it! I will!'

'Go on, then,' Major Von Mundel taunted him, his cold blue eyes like chips of ice.

There was a click as Arthur cocked the gun, ready to fire.

'Stop it!' Dora cried. 'Please!' Still Major Von Mundel didn't move.

She heard footsteps coming lightly down the passageway, and a moment later Kitty Jenkins put her head round the door.

'Nurse Riley, the post-op–' She saw her brother. 'Arthur?'

Dora saw Arthur lose his concentration for a moment, and seized her chance. Springing forward, she made a desperate lunge for the gun.

'Honestly, Helen, I don't know why you don't just forget it.'

There was an edge of impatience to Clare's voice as she set up the drip stand. 'You did everything you could, you even made her a peace offering, and all she did was throw it back in your face. I'm telling you, she simply isn't worth it.'

'I know, but...' Helen sighed. 'You didn't see her. She was so adamant she hadn't done it. Even

360

when I told her I didn't mind, that I was happy David and I were talking again, she still denied it all.'

'What?' Clare turned, her face rigid. 'You're speaking to David again?'

'Well, not exactly speaking. But I did reply to his letter.'

'You didn't tell me!'

'Didn't I? It must have slipped my mind.' Helen shrugged. 'Anyway, I felt I had to write to him. Honestly, Clare, it was such a lovely letter he sent me.'

Helen had honestly expected him to hate her, to shun her after what had happened. But David's letter was so full of love and understanding, it made her realise that he truly cared about her.

It made her dare to hope that there might be a chance for them after all.

'So that's it?' Clare said coldly. 'It's all back on?'

'I wouldn't say that. I don't know what's going to happen, but I've said I'll meet him when he comes back to England–' She broke off, seeing Clare's face. 'What is it? What's the matter?'

'Nothing.' Clare turned away from her, testing the drip. 'I just thought you would have told me all this, that's all. Since I'm supposed to be your best friend.'

'I was going to,' Helen said.

'When? When were you going to tell me? Tomorrow? The next day? Or were you going to wait until he came home and you didn't need me any more?'

Helen frowned. 'Clare–' she started to say.

That was when the gunshot rang out.

Chapter Forty-Four

The ward was in uproar when Helen arrived. Kitty Jenkins was sobbing in Miss Sloan's arms, and most of the men were out of bed, gathered around the end of the ward. Helen looked around for the guards but they were nowhere to be found.

'What on earth is going on here? Get these men back to bed immediately!' she shouted. No one moved.

Most of the men were clustered around the kitchen doorway. Helen shoved her way through them. As they parted, she saw Major Von Mundel in the kitchen, kneeling on the floor, cradling Dora in his arms. Blood pooled on the tiles around them, soaking through his grey prison uniform.

'No!' Helen forgot herself and everyone around her, as she threw herself down beside him. 'Oh God, Dora!'

Dora's eyes fluttered open and she managed a wan smile. 'Hello, Sister.' Her cap had slipped, spilling red curls around her white face. She put up a shaky hand to set it straight, then cried out in pain.

'Here, let me.' Helen reached over and tucked her friend's curls inside the cap, her face averted from the spreading crimson stain on the starched bib of her apron. The coppery tang of blood filled her nose and mouth.

She felt her head begin to swim. This couldn't

be happening. It was an awful dream and in a moment she would wake up...

'The bullet passed through her, but it has damaged her collarbone.' Major Von Mundel's voice was quiet and precise, cutting a clear path through her panic. 'But I believe the subclavian artery has been damaged. We need to stop the bleeding.'

Helen blinked stupidly at his hand, jammed under Dora's arm. As she forced her head to clear, she realised he was trying to stem the blood that flowed from the open wound on her shoulder.

Tourniquet. The word came into her brain but for a moment she could do nothing but stare at her friend. She was gasping for breath, a blueish tinge around her lips.

'*Oberschwester?*' Major Von Mundel snapped, bringing her sharply to her senses again.

Helen jumped to her feet and turned to the men standing around the door. 'Get back to your beds, all of you!' she snapped. They stayed rooted to the spot, staring at her with wide, blank eyes.

'*Bett!*' Von Mundel barked, and they all fled.

Helen turned to Kitty and Miss Sloan, still standing in the middle of the ward with their arms wrapped around each other. 'Don't just stand there! Jenkins, set a trolley with dressings. Sloan, make up a bed in Room Three.'

Without waiting for a reply, she went to the supplies cupboard and found a length of bandage which she brought back to Major Von Mundel. Together they fashioned a tourniquet around the top of Dora's arm.

It must have only been a few seconds before the bleeding slowed down, but it felt like a lifetime.

Neither of them spoke. All Helen could hear was the crashing of her own heartbeat in her ears.

Kitty wheeled in the dressings trolley, and Helen quickly set about cleaning and dressing the wound on Dora's shoulder. She had dressed a thousand wounds as a field nurse, but suddenly her hands were clumsy, her fingers fumbling over the swabs. All the time she could feel Major Von Mundel watching her keenly.

Dora laughed faintly. 'Honestly, Sister, you're as bad as a probationer–' she started to say, but her words were lost in a panicky gulp of breath.

'Her chest seems very weak,' Major Von Mundel said.

Helen's eyes met his. She knew they were both thinking the same thing. The damage to her collar-bone had torn a hole in the pleura, causing her lung to collapse.

'I'll check her pulse,' she said.

Once again, she was aware of him watching her anxiously.

'The apex beat is displaced, yes?' Helen nodded. '*Verdammt!*' he hissed.

'She needs oxygen–'

'*Nein, Oberschwester.* Oxygen will not be enough. She needs aspiration.'

Helen looked from him to Dora. 'I'll fetch the doctor.'

She called down to theatre, but the sister told her that both Dr Abbott and Dr Marsh were in the middle of surgery The only doctor available was Dr Philpott, a second year medical student with no real experience of surgical procedures.

'I can do it,' Major Von Mundel said, when

Helen returned.

'You can't. It's against the rules.'

'Your friend is dying, *Oberschwester*. What are rules, at a time like this?'

Helen looked down at Dora, fighting for breath. He was right, she was dying. Another few minutes and it would be too late.

But to save her, she would have to do the very thing she had sworn never to do again. She had to put her trust in a German.

She shook her head. 'It's not safe–'

'You think I would ever do anything to hurt Nurse Riley?' His voice was edged with steel. 'I owe her my life, *Oberschwester*. The least I can do is try to save hers.' He met Helen's gaze, his eyes cold. 'I intend to perform this procedure, whether you want me to or not,' he said. 'It would be better if you helped me, but if you want to go and fetch a guard, or one of the porters to come and take me away, then please do so. But make up your mind, as we do not have much time, I think.'

Helen looked from the Major's arrogant face to Dora's and back again.

'Do it,' she said.

Major Von Mundel was clean, quick and more precise than any surgeon Helen had ever seen. He worked with icy dispassion, inserting the needle and then the tube into Dora's chest, releasing the air from the chest cavity. Helen could almost see the life ebbing back into her friend, the blue fading from around her lips as her chest went down.

Dr Philpott arrived just as they were finishing off the procedure. Helen steeled herself, ready for a dressing-down for what she had done. But the young man seemed relieved that he hadn't had to do it himself.

'It all looks in order,' he said, inspecting the wound.

Helen suspected he had no idea what he was looking at.

'She will need something for the pain,' Major Von Mundel said.

'Of course. I'll prescribe some morphia. A quarter of a gram should do it, I think?' He glanced at Major Von Mundel for confirmation. The Major gave a barely perceptible nod.

Once Dora was settled in bed in the private room, Helen went to sit with her. Dora seemed in very high spirits for someone who had brushed with death.

'I knew I was in good hands,' she grinned.

'I'm not so sure!' Helen held up her hands to show Dora her trembling fingers. 'I don't think I've stopped shaking since I saw you on that kitchen floor.'

'Just as well it was Major Von Mundel sticking the needle in and not you, then!' Dora smiled. 'I said you could trust him, didn't I?'

'Yes,' Helen agreed quietly. 'Yes, you did.'

'I know he might seem like a bit of a cold fish, but he's got a good heart, I reckon.'

'I'll take your word for it.'

Helen left Dora sleeping and crept out of the room. As she passed down the ward, she spotted Major Von Mundel in the passageway. He was leaning against the doorframe, staring into the kitchen, a look of blank horror on his face.

He must have heard her approach, because he

turned round quickly.

'Pardon me, *Oberschwester*,' he muttered, hurrying past her. He kept his head down, but not before Helen glimpsed the tears running down his face.

So much for being a cold fish, she thought.

'Stille Nacht, Heilige Nacht... Alles schläft; einsam wacht...'

Dora opened her eyes, lost in confusion. At first she thought she was dreaming. The room was in darkness, the blackout blinds drawn. And there were the voices, faint but unmistakable, coming from somewhere outside the door.

She struggled to sit up, as the door opened and there was Helen silhouetted against the dim light from the passageway.

'You're awake,' she said.

Dora rubbed her eyes. 'How long have I been here?'

'A couple of hours. I didn't want to disturb you, so I thought I'd let you sleep. How are you feeling?'

'Sore.' That was an understatement. Her shoulder seemed to be filled with throbbing fire.

'I can give you some more morphia for that.' Helen picked up her wrist and took her pulse. Outside the voices continued.

'Stille Nacht, Heilige Nacht...'

Perhaps it was the morphia, Dora thought. Helen didn't seem aware of them at all as she busily checked her temperature.

'We've moved you to the sick bay,' she said. 'We thought you'd be more comfortable here than on the POWs' ward.'

Dora nodded, taking it in. 'How long will I have to stay here?'

'Another two or three weeks, according to the doctor. That's if the X-ray doesn't show any more damage.'

'Three weeks?' Dora was aghast. 'That's longer than I've ever stayed in bed in my life!'

'Well, you'll have to get used to it,' Helen said. 'It's about time someone looked after you for a change, instead of the other way round.'

Dora frowned. 'We'll have to see about that, won't we?'

'Stop being so stubborn, Dora Riley!'

Helen's words pulled them both up short. They were almost exactly the last words Helen had thrown at her, before–

As if she could read her mind, Helen quietly said, 'I'm sorry.'

'It doesn't matter now–'

'It does,' Helen insisted. She lowered her head. 'Clare admitted it was her who wrote that letter and pretended it was from you,' she said. 'I think she felt so awful after what happened to you...' She trailed off.

'So you believe me now, do you?' Dora couldn't keep the bitterness out of her voice. But she regretted it the moment she saw the wretched expression on her friend's face.

'I'm sorry. I should have known you wouldn't break a promise,' Helen said.

'I'm not the only one you should have trusted.'

Helen nodded. 'I know.'

'How is the Major?'

'Utterly furious with you for risking your life to take that gun off Arthur Jenkins. And so am I,' she said sternly. 'He reckons you saved his life.'

'And he saved mine,' Dora smiled.

They were both silent for a moment.

'Stille Nacht, heilige Nacht, Gottes Sohn, o wie lacht...'

'When can I see my family?' Dora asked.

'Tomorrow,' Helen said. 'Get some rest tonight.'

Dora chewed her lip. How would her children manage without her? And her mum, and Nanna Winnie?

Once again, Helen seemed to read her mind. 'They'll be fine,' she said. 'Worry about yourself for a change.' She checked her watch. 'I'm going off duty in a minute, but I'll make sure to bring you that morphia before I go. Is there anything else you need?'

Dora frowned. 'There is one thing,' she said.

'What's that?'

'You can tell me if I'm going mad or not. Only I swear I can hear someone singing a Christmas carol...'

Helen smiled, and opened the door. Outside, in the gloom of the passageway, Dora could make out the dim outlines of half a dozen men in grey prison uniforms.

'Matron gave them special permission to leave the ward, but I think they would have probably come anyway,' Helen said. 'They wanted to do something special for you. They said it's your favourite?'

Dora nodded. 'It is.'

'I tried to tell them Christmas carols weren't

appropriate at Easter, but they wouldn't listen.' Helen rolled her eyes.

'Oh, I dunno.' Dora settled happily back against the pillows. 'I reckon Christmas carols are nice any time of the year.'

Chapter Forty-Five

They sat in the police station until nearly midnight. Kitty, her mother and her father, all sitting in a row, staring at the wall in front of them. The brickwork was painted a shiny grey-green colour, pasted over with various signs and notices, some of them old, yellowing and curling at the corners.

To their left, the duty sergeant stood behind his desk, dealing with the various people who came in. There was a woman who'd lost her cat, another who'd lost her purse. A policeman came in, manhandling a young boy who'd been caught picking a pocket on Roman Road. Later in the evening, the rowdy drunks were hauled in, swearing and falling over their feet and still trying to swing punches at each other.

But it was to the right, a door marked Private, that Kitty and her parents turned their attention. That was where they'd taken Arthur three hours earlier. And there had been no word of him since.

'That poor girl,' her mother said quietly. 'She will be all right, won't she?'

Kitty nodded. 'She was conscious and being transferred to sick bay when I left.'

But that still didn't take away the sickening picture Kitty had of her sprawled on the floor, cradled in Major Von Mundel's arms, blood soaking through the starched white of her uniform. She knew how close Dora had come to death.

But she couldn't tell her mother that. Florrie Jenkins was upset and worried enough.

'I don't understand it,' her mother said. 'Why would our Arthur do something like that? It doesn't make sense. He's such a good boy...'

If you think that, then you don't know him. Kitty bit back the retort. Her brother had turned into a twisted bully.

And we all know where he gets it from. She glanced sideways at her father. Horace Jenkins sat with his hands resting on his knees, staring at the floor.

'It's been such a long time. I do wish someone would come and tell us what's going on.' Her mother glanced towards the door. 'Perhaps you should have a word with that sergeant, Horace? He might know—'

'They'll tell us when they're good and ready,' her father said gruffly. 'No point in troubling anyone.'

'But I can't bear to think of Arthur being locked up in a cell—'

'It's no more than he deserves,' Kitty muttered.

Her mother turned to her, shocked. 'That's your brother you're talking about!'

'He's no brother of mine. Not after what he did.'

'It was a moment of madness, that's all—'

'You didn't see him, Mum!' Every time Kitty closed her eyes she could see Arthur standing there, levelling their father's old service revolver at Major Von Mundel. 'If Dora Riley hadn't got

371

in the way he would have killed him, I'm sure of it. And then he would have hanged for it.'

'Don't!' Her mother burst into tears, fumbling for her handkerchief.

'Now look what you've done!' Her father turned on her. 'Don't you think you've done enough damage, without causing more trouble?'

'Me?' Kitty stared at him. 'I'm not the one behind bars.'

'No, but you're the one who drove him to it!' Her father's eyes glittered with anger. 'If you hadn't taken up with that bloody German, none of this would have happened!'

'And if you hadn't gone on and on about Ray, and how we needed to get revenge on the Germans for what happened, he would never have picked up that gun in the first place!'

'Ahem.' The desk sergeant cleared his throat and sent them a severe look. 'Quiet, please, or I'll send you home.'

Her father lowered his voice. 'I didn't expect him to do something like this, did I? I only wanted him to sign up, to do his bit like anyone else–'

'He couldn't, could he? They didn't want him.'

'What?'

'They turned him down, Dad. Unfit for service.'

Her father frowned. 'He didn't tell me...'

'No, because he was too ashamed. He knew how much you wanted him to go and fight, and he felt he'd let you down.' Kitty saw her father's face fall, but she didn't care. He deserved to hear the truth, even if it hurt him. 'You know how Arthur worships you. He wanted to make you proud. So he took that gun and went to shoot the only German he could find.'

Her father stared down at his feet, shaken. 'He should have told me.'

'How could he?' Kitty faced him angrily. 'You'd only compare him to Ray, make him feel like he was less of a man than his brother–'

The door to their right swung open, and they all shot to their feet as Arthur appeared, flanked by a police constable. He looked white-faced and much younger than his eighteen years. For a moment, even Kitty felt a pang of pity for him.

'We're releasing him on bail,' the policeman said. 'Pending further charges.'

'What will happen to him?' her father asked.

'That's up to the court to decide, ain't it? But I don't suppose the judge will take kindly to someone running round a hospital, waving a gun around.' He cuffed the back of Arthur's head. 'Be on your way, lad, and try to stay out of trouble.'

Arthur didn't reply. He looked sick and wretched.

'Come on,' Horace Jenkins said. 'Let's get you home.'

They made their way home in silence through the darkened, empty streets. Her father and Arthur trudged ahead, neither of them looking at each other. Kitty and her mother trailed behind.

'He could go to prison, couldn't he?' her mother said. Kitty didn't reply. 'Oh Kitty, what's happened to this family? We used to be so happy. Now Ray's dead, and Arthur might go to prison, and you've left home–'

'I didn't leave,' Kitty reminded her. 'Dad threw me out, remember?'

'I know,' her mother sighed. 'I think he regrets it now. He misses you, Kit. We all do.'

'It's too late for that, isn't it?'

'Is it?' Her mother looked at her anxiously. 'Do you really think it's too late to put this family back together?'

Kitty stared bleakly ahead of her at her father, walking beside his son.

Her mother fell silent the rest of the way home. Once they were indoors, Horace Jenkins frog-marched his son into the parlour and pushed him down on to a hard wooden chair.

'What have you got to say for yourself?' he demanded.

Arthur hung his head. 'I'm sorry,' he mumbled.

'I should think so, too. Do you know how much worry you've caused your mother? And what's all this about you being turned down for the army?' he asked.

Arthur shot Kitty a mutinous look. 'You told him!'

'He'd have to know sometime,' she shrugged.

'That's right,' Horace said. 'But I'd much rather have heard about it from my own son.'

Arthur gnawed moodily on his thumbnail. 'I'm sorry. I wasn't good enough.'

'Now then, I won't have that talk,' her father said briskly. 'There are ways and means around these things, lad, as I would have told you if you'd come to me in the first place. If we could go down to the doctor's first thing in the morning, I'm sure we could get him to sign you fit. He's not like those army doctors; he knows you—'

'No.'

Kitty turned round. Her mother stood in the doorway, wearing an expression of determination she had never seen before.

Horace frowned over his shoulder at the interruption. 'Don't disturb me, Mother, I'm talking to our son–'

'And I'm talking to you!' Florrie advanced into the room. 'I'm not having it. If the army doesn't want him, then that's fine by me. I don't want to see another of my sons going off to fight, and I don't know why you'd want to, either.'

Horace stared at her, lost for words. 'It's his duty–'

'Bloody duty!'

Kitty blinked. She had never heard her mother use such language. But then, she'd never heard her raise her voice, either. 'That's all we heard from you, Horace Jenkins. Kitty's right, that's how all this started, with you pushing him all the time, trying to get him to live up to your expectations.'

'Now you listen to me–'

'No, you listen to me for a change.' Florrie Jenkins confronted her husband. They made a strange picture, her standing nose to his puffed out chest, but Horace was no match for her utter defiance. 'We all know what this is really about, don't we? But you're not going to bring Ray back, Horace, no matter how many Germans die.' She swallowed hard, and Kitty could see her fighting down her emotion. 'And you're not going to make yourself feel better by hating and being angry, either. All you're doing is driving the family apart.' She looked up at him imploringly. 'I've already lost one child. I don't want to lose my son and my daughter, too.'

Horace stared down at her, for once lost for words. Kitty thought she could see a glitter of tears in his eyes.

'And as for you–' Florrie turned on Arthur, who shrank back in his seat. 'What do you think your brother would say about what you've done? Do you think he'd be proud of you? I'll tell you, shall I? He'd be disgusted with you. He'd be disgusted with all of us for what we've become since he went.' She jabbed her finger in her son's chest. 'So I don't want to hear you spouting any more nonsense, is that understood? And that goes for the rest of you, too.' She swung round to face them all. 'And you–' she pointed at Kitty. 'I want you to move back home.'

Kitty automatically glanced at her father. 'Is that all right, Dad?'

Horace opened his mouth to speak, but her mother interrupted. 'Oh, don't look at him. It's my house, too. I can say what goes. Isn't that right, Father?'

Horace Jenkins looked sullen. 'No one seems to care what I think,' he mumbled.

Kitty looked at her mother, and saw her wink. Florrie Jenkins had found her voice again, and not a moment too soon.

Chapter Forty-Six

May 1945

On a warm Tuesday in May, the day after Germany surrendered to the Allies, Dora was finally allowed to leave the hospital.

She had her suitcase open on the bed and was trying to pack it when Helen came in.

'Here, let me help you,' she said, but Dora waved her away.

'It's all right, I can manage–' she started to say, then she caught Helen's look. 'I'm being stubborn again, aren't I?'

Helen smiled ruefully. 'Just a bit.'

'Oh, all right then. You can help.'

As Helen folded up Dora's nightdress, she said, 'I expect you'll be glad to be going home at last?'

'I'll say!' She had missed her family more than she could ever have imagined. All she wanted was to go home and hug her twins, and have a nice cup of tea and a natter with her mum.

She looked around the sick bay, her home for just over a month. 'I won't be sad to see the back of this place.'

'That's charming!' Helen did her best to look hurt. 'And after the way we've looked after you all these weeks.' She straightened up, her hands on her hips. 'Well, we'll be glad to see the back of you, too, Dora Riley. I've never nursed such a difficult patient. You never do as you're told.'

Dora laughed. 'What did you expect? Never mind, you can get your revenge when I'm back on the ward.'

Helen's expression grew serious. 'I'm not sure there will be a POWs' ward for much longer.'

'No, there probably won't.' Dora was thoughtful. 'I suppose you'll be glad about that?' she said to Helen. 'You never did like nursing them, did you?'

'No,' Helen agreed, then added, 'but the funny thing is I've grown rather fond of them. I've realised I was wrong to hate them all, just because of what one person did. There's good and bad in everyone, isn't there?'

Her gaze dropped to Dora's injured shoulder, and Dora understood what she was thinking. It wasn't a German who had pulled that gun on her.

'I'm glad you think like that,' she said. Perhaps they were both healing in their own way, she thought.

Helen fastened Dora's suitcase and hauled it off the bed. 'Come on, then. Mustn't keep you from your family any longer, must we?'

She headed to the door, but Dora hung back. 'Do you mind? There's someone I'd like to see before I go.'

Helen sent her a look of understanding. 'Try to be quick, won't you?'

Dora hadn't been up to the POWs' ward since the day of the shooting. Her stomach fluttered as she walked through the double doors. She had thought she was getting over it, but if she closed her eyes she could see herself back in the kitchen,

378

staring transfixed down the barrel of Arthur Jenkins' gun.

She saw Miss Sloan hurrying towards her, and pulled herself together.

'Oh, Nurse Riley, how lovely to see you,' she smiled, exposing prominent teeth. 'How are you, my dear?'

'Getting better, thank you. They're sending me home today.' Dora gazed around the ward. 'I was looking for Major Von Mundel.'

Miss Sloan frowned. 'Now let me see, he was here a minute ago–'

'I am here.'

He strode down the length of the ward towards them. With his tall figure and upright bearing, he managed to make his grey prison garb look like the smartest officer's dress uniform.

Dora felt a small shock at how much she had missed him.

'Nurse Riley,' he greeted her in his usual stiff, formal manner. 'How are you? You are looking much better, I think.'

'I feel better, thank you.'

'I am sorry I have not been able to visit you. I wanted to, but I was not granted permission.' A shadow of sadness passed over his face.

Dora changed the subject, asking about the other patients on the ward. They spent a few pleasant minutes discussing *Gefreiter* Schroeder's bronchitis, and *Unteroffizier* Lange's ongoing bowel problems, and Major Von Mundel told her about a couple of the more interesting cases that had been admitted since she had been away.

As he was speaking, Kitty Jenkins went past,

379

pushing a trolley set with dressings. She sent Dora a sideways glance and hurried on, her head down.

'She doesn't seem very pleased to see me,' Dora observed.

'She is a little embarrassed, I think.'

'It wasn't her fault.'

'I know, but it is still difficult for her, no?'

'I suppose so.' Dora watched Kitty from the other end of the ward. 'I wonder how Arthur is getting on up in Durham?'

Major Von Mundel's lip curled. 'I neither know nor care,' he said.

'And yet you didn't get him locked up while you had the chance?' Dora had refused to press charges against Arthur, but she was surprised when she found out Major Von Mundel had done the same. The police had not prosecuted, but his family had thought it best to send him up north to stay with one of his father's cousins. The last Dora had heard from her mother, Arthur had got a job as a miner.

Major Von Mundel shook his head. 'What would be the point?' he said. 'The boy's family has suffered enough, losing one son. I would not want to be responsible for them losing another.' He looked at Dora. 'It is a time for forgiveness, Sister Riley. If we can't forget the past, how can we ever have a future?'

'I suppose you're right.' Dora went to the window and gazed out. Below her, the porters were busy stringing Union Jack flags from one side of the courtyard to the other while Mr Hopkins stood at the foot of the ladder, barking orders. Nurses pushed patients in wheelchairs out in the sunshine, everyone smiling and laughing.

Major Von Mundel came to stand beside her. 'It seems as if everyone is celebrating,' he observed.

Dora sent him a sideways glance.

'What will happen now?' she asked.

'I do not know.' His face was wistful.

'Will you be going home?'

'I am not sure I have a home to go to, any more.' His mouth twisted. 'But I think perhaps I will be allowed to return to my children next year, or the year after.'

'Next year? That's a long time to wait.'

'I have already waited for many years, Nurse Riley. What are another few months?'

Dora gazed at his profile, the sun falling on the sharp bones of his angular face. It had hurt her enough to be away from her children for a month. She couldn't imagine being separated from them for so many years.

Helen appeared at the doors with Dora's suitcase. 'It is time for you to go, I think,' Major Von Mundel said.

Panic assailed her. *I don't want to go,* she thought. But she hid her feelings behind a carefully neutral expression. 'Yes,' she said.

He held out his hand. '*Auf Wiedersehen,* Nurse Riley. Who knows, perhaps our paths will cross again one day?'

'*Auf Wiedersehen,* Major Von Mundel.'

He winced. 'Such a terrible accent!'

Dora laughed. Then, on impulse, she reached up and planted a kiss on his cheek.

The other men whooped and laughed. Major Von Mundel stepped back as if she'd slapped him.

'Ta ta, Major!' Dora walked away, and didn't look back until she reached the door. When she did, Major Von Mundel was still standing in the middle of the ward, his hand pressed to his cheek.

Helen walked down with her to the front doors. 'Shall I ask Mr Hopkins to call a taxi for you?' she asked.

Dora laughed. 'Taxi? Blimey, do you think I'm made of money?' She shook her head. 'No thanks, the fresh air will do me good. I need it after being cooped up in that hospital bed for a month.'

Helen handed over her suitcase, being careful to put it in Dora's good hand.

'Take care,' she said. 'And I'll see you soon. But not too soon, mind. I don't want you coming back to work until you're fully fit.'

'Don't worry, I won't!' Dora called back, waving as she walked away.

On the way home, she took a detour to Griffin Street. As she approached Mrs Price's house, she saw a Union Jack hanging from the upstairs window. Dora's heart lifted at the sight of it, proudly fluttering over the flattened street below.

'I told you I'd do it, didn't I?' Mrs Price called out to her, waving from the window. 'I told you I'd put the flags out in Griffin Street!'

'So you did, Mrs P. And it looks smashing.'

Mrs Price beamed. 'Glad to see you up and about, girl. You feeling better?'

'I am. I'm just on my way home now.'

'Oh, I won't keep you, then. But tell your mum I'll be popping round for a cuppa later, to celebrate.'

'I will.'

They had been living in Albion Road for two years but Dora had never thought of it as home until she turned the corner and saw the crumbling old terrace, strung with flags. Children played on the cobbled street, chasing each other and knocking down rusty tin cans with a ball.

Dora stood at the end of the street and felt hot tears stinging her eyes. *Daft beggar,* she thought, wiping her face with her sleeve. *What will the neighbours think?*

She let herself in the back door and ran up the stairs two at a time. 'I'm home–' she called out, then stopped in her tracks when she saw the figure sitting at the kitchen table.

'Hello, Dora,' Lily said, looking up from the pan of potatoes she was peeling.

'Lily?' Dora wasn't sure which astonished her more, that her sister-in-law had returned or that she was making herself useful.

Before she could say any more, her mother came in the door behind her with the twins and Mabel. Walter and Winnie immediately launched themselves at her, clamouring for a cuddle. Mabel watched them slyly from the doorway, sucking on a boiled sweet.

'We've just been to get a loaf of bread from the shop,' Rose said breathlessly. 'We saw you coming up the street but we couldn't catch you up. Mind your mum's arm,' she warned Walter. 'She's still poorly, you know.'

'I don't mind.' Dora hugged her son fiercely. No pain was great enough to stop her holding them. After everything she had been through, she didn't think she would ever let them go again.

'Now then, what's all this noise?' Nanna Winnie bustled in. 'Oh, it's you.' She looked Dora up and down. 'I wondered when you'd turn up.'

'Lovely to see you, too, Nanna,' Dora grinned.

'I don't know,' Nanna said, lowering herself carefully into her usual rocking chair. 'This place is like Piccadilly Circus, with all the comings and goings.' She glared at Lily as she said it.

'I'll make some tea, shall I?' Rose offered. 'You'd like a nice cuppa, wouldn't you, Dor?'

'I'd love one, Mum.'

'I'll make it.' Lily dropped a potato into the pan of water and hurried off to the scullery,

Dora turned to her mother. 'What's she doing here?' she whispered.

'You might well ask,' Nanna said darkly.

Rose turned her back so that Mabel couldn't see her. 'Hank left her, so she came home.'

'No!'

'It's true,' Nanna said. 'She's got more bloody front than Margate, that one! Can you imagine it? Running off with your fancy man and then crawling back to your husband's family?'

'Shh!' Rose hissed, shooting a quick glance at Mabel. 'She'll hear you. She already feels bad enough about it.'

'And so she should!' Nanna hissed back.

Dora was still trying to take it all in. 'What does Bea think about it?' she asked. Knowing her sister, she could imagine there must have been fisticuffs. She was surprised Lily had any face left.

'She wasn't as bad as we thought she'd be,' Rose said. 'Oh, they had a blazing row and Bea pulled out a couple of handfuls of her hair, but then she calmed down. Between you and me, I think she's happy Hank ditched her. And she's been making sure Lily's sorry about it.'

'I can imagine,' Dora said ruefully.

She took her suitcase into the bedroom and started unpacking. The twins came to help her, bouncing on the bed around her.

'Stop it, you little monkeys!' Dora said, but she was too happy to see them to scold them.

Lily slunk in, carrying a teacup. 'I've brought you your tea,' she said. Her mournful expression was beginning to grate on Dora.

'Cheer up, for gawd's sake, Lily! It's VE day. We're supposed to be celebrating, ain't we?'

Lily eyed her warily. 'I wasn't sure what you'd say about me coming home.'

'Well, I ain't going to pull your hair out like Bea, so don't worry about that.'

Lily put her hand to her scalp. 'I'm sorry,' she mumbled.

'It ain't me you should be apologising to, is it?'

Lily stared down at the worn rug. 'You've got to understand how I felt,' she whined. 'I was lonely and miserable and Hank – took advantage of me.'

'So it's his fault, is it?'

'I didn't say that, did I? I know what I did was wrong, but like I said, I was lonely. I didn't know if Pete was ever going to come home or not...'

Dora sipped her tea to stop herself saying anything. How did that make a difference? she wondered. She would have waited for Nick until her dying day.

'Anyway, I made a mistake,' Lily said quietly.

She lifted her gaze to meet Dora's. 'You won't tell Peter, will you?'

Dora laughed shortly. 'You're having a laugh, ain't you? You'll never keep a secret like that in this house. Not with Bea and Nanna around, at any rate. Besides, it's not fair to lie to him. You'll have to tell him, Lily. Before he finds out from someone else.'

'I – I will.' Lily lowered her eyes demurely.

And he'll forgive you, Dora thought. You'll look at him with those big doe eyes of yours and spin him a line about how a smooth-talking GI took advantage of you, and you'll have him twisted round your little finger in no time.

But then the anger left her. The war had done some strange things to people, made them think and act in ways they might never have imagined. Like poor Arthur Jenkins, for instance.

She looked at Lily's downcast face. Major Von Mundel was right, she thought. If they didn't forget about the past, they would have no future.

Chapter Forty-Seven

December 1945

There wasn't another soul in Victoria Park. The bitter weather and falling snow had kept everyone else away.

It was a shame, Kitty thought, because the park looked so beautiful this winter. The anti-aircraft guns had been taken away, and the barrage balloons no longer loomed ominously overhead. Everything seemed at perfect peace, coated in a thick blanket of white. The bare branches of the trees looked as if they had been lavishly iced.

The snow crunched under her boots as she made her way to the lake where she and Stefan always met. Usually she would be looking forward to turning the corner and seeing him, but today her stomach was a knot of anxiety.

Today might be the last time she ever saw him.

He was waiting for her beside the lake, staring out over the expanse of frozen water. Kitty took one look at his grim profile, and her heart sank.

He turned as she approached, breaking into a smile when he saw her. With his heavy coat over his prison uniform, he looked like any other man waiting for his sweetheart.

Except they weren't like any other couple. Their meetings were always carefully planned and far too fleeting.

'*Liebling*.' He took her in his arms and kissed her. 'I wasn't sure you would come, as it is so cold.'

'As if I'd let a bit of snow stop me!'

'It is beautiful, *nein?*' He turned his gaze back over the lake. 'The water has turned to ice. Look at the ducks, marching in a line across it.'

Kitty looked, but her mind was elsewhere. She knew Stefan and some of the other POWs had been summoned to see the men from the government, to discuss what would happen to them.

She stamped her feet and tucked her gloved hands in her pockets. She wanted to ask Stefan and yet at the same time she didn't want to know, in case it was bad news.

'It is too cold to stand. We will walk, yes?' He took her hand. They strolled away from the lake, down towards the bandstand. The grove of poplars stood tall and straight, like sentries, watching over them. There always seemed to be someone watching them, Kitty thought resentfully.

Finally, she couldn't stand it any longer. 'Did you speak to those men? What did they say?'

Stefan let out a heavy sigh. 'Yes, I spoke to them.'

'And?'

'And they asked me all kinds of questions about my political beliefs, and told me if I gave them the right answers I could go home.'

Kitty let out the breath she had been holding in. She should be pleased for him, she told herself. It was what he had always wanted, to be allowed to go home.

And yet she couldn't help feeling a twist of misery at the thought of never seeing him again.

'What did you tell them?'

'I told them that if I was sent back to Serbia I could not promise to behave myself. I told them I thought I might be a grave threat to their country. They made lots of notes and scratched their heads, and in the end they decided I should stay here, where they could keep an eye on me.'

Kitty shot him a sideways look. 'But I don't understand. You could have gone home?'

'Then I wouldn't be with you,' he said simply.

'But it's what you wanted.'

'Not any more. I would rather be a prisoner with you than a free man without you, *Fraulein*.'

Kitty said nothing as they walked, trying to take it in.

'You are disappointed?' Stefan frowned at her. 'You wanted me to go home, perhaps?'

'No! Oh no, not at all. I'm just – surprised, that's all.'

'Surprised that I would give up my freedom for love?' His mouth twisted ruefully. 'Believe me, *Fraülein*, no one is more surprised than I about that! But perhaps in another year or so I will be free. Then I will be able to stay here.'

'I hope so.' She squeezed his hand.

They went on walking, past the bandstand and around the fountain, then back to the lake. As they approached the water's edge, Kitty's stomach clenched, knowing they would soon have to say goodbye.

She tried not to think about it, as they talked about Christmas. Kitty told him that Arthur was coming home for Christmas, and bringing the girl he was courting.

'Mum's in a terrible flap about it. She's been cleaning and cooking for days. Anyone'd think one of the royal princesses was coming to visit.'

'It must be serious, if he's bringing her home?'

Kitty looked at him. 'It isn't fair,' she said. 'I wish I could bring you home for Christmas.'

Stefan shook his head. 'You know that is not possible, *liebling*. I am not allowed to visit your house, it is against the camp rules.'

And even if it wasn't, my father would never allow it, Kitty thought.

They had reached an uneasy truce over the past few months since Kitty had moved home. Her father had learned to accept Stefan's existence, even if he still winced whenever Kitty said his name. But he wasn't ready to meet him.

Her mother was a different story. Much to Kitty's – and her father's – astonishment, Florrie Jenkins had defied her husband and met Stefan. They had all had tea together in a café, and Florrie was utterly charmed by him.

'You hold on to him, my girl,' she had told Kitty afterwards. 'He's a good one.'

'That reminds me,' she said. 'Mum's made you a Christmas cake.' She took the package out of her bag and handed it to him.

'Thank you. I'm sure they will appreciate it back at the camp.'

'And this is from me.' Kitty shyly handed him another package, wrapped up in brown paper. She'd done her best to make it look festive, drawing Christmas trees all over it. 'It isn't much,' she said, as she watched him unwrapping it. 'Just some socks and gloves I knitted...'

'They are beautiful, *liebling*. I will treasure them.' He reached into his pocket. 'I also have a gift for you...' He pulled a box out of his pocket. 'I am sorry I could not wrap it, but perhaps you will not mind.'

'For me?' She took the box he handed her. It was an exquisite wooden jewellery box, the lid carved with her name inside a heart. 'It's beautiful,' she breathed.

'I wish I could tell you I made it, but sadly I am not that skilled,' Stefan sighed. 'One of the other prisoners made it for me. But I did make what is inside...'

'There's something inside?'

'Open it and see.'

Kitty could feel Stefan watching her eagerly as she opened the lid of the wooden box. Nestling inside was a ring, carefully fashioned from a twist of wire and decorated with a single red bead.

'I made it from a piece of barbed wire I found.' He smiled. 'Something beautiful, from something so ugly. I thought it sounded like us, *nein?*'

'Something beautiful from something ugly... You're right, it does sound like us.' Kitty took off her gloves and went to put on the ring, then hesitated. 'But which finger should I wear it on?'

Stefan took the ring from her and placed it gently on her right hand. 'Here, for now,' he said. 'Until I can buy you a proper ring and make you my wife.'

She looked up at him, smiling. 'Is that a proposal?'

He looked shy. 'I think it is, *Fraülein.*'

They walked together to the gate. As they approached the street, Stefan slipped his hand from hers.

'Well, *Fraülein,* this is where we must part,' he said.

He pulled her into his arms and kissed her. Kitty clung to him, desperately trying to memorise the smell of him, the feel of his strong arms around her, his body close to hers. She didn't know how long it would be before she saw him again, and she needed to soak up as much as she could before she had to let him go.

'Now, *Fraülein.*' Stefan gently disentangled her arms from around his waist, his expression mock severe. 'We will see each other soon.'

'Will we? Every time we say goodbye, I'm so afraid it will be the last time I see you.'

'You know I will always find my way back to you, *Fraülein.*' He lifted her right hand to his lips and kissed her gloved hand over the barbed wire ring. 'Every time you feel afraid, you must look at this and remember you do not have long to wait.'

He leaned over and planted another light kiss on her lips. *'Eines tages, liebling.* One day.'

She nodded, biting back her tears. 'One day.'

Outside the park, life went on. As Kitty trudged home through the snow, she couldn't help noticing all the other couples, walking hand in hand or with their arms round each other. Laughing, enjoying being in love, and not caring who saw them. She felt a stab of jealousy, wishing it could be like that for her and Stefan.

Eines tages. One day.

She took off her gloves and slipped the ring from her right hand to the third finger of her left.

She would wait. For as long as it took.

Chapter Forty-Eight

'Stand still, for gawd's sake. I'll never get this hem straight if you keep fidgeting about!' Dora muttered through a mouthful of pins.

'Sorry.' Helen was still for a few seconds, then shifted from foot to foot again. 'I wish I had something new to wear. This dress is so old I'm surprised it's not falling apart!'

'Don't you worry, I'll soon have it looking as good as new.' Dora smiled up at her friend, towering over her as she knelt on the floor. They were in Helen's room at the nurses' home, and she was trying to get her friend ready to go and meet David again for the first time in two years.

She didn't think she had ever seen her friend so nervous. In the usual way of things, very little ruffled Helen Dawson.

'Thank you for helping me,' she said. 'I tried to do it myself, but my hands were shaking so much I couldn't hold the needle.'

'There, that's done.' Dora stuck in the last pin. 'Now take it off and I'll stitch it for you.'

Helen glanced at the clock. 'Will you have time? I should be at the station in half an hour.'

'Well, you can't go and meet David with pins in your frock, can you? I'll be quick, I promise. I was the fastest hand-stitcher at Gold's Garments before I trained as a nurse.'

Helen slipped off her dress and stood shivering in her thin slip. She had lost weight, Dora thought. Her long, pale limbs were as slender as a child's.

'Have you eaten today?' Helen shook her head. 'You should have something, you know. You'll feel faint otherwise.'

'I couldn't eat, I'm too nervous.' Helen went to the mirror above the chest of drawers and frowned at her reflection. 'Does my hair look all right? Should I have pinned it up, or would it be better down, do you think?'

Dora sighed. 'You look smashing, Helen. Besides, I'm sure David won't mind what you look like. You could turn up wearing a sack and he'd still be thrilled to see you.'

Helen smiled ruefully. 'You think I'm being silly, don't you? I'm just so scared – that he might not want me any more.'

'Of course he wants you. He loves you.'

Dora saw the shadow of doubt that crossed Helen's face and knew exactly what she was thinking. She knew only too well what it was like to look in the mirror and see someone dirty and blighted, and to wonder how anyone could ever love her. She only hoped David could help take away some of the shame, the way Nick's love had taken away hers.

'I wish you could come with me,' Helen said.

'It's you David's come to see, not me.'

'He wouldn't mind. And I wouldn't be nearly so nervous if you were with me. Please, Dora?'

Dora shook her head. 'I don't think that would be right,' she said quietly.

The truth was, she couldn't bear the thought of standing on that station platform with all the other wives and sweethearts, watching all those joyful reunions with their loved ones, and knowing Nick would never be with them.

Helen must have read the look on her face because she said, 'Oh Dora, I'm so sorry, I didn't think–'

'It's all right.'

'But here I am, fussing on about my dress and my hair, and all the time you–'

'It's all right, honestly.' Dora silenced her with a quick, bracing smile. 'I'm not the only one, am I? Besides,' she added, looking back at her sewing, 'I've got somewhere else to go after this.'

She kept her attention focused on her needle, flashing in and out of the fabric, and hoped Helen wouldn't ask any more. She didn't think she could keep up the front for much longer.

'It's very kind of you to help me,' Helen said. 'I – know I haven't always been very kind to you over the past year, have I?'

'It's all over now.'

Helen went to the window and looked out. 'Do you remember this time last year? The way I treated you over those Christmas decorations, and the carol singing?'

Dora glanced up at her friend. Helen's back was turned as she gazed out at the grey, snowy landscape. 'You were upset,' she said.

'I was monstrous.' She hugged herself tighter. 'Sometimes when I look back at it, I can hardly believe it was me...'

Neither can I, Dora thought. 'As I said, it's all in the past now.'

Helen paused, then said, 'Do you know what happened to Major Von Mundel?'

'The last I heard, he was being transferred to another camp on the south coast.'

'I thought you might have stayed in touch with him?'

Dora shook her head. They had never written to each other, and that was probably for the best, she thought. They had travelled along the same path for a while, and he would always stay in her heart as a treasured friend, but now it was right that they should continue their journeys alone.

She only hoped that his journey would take

him home. He deserved to be reunited with his family.

'There, it's finished.' Dora held up the dress. 'Now hurry up and get it on. You don't want to keep David waiting, do you?'

Helen slipped into the dress and looked at herself in the mirror. 'Are you sure I look all right?' she said anxiously.

'You look beautiful,' Dora said, and meant it. With her tall, slender figure and dramatic dark colouring, Helen could never look anything else.

'What if he thinks I've changed?' Panic rose in Helen's voice. 'What if he's changed?'

'You won't know that until you see him, will you?'

'Yes, but what will I say to him?'

'I'm sure you'll think of something. Now hurry up, or you'll be late.'

Helen started to put on her coat, then stopped. 'I can't,' she said. 'I don't know how to be...' She looked stricken.

'Just be the girl he fell in love with,' Dora said. She helped Helen into her coat and reached up to arrange her friend's hat. She could feel the rapid rise and fall of Helen's chest, her breath coming in short, panicky gasps. For a moment she wondered if she should go with her to the station, just to make sure she was all right.

But she couldn't. Even she couldn't keep up a brave face for that long.

'Good luck,' she whispered, squeezing her hand. 'You'll be fine, honestly.'

Just be the girl he fell in love with.

That was easier said than done, Helen thought as she stood on the crowded platform, waiting for the train to come in. The sky was the colour of wet cement, heavy with the promise of more snow. Underneath her feet, the snow had been churned to a dark, icy slush. It was all she could do to hold herself upright as bodies pressed on her from all sides.

The air tingled with happy excitement. In a few minutes the train would come in, bringing husbands and fathers and brothers and lovers home.

And David.

Helen shivered inside her coat. What would he think of her? Would he look at her and see the girl he used to know? Or would he see the scarred, damaged woman she had become?

Beside her, a woman fussed with her children, buttoning up their coats and smoothing down their hair. Her face was flushed with excitement.

'Won't be long now,' she said. 'Then you'll see Daddy again.'

Helen's head began to swim. In spite of the icy weather, she felt hot inside her coat. She wished she'd taken Dora's advice and eaten before she came out, but her stomach had been too tightly knotted.

If only Dora had come with her. But Helen knew it would have been selfish of her to press it. The poor girl was finding it hard enough to cope.

She would have asked Clare, but they hadn't spoken much since she'd been posted to a military convalescent home in Hampshire three months earlier. It was Clare who had withdrawn from their friendship. Helen had tried to tell her that she didn't bear a grudge over her writing to David, but she sensed Clare was embarrassed about her behaviour, and the lies she had told. At any rate, Helen hoped her friend could find some happiness, wherever she was.

The train was coming in. People began to surge forward. Helen tried to stand her ground, but the press of the crowd carried her forward. She felt the rush of blood to her head and knew she should sit down, but she couldn't fight her way back through the tide of bodies.

Panic closed her throat and her vision started to blur. She couldn't breathe past the tight band around her chest. She tried to turn back but she lost her footing on the slippery ground and her legs went from under her. As she sank to the ground, her last thought was that she would be trampled underfoot.

Then, by some miracle, hands came down, hauling her to her feet.

'Let her through, she's fainted,' someone called out.

The crowd parted and Helen felt herself being half carried, half propelled towards a bench.

'She looks pale. Someone fetch her a glass of water!'

'Has anyone got any smelling salts?'

'I'm quite all right, really. I just need to sit down for a minute–' Helen tried to say, but her breath was coming so fast the words wouldn't come out.

And then she was vaguely aware of the crowd parting again, and a voice calling out, 'Let me through, please. I'm a doctor.'

The next thing she saw was David's bespectacled face looking down at her, wearing a look of frank astonishment. 'Helen?'

She gave him a wobbly smile. 'Hello, David.'

At least she didn't have to worry about what to say to him, or how to greet him. Whatever ice there might have been between them was already well and truly broken.

They laughed about it afterwards, as David bought her a reviving cup of tea in the station tea shop.

'Heaven knows what everyone must have thought when you kissed me!' Helen said.

'They probably assumed it was some unorthodox new medical method I'd picked up in France,' David said. 'Not that I'd ever like to try it on a sergeant major,' he added. His face was straight, but there was a glint of amusement in his brown eyes.

He hadn't changed, Helen thought with relief. He was still the same darling, lovable David she'd always known.

And to her surprise, she felt like the same girl, too. For the first time since the war started, she began to remember what it was like to be young and in love.

'How are you feeling now?' he asked, full of gentle concern. 'Are you all right?'

'Much better, thank you,' she said.

He reached across the table, clasping her hands in his. 'I'm glad you came to meet me.'

'I nearly didn't,' she admitted, looking down at their entwined fingers. 'Dora made me.'

'And when Nurse Riley tells you to do something, you don't say no, do you?' He grinned. Then he seemed to remember something and asked, 'Is Dora here? Did she come with you?'

'No, why?'

He paused for a moment, his expression thoughtful. Then he shook his head. 'It doesn't matter. I expect she'll find out soon enough.'

His smile intrigued her. 'Find out what?' she asked.

'Nothing. I don't want to spoil the surprise.' He lifted her hands to his lips and kissed them. 'Oh, Helen. I've missed you so much.'

Helen withdrew her hands from his slowly. 'David–'

'Don't,' he begged. 'Don't spoil the moment, please?'

'But we need to talk–'

'I know. And we will, I promise.' His gaze held hers, full of understanding. 'I want to hear everything, Helen. But not now. There's plenty of time for talking, isn't there? I mean, we've got all the time in the world. Haven't we?'

Helen smiled at their hands, linked together. He was right, she thought. They had all the time in the world.

Chapter Forty-Nine

Griffin Street was coated in a thick blanket of untouched snow. The twins loved it, tumbling about, pushing each other over and throwing snowballs. The still air rang with their laughter.

'Be careful,' Dora warned as she trudged after them, her feet sinking into the deep whiteness. 'Watch where you're treading, the ground's a bit uneven under all this snow.'

'Are we going to see Mrs Price?' Walter asked.

Dora shook her head. 'Mrs Price is gone, love,' she said quietly.

It was such a shame. Once the feisty old lady had kept her promise to hang out the flags on VE day, she seemed to run out of steam. When winter arrived, she succumbed once again to the flu, but this time she didn't survive it.

She had died two days earlier in the hospital, with Dora at her bedside.

'What about Timmy?' Winnie wanted to know.

'That's why we've come, to fetch him.' Dora held up the basket she'd brought with her. Once again, she'd come to fulfil her promise to old Mrs Price, to take care of her precious cat.

'Can he come back home to live with us?' Winnie's face shone with excitement.

'Yes, if we can find him.'

The twins immediately set off with a fresh purpose, roaming up and down the street, calling out Timmy's name. But he was nowhere to be found.

'He might be hiding in the house,' Walter said.

'I think you might be right,' Dora said. 'Let's go and look, shall we?'

They let themselves in through the back door. Inside, the house was dark, freezing and reeked of damp.

Dora and Winnie stepped into the kitchen, but Walter lingered on the back step.

'What's the matter?' Dora asked.

'Can I stay out here?' Walter said, his voice tremulous.

'He's scared, ain't you?' his sister teased him. 'You frightened the ghost of Mrs Price is going to get you? Wooo!' She loomed up at her brother, her arms raised above her head.

'Get off!' Walter shoved her away.

'Don't tease your brother, Win,' Dora said absently, still looking around. She went into the front room, where Mrs Price had slept, and searched under the bed. There was a slightly whiffy china chamber pot, but no sign of the cat.

'He might've gone upstairs,' Winnie suggested.

Dora peered up the darkened staircase. 'Timmy! Come down, you daft cat!' There was no sound.

'Do we have to go up there?' Walter whispered, his eyes wide and fearful.

'I'll go,' Dora said. 'You two stay down here.'

'Come on, let's go and build a snowman,' Winnie said, tugging at her brother's sleeve.

'Don't go too far,' Dora called after them as they disappeared out of the back door. 'And if you hear an air raid–'

She stopped herself. The sirens had been silent for more than six months, but Dora still woke in the night, listening for them. She wondered how long it would be before she could trust that her children wouldn't be in danger out of her sight.

It had taken her a long time to get used to war, with its rationing and restrictions, the blackouts and the bombings. And it seemed as if it would take just as long to get used to peace, too.

She went upstairs. The top part of the house had not been used in years. Mrs Price had lived and slept in the two rooms downstairs, to keep warm, and rarely ventured upstairs. The windows were still covered with heavy blackout curtains.

The floorboards were soft with damp under her feet. Dora trod carefully, anxious not to put her foot through. As she swung her torch beam left and right, the light picked out what seemed to be ghosts looming up at her out of the darkness. It took a moment for her to realise they were only sheets thrown over the furniture to protect it.

'Timmy?' Her voice sounded loud in the gloom. She waited, straining her ears to listen for the faintest mew. Perhaps the daft cat had got himself trapped somewhere...

And then she heard the creak of footsteps, coming up the stairs.

Dora swung round towards the sound. Her first thought was that it must be the twins. But then she heard their childish shrieks coming from outside. They sounded more distant than before. They must have defied her and wandered into the next street. From the sound they were making, they must have found some other children to play with.

The footsteps were coming nearer. A ghost? Dora dismissed the thought. Ghosts didn't wear boots. No, it was probably another looter, who'd heard Mrs Price was dead and come to see what they could find.

Well, I'll give them something they're not expecting, she thought. She switched off her torch and turned it round in her hand, ready to attack.

The figure appeared, a tall, dark shape silhouetted against the dim daylight coming from downstairs.

Then he spoke. 'Still looking for that ruddy cat, Dora?'

Dora stared at him, the torch still raised, ready to strike. 'Nick?'

He looked up at the weapon in her hand. 'That's a nice way to greet your old man, I must say. I manage to get through six years of war, only to be brained by my own wife!'

Dora stared at him. She was worried if she spoke she would wake up and he would disappear.

'I don't understand–' she murmured. 'I thought you were dead. I got a letter–'

'As you can see, I'm alive and well.'

'They told me you were dead. I got a letter–'

'That's what everyone thought. It's a long story.'

He moved past her to the window and tried to pull the blackout curtains. The plaster crumbled and the curtain rail came down, showering them both in lumps of damp dust. But at least it allowed some weak light in through the grimy glass.

Dora stared at him. She could feel the solid warmth of his body, hear him breathing. But still she could scarcely believe it.

'What happened to you? I heard your unit was attacked–'

He looked grim. 'As I said, it's a long story,' he said. He seemed reluctant to tell it, and Dora wasn't sure she was ready to hear it, either.

'But you're here now,' she said. It was more of a question than a statement. She still couldn't trust her eyes. She hardly dared blink in case he disappeared again.

'I'm here now.' He reached out his hand. Dora tentatively touched his fingers. She wanted to throw herself into his arms but she was still paralysed by shock.

Nick seemed to feel the same. Dora could see in his eyes that there was a torrent of emotion he was trying to hold back.

'What's been going on here while I've been gone?' he asked lightly.

'Not much.'

'Really?' His brows rose. 'And that's what you call getting shot? Not much?'

She stared at him. 'How did you–'

'I met David McKay on the train. He'd heard about it from Helen Dawson, in her letter.' He looked down at her, his eyes full of concern. 'How are you?'

For a moment she didn't reply. It seemed so unreal, to be having a mundane conversation with a man she had thought was dead. It was certainly nothing like the conversations she had with him when she lay awake at night.

But perhaps they would come later. Now it was all she could do to act normal.

'I'm all right now.' She flexed her arm to prove it. 'I wish I'd been here to take care of you.'

'You're here now.'

'Yes, I'm here now. And I ain't going anywhere.'

'Do you promise?'

'I promise. And I always keep my promises, don't I?'

The self-control Dora had been holding on to for so long finally gave way, and she allowed herself to fall into his embrace. His arms went round her, holding her close. She pressed her face against the solid wall of his chest, breathing in the familiar

405

smell of him.

'You'd better never leave me again, Nick Riley!' she whispered, her tears soaking through his shirt. 'You're staying here, where you belong.'

'You try and stop me,' he whispered into her hair.

She didn't know how long they stood, locked together with their arms around each other. But suddenly Dora was aware of something brushing against her leg. She jumped back with a cry of fright, and looked down to see a slim ginger body winding itself sinuously around her.

Nick sighed with frustration. 'That ruddy cat!'

'Now, that's no way to talk about your new pet!' She pulled away from him and scooped Timmy into her arms. 'Looks like the whole family's back together again,' she said.

Nick put his arm around her shoulders. 'Then let's go home,' he said.

Dora smiled up at him. 'Let's go home.'

The publishers hope that this book has given you enjoyable reading. Large Print Books are especially designed to be as easy to see and hold as possible. If you wish a complete list of our books please ask at your local library or write directly to:

Magna Large Print Books
Magna House, Long Preston,
Skipton, North Yorkshire.
BD23 4ND

This Large Print Book for the partially sighted, who cannot read normal print, is published under the auspices of

THE ULVERSCROFT FOUNDATION